James Parton

General Jackson

James Parton

General Jackson

ISBN/EAN: 9783337324940

Printed in Europe, USA, Canada, Australia, Japan

Cover: Foto ©Raphael Reischuk / pixelio.de

More available books at **www.hansebooks.com**

GREAT COMMANDERS

★ ★ ★ ★

GENERAL JACKSON

BY

JAMES PARTON

NEW YORK
D. APPLETON AND COMPANY
1897

PREFACE.

THE military life of Andrew Jackson lasted nine years, of which about two years were passed in the field. He was in no proper sense of the word a professional soldier, and he resented the phrase "military chieftain" which Henry Clay, knowing its irritating power, so often applied to him. He was simply a Tennessee farmer and militia-general who, when his country was invaded, led his neighbors and fellow-citizens to its defense. In doing this duty of a citizen he displayed military talents which friends and foes agreed in pronouncing extraordinary.

His old comrade and friend, a near neighbor for half a lifetime, the late Major William B. Lewis, a gentleman competent to judge in such matters, used to say, as he talked of the Creek and New Orleans campaigns, that Andrew Jackson, in point of native military capacity, was the peer of the great generals of the world—Cæsar, Cromwell, Frederick, Bonaparte, or Wellington—and in support of this opinion he would adduce many curious facts and traits that could be known only to an intimate and confidential companion.

This was the judgment of a friend, though a friend not blind to the limitations of his old commander. I have before me the testimony of an enemy, one who had personally felt the force of the stroke which General Jackson's puissant arm could deal. As late as 1888 there were two survivors of the British army that invaded Louisiana in 1814 and took part in the action of January 8, 1815. One of these was the late Earl of Albemarle; the other, Rev. George R. Gleig, who was for many years chaplain-general to the British forces, but served as a lieutenant of foot in the expedition against New Orleans. Mr. Gleig was the "subaltern" whose excellent narrative of the expedition is occasionally quoted in this volume. A short time before his death he wrote thus to his American friend, General James Grant Wilson, the editor of this series of volumes:

"When I look back upon the means which General Jackson adopted to cover New Orleans, and remember the materials of which his army was composed, I can not but regard his management of that campaign as one of the most masterly of which history makes mention. His night attack on our advanced guard was as bold a stroke as ever was struck. It really paralyzed all our future operations; for, though unsuccessful, it taught us to hold our enemy in respect, and in all future movements to act with an excess of caution. The use, also, which he made of the river was admirable. Indeed, I am inclined to think that to him the generals who came after him were indebted for the perception of the great advantages to which the command of rivers may be turned. And do not let us forget that he had little else to oppose to Wellington's veterans, fresh from their triumphs in Spain and the south of France, except raw levies. Altogether I think of Jackson as, next to Washington, the greatest general America has produced."

To the last of his days—and he lived to be past ninety-one—he retained these impressions unimpaired. General Wilson, in conversation, would call the old gentleman's attention to the brilliant achievements of

Grant, Sherman, Sheridan, and others, but could never convince him that either of them showed military capacity superior to that of the general who had given him and his comrades such a world of trouble seventy years before.

"No," he would say, "Jackson did everything that could be done to repel an attack that ought to have proved successful. His beating up our bivouac on the night of our landing was a master stroke, and, had his troops been such as yours became during your civil war, he would have destroyed us." This is the judgment of a soldier who saw and felt during some terrible weeks what it is in war to have a real general in command on the other side.

No one can carefully examine the record without discovering that Andrew Jackson possessed the indispensable qualities of a commanding general: in all circumstances imperturbably brave; confident in himself, but open to suggestion and to argument; bold when boldness was wise, but as wary as an Indian until he saw his way to victory clear; vigilant, prompt, persistent, indefatigable, and aware of the importance of little things. He had for his soldiers the paternal feeling which we observe in all the great generals, as we do also in the great captains of industry; yet he could be a stern and ruthless disciplinarian. There is a passage in his farewell address to the army in 1821 where he speaks of the bounty-jumpers of his day, who found it "a source of speculation to go from rendezvous to rendezvous, enlisting, receiving the bounty, and deserting, all the way from Boston to New Orleans." The passage, if it had been acted upon during the late war, would have saved a vast amount of suffering and waste.

Two of his favorite maxims denote the soldier: "In war, till everything is done, nothing is done"; and this also, "When you have a thing to do, take all the time for thinking that the circumstances allow, but when the time has come for action, stop thinking."

[THE last literary work of James Parton was the preparation of this brief biography of General Jackson. It was completed in August, 1891. Two months later, a long career of literary industry was closed by his death at the ripe age of seventy. An indefatigable worker, he produced many valuable American biographies, of which his earliest—a Life of Horace Greeley —was perhaps the most popular. Although less ambitious in scope than some of Mr. Parton's previous volumes, his last work, like his first, presents a fair estimate of its subject, and seems free from the natural tendency of biographers, which Macaulay sneeringly designates "the disease of admiration." Altogether the book appears to be a model miniature biography, possessing throughout all the interest of a romance. It would seem that this story of the career of the great American commander can not fail to add to Mr. Parton's literary reputation. EDITOR.]

CONTENTS.

GENERAL JACKSON.

CHAPTER I.

PARENTAGE AND EDUCATION.

IN 1765, Andrew Jackson, the father of the Andrew Jackson whose career we are about to relate, emigrated, with his wife and two sons, from Carrickfergus, in the north of Ireland, to South Carolina. His sons were named Hugh and Robert; Andrew was not yet born. In his native country he had cultivated a few hired acres, and his wife had been a weaver of linen. Like most of the inhabitants of the north of Ireland, he was of Scottish origin; but his ancestors had lived for five generations in the neighborhood of Carrickfergus; lowly, honest people, tillers of the soil and weavers; radical Whigs in politics, Presbyterians in religion. He was accompanied to America by three of his neighbors, James, Robert, and Joseph Crawford, the first-named of whom was his brother-in-law. The peace between France and England, signed two years before, which ended the "old French War"—the war in which Braddock was defeated and Canada won—had restored to mankind their highway, the ocean, and given an impulse to emigration from the Old World to the New. From the north of Ireland large numbers sailed away to the land of promise. Five sisters of Mrs. Jackson had gone, or were soon going. Samuel Jackson, a brother of Andrew, afterward went, and established himself in Philadelphia, where he long lived, a respectable citizen. Mrs. Suffren, a daughter of another brother, followed in later years, and settled in the city of New York, where she has living descendants.

The party of emigrants from Carrickfergus landed at Charleston, and proceeded without delay to the Waxhaw settlement, a hundred and sixty miles to the northwest of Charleston, where many of their kindred and countrymen were already established. This settlement was, or had been, the seat of the Waxhaw tribe of Indians.

A proof of the poverty of Andrew Jackson is this: the Crawfords, who came with him from Ireland, bought lands near the center of the settlement, on the Waxhaw Creek itself—lands which still attest the wisdom of their choice; but Jackson settled seven miles away, on new land, on the banks of Twelve Mile Creek, another branch of the Catawba. The place is now known as "Pleasant Grove Camp Ground," and the particular land once occupied by the father of General Jackson is still pointed out by the old people of the neighborhood.

For two years Andrew Jackson and his family toiled in the Carolina woods. He had built his log-house, cleared some fields, and raised a crop. Then, the father of the family, his work all incomplete, sickened and died: his two boys being still very young, and his wife far advanced in pregnancy. This was early in the spring of 1767.

The bereaved family of the Jacksons never returned to their home on the banks of Twelve Mile Creek, but went from the churchyard to the house, not far off, of one of Mrs. Jackson's brothers-in-law, George McKemey by name, whose remains now repose in the same old burying-ground. A few nights after there was a swift sending of messengers to the neighbors, and a hurrying across the fields of friendly women; and before the sun rose a son was born, the son whose career and fortunes we have undertaken to relate. It was in a small log-house, in the province of North Carolina, less than a quarter of a mile from the boundary-line between North and South Carolina, that the birth took place. Andrew Jackson, then, was born in Union County, North Carolina, on the 15th of March, 1767.

General Jackson always supposed himself to be a native of South Carolina. "Fellow-citizens of my *native* State!" he exclaims, at the close of his proclamation to the nullifiers of South Carolina; but it is as certain as any fact of the kind can be that he was mistaken. The clear and uniform tradition of the neighborhood, supported by a great mass of indisputable testimony, points to a spot in *North* Carolina, but only a stone's-throw from the line that divides it from South Carolina, as the birthplace of Andrew Jackson.

In the family of his Uncle Crawford, Andy Jackson (for by this familiar name he is still spoken of in the neighborhood) spent the first ten or twelve years of his life. Mr. Crawford was a man of considerable substance for a new country, and his family was large. He lived in South Carolina, just over the boundary-line, near the Waxhaw Creek, and six miles from the Catawba River. The land there lies well for farming; level, but not flat; undulating, but without hills of inconvenient height. The soil is a stiff, red clay, the stiffest of the stiff and the reddest of the red; the kind of soil which bears hard usage, and makes the very worst winter roads anywhere to be found on this planet. Except where there is an interval of fertile soil, the country round about is a boundless continuity of pine woods, wherein to this day wild turkeys and deer are shot, and the farmers take their cotton to market in immense wagons of antique pattern, a journey of half a week, and camp out every night. As evening closes in, the passing traveler sees the mules, the negro driver, the huge covered wagon, the farmer, and sometimes his wife with an infant, grouped in the most strikingly picturesque manner, in an opening of the forest, around a blazing fire of pine knots that light up the scene like an illumination. In such a country as this, with horses to ride, and cows to hunt, and journeys to make, and plenty of boys, black and white, to play with, our little friend spent his early years.

In due time the boy was sent to an "old-field school," an institution not much unlike the roadside schools in Ireland of which we read. The Northern reader is perhaps not aware that an "old field" is not a field at all, but a pine forest. When crop after crop of cotton, without rotation, has exhausted the soil, the fences are taken away, the land lies waste, the young pines at once spring up and soon cover the whole field with a thick growth of wood. In one of these old fields the rudest possible shanty of a log house is erected, with a fireplace that extends from side to side and occupies a third of the interior. In winter the interstices of the log walls are filled up with clay, which the restless fingers of the boys make haste to remove in time to admit the first warm airs of spring. An itinerant schoolmaster presents himself in a neighborhood; the responsible farmers pledge him a certain number of pupils, and an old-field school is established for the season. Reading, writing, and arithmetic were all the branches taught in the early days.

But Mrs. Jackson had more ambitious views for her youngest son. She aimed to give him a liberal education, in the hope that he would one day become a clergyman in the Presbyterian Church. It is probable that her condition was not one of absolute dependence. The tradition of the neighborhood is, that she was noted the country round for her skill in spinning flax, and that she earned money by spinning to pay for Andrew's schooling. It is possible, too, that her relations in Ireland may have contributed something to her support.

Andy was a wild, frolicsome, willful, mischievous, daring, reckless boy; generous to a friend, but never content to submit to a stronger enemy. He was passionately fond of those sports which are mimic battles; above all, wrestling.

If our knowledge of the school-life of Jackson is scanty, we are at no loss to say what he learned and what he failed to learn at school. He learned to read, to write, to cast accounts—little more. If he began, as he may have done, to learn by heart, in the old-fashioned way, the Latin grammar, he never acquired enough of it to leave any traces of classical knowledge in his mind or his writings. In some of his later letters there may be found, it is true, an occasional Latin phrase of two or three words, but so quoted as to show ignorance rather than knowledge. He was never a well-informed man. He never was addicted to books. He never learned to write the English language correctly, though he often wrote it eloquently and convincingly. He never learned to spell correctly, though he was a better speller than Frederick II, Marlborough, Napoleon, or Washington. Few men of his day, and no women, were correct spellers.

He was nine years old when the Declaration of Independence was signed. By the time the war approached the Waxhaw settlement, bringing blood and terror with it, leaving desolation behind it, closing all schoolhouses, and putting a stop to the peaceful labors of the people,

2

Andrew Jackson was little more than thirteen. His brother Hugh, a man in stature if not in years, had not waited for the war to come near his home, but had mounted his horse a year before and ridden southward to meet it. He was one of the troopers of that famous regiment to raise and equip which, its colonel, William Richardson Davie, spent the last guinea of his inherited estate. Under Colonel Davie, Hugh Jackson fought in the ranks of the battle of Stono, and died, after the action, of heat and fatigue. His brother Robert was a strapping lad, but too young for a soldier, and was still at home with his mother and Andrew when Tarleton and his dragoons thundered along the red roads of the Waxhaws, and dyed them a deeper red with the blood of the surprised militia.

CHAPTER II.

IT was on the 29th of May, 1780, that Tarleton, with three hundred horsemen, surprised a detachment of militia in the Waxhaw settlement and killed one hundred and thirteen of them, and wounded a hundred and fifty. The wounded, abandoned to the care of the settlers, were quartered in the houses of the vicinity; the old log Waxhaw meeting-house itself being converted into a hospital for the most desperate cases. Mrs. Jackson was one of the kind women who ministered to the wounded soldiers in the church, and under that roof her boys first saw what war was. The men were dreadfully mangled. Some had received as many as thirteen wounds, and none less than three. For many days Andrew and his brother assisted their mother in waiting upon the sick men; Andrew, more in rage than pity, burning to avenge their wounds and his brother's death.

Tarleton's massacre at the Waxhaws kindled the flames of war in all that region of the Carolinas. Many notable actions were fought, and some striking though unimportant advantages were gained by the patriot forces. Andrew Jackson and his brother Robert were present at Sumter's gallant attack upon the British post of Hanging Rock, near Waxhaw, where the patriots half gained the day, and lost it by beginning too soon to drink the rum they captured from the enemy. The Jackson boys rode on this expedition with Colonel

Davie, a most brave, self-sacrificing officer, who, as we have said, commanded the troop of which Hugh Jackson was a member when he died, after the battle of Stono. Neither of the boys was attached to Davie's company, nor is it likely that Andrew, a boy of thirteen, did more than witness the affair at Hanging Rock.

This Colonel Davie, Hugh Jackson's old commander, was the man, above all others who led Carolina troops in the Revolution, that the Jackson boys admired. He was a man after Andrew's own heart—swift but wary, bold in planning enterprises but most cautious in execution, sleeplessly vigilant, untiringly active—one of those cool, quick men who apply mother-wit to the art of war; who are good soldiers because they are earnest and clear-sighted men. So far as any man was General Jackson's model soldier, William Richardson Davie, of North Carolina, was the individual.

The boys rejoined their mother at the Waxhaw settlement. On the 16th of August, 1780, occurred the great disaster of the war in the South, the defeat of General Gates. The victor, Cornwallis, moved three weeks after, with his whole army, toward the Waxhaws; which induced Mrs. Jackson and her boys once more to abandon their home for a safer retreat north of the scene of war.

In February, 1781, the country about the Waxhaws again being tranquil, because subdued, Mrs. Jackson, her sons, and many of her neighbors returned to their ravaged homes. Andrew soon after passed his fourteenth birthday, an overgrown youth, as tall as a man, but weakly from having grown too fast. Then ensued a spring and summer of small, fierce, intestine warfare— a war of Whig and Tory, neighbor against neighbor, brother against brother, and even father against son.

Without detaining the reader with a detail of the

Revolutionary history of the Carolinas, I yet desire to show what a war-charged atmosphere it was that young Andrew breathed during this forming period of his life, especially toward the close of the war, after the great operations ceased.

The people in the upper country of the Carolinas little expected that the war would ever reach settlements so remote, so obscure, so scattered as theirs; and it did not for some years. When at last the storm of war drew near their borders, it found them a divided people. The old sentiment of loyalty was still rooted in many minds. There were many who had taken a recent and special oath of allegiance to the king, which they considered binding in all circumstances. They were Highlanders, clannish and religiously loyal, who pointed to the text, "Fear God and honor the king," and overlooked the fact that the biblical narrative condemns the Jews for desiring a kingly government. There were Moravians and Quakers, who conscientiously opposed all war. There were Catholic Irish, many of whom sided with the king. There were Protestant Scotch-Irish, Whigs and agitators in the old country, Whigs and fervent patriots in the new. There were placeholders, who adhered to their official bread and dignity. There were trimmers, who espoused the side that chanced to be strongest. The approach and collision of hostile forces converted most of these factions into belligerents, who waged a most fierce and deadly war upon one another, renewing on this new theatre the border wars of another age and country.

The time came when Andrew and his brother began to play men's parts in the drama. Without enlisting in any organized corps, they joined small parties that went out on single enterprises of retaliation, mounted on their own horses and carrying their own weapons.

The activity and zeal of the Waxhaw Whigs coming to the ears of Lord Rawdon, whom Cornwallis had left in command, he dispatched a small body of dragoons to aid the Tories of that infected neighborhood. The Waxhaw people, hearing of the approach of this hostile force, resolved upon resisting it in open fight, and named the Waxhaw meeting-house as the rendezvous. Forty Whigs assembled on the appointed day, mounted and armed, and among them were Robert and Andrew Jackson. In the grove about the old church these forty were waiting for the arrival—hourly expected—of another company of Whigs from a neighboring settlement. The British officer in command of the dragoons, apprised of the rendezvous by a Tory of the neighborhood, determined to surprise the patriot party before the two companies had united. Before coming in sight of the church, he placed a body of Tories wearing the dress of the country far in advance of his soldiers, and so marched upon the devoted band. The Waxhaw party saw a company of armed men approaching, but, concluding them to be their expected friends, made no preparations for defense. Too late the error was discovered. Eleven of the forty were taken prisoners, and the rest sought safety in flight, fiercely pursued by the dragoons. The brothers were separated. Andrew found himself galloping for life and liberty by the side of his cousin, Lieutenant Thomas Crawford, a dragoon close behind them, and others coming rapidly on. They tore along the road awhile, and then took to a swampy field, where they came soon to a wide slough of water and mire, into which they plunged their horses. Andrew floundered across, and on reaching dry land again looked round for his companion, whose horse had sunk into the mire and fallen. He saw him entangled, and trying vainly to ward off the blows of his pursuers with his sword. Before Andrew could turn to assist him the lieutenant received a severe wound in the head, which compelled him to give up the contest and surrender. The youth put spurs to his horse and succeeded in eluding pursuit. Robert, too, escaped unhurt, and in the course of the day the brothers were reunited, and took refuge in a thicket, in which they passed a hungry and anxious night.

The next morning the pangs of hunger compelled them to leave their safe retreat and go in quest of food. The nearest house was that of Lieutenant Crawford. Leaving their horses and arms in the thicket, the lads crept toward the house, which they reached in safety. Meanwhile, a Tory traitor of the neighborhood had scented out their lurking-place, found their horses and weapons, and set a party of dragoons upon their track. Before the family had a suspicion of danger, the house was surrounded, the doors were secured, and the boys were prisoners.

A scene ensued which left an impression upon the mind of one of the boys which time never effaced. Regardless of the fact that the house was occupied by the defenseless wife and young children of a wounded soldier, the dragoons, brutalized by this mean partisan warfare, began to destroy, with wild riot and noise, the contents of the house. Crockery, glass, and furniture were dashed to pieces, beds emptied, the clothing of the family torn to rags; even the clothes of the infant that Mrs. Crawford carried in her arms were not spared. While this destruction was going on, the officer in command of the party ordered Andrew to clean his high jack-boots, which were well splashed and crusted with mud. The boy replied, not angrily, though with a certain firmness and decision, in something like these words:

"Sir, I am a prisoner of war, and claim to be treated as such."

The officer aimed a desperate blow at the boy's head with his sword. Andrew broke the force of the blow with his left hand, and thus received two wounds—one deep gash on his head and another on his hand, the marks of both of which he carried to his grave. The officer, after achieving this gallant feat, turned to Robert Jackson and ordered him to clean the boots. Robert also refused. The valiant Briton struck the young man so violent a sword-blow upon the head, as to prostrate and disable him.

Andrew was ordered to mount, and to guide some of the party to the house of a noted Whig of the vicinity named Thompson. Threatened with instant death if he failed to guide them aright, the youth submitted, and led the party in the right direction. A timely thought enabled him to be the deliverer of his neighbor instead of his captor. Instead of approaching the house by the usual road, he conducted the party by a circuitous route, which brought them in sight of the house half a mile before they reached it. Andrew well knew that, if Thompson was at home, he would be sure to have some one on the lookout, and a horse ready for the road. On coming in sight of the house he saw Thompson's horse, saddled and bridled, standing at a rack in the yard, which informed him both that the master was there and that he was prepared for flight. The dragoons dashed forward to seize their prey. While they were still some hundreds of yards from the house, Andrew had the delight of seeing Thompson burst from his door, run to his horse, mount, and plunge into a foaming, swollen creek that rushed by his house. He gained the opposite shore, and, seeing that the dragoons dared not attempt the stream, gave a shout of defiance and galloped into the woods.

The elation caused by the success of his stratagem

was soon swallowed up in misery. Andrew and Robert Jackson, Lieutenant Thomas Crawford, and twenty other prisoners, all the victims of this raid of the dragoons into the Waxhaws, were placed on horses stolen in the same settlement and marched toward Camden, South Carolina, a great British depot at the time, forty miles distant. It was a long and agonizing journey, especially to the wounded, among whom were the Jacksons and their cousin. Not an atom of food nor a drop of water was allowed them on the way. Such was the brutality of the soldiers, that when these miserable lads tried to scoop up a little water from the streams which they forded, to appease their raging thirst, they were ordered to desist.

At Camden their situation was one of utter wretchedness. Two hundred and fifty prisoners in a contracted inclosure drawn around the jail; no beds of any description; no medicine; no medical attendance, nor means of dressing the wounds; their only food a scanty supply of bad bread. They were robbed even of part of their clothing, besides being subject to the taunts and threats of every passing Tory. The three relatives, it is said, were separated as soon as their relationship was discovered. Miserable among the miserable; gaunt, yellow, hungry, and sick; robbed of his jacket and shoes; ignorant of his brother's fate; chafing with suppressed fury, Andrew passed now some of the most wretched days of his life. Ere long the smallpox—a disease unspeakably terrible at that day, more terrible than cholera or plague has ever been—broke out among the prisoners, and raged unchecked by medicine and unalleviated by any kind of attendance or nursing. The sick and the well, the dying and the dead, those shuddering at the first symptoms and those putrid with the disease, were mingled together; and all but the dead were equally miserable.

For some time Andrew escaped the contagion. He was reclining one day in the sun, near the entrance of the prison, when the officer of the guard, attracted, as it seemed, by the youthfulness of his appearance, entered into conversation with him. The lad soon began to speak of that of which his heart was full—the condition of the prisoners and the bad quality of their food. He remonstrated against their treatment with such energy and feeling that the officer seemed to be moved and shocked, and, what was far more important, he was induced to ferret out the villainy of the contractors who had been robbing the prisoners of their rations. From the day of Andrew's remonstrance the condition of the prisoners was ameliorated; they were supplied with meat and better bread, and were otherwise better cared for.

Andrew's spirits sank under this accumulation of miseries, and he began to sicken with the first symptoms of the smallpox. Robert was in a condition still worse. The wound in his head had never been dressed, and had not healed. He, too, reduced as he was, began to shiver and burn with the fever that announces the dread disease. Another week of prison life would have probably consigned both these boys to the grave. But they had a friend outside the prison—their mother, who at this crisis of their fate strove with the might of love for their deliverance. Learning their forlorn condition, this heroic woman went to Camden, and succeeded, after a time, in effecting an exchange of prisoners between a Waxhaw captain and the British general. The Whig captain gave up thirteen soldiers whom he had captured in the rear of the British army, and received in return the two sons of Mrs. Jackson and five of her neighbors. When the little family were reunited in the town of Camden, the mother could but gaze upon her boys with astonishment and horror—so worn and wasted were they with hunger, wounds, and disease. Robert could not stand, or even sit on horseback, without support.

The mother, however, had no choice but to get them home immediately. Two horses were procured. One she rode herself. Robert was placed upon the other, and held in his seat by the returning prisoners to whom Mrs. Jackson had just given liberty. Behind the sad procession poor Andrew dragged his weak and weary limbs, bareheaded, barefooted, without a jacket, his only two garments torn and dirty. The forty miles of lonely wilderness that lay between Camden and Waxhaw were nearly traversed, and the fevered lads were expecting in two hours more to enjoy the bliss of repose, when a chilly, drenching, merciless rain set in. When this occurred, the smallpox had reached that stage of development when, after having raged within the system, it was about to break out in those loathsome sores which give vent to the disease. The boys reached home and went to bed. In two days Robert Jackson was a corpse and his brother Andrew a raving maniac. A mother's nursing, medical skill, and a constitution sound at the core, brought the youth out of this peril, and set him upon the way to slow recovery. He was an invalid for several months.

In the summer of 1781 a great cry of anguish and despair came up to Waxhaw from the Charleston prisonships, wherein, among many hundreds of other prisoners, were confined some of the sons of Mrs. Jackson's sisters, and other friends and neighbors of hers from the Waxhaw country. Mrs. Jackson had seen at Camden what prisoners of war may suffer. She had also seen what a little vigor and tact can effect in the deliverance of prisoners. Andrew was no sooner quite out of danger than his brave mother resolved to go to Charleston (distant one hundred and sixty miles) and do what she could for the comfort of the prisoners there. The tradition of the neighborhood now is that she performed the entire journey on foot, in company with two other women of like mind and purpose. It is more probable, however, and so thought General Jackson, that these gallant women rode on horseback, carrying with them a precious store of gifts and rural luxuries and medicines for the solace of their imprisoned relatives, and bearing tender messages and precious news from home. Protected by being unprotected, they reached Charleston in safety, gained admission to the ships, emptied their hearts and saddle-bags, and brought such joy to the haggard prisoners as only prisoners know when women from home visit them.

And there the history of this expedition ends. This only is further known of it, or will ever be: While stopping at the house of a relative, William Barton by name, who lived two miles and a half from Charleston, Mrs. Jackson was seized with the ship fever, and, after a short illness, died, and was buried on the open plain near by.

And so Andrew, before reaching his fifteenth birthday, was an orphan; a sick and sorrowful orphan; a homeless and dependent orphan.

CHAPTER III.

CORNWALLIS surrendered at Yorktown on the 19th of October, 1781. Savannah remained in the enemy's hands nine months, and Charleston fourteen months after that event ; but the war, in effect, terminated then, North and South. The Waxhaw people who survived returned to their homes, and resumed the vocations which the war had interrupted.

With returning health returned the frolicsome spirit of the youth, which now began to seek gratification in modes less innocent than the sportive feats of his schoolboy days. Several Charleston families of wealth and social eminence were living in the neighborhood, waiting for the evacuation of their city. With the young men of these families Jackson became acquainted, and led a life with them, in the summer and autumn of 1782, that was more merry than wise. He was betrayed by their example and his own pride into habits of expense, which wasted his small resources. That passion for horses, which never left him, began to show itself. He ran races and rode races, gambled a little, drank a little, fought cocks occasionally, and comported himself in the style usually affected by dissipated young men of that day.

In December, 1782, to the joy and exultation of all the Southern country, Charleston was evacuated, and its scattered Whig families were free to return to their homes. Andrew, finding the country dull after the departure of his gay companions, suddenly resolved to follow them to the city. He mounted his horse, a fine and valuable animal that he had contrived to possess, and rode to Charleston through the wilderness. There, it appears, he remained long enough to expend his slender stock of money and run up a long bill with his landlord. He was saved from total ruin by a curious incident, which is thus related by one who heard it from himself : " He had strolled one evening down the street and was carried into a place where some persons were amusing themselves at a game of dice, and much betting was in progress. He was challenged for a game by a person present, by whom a proposal was made to stake two hundred dollars against the fine horse on which Jackson had come to Charleston. After some deliberation he accepted the challenge. Fortune was on his side ; the wager was won and paid. He forthwith departed, settled his bill next morning, and returned to his home. ' My calculation,' said he, speaking of this incident, ' was that, if a loser in the game, I would give the landlord my saddle and bridle, as far as they would go toward the payment of his bill, ask a credit for the balance, and walk away from the city ; but being successful, I had new spirits infused into me, left the table, and from that moment to the present time I have never thrown dice for a wager.' "

Upon the return of the young man to the home of his childhood he evidently took hold of life more earnestly than he had done before. He made some attempts, it is said, to continue his studies. Three entirely credible informants testify that Andrew Jackson was a schoolmaster at this period of his life. Nothing is more certain than that part of the small cash capital upon which he started in his career was earned amid the hum and bustle of an old-field school. It is the more certain, as the uniform tradition of the Waxhaw country is that he was a very poor young man, who inherited nothing from his father, because his father had nothing to leave. The tradition at Charlotte is, that when young Andrew attended Queen's College he often passed down the street to school with his trousers too ragged to keep his shirt from flying in the wind.

For a year certainly, and probably for two years, after Andrew's return from Charleston he remained in the Waxhaw country, employed either in teaching school or in some less worthy occupation. Peace was formally proclaimed in April, 1783. Some time between the proclamation of peace and the winter of 1784–'85, Andrew Jackson resolved upon studying law. In that winter he gathered together his earnings and whatéver property he may have possessed, mounted his horse again, and set his face northward in quest of a master in the law under whom to pursue his studies. He rode to Salisbury, North Carolina, a distance of seventy-five miles from the Waxhaws.

At Salisbury he entered the law office of Mr. Spruce McCay, an eminent lawyer at that time, and in later days a judge of high distinction, who is still remembered with honor in North Carolina.

In one of the back streets of this old town, on the lawn in front of one of its largest and handsomest mansions, close to the street and to the left of the gate, stood, in 1858, a little box of a house fifteen feet by sixteen, and one story high. It was built of shingles, several of which had decayed and fallen off. This little decaying house of shingles was the law office of Spruce McCay when Andrew Jackson studied law under him at Salisbury, in 1785 and 1786. The mansion behind it stands on the site of the house in which Mr. McCay lived at the time, and the property is still owned and occupied by a near connection of his, who has preserved the old office from regard to his memory.

Our student completed his preparation for the bar in the office of Colonel John Stokes, a brave soldier of the Revolution, and afterward a lawyer of high repute, from whom Stokes County, North Carolina, took its name. Colonel Stokes was one of those who fell covered with wounds at the Waxhaw massacre in 1780, and may have been nursed in the old meeting-house by Mrs. Jackson and her sons. Before the spring of 1787, about two years after beginning the study of the law, Andrew Jackson was licensed to practice in the courts of North Carolina. He was twenty years of age when he completed the preliminary part of his education at Salisbury. He had grown to be a tall fellow. He stood six feet and an inch in his stockings. He was remarkably slender for that robust age of the world, but he was also remarkably erect, so that his form had the effect of symmetry without being symmetrical. His movements and carriage were graceful and dignified. In the accomplishments of his day and sphere he excelled the young men of his own circle, and was regarded by them as their chief and model. He was an exquisite horseman, as all will agree who ever saw him on horseback. Jefferson tells us that General Washington was the best horseman of his time, but he could scarcely have been a more graceful or a more daring rider than Jackson. From early boyhood to extreme old age he was the master and friend of horses.

He was far from handsome. His face was long, thin, and fair; his forehead high and somewhat narrow; his hair, reddish-sandy in color, was exceedingly abundant, and fell down low over his forehead. The bristling hair of the ordinary portraits belongs to the latter half of his life. There was but one feature of his face that was not commonplace—his eyes, which were of a deep blue, and capable of blazing with great expression when he was roused.

The truth is, this young man was one of those who convey to strangers the impression that they are "somebody"; who naturally, and without thinking of it, take the lead; who are invited or permitted to take it as a matter of course.

Finding no opportunity to practice his profession in the old settlements, young Jackson resolved to join a large party of emigrants bound for that part of the Western country which is now the State of Tennessee, but which was then Washington County, North Carolina. John McNairy, a friend of Jackson's, had been appointed judge of the Superior Court for that vast region, and Jackson was invested with the office of solicitor, or public prosecutor, for the same district. This office was not in request, nor desirable. It was, in fact, difficult to get a suitable person to accept an appointment of the kind, which was to be exercised in a wilderness five hundred miles distant from the populous parts of North Carolina, and where the office of prosecutor was sure to be unpopular, difficult, and dangerous. Thomas Searcy, another of Jackson's friends, received the appointment of clerk of the court. Three or four more of his young acquaintances, lawyers and others, resolved to go with him and seek their fortune in the new and vaunted country of the West. The party rendezvoused at Morganton in the spring or early summer of 1788, mounted and equipped for a ride over the mountains to Jonesboro, then the chief settlement of East Tennessee, and the first halting-place of companies bound to the lands on the Cumberland River.

The judge and his party remained several weeks at

3

Jonesboro, waiting for the assembling of a sufficient number of emigrants, and for the arrival of a guard from Nashville to escort them. Nashville is one hundred and eighty-three miles from Jonesboro. The road ran through a gap in the Cumberland Mountains, and thence entered a wilderness more dangerously infested with hostile Indians than any other portion of the Western country, not even excepting the dark and bloody land of Kentucky.

Before the end of October, 1788, the long train of emigrants, among whom was Mr. Solicitor Jackson, reached Nashville, to the great joy of the settlers there, to whom the annual arrival of such a train was all that an arrival can be—a thrilling event, news from home, reunion with friends, increase of wealth, and additional protection against a foe powerful and resolute to destroy.

The settlement grew apace, however. When Jackson arrived, the stations along the Cumberland may have contained five thousand souls or more. But the place was still an outpost of civilization, and so exposed to Indian hostility that it was not safe to live five miles from the central stockade—a circumstance that influenced the whole career and life of our young friend the newly-arrived solicitor.

When young Jackson reached the settlement he found the Widow Donelson living there in a blockhouse, somewhat more commodious than any other dwelling in the place; for she was a notable housekeeper, as well as a woman of property. With her then lived her daughter Rachel and her Kentucky husband, Lewis Robards.

The presence of the young lawyer at Nashville was most opportune. The only licensed lawyer in West Tennessee was engaged exclusively in the service of debtors, who, it seems, made common cause against the common enemy, their creditors. Jackson came not as a lawyer merely, but as the public prosecutor, and there was that in his bearing which gave assurance that he was the man to issue unpopular writs and give them effect.

In the four terms of 1794 there were three hundred and ninety-seven cases before the same court, in two hundred and twenty-eight of which Jackson acted as counsel. And during these and later years he practiced at the courts of Jonesboro, and other towns in East Tennessee.

In the year 1791 the prosperous young solicitor, after a courtship of an extraordinary character. was married to Mrs. Rachel Robards, the daughter of that brave old pioneer, John Donelson.

As Tennessee prospered (and it prospered rapidly after the Indians were subdued, in 1794), the district attorney could not but prosper with it. The land records of 1794, 1795, 1796, and 1797 show that it was during those years that Jackson laid the foundation of the large estate which he subsequently acquired. Those were the days in which a lawyer's fee for conducting a suit of no great importance might be a square mile of land, or, in Western phrase, a "six-forty." Jackson appears frequently in the records of the years named as the purchaser and assignee of sections of land. He bought six hundred and fifty acres of the fine tract which afterward formed the Hermitage farm for eight hundred dollars— a high price for that day. By the time that Tennessee entered the Union, in 1796, Jackson was a very extensive landowner, and a man of fair estate for a frontiersman.

The office of public prosecutor, held by Andrew Jackson during the first seven or eight years of his residence in Tennessee, was one that a man of only ordinary nerve and courage could not have filled. It set in array against him all the scoundrels in the Territory. Those

were the times when a notorious criminal would defy
the officers of justice, and keep them at bay for years at
a time; when a district attorney who made himself too
officious was liable to a shot in the back as he rode to
court; when two men, not satisfied with the court's
award, would come out of the court-house into the public square and fight it out in the presence of the whole
population, judge and jury, perhaps, looking on; when
the public prosecutor was apt to be regarded as the man
whose office it was to spoil good sport and interfere between gentlemen.

CHAPTER IV.

IN November, 1795, the Governor of the Territory announced, as the result of a census ordered by the Legislature, that Tennessee contained seventy-seven thousand two hundred and sixty-two inhabitants, of whom ten thousand six hundred and thirteen were slaves. He therefore called upon the people to elect delegates to a convention for making a Constitution, and named January 11, 1796, as the day for their assembling at Knoxville. The convention met accordingly, fifty-five members in all, five from each of the eleven counties. The five members sent from Davidson County were John McNairy, Andrew Jackson, James Robertson, Thomas Hardeman, and Joel Lewis.

The State was promptly organized. A Legislature was elected, and " Citizen John Sevier," we are officially informed, was chosen the first Governor. On the 1st of June, 1796, Tennessee became the sixteenth member of the confederacy. Three presidential electors were chosen, who cast the vote of the State for Jefferson and Burr. As yet, Tennessee was entitled to but one member of the House of Representatives. Early in the fall of 1796 Andrew Jackson was elected by the people to serve them in that honorable capacity. Soon after—for the journey was a long one, and more difficult than long —he mounted his horse and set out for Philadelphia, distant nearly eight hundred miles.

The member from Tennessee reached Philadelphia at one of those periods of commercial depression to which the country has always been liable. The financial reader is aware that the suspension of specie payments by the Bank of England, which lasted twenty-two years, began in February, 1797, about two months after Jackson's arrival in Philadelphia.

On the third day of the session, a quorum of the Senate having reached Philadelphia, and both Houses being assembled in the Representatives' chamber, Jackson saw General Washington, an august and venerable form, enter the chamber and deliver his last speech to Congress; heard him recommend the gradual creation of a navy for the protection of American commerce in the Mediterranean against the pirates of Algiers; heard him modestly—almost timidly—suggest that American manufactures ought to be at least so far encouraged and aided by Government as to render the country independent of foreign nations in time of war; heard him recommend the establishment of boards of agriculture, a national university, and a military academy; heard him mildly object to the policy of paying low salaries to high officers, to the exclusion from high office of all but men of fortune; and heard him denounce the spoliations of our commerce by cruisers sailing under the flag of the French Republic.

At that day it was customary for each House to prepare, and in person deliver, a formal reply to the President's opening speech. An address was drawn up which concluded with a series of paragraphs highly eulogistic not merely of the retiring President but of his administration. The more radical Democrats, of whom Jackson was one, objected, and, after two days' animated discussion, Edward Livingston brought the debate to an end by distinctly moving to strike out the words, "wise, firm, and patriotic administration ", and to insert in their place, "your firmness, wisdom, and patriotism." The question was taken on Mr. Livingston's amendment, and decided in the negative. The whole address was then read with the slight amendments previously ordered, and the question was about to be submitted as to its final acceptance, when Mr. Thomas Blount, of North Carolina, demanded the yeas and nays, in order that posterity might see that he did not consent to the address. The yeas and nays were then taken, with this result: For accepting the address, sixty-seven votes; against its acceptance, twelve. The following gentlemen voted against it: Thomas Blount, Isaac Coles, William B. Giles, Christopher Greenup, James Holland, Andrew Jackson, Edward Livingston, Matthew Locke, William Lyman, Samuel Maclay, Nathaniel Macon, and Abraham Venable.

Jackson's vote on this occasion merely shows that in 1796 he belonged to the most radical wing of the Jeffersonian party, the "Mountain" of the House of Representatives.

On Thursday, December 29, 1796, the member from Tennessee first addressed the House. In 1793, while Tennessee was still a Territory under the Federal Government, General Sevier, induced thereto by extreme provocation and the imminent peril of the settlements, led an expedition against the Indians without waiting for the authorization of the General Government. One of those who served on this expedition was a young student by the name of Hugh L. White, afterward judge, senator, and candidate for the presidency. Young White killed a great chief, the Kingfisher, in battle. After the return of the expedition it became a question whether the Government would pay the expenses of an expedition which it had not authorized. To test the question, Hugh L. White sent a petition to Congress asking compensation for his services. On the day named above the subject came before the Committee of the Whole House, when a report on Mr. White's petition, from the Secretary of War, was read. The report recounted the facts, and added that it was for the House to decide whether the provocation and danger were such as to justify the calling out of the troops. Whereupon "Mr. A. Jackson," in a few energetic remarks, defended the claims of his fellow-citizens. The debate continued for a considerable time, Jackson occasionally interposing explanations, and replying to the objections of members. The result of his exertions was, that the subject was referred to a select committee of five, Mr. A. Jackson chairman; who reported, of course, in favor of the petitioner, and recommended that the sum of twenty-two thousand eight hundred and sixteen dollars be appropriated for the payment of the troops, which was done.

The member from Tennessee did not again address the House of Representatives. His name appears in the records thenceforth only in the lists of yeas and nays.

Congress adjourned on the 3d of March, and Andrew Jackson took a final farewell of the House, for at the war session of the following summer he did not appear. His conduct in the House of Representatives was keenly approved by Tennesseeans.

A vacancy in the Senate of the United States occurring this year, Andrew Jackson received the appointment, and returned to Philadelphia in the autumn of 1797, a Senator.

In April, 1798, Senator Jackson asked and obtained leave of absence for the remainder of the session. He went home to Nashville, and immediately resigned his seat in the Senate.

Early in the year 1798, then, Andrew Jackson returned to his home on the banks of the Cumberland, a private citizen, and intending to remain such. But it seems he could not yet be spared from public life. Soon after his return to Tennessee he was elected by the Legislature to a seat on the bench of the Supreme Court of the State—a post which he said he accepted in obedience to his favorite maxim, that the citizen of a free commonwealth should never seek and never decline public duty. The office assigned him was next in consideration, as in emolument, to that of Governor; the Governor's salary being seven hundred and fifty dollars a year, and the judge's six hundred. He retained the judgeship for six years, holding courts in due succession at Jonesboro, Knoxville, Nashville, and at places of less importance, dispensing the best justice of which he was master.

It was while Jackson was judge of the Supreme Court of Tennessee that his feud with Governor Sevier came to an issue. First, there was a coolness between the two men; then altercations; then total estrangement; then loud, recriminating talk on both sides, reported to both; then various personal encounters, of which I heard in Tennessee so many different accounts that I was convinced no one knew anything about them. At last, in the year 1801, Jackson gained an advantage over Sevier which was peculiarly calculated to wound, disgust, and exasperate the impetuous old soldier, victor in so many battles. Sevier was then out of office. The major-generalship of militia was vacant, and the two belligerents were candidates for the post, which at that time was keenly coveted by the very first men in the State. Nor was it then merely an affair of title, regimentals, and showy gallopings on the days of general muster. There were then Indians to be kept in awe, as well as constant rumors and threatenings of war with France or England. The office of major-general was in the gift of the field officers, who were empowered by the Constitution to select their chief. The canvassings and general agitation which preceded the election on this occasion may be imagined. The day came. The election was held. There was a tie, an equal number of votes being cast for Jackson and Sevier. In such a conjuncture the Governor of the State, being, from his office, commander-in-chief of the militia, had a casting vote. Governor Roane gave his vote for Jackson, who thus became the major-general, to the discomfiture of the other competitor.

Jackson, as we have seen, accepted the judgeship of the Supreme Court, intending to carry on the business of a merchant, and to snatch time enough between his courts to make an occasional journey to Philadelphia for the purchase of a fresh supply of goods. For a while all went well with him; but eventually came the crash and panic of 1798 and 1799. Notice was forwarded to Jackson to provide for the payment of the notes with which he had bought his stock of goods. This was a staggering blow, not only because the amount of the loss was large, but because the notes had to be paid in money—*real* money, money that was current in Philadelphia—which, of all commodities, was the one most scarce in the new States of the far West. To the honor of Andrew Jackson be it recorded, that each of these large notes was paid, principal and interest, on the day of its maturity.

Andrew Jackson was a man singularly averse to anything complicated, and of all complications the one under which he was most restive was debt. So, about the year 1804, he resolved upon simplifying or "straightening out" his affairs and commencing life anew. He resigned his judgeship. He sold his house and improved farm on Hunter's Hill. He sold twenty-five thousand acres, more or less, of his wild lands in other parts of the State. He paid off all his debts. He removed with his negroes, to the place now known as the Hermitage, and lived once more in a house of logs. He went more extensively into mercantile business than ever.

Jackson was now a man with many irons in the fire. First, there was his farm, cultivated by slaves, superintended by Mrs. Jackson in the absence of her lord. The large family of slaves, one hundred and fifty in number, of which he died possessed, were mostly descended from the few that he owned in his storekeeping days. He was a vigilant and successful farmer. To use the language of the South, " He made good crops." He was proud of a well-cultivated field. Every visitor was invited to go the rounds of his farm and see his cotton, corn, and wheat, his horses, cows, and mules. He had also a backwoodsman's skill in repairing and contriving, and spent many a day in putting an old plow in order or finishing off a new cabin.

On his plantation he had a cotton gin, a rarity at that day, upon which there was a special tax of twenty dollars a year. The tax-books of Davidson County show that in 1804 there were but twenty-four gins in the county, of which Andrew Jackson was the owner of one. This cotton gin served to clean his own cotton, the cotton of his neighbors, and that which he took in exchange for goods.

General Jackson's fine horses were also a source of profit to him. At that period a good horse was among the pioneer's first necessities and most valued possessions; and to this day the horse is a creature of far more importance at the South, where every one rides and must ride on horseback, than at the North, where riding is the luxury of the few.

Soon after Jackson left the bench he set off for a tour in Virginia, then universally renowned for her breed of horses, with the sole object of procuring the most perfect horse in the country. The far-famed Truxton was the result of this journey—Truxton, winner of many a well-contested race and progenitor of a line of Truxtons highly prized in Tennessee to this hour.

CHAPTER V.

THE Revolutionary War introduced among the people of rustic America the practice of resorting to arms for the settlement of quarrels. Every man who had worn a sash or even shouldered a musket in that contest seems to have hugged the delusion that he was thenceforth subject to the code of honor. He retained the title and affected the tone of a soldier. I call it affectation, believing that no man with Saxon blood dominant in his veins ever yet fought a duel without being distinctly conscious that he was doing a very silly thing. Yet there never existed a people so given to dueling and other domestic battling as the people of the South and West from 1790 to 1810. In Charleston, about the year 1800, we are told, there was a club of duelists, in which every man took precedence according to the number of times he had been "out"—so difficult was it for the duelists to support the reproaches of their own good sense. "I believe," says General William Henry Harrison, "that there were more duels in the Northwestern army between the years 1791 and 1795 than ever took place in the same length of time, and among so small a body of men as composed the commissioned officers of the army, either in America or any other country."

As late as 1834, Miss Martineau tells us there were more duels fought in the city of New Orleans than there are days in the year—"fifteen on one Sunday morning";

"one hundred and two between the 1st of January and the end of April."

In the interior settlements, if dueling was rarer, fighting of a less formal and deadly character was so common as to excite scarcely any notice or remark. It was taken for granted, apparently, that whenever a number of men were gathered together for any purpose whatever there must be fighting. The meetings of the Legislature, the convening of courts, the assemblages out of doors for religious purposes, were all alike the occasion both of single combats and general fights. "The exercises of a market day," says the Rev. Mr. Milburn, "were usually varied by political speeches, a sheriff's sale, half a dozen free fights, and thrice as many horse-swaps."

Let most of the old Jacksonian quarrels pass into oblivion. Some of them, however, were of such a nature, and are so notorious, that they can not be omitted in any fair account of his career. We have now arrived at one of these. The series of trivial and absurd events which led to the horrible tragedy of the Dickinson duel —events which, but for that tragic ending, would be nothing more than amusing illustrations of the manners of a past age—now claim our attention.

For the autumn races of 1805, a great match was arranged between General Jackson's Truxton and Captain Joseph Ervin's Plowboy. The stakes were two thousand dollars, payable on the day of the race in notes, which notes were to be then due; forfeit, eight hundred dollars. Six persons were interested in this race: on Truxton's side, General Jackson, Major W. P. Anderson, Major Verrell, and Captain Pryor; on the side of Plowboy, Captain Ervin and his son-in-law, Charles Dickinson. Before the day appointed for the race arrived Ervin and Dickinson decided to pay the forfeit and withdraw their

horse, which was amicably done, and the affair was supposed to be at an end.

About this time a report reached General Jackson's
ears that Charles Dickinson had uttered disparaging
words of Mrs. Jackson, which was with Jackson the sin
not to be pardoned. Dickinson was a lawyer by profession, but, like Jackson, speculated in produce, horses,
and, it is said, in slaves. He was well connected, possessed considerable property, and had a large circle of
gay friends. He is represented as a somewhat wild, dissipated young man, yet not unamiable, nor disposed
wantonly to wound the feelings of others. When excited
by drink, or by any other cause, he was prone to talk
loosely and swear violently, as drunken men will. He
had the reputation of being the best shot in Tennessee.
Upon hearing this report, General Jackson called on
Dickinson and asked him if he had used the language
attributed to him. Dickinson replied that if he had, it
must have been when he was drunk. Further explanations and denials removed all ill feeling from General
Jackson's mind, and they separated in a friendly manner.

A second time, it is said, Dickinson uttered offensive
words respecting Mrs. Jackson in a tavern at Nashville,
which were duly conveyed by some meddling parasite
to General Jackson. Jackson, I am told, then went to
Captain Ervin and advised him to exert his influence
over his son-in-law, and induce him to restrain his
tongue and comport himself like a gentleman in his
cups. "I wish no quarrel with him," said Jackson; "he
is used by my enemies in Nashville, who are urging him
on to pick a quarrel with me. Advise him to stop in
time." It appears, however, that enmity grew between
these two men. In January, 1806, when the events occurred that are now to be related, there was the worst
possible feeling between them.

Deadly enmity existing between Jackson and Dickinson, a very trivial event was sufficient to bring them into collision. A young lawyer of Nashville, named Swann, misled by false information, circulated a report that Jackson had accused the owners of Plowboy of paying their forfeit in notes other than those which had been agreed upon—notes less valuable because not due at the date of settling. General Jackson, in one of his letters to Mr. Swann, went out of his way to assail Charles Dickinson by name, calling him "a base poltroon and cowardly talebearer," requesting Swann to show Dickinson these offensive words, and offering to meet him in the field if he desired satisfaction for the same. Upon reading the letter, Dickinson published a card which contained these words:

"I declare him, notwithstanding he is a major-general of the militia of Mero district, to be a worthless scoundrel, 'a poltroon and a coward'—a man who, by frivolous and evasive pretexts, avoided giving the satisfaction which was due to a gentleman whom he had injured. This has prevented me from calling on him in the manner I should otherwise have done, for I am well convinced that he is too great a coward to administer any of those anodynes he promised me in his letter to Mr. Swann."

Jackson instantly challenged Dickinson. The challenge was promptly accepted. Friday, May 30, 1806, was the day appointed for the meeting; the weapons, pistols; the place, a spot on the banks of the Red River, in Kentucky.

The place appointed for the meeting was a long day's ride from Nashville. Thursday morning, before the dawn of day, Dickinson stole from the side of his young and beautiful wife, and began silently to prepare for the journey.

He mounted his horse and repaired to the rendezvous where his second and half a dozen of the gay blades of Nashville were waiting to escort him on his journey. Away they rode, in the highest spirits, as though they were upon a party of pleasure. Indeed, they made a party of pleasure of it. When they stopped for rest or refreshment, Dickinson is said to have amused the company by displaying his wonderful skill with the pistol. Once, at a distance of twenty-four feet, he fired four balls, each at the word of command, into a space that could be covered by a silver dollar. Several times he cut a string with his bullet from the same distance. It is said that he left a severed string hanging near a tavern, and said to the landlord, as he rode away, "If General Jackson comes along this road, show him *that!*"

Very different was the demeanor of General Jackson and the party that accompanied him. His second, General Thomas Overton, an old Revolutionary soldier, versed in the science. and familiar with the practice of dueling, had reflected deeply upon the conditions of the coming combat, with the view to conclude upon the tactics most likely to save his friend from Dickinson's unerring bullet. For this duel was not to be the amusing mockery that some modern duels have been. This duel was to be *real.* It was to be an affair in which each man was to strive with his utmost skill to effect the purpose of the occasion—disable his antagonist and save his own life. As the principal and the second rode apart from the rest, they discussed all the chances and probabilities with the single aim to decide upon a course which should result in the disabling of Dickinson and the saving of Jackson. The mode of fighting which had been agreed upon was somewhat peculiar. The pistols were to be held downward until the word was given to fire; then each man was to fire as soon as he pleased. With such an arrangement it was scarcely possible that both the pistols should be discharged at the same moment. There was a chance, even, that by extreme quickness of movement one man could bring down his antagonist without himself receiving a shot. The question anxiously discussed between Jackson and Overton was this: Shall we try to get the first shot, or shall we permit Dickinson to have it? They agreed, at length, that it would be decidedly better to *let* Dickinson fire first.

Jackson ate heartily at supper that night, conversing in a lively, pleasant manner, and smoked his evening pipe as usual. Jacob Smith remembers being exceedingly well pleased with his guest, and, on learning the cause of his visit, heartily wishing him a safe deliverance. Before breakfast on the next morning the whole party mounted and rode down the road that wound close along the picturesque banks of the stream. The horsemen rode about a mile along the river, then turned down toward the river to a point on the bank where they had expected to find a ferryman. No ferryman appearing, Jackson spurred his horse into the stream and dashed across, followed by all his party. They rode into the poplar forest two hundred yards or less, to a spot near the center of a level platform or river bottom, then covered with forest, now smiling with cultivated fields. The horsemen halted and dismounted just before reaching the appointed place. Jackson, Overton, and a surgeon who had come with them from home walked on together, and the rest led their horses a short distance in an opposite direction.

"How do you feel about it now, general?" asked one of the party, as Jackson turned to go.

"Oh, all right," replied Jackson, gayly; "I shall wing him, never fear."

Dickinson's second won the choice of position, and Jackson's the office of giving the word. The astute Overton considered this giving of the word a matter of great importance, and he had already determined how he would give it if the lot fell to him. The eight paces were measured off and the men placed. Both were perfectly collected. All the politenesses of such occasions were very strictly and elegantly performed. Jackson was dressed in a loose frock-coat, buttoned carelessly over his chest and concealing in some degree the extreme slenderness of his figure. Dickinson was the younger and handsomer man of the two. But Jackson's tall, erect figure, and the intensity of his demeanor, it is said, gave him a most superior and commanding air, as he stood under the tall poplars on this bright May morning, silently awaiting the moment.

"Are you ready?" said Overton.

"I am ready," replied Dickinson.

"I am ready," said Jackson.

The words were no sooner pronounced than Overton, with a sudden shout, cried, using his old-country pronunciation:

"Fere!"

Dickinson raised his pistol quickly and fired. Overton, who was looking with anxiety and dread at Jackson, saw a puff of dust fly from the breast of his coat, and saw him raise his left arm and place it tightly across his chest. He is surely hit, thought Overton, and in a bad place, too. But no; he does not fall. He raised his pistol. Overton glanced at Dickinson. Amazed at the unwonted failure of his aim, and apparently appalled at the awful figure and face before him, Dickinson had unconsciously recoiled a pace or two.

"Great God!" he faltered, "have I missed him?"

"Back to the MARK, sir!" shrieked Overton with his hand upon his pistol.

Dickinson recovered his composure, stepped forward to the peg, and stood with his eyes averted from his antagonist. All this was the work of a moment, though it requires many words to tell it.

General Jackson took deliberate aim and pulled the trigger. The pistol neither snapped nor went off. He looked at the trigger, and discovered that it had stopped at half-cock. He drew it back to its place and took aim a second time. He fired. Dickinson's face blanched; he reeled; his friends rushed toward him, caught him in their arms, and gently seated him on the ground, leaning against a bush. They stripped off his clothes. The blood was gushing from his side in a torrent. The ball had passed through the body, below the ribs. Such a wound could not but be fatal.

Overton went forward and learned the condition of the wounded man. Rejoining his principal, he said, "He won't want anything more of you, general," and conducted him from the ground. They had gone a hundred yards, Overton walking on one side of Jackson, the surgeon on the other, and neither speaking a word, when the surgeon observed that one of Jackson's shoes was full of blood.

"My God! General Jackson, are you hit?" he exclaimed, pointing to the blood.

"Oh! I believe," replied Jackson, "that he has pinked me a little. Let's look at it. But say nothing about it there," pointing to the house.

He opened his coat. Dickinson's aim had been perfect. He had sent the ball precisely where he supposed Jackson's heart was beating. But the thinness of his body and the looseness of his coat combining to deceive Dickinson, the ball had only broken a rib or two and raked the breast-bone. It was a somewhat painful, bad-looking wound, but neither severe nor dangerous, and he was able to ride to the tavern without much inconvenience. Upon approaching the house he went up to one of the negro women who was churning and asked her if the butter had come. She said it was just coming. He asked for some buttermilk. While she was getting it for him she observed him furtively open his coat and look within it. She saw that his shirt was soaked with blood, and she stood gazing in blank horror at the sight, dipper in hand. He caught her eye, and hastily buttoned his coat again. She dipped out a quart measure full of buttermilk and gave it to him. He drank it off at a draught; then went in, took off his coat, and had his wound carefully examined and dressed. That done, he dispatched one of his retinue to Dr. Catlett, to inquire respecting the condition of Dickinson, and to say that the surgeon attending himself would be glad to contribute his aid toward Mr. Dickinson's relief. Polite reply was returned that Mr. Dickinson's case was past surgery. In the course of the day General Jackson sent a bottle of wine to Dr. Catlett for the use of his patient.

But there was one gratification which Jackson could not, even in such circumstances, grant him. A very old friend of General Jackson writes to me thus: "Although the general had been wounded, he did not desire it should be known until he had left the neighborhood, and had therefore concealed it at first from his own friends. His reason for this, as he once stated to me, was, that as Dickinson considered himself the best shot in the world, and was certain of killing him at the first fire, he did not want him to have the gratification even of knowing that he had touched him."

Poor Dickinson bled to death.

General Jackson's wound proved to be more severe

and troublesome than was at first anticipated. It was nearly a month before he could move about without inconvenience, and when the wound healed it healed falsely; that is, some of the viscera were slightly displaced, and so remained. Twenty years after, this forgotten wound forced itself upon his remembrance, and kept itself there for many a year.

It is not true, as has been alleged, that this duel did not affect General Jackson's popularity in Tennessee. It followed quick upon his feud with Governor Sevier, and both quarrels told against him in many quarters of the State. And though there were large numbers whom the nerve and courage which he had displayed in the duel blinded to all considerations of civilization and morality, yet it is certain that at no time between the years 1806 and 1812 could General Jackson have been elected to any office in Tennessee that required a majority of the voters of the whole State. Beyond the circle of his own friends, which was large, there existed a very general impression that he was a violent, overbearing, passionate man.

CHAPTER VI.

AT HOME.

BETWEEN the fighting of this bloody duel and the beginning of the War of 1812 there is not much to relate of General Jackson. A few incidents and anecdotes of his private life may detain us a moment from the stirring scenes of his military career.

He removed, as we have before related, from Hunter's Hill, about the year 1804, to the adjoining estate, which he named the Hermitage. The spacious mansion now standing on that estate, in which he resided during the last twenty-five years of his life, was not built until about the year 1819. A square, two-story blockhouse was General Jackson's first dwelling-place on the Hermitage farm. This house, like many others of its class, contained three rooms—one on the ground floor and two upstairs. To this house was soon added a smaller one, which stood about twenty feet from the principal structure, and was connected with it by a covered passage. This was General Jackson's establishment from 1804 to 1819.

In an establishment so restricted General Jackson and his good-hearted wife continued to dispense a most generous hospitality. A lady of Nashville told me that she has often been at the Hermitage in those simple old times, when there was in each of the four available rooms not a guest merely but a family; while the young men and solitary travelers who chanced to drop in disposed of themselves on the piazza, or any other half shelter about the house. "Put down in your book," said one of General Jackson's oldest neighbors, "that the general was the prince of hospitality; not because he entertained a great many people, but because the poor, belated peddler was as welcome as the President of the United States, and made so much at his ease that he felt as though he had got home."

On May 29, 1805, Colonel Burr, then making his first tour of the Western country, visited the thriving frontier town of Nashville. Throughout the West Burr was received as the great man, and nowhere with such distinction as at Nashville. People poured in from the adjacent country to see and welcome so renowned a personage. Flags, cannons, and martial music contributed to the *éclat* of his reception. An extemporized but superabundant dinner concluded the ceremonies, in the course of which Burr addressed the multitude with the serious grace that usually marked his demeanor in public. Could Jackson be absent from such an ovation—Jackson, who had been with the great man in Congress, and worked in concert with him for Tennessee? On the morning of this bright day General Jackson mounted one of his finest horses and rode to Nashville, attended by a servant leading a milk-white mare. In the course of the dinner General Jackson gave a toast, "Millions for defense, but not one cent for tribute!" and when Colonel Burr retired from the apartment General Overton proposed his health to the company. General Jackson returned home at the close of the day, accompanied by Colonel Burr, who was to be his guest during his stay in that vicinity. Burr remained only five days at the Hermitage, but promised to make a longer visit on his return.

On August 6, 1805, Burr visited the Hermitage again on his return from New Orleans, as he had promised. Of this visit, which lasted eight days, we have no knowledge except that derived from Burr's diary: "Arrived at Nashville on the 6th August. For a week I have been lounging at the house of General Jackson, once a lawyer, after a judge, now a planter; a man of intelligence, and one of those prompt, frank, ardent souls whom I love to meet. The general has no children, but two lovely nieces made a visit of some days, contributed greatly to my amusement, and have cured me of all the evils of my wilderness jaunt. If I had time I would describe to you these two girls, for they deserve it. To-morrow I move on toward Lexington." There is no doubt as to the topic upon which Colonel Burr and General Jackson chiefly conversed on this occasion. There was but one topic then in the Western country—the threatened war with Spain.

Colonel Burr returned to the East. Months passed, during which Jackson and Burr occasionally corresponded.

In September, 1806, three months after the duel with Dickinson, Colonel Burr was again the guest of General Jackson. On this occasion he had brought to the Western country, and left on Blennerhassett Island, his daughter Theodosia, intending never again to return to the Eastern States. He was in the full tide of preparation for descending to the lower country. The morning after his arrival at the Hermitage, General Jackson, on hospitable thoughts intent, wrote to a friend in Nashville the following note: "Colonel Burr is with me; he arrived last night. I would be happy if you would call and see the colonel before you return. Say to General O. that I shall expect to see him here on to-morrow with you. Would it not be well for us to do something as a mark of attention to the colonel? He has always been and is still a true and trusty friend to Tennessee. If General Robertson is with you when you receive this, be good enough to say to him that Colonel Burr is in the country. I know that General Robertson will be happy in joining in anything that will tend to show a mark of respect to this worthy visitant."

After a stay of a few days Colonel Burr left Tennessee to take up the threads of his enterprise in Kentucky and Ohio.

October passed by. On the 3d of November, General Jackson, in his character of business man, received from Burr some important orders : one for the building, on Stone's River, at Clover Bottom, of five large boats, such as were then used for descending the Western rivers, and another for the gradual purchase of a large quantity of provisions for transportation in those boats. A sum of money, in Kentucky bank-notes, amounting to three thousand five hundred dollars, accompanied the orders. General Jackson, nothing doubting, and never reluctant to do business, took Burr's letter of directions and the money to his partner, John Coffee, and requested him to contract at once for the boats and prepare for the purchase of the provisions. Coffee proceeded forthwith to transact the business. I notice, also, that Patton Anderson, one of Jackson's special intimates, was all activity in raising a company of young men to accompany Burr down the river. I observe, too, that Anderson's expenses were paid out of the money sent by Burr to Jackson ; at least, in the account rendered to Burr by Jackson and Coffee at the final settlement there is an item of seven hundred dollars cash paid to Anderson. Anderson succeeded in getting seventy-five young men to enlist in his company.

It was not until the 10th of November, a week after the receipt of Burr's orders and money, that General Jackson, according to his own account, began to think there might be some truth in the reports which attributed to Burr unlawful designs—reports which he had previously regarded only as new evidences of the malice of Burr's political enemies and his own.

But about the date mentioned, while General Jackson and his partners were full of Burr's business, a friend of Jackson's visited the Hermitage, who succeeded in convincing him that some gigantic scheme of iniquity was on foot in the United States—a conspiracy for the dismemberment of the Union—and that it was possible, nay, almost probable, that Colonel Burr's extensive preparations of boats, provisions, and men had some connection with this nefarious plan. The President's proclamation, denouncing Burr, soon followed.

It fell to the lot of General Jackson, as commanding officer of militia, to take the lead in the measures designed to procure the arrest of Burr and his confederates. The general made great exertions to accomplish this object, but Burr had gone beyond pursuit. It was widely believed at the time that General Jackson was involved in the unlawful part of Burr's schemes, but there was not the slightest ground for such a belief, and nothing can be more complete than the chain of testimony that establishes his innocence. A few months later we find him at Richmond, whither he had been summoned as a witness in the trial of Burr. There he harangued the crowd in the Capitol Square, defending Burr, and angrily denouncing Jefferson as a persecutor. He made himself so conspicuous as Burr's champion at Richmond, that Mr. Madison, the Secretary of State, took offense at it, and remembered it to Jackson's disadvantage five years later, when he was President of the United States, with a war on his hands. For the same reason, I presume, it was that Jackson was not called upon to give testimony upon the trial. Burr, it seems, was equally satisfied with Jackson. Blennerhasset, in that part of his diary which records his prison interviews with Burr, says: " We passed to the topics of our late adventures on the Mississippi, in which Burr said little, but declared he did not know of any reason to blame General Jackson, of Tennessee, for anything he had done or omitted. But he declares he will not lose a day after the favorable issue at the Capitol (his acquittal)—of which he has no doubt—to direct his entire attention to setting up his projects (which have only been suspended) on a better model, 'in which work,' he says, 'he has even here made some progress.'" Jackson, on his part, went all lengths in defense of Burr; nor was it possible for him to support any man in any other way. Toward Wilkinson, whom he regarded as the betrayer of Burr, his anger burned with such fury, that if the two men had met in a place convenient the meeting could hardly have had any other result than a—"difficulty."

About the year 1809 it chanced that twins were born to one of Mrs. Jackson's brothers, Savern Donelson. The mother, not in perfect health, was scarcely able to sustain both these newcomers. Mrs. Jackson, partly to relieve her sister and partly with the wish to provide a son and heir for her husband, took one of the infants, when it was but a few days old, home to the Hermitage. The general soon became extremely fond of the boy, gave him his own name, adopted him, and treated him thenceforth, to the last hour of his life, not as a son merely but as an only son. This boy was the late Andrew Jackson, inheritor of the general's estate and name, master of the Hermitage until it became the property of the State of Tennessee. A few years later another little nephew of Mrs. Jackson's, the well-known Andrew Jackson Donelson, became an inmate of the Hermitage, and was educated by General Jackson.

CHAPTER VII.

IN THE FIELD.

At the beginning of the War of 1812 there was not a militia general in the Western country less likely to receive a commission from the General Government than Andrew Jackson. There were unpleasant traditions and recollections connected with his name in Mr. Madison's Cabinet, as we know.

There were those, however, who were strongly convinced that General Jackson was the very man, of all who lived in the valley of the Mississippi, to be intrusted with its defense. Aaron Burr thought so for one. He had just returned to New York, after his four years' exile, when the war began. "I know," said Colonel Burr, "that my word is not worth much with Madison ; but you may tell him from me that there is an unknown man in the West, named Andrew Jackson, who will do credit to a commission in the army if conferred on him." This remarkable prediction of what was soon verified, and proof of Burr's knowledge of the then obscure individual he recommended to notice, occurred before General Jackson had probably ever heard a volley of musket balls, or performed any part to indicate his future military distinction.

It was General Jackson's promptitude in tendering his services and the services of his division, and that alone, which softened the repugnance of the President and his Cabinet. The war was declared on the 12th of

June. Such news is not carried, but flies, and so may have reached Nashville by the 20th. On the 25th, General Jackson offered to the President, through Governor Blount, his own services and those of twenty-five hundred volunteers of his division. A response to the declaration of war so timely and practical could not but have been extremely gratifying to an administration (never too confident in itself) that was then entering upon a contest to which a powerful minority was opposed, and with a presidential election only four months distant. The reply of the Secretary of War, dated July 11th, was as cordial as a communication of the kind could be. The President, he said, had received the tender of service by General Jackson and the volunteers under his command " with peculiar satisfaction." " In accepting their services," added the Secretary, "the President can not withhold an expression of his admiration of the zeal and ardor by which they are animated." Governor Blount was evidently more than satisfied with the result of the offer; he publicly thanked General Jackson and the volunteers for the honor they had done the State of Tennessee by making it.

Thus we find General Jackson's services accepted by the President before hostilities could have seriously begun. The summer passed, however, and the autumn came, and still he was at home upon his farm.

After Hull's failure in Canada, fears were entertained that the British would direct their released forces against the ports of the Gulf of Mexico, particularly New Orleans, where General James Wilkinson still commanded. On October 21st the Governor of Tennessee was requested to dispatch fifteen hundred of the Tennessee troops to the re-enforcement of General Wilkinson. On November 1st Governor Blount issued the requisite orders to General Jackson, who entered at once upon the task of preparing for the descent of the river with his volunteers.

The 10th of December was the day appointed for the troops to rendezvous at Nashville. The climate of Tennessee, generally so pleasant, is liable to brief periods of severe cold. Twice within the memory of living persons the Cumberland has been frozen over at Nashville, and as often snow has fallen there to the depth of a foot. It so chanced that the day named for the assembling of the troops was the coldest that had been known at Nashville for many years, and there was deep snow on the ground. Such was the enthusiasm, however, of the volunteers, that more than two thousand presented themselves on the appointed day. The general was no less puzzled than pleased by this alacrity. Nashville was still little more than a large village, not capable of affording the merest shelter to such a concourse of soldiers — who, in any weather not extraordinary, would have disdained a roof. There was no resource for the mass of the troops but to camp out. Fortunately, the quartermaster, Major William B. Lewis, had provided a thousand cords of wood for the use of the men—a quantity that was supposed to be sufficient to last till they embarked. Every stick of the wood was burned the first night in keeping the men from freezing. From dark until nearly daylight the general and the quartermaster were out among the troops, employed in providing for this unexpected and perilous exigency—seeing that drunken men were brought within reach of the fire, and that no drowsy sentinel slept the sleep of death.

The extreme cold soon passed away, however, and the organization of the troops proceeded. In a few days the little army was in readiness: one regiment of cavalry, commanded by Colonel John Coffee, six hundred and seventy in number; two regiments of infantry, fourteen hundred men in all, one regiment commanded by Colonel William Hall, the other by Colonel Thomas H. Benton. Major William B. Lewis, the general's neighbor and friend, was the quartermaster. William Carroll, a young man from Pennsylvania, a new favorite of the general's, was the brigade inspector. The general's aide and secretary was John Reid, long his companion in the field, afterward his biographer. The troops were of the very best material the State afforded—planters, business men, their sons and grandsons—a large proportion of them descended from Revolutionary soldiers who had settled in great numbers in the beautiful valley of the Cumberland. John Coffee was a host in himself—a plain, brave, modest, stalwart man, devoted to his chief, to Tennessee, and to the Union. He had been recently married to Polly Donelson, the daughter of Captain John Donelson, who had given them the farm on which they lived.

On the 7th of January all was ready. The infantry embarked, and the flotilla dropped down the river. Colonel Coffee and the mounted men marched across the country, and were to rejoin the general at Natchez. " I have the pleasure to inform you," wrote Jackson to the Secretary of War just before leaving home, " that I am now at the head of 2,070 volunteers, the choicest of our citizens, who go at the call of their country to execute the will of the Government, who have no constitutional scruples, and, if the Government orders, will rejoice at the opportunity of placing the American eagle on the ramparts of Mobile, Pensacola, and Fort St. Augustine, effectually banishing from the Southern coasts all British influence."

Down the Cumberland to the Ohio; down the Ohio to the Mississippi; down the Mississippi toward New Orleans; stopping here and there for supplies; delayed for days at a time by the ice in the swift Ohio; grounding a boat now and then; losing one altogether—the fleet pursued its course, crunching through the floating masses, but making fair progress, for the space of thirty-nine days.

The weather was often very cold and tempestuous, and the frail boats afforded only an imperfect shelter; but all the little army, from the general to the privates, were in the highest spirits, and burned with the desire to do their part in restoring the diminished prestige of the American arms; to atone for the shocking failures of the North by making new conquests at the South. On the 15th of February, at dawn of day, they had left a thousand miles of winding stream behind them, and saw before them the little town of Natchez. The fleet came to. The men were rejoiced to hear that Colonel Coffee and his mounted regiment had already arrived in the vicinity.

Here General Jackson received a dispatch from General Wilkinson requesting him to halt at Natchez, as neither quarters nor provisions were ready for them at New Orleans, nor had an enemy yet made his appearance in the Southern waters. Wilkinson added, that he had received no orders respecting the Tennesseeans, knew not their destination, and should not think of yielding his command "until regularly relieved by superior authority." Jackson assented to the policy of remaining at Natchez for further instructions; but with regard to General Wilkinson's uneasiness on the question of rank he said, in his reply, "I have marched with the true spirit of a soldier, to serve my country at any and every point where service can be rendered," and "the detachment under my command shall be kept in complete readiness to move to any point at which an enemy may appear, at the shortest notice." So, at

5

Natchez, the troops disembarked, and, encamping in a pleasant and salubrious place a few miles from the town, passed their days in learning the duties of the soldier.

The month of February passed away and still the army was in camp, employed in nothing more serious than the daily drill. No one knew when they were to move, where they were to go, nor what they were to do. The commanding general was not a little impatient, and even the more placid Colonel Coffee longed to be in action.

At length, on a Sunday morning toward the end of March, an express from Washington reached the camp, and a letter from the War Department was placed in the general's hands. We can imagine the intensity of feeling with which he tore it open and gathered its purport, and the fever of excitement which the news of its arrival kindled throughout the camp. The communication was signed " J. Armstrong." Eustis, then, was out of office. Yes, he left the department February 4th, and this letter was written by the new Secretary two days after. But its contents? Was it the perusal of this astounding letter that caused the general's hair to stand on end, and remain forever after erect and bristling, *un*like the quills upon the fretful porcupine? Fancy, if you can, the demeanor, attitude, countenance, of this fiery and generous soldier, as he read and re-read, with ever-growing wonder and wrath, the following epistle:

" SIR: The causes of embodying and marching to New Orleans the corps under your command having ceased to exist, you will, on the receipt of this letter, consider it as dismissed from public service, and take measures to have delivered over to Major-General Wilkinson all the articles of public property which may have been put into its possession. You will accept for yourself and the corps the thanks of the President of the United States."

Dismissed without pay, without means of transport, without provision for the sick? How could he dismiss men so far from home, to whom, on receiving them from their parents, he had promised to be a father, and either to restore them in honor to their arms, or give them a soldier's burial?

His resolution was taken on the instant *never* to disband his troops till he had led them back to the borders of their own State! The very day on which the order arrived the general issued the requisite directions for the preparation of wagons, provisions, and ammunition. On the next day he dispatched letters, indignant and explanatory, to the Secretary of War, to Governor Blount, to the President, and to General Wilkinson. He attributed the strange conduct of the Government to every cause but the right one—its own inexperience, and the difficulty of directing operations at places so remote from the seat of Government.

At the last moment came the orders of the Government (which ought to have accompanied the order to disband) directing the force under General Jackson to be paid off, and allowed pay and rations for the journey home. It was too late. The general was resolved, whatever might betide, to conduct the men back to their homes, in person, as an organized body. " I shall commence the line of march," he wrote to Wilkinson, " on Thursday, the 25th. Should the contractor not feel himself justified in sending on provisions for my infantry, or the quartermaster wagons for the transportation of my sick, I shall dismount the cavalry, carry them on, and provide the means for their support out of my private funds. If that should fail, I thank my God we have plenty of horses to feed my troops to the Tennessee, where I know my country will meet me with ample supplies. These brave men, at the call of their country, voluntarily rallied round its insulted standard. They followed me to the field. I shall carefully march them back to their homes. It is for the agents of the Government to account to the State of Tennessee and the whole world for their singular and unusual conduct to this detachment."

This resolve of his to disobey his Government for their sakes, and the manner in which he executed that resolve, raised his popularity to the highest point. When the little army set out from Natchez for a march of five hundred miles through the wilderness, there were a hundred and fifty men on the sick list, of whom fifty-six could not raise their heads from the pillow. There were but eleven wagons for the conveyance of these. The rest of the sick were mounted on the horses of the officers. The general had three excellent horses, and gave them all up to the sick men, himself trudging along on foot with the brisk pace that was usual with him. Day after day he tramped gayly along the miry forest roads, never tired, and always ready with a cheery word for the others. They marched with extraordinary speed, averaging eighteen miles a day, and performing the whole journey in less than a month; and yet the sick men rapidly recovered under the reviving influences of a homeward march. "Where am I?" asked one young fellow who had been lifted to his place in a wagon when insensible and apparently dying. "On your way *home!*" cried the general, merrily; and the young soldier began to improve from that hour, and reached home in good health.

On approaching the borders of the State the general

again offered his services to the Government to aid in, or conduct, a new invasion of Canada. His force, he said, could be increased if necessary, and he had a few standards wearing the American eagle that he should be happy to place upon the enemy's ramparts. But the desired response came not; and so, on the 22d of May, the last of his army was drawn up on the public square of Nashville waiting only for the word of command to disperse to their homes.

The troops were dismissed, exulting in their commander, and spreading wide the fame of his gallant and graceful conduct. " Long will their general live in the memory of the volunteers of West Tennessee," said the Nashville Whig, a day or two after the troops were disbanded, " for his benevolent, humane, and fatherly treatment of his soldiers. If gratitude and love can reward him, General Jackson has them. It affords us pleasure to say that we believe there is not a man belonging to the detachment but what loves him. His fellow-citizens at home are not less pleased with his conduct. We fondly hope his merited worth will not be overlooked by the Government."

These events were not regarded at Washington in the light they were at Nashville. The " Government " came very near making up its mind to let the general bear the responsibilities which he had incurred. Colonel Benton says: " We all returned; were discharged; dispersed among our homes, and the fine chance on which we had so much counted was all gone. And now came a blow upon Jackson himself—the fruit of the moneyed responsibility which he had assumed. His transportation drafts were all protested—returned upon him for payment, which was impossible, and directions to bring suit. This was the month of May. I was coming on to Washington on my own account, and cordially took charge of Jackson's case. Suits were delayed until the result of his application of relief could be heard. I arrived at this city. Congress was in session—the extra session of the spring and summer of 1813. I applied to the members of Congress from Tennessee; they could do nothing. I applied to the Secretary of War; he did nothing.

"Weeks had passed away, and the time for delay was expiring at Nashville. Ruin seemed to be hovering over the head of Jackson, and I felt the necessity of some decisive movement. I was young then, and had some material in me—perhaps some boldness, and the occasion brought it out. I resolved to take a step, characterized in the letter which I wrote to the general as '*an appeal from the justice to the fears of the Administration.*' I remember the words, though I have never seen the letter since. I drew up a memoir, addressed to the Secretary of War, representing to him that these volunteers were drawn from the bosoms of almost every substantial family in Tennessee; that the whole State stood by Jackson in bringing them home; and that the State would be lost to the Administration if he was left to suffer. It was upon this last argument that I relied—all those founded on justice having failed.

"It was on a Saturday morning, June 12th, that I carried this memoir to the War Office and delivered it. Monday morning I came back early to learn the result of my argument. The Secretary was not yet in. I spoke to the chief clerk (who was afterward Adjutant-General Parker), and inquired if the Secretary had left any answer for me before he left the office on Saturday. He said No, but that he had put the memoir in his side-pocket—the breast-pocket—and carried it home with him, saying he would take it for his Sunday's consideration. That encouraged me—gave a gleam of hope and a feeling of satisfaction. I thought it a good subject for his Sunday's meditation. Presently he arrived. I stepped in before anybody to his office.

"He told me quickly and kindly that there was much reason in what I had said, but that there was no way for him to do it ; that Congress would have to give the relief. I answered him that I thought there was a way for him to do it: it was, to give an order to General Wilkinson, Quartermaster-General in the Southern Department, to pay for so much transportation as General Jackson's command would have been entitled to if it had returned under regular orders. Upon the instant he took up a pen, wrote down the very words I had spoken, directed a clerk to put them into form, and the work was done. The order went off immediately, and Jackson was relieved from imminent impending ruin and Tennessee remained firm to the Administration."

Meanwhile, General Jackson was drawn, much against his will, into a "difficulty" with Jesse Benton, a brother of Colonel Thomas H. Benton, who had just rendered him so important a service. He had even served as second in a duel between Colonel Carroll and Jesse Benton, in which Benton had been wounded. It happened, too, that Colonel Benton heard this strange news at the most unfortunate moment. He had completed his business at Washington, had sent on to Tennessee the news of his great success, and was about to return home, when he heard of this duel, and heard, too, that General Jackson had gone to the field not as his brother's friend but as the second of his brother's antagonist! Soon came wild letters from Jesse, so narrating the affair as to place the conduct of General Jackson in the worst possible light. Officious friends of the Bentons, foes to Jackson and to Carroll, wrote to Colonel Benton in a similar strain, adding fuel to the fire of his indignation. Benton wrote to Jackson denouncing his conduct in offensive terms. Jackson replied, in effect, that before addressing him in that manner Colonel Benton should have inquired of *him* what his conduct really had been—not listened to the tales of designing and interested parties. Benton wrote still more angrily. He said that General Jackson had conducted the duel in a "savage, unequal, unfair, and base manner." On his way home through Tennessee, especially at Knoxville, he inveighed bitterly and loudly, in public places, against General Jackson, using language such as angry men *did* use in the Western country fifty years ago.

Jackson had liked Thomas Benton, and remembered with gratitude his parents, particularly his mother, who had been gracious and good to him when he was a "raw lad" in North Carolina. Jackson was therefore sincerely unwilling to break with him, and manifested a degree of forbearance which it is a pity he could not have maintained to the end. He took fire at last, threw old friendship to the winds, and swore by the Eternal that he would horsewhip Tom Benton the first time he met him.

On reaching Nashville Colonel Benton and his brother Jesse did not go to their accustomed inn, but stopped at the City Hotel, to avoid General Jackson, unless he chose to go out of his way to seek them. This was on the 3d of September. In the evening of the same day it came to pass that General Jackson and Colonel Coffee rode into town, and put up their horses as usual, at the Nashville Inn.

The next morning, about nine, Colonel Coffee proposed to General Jackson that they should stroll over to the post-office. They started. The general carried with him, as he ordinarily did, his riding-whip. He also wore a smallsword, as all gentlemen once did, and as official persons were accustomed to do in Tennessee as late as the War of 1812. As they drew near they observed that Jesse Benton was standing before the hotel near his brother. On coming up to where Colonel Benton stood, General Jackson turned suddenly toward him, with his whip in his right hand, and, stepping up to him, said:

"Now, you d——d rascal, I'm going to punish you. Defend yourself!"

Benton put his hand into his breast-pocket and seemed to be fumbling for his pistol. As quick as lightning Jackson drew a pistol from a pocket behind him, and presented it full at his antagonist, who recoiled a pace or two. Jackson advanced upon him. Benton continued to step slowly backward, Jackson close upon him, with a pistol at his heart, until they had reached the back door of the hotel and were in the act of turning down the back piazza. At that moment, just as Jackson was beginning to turn, Jesse Benton entered the passage behind the belligerents, and, seeing his brother's danger, raised his pistol and fired at Jackson. The pistol was loaded with two balls and a large slug. The slug took effect in Jackson's left shoulder, shattering it horribly. One of the balls struck the thick part of his left arm, and buried itself near the bone. The other ball splintered the board partition at his side. The shock of the wounds was such that Jackson fell across the entry and remained prostrate, bleeding profusely.

Coffee had remained just outside, meanwhile. Hearing the report of the pistol, he sprang into the entry, and, seeing his chief prostrate at the feet of Colonel Benton, concluded that it was *his* ball that had laid him low. He rushed upon Benton, drew his pistol, fired, and missed. Then he "clubbed" his pistol, and was about to strike, when Colonel Benton, in stepping backward, came to some stairs of which he was not aware and fell headlong to the bottom. Coffee, thinking him *hors de combat*, hastened to the assistance of his wounded general.

Faint from the loss of blood, Jackson was conveyed to a room in the Nashville Inn, his wound still bleeding fearfully. Before the bleeding could be stopped, two mattresses, as Mrs. Jackson used to say, were soaked through, and the general was reduced almost to the last gasp. All the doctors in Nashville were soon in attendance, all but one of whom, and he a young man, recommended the amputation of the shattered arm. " I'll keep my arm," said the wounded man, and he kept it. No attempt was made to extract the ball, and it remained in the arm for twenty years. The ghastly wounds in the shoulder were dressed, in the simple manner of the Indians and pioneers, with poultices of slippery elm and other products of the woods. The patient was utterly prostrated with the loss of blood. It was two or three weeks before he could leave his bed.

After the retirement of the general's friends the Bentons remained for an hour or more upon the scene of the affray, denouncing Jackson as an assassin, and a defeated assassin. They defied him to come forth and renew the strife. Colonel Benton made a parade of breaking Jackson's smallsword, which had been dropped in the struggle and left on the floor of the hotel. He broke it in the public square, and accompanied the act with words defiant and contemptuous, uttered in the loudest tones of his thundering voice. The general's friends, all anxiously engaged around the couch of their bleeding chief, disregarded these demonstrations at the time, and the brothers retired, victorious and exulting.

Shortly after the affray Colonel Benton went to his home in Franklin, Tennessee, beyond the reach of

"Jackson's puppies." He was appointed lieutenant-colonel in the regular army, left Tennessee, resigned his commission at the close of the war, emigrated to Missouri, and never again met General Jackson till 1823, when both were members of the Senate of the United States. Jesse Benton, I may add, never forgave General Jackson, nor could he ever excuse his brother for forgiving the general. Publications against Jackson by the angry Jesse, dated as late as 1828, may be seen in old collections of political trash.

CHAPTER VIII.

THE MASSACRE AT FORT MIMS.

AUGUST 30, 1813, was the date of this most terrible event. The place was a fort, or stockade-of-refuge, on the shores of Lake Tensaw, in the southern part of what is now the State of Alabama.

One Samuel Mims, an old and wealthy inhabitant of the Indian country, had inclosed with upright logs an acre of land, in the middle of which stood his house, a spacious one-story building, with sheds adjoining. The inclosure, pierced with five hundred portholes three and a half feet from the ground, was entered by two heavy, rude gates, one on the eastern, and one on the western side. In a corner, on a slight elevation, a blockhouse was begun but never finished. When the country became thoroughly alarmed by the hostility of the Indians, the inhabitants along the Alabama River, few in number and without means of defense, had left their crops standing in the fields and their houses open to the plunderer, and had rushed to the blockhouses and stockades, of which there were twenty in a line of seventy miles. The neighbors of Mr. Mims resorted to his inclosure, each family hastening to construct within it a rough cabin for its own accommodation.

As soon as the fort—for fort it was called—was sufficiently prepared for their reception, Governor Claiborne, of New Orleans, dispatched one hundred and seventy-five volunteers to assist in its defense, under the command of Major Daniel Beasley. Already, from the neighborhood, seventy militiamen had assembled at the fort, besides a mob of friendly Indians and one hundred and six negro slaves. Upon taking the command, Major Beasley, to accommodate the multitude which thronged to the fort, had enlarged it by making a new line of picketing sixty feet beyond the eastern end, but left the old line of stockades standing, thus forming two inclosures.

On the morning of the fatal day, though Major Beasley had spared some of his armed men for the defense of neighboring stations, Fort Mims contained five hundred and fifty-three souls—a mass of human beings crowded together in a flat, swampy region, under the broiling sun of an Alabama August. Of these, more than one hundred were white women and children.

Many days had passed—long, hot, tedious days— and no Indians were seen. The first terror abated. The higher officers, it seems, had scarcely believed at all in the hostile intentions of the Creeks, and were inclined to make light of the general consternation. At least, they were entirely confident in their ability to defend the fort against any force that the Indians could bring against it. The motley inmates gave themselves up to fun and frolic. A rumor would occasionally come in with alarming news of Indian movements, and for a few hours the old caution was resumed, and the men would languidly work on the defenses. But still the hourly scouts sent out by the commander could discover no traces of an enemy, and the hot days and nights still wore away without alarm.

On August 29th, two slaves, who had been sent out to watch some cattle that grazed a few miles from the fort, came rushing breathless through the gate, reporting that they had seen twenty-four painted warriors. A general alarm ensued, and the garrison flew to their stations. A party of horse, guided by the negroes, galloped to the spot, but could neither find Indians nor discover any of the usual traces of their presence. Upon their return one of the negroes was tied up and severely flogged for alarming the garrison by what Major Beasley supposed to be a sheer fabrication. The other negro would also have been punished but for the interference of his master, who believed his tale; at which interference the major was so much displeased that he ordered the gentleman, with his large family, to leave the fort on the following morning. Never did such a fatal infatuation possess the mind of a man intrusted with so many human lives.

The 30th of August arrived. At ten in the morning the commandant was sitting in his room writing to Governor Claiborne a letter (which still exists) to the effect that he need not concern himself in the least respecting the safety of Fort Mims, as there was no doubt of its impregnability against any Indian force whatever. Both gates were wide open. Women were preparing dinner. Children were playing about the cabins. Soldiers were sauntering, sleeping, playing cards. The owner of the frightened negro had now consented to his punishment rather than leave the fort, and the poor fellow was tied up expecting soon to feel the lash. His companion, who had been whipped the day before, was tending cattle at the same place where again he saw, or thought he saw, painted warriors; and, fearing to be whipped again if he reported the news, he fled to the next station some miles distant.

All this calm and quiet morning, from before daylight until noon, there lay, in a ravine only four hundred yards from the fort's eastern gate, one thousand Creek warriors, armed to the teeth, and hideous with war-paint and feathers. Weathersford, the crafty and able chieftain, had led them from Pensacola, where the British had supplied them with weapons and ammunition, to this well-chosen spot, where they crouched and waited through the long slow morning, with the devilish patience with which savages and tigers can wait for their prey. So dead was the silence in the ravine that the birds fluttered and sang as usual in the branches above the dusky, breathing mass. Five prophets with blackened faces, with medicine-bags and magic rods, lay among them, ready at the signal to begin their incantations and stimulate the fury of the warriors.

At noon a drum in the fort beat to dinner. Officers and men, their arms laid aside, all unsuspicious of danger, were gathering to the meal in various parts of the stockade. That dinner-drum was the signal which Weathersford had cunningly chosen for the attack. At the first tap the silent ravine was alive with Indians, who leaped up and ran in a tumultuous mass toward the eastern gate of the devoted fort. The head of the throng had reached a field one hundred and fifty yards across that lay before the gate, had raised a hideous whoop, and were streaming across the field, before a sentinel saw or heard them. Then arose the terrible cry, "*Indians! Indians!*" and there was a rush of women and children to the houses, and of men to the gates and portholes. Major Beasley was one of the first at the gate, and made a frantic attempt to close it; but sand had washed into the gateway, and ere the obstruction could be removed the savages poured in, felled the commander to the earth with clubs and tomahawks, and ran over his bleeding body into the fort. He crawled behind the gate, and in a few minutes died, exhorting his men with his last breath to make a resolute resistance. At once the whole of that part of the fort which had been lately added, and which was separated from the main inclosure by the old line of pickets, was filled with Indians, hooting, howling, dancing among the dead bodies of many of the best officers and men of the little garrison. The poor negro, tied up to be whipped for doing all he could to prevent this catastrophe, was killed as he stood waiting for his punishment.

The situation was at once simple and horrible. Two inclosures adjoining, with a line of portholes through the log partition—one inclosure full of men, women, children, friendly Indians and negroes, the other filled with howling savages, mad with the lust of slaughter; both compartments containing sheds, cabins, and other places for refuge and assault; the large open field without the eastern gate covered with what seemed a countless swarm of naked fiends hurrying to the fort; all avenues of escape closed by Weathersford's foresight and vigilance; no white station within three miles, and no adequate help within a day's march; the commandant and some of his ablest officers trampled under the feet of the savage foe—such was the posture of affairs at Fort Mims a few minutes after noon on this dreadful day.

The garrison, partly recovering their first panic, formed along the line of portholes and fired some effective volleys, killing with the first discharge the five prophets who were dancing, grimacing, and howling among the assailants in the smaller inclosure. These men had given out that they were invulnerable. American bullets were to split upon their sacred persons and pass off harmless. Their fall so abated the ardor of the savages that their fire slackened, and some began to retreat from the fort. But new crowds kept coming up, and the attack was soon renewed in all its first fury.

The garrison, with scarcely an exception, behaved as

men should do in circumstances so terrible and desperate. One Captain Bailey took the command after the death of Major Beasley, and infused the fire of his own indomitable spirit into the hearts of the whole company, adding an example of cool valor to encouraging words. The garrison maintained a ceaseless and destructive fire through the portholes and from the houses. It happened more than once that, at a simultaneous discharge through a porthole, both the Indian without and the white man within were killed. Even the boys and some of the women assisted in the defense; and few of the women gave themselves up to terror while there remained any hope of preserving the fort. Some of the old men broke holes in the roof of the large house and did good execution upon the savages outside of the stockade. The noise was terrific. All the Indians who could not get at the portholes to fight seemed to have passed the hours of this horrible day in dancing round the fort, screaming, hooting, and taunting the inmates with their coming fate.

Amid scenes like these three hours passed, and still the larger part of the fort remained in the hands of the garrison, though many a gallant soldier had fallen, and the rooms of the large house were filled with wounded men and ministering women. The heroic Bailey still spoke cheerily. He said that Indians never fought long when they were bravely met; they would certainly abandon the assault if the garrison continued to resist. He tried to induce a small party to make a sortie, fight their way to the next station, and bring a force to attack the enemy in the rear. Failing in this, he said he would go himself, and began to climb the picketing, but was pulled back by his friends, who saw the madness of the attempt. About three o'clock the Indians seemed to tire of the long contest. The fire slackened, the howl-

ings subsided, the savages began to carry off the plunder from the cabins in the lesser inclosure, and hope
revived in many a despairing heart. But Weathersford
at this hour rode up on a large black horse, and, meeting a throng of the retreating plunderers, upbraided
them in an animated speech, and induced them to return
with him to the fort and complete its destruction.

And now fire was added to the horrors of the scene!
By burning arrows and other expedients the house of
Mr. Mims was set on fire, and soon the whole structure,
with its extensive outbuildings and sheds, was wrapped
in flames; while the shrieks of the women and children
were heard, for the first time, above the dreadful din
and whoop of the battle. One after another the smaller
buildings caught, until the whole inclosure was a roaring sea of flame, except one poor corner, where some
extra picketing formed a last refuge to the surviving
victims. Into this inclosure hurried a crowd of women,
children, negroes, old men, wounded soldiers, trampling
one another to death—all in the last agonies of mortal
terror. The savages were soon upon them, and the
work of slaughter—fierce, unrelenting slaughter—began.
Children were seized by the feet and their brains dashed
out against the pickets. Women were cut to pieces.
Men were tomahawked and scalped. Some poor Spaniards, deserters from Pensacola, were kneeling along the
pickets, and were tomahawked one after another as
they knelt. Weathersford, who was not a savage, but
a misguided hero and patriot, worthy of Tecumseh's
friendship, did what Tecumseh would have done if he
had been there: he tried to stop this horrid carnage.
But the Indians were delirious and frantic with the love
of blood, and would not stay their murderous hands while
one of that mass of human victims continued to live.

At noon that day, as we have seen, five hundred and

fifty-three persons were inmates of Fort Mims. At sunset, four hundred mangled, scalped and bloody corpses were heaped and strewed within its wooden walls. Not one white woman, not one white child, escaped. Twelve of the garrison, at the last moment, by cutting through two of the pickets, got out of the fort and fled to the swamp. A large number of the negroes were spared by the Indians and kept for slaves. A few half-breeds were made prisoners. Captain Bailey, severely wounded, ran to the swamp, and died by the side of a cypress stump. A negro woman, with a ball in her breast, reached a canoe on Lake Tensaw and paddled fifteen miles to Fort Stoddart, and bore the first news of the massacre to Governor Claiborne. Most of the men who fled from the slaughter wandered for days in the swamps and forests, and only reached places of safety, nearly starved, after many a hair-breadth escape from the Indians. Some of them were living forty years ago, from whose lips Mr. A. J. Pickett, the historian of Alabama, gathered most of the particulars which have been briefly related here.

The garrison sold their lives as dearly as they could. It is thought that four hundred of Weathersford's band were killed and wounded. That night the savages, exhausted with their bloody work, appear to have slept near the scene of the massacre. Next day they returned to bury their dead, but, fatigued with the number, gave it up and left many exposed. Ten days after, Major Kennedy reached the spot with a detachment of troops to bury the bodies of the whites, and found the air dark with buzzards, and hundreds of dogs gnawing the bodies. In two large pits the troops, shuddering now with horror and now fierce for revenge, succeeded at length in burying the remains of their countrymen and countrywomen. Major Kennedy said in his report : " Indians, negroes, white men, women, and children, lay in one promiscuous ruin. All were scalped, and the females of every age were butchered in a manner which neither decency nor language will permit me to describe. The main building was burned to ashes, which were filled with bones. The plains and woods around were covered with dead bodies. All the houses were consumed by fire except the blockhouse and a part of the pickets. The soldiers and officers with one voice called on Divine Providence to revenge the death of our murdered friends."

Such was the massacre at Fort Mims. The news flew upon the wings of the wind. From Mobile to the borders of Tennessee, from the vicinity of New Orleans almost to the coast of Georgia, there was felt to be no safety for the white man except in fortified posts; nor certain safety even in them. In the country of the Alabama River and its branches, every white man, woman, and child, every friendly half-breed and Indian, hurried to the stockades or fled in wild terror toward Mobile. "Never in my life," wrote an eyewitness, "did I see a country given up before without a struggle. Here are the finest crops my eyes ever beheld made and almost fit to be housed, with immense herds of cattle, negroes, and property, abandoned by their owners almost on the first alarm." Within the stockades diseases raged, and hundreds of families, unable to get within those inclosures, lay around the walls, squalid, panic-stricken, sick, and miserable. Parties of Indians roved about the country rioting in plunder. After burning the houses and laying waste the plantations, they would drive the cattle together in herds, and either destroy them in a mass or drive them off for their future use. The horses were taken to facilitate their marauding, and their camps were filled with the luxuries of the planters' houses. Governor Claiborne, a generous and feeling man, was at his wits' end. From every quarter came the most urgent and pathetic demands for troops. Not a man could be spared, for no one knew where next the exultant savages would endeavor to repeat the catastrophe of Fort Mims; and in the best-defended forts there were five non-combatants to one soldier. For some weeks of the autumn of 1813 it really seemed as if the white settlers of Alabama, including those of Mobile itself, were on the point of being exterminated.

The news of the massacre at Fort Mims was thirty-one days in reaching New York. It is a proof how occupied were the minds of the people in the Northern States with great events, that the dread narrative appeared in the New York papers only as an item of war news of comparatively small importance. The last prodigious acts in the drama of Napoleon's decline and fall were watched with absorbing interest. The news of Perry's victory on Lake Erie had just thrilled the nation with delight and pride, and all minds were still eager for every new particular. Harrison's victory on the Thames over Proctor and Tecumseh soon followed. The lamentable condition of the Southern country was therefore little felt at the time beyond the States immediately concerned. Perry and Harrison were the heroes of the hour. Their return from the scene of their exploits was a continuous triumphal *fête*.

In a room at Nashville, a thousand miles from these splendid scenes, lay a gaunt, yellow-visaged man, sick, defeated, prostrate, with his arm bound up and his shoulders bandaged, waiting impatiently for his wounds to heal and his strength to return. Who then thought of him in connection with victory and glory? Who supposed that he, of all men, was the one destined to cast into the shade those favorites of the nation, and shine out as the prime hero of the war?

CHAPTER IX.

THERE must have been swift express riding in those early days of September, and as stealthy as swift through the Indian country ; for, on the 18th of the month, nineteen days after the massacre, we find the people of Nashville assembled in town meeting to deliberate upon the event, the Rev. Mr. Craighead in the chair.

The news of the massacre produced everywhere in Tennessee the most profound impression. Pity for the distressed Alabamans, fears for the safety of their own borders, rage against the Creeks, so long the recipients of governmental bounty, united to inflame the minds of the people. But one feeling pervaded the State. With one voice it was decreed that the entire resources and the whole available force of Tennessee should be hurled upon the savage foe, to avenge the massacre and deliver the Southern country.

A striking narrative of the proceedings of the Legislature on this occasion, and of the nerve, vigor, and resolution of the prostrate Jackson, lies before me, from the pen of Mr. Enoch Parsons, then a member of the Senate of Tennessee. "I arrived at Nashville," says this gentleman, " on the Saturday before the third Monday in September, 1813. I found in the public square a very large crowd of people, and many fine speeches were making to the people, and the talking part of a war was never better performed. I was invited out to the place where the orators were holding forth, and invited to address the people. I declined the distinction. The talking ended, and resolutions were adopted, the substance of which was that the enlightened Legislature would convene on the next Monday, and they would prepare for the emergency.

"The Legislature was composed of twenty Senators and forty Representatives, some of them old, infirm men. As soon as the Houses were organized, at my table I wrote a bill, and introduced it, to call out three thousand five hundred men, under the general entitled to command, and place them in the Indian nation, so that they might preserve the Mississippi Territory from destruction and prevent the friendly Indians from taking the enemy's side, and to render service to the United States until the United States could provide a force. The bill pledged all the revenue of the State for one hundred years to pay the expense, and authorized the Governor to borrow money from any source he could, and at the lowest rate he could, to defray the expenses of the campaign. The Secretary of State, William G. Blount, Major John Russell, a Senator, and myself, signed or indorsed the Governor's note for twenty thousand dollars, and the old patriotic State Bank lent the money which the note called for.

"At this time General Jackson was lying, as he had been between ten and twenty days, with the wounds received in the battle with the Bentons and others, and had not been out of his room, if out of his bed. The Constitution of the State would not allow the bill to become a law until it had passed in each House three times on different days. The bill was therefore passed in each House on Monday, and lay in the Senate for Tuesday.

"After the adjournment of the Houses on Monday, as I passed out of the Senate-chamber, I was accosted by a gentleman and presented with General Jackson's compliments and a request that I should see him forthwith. I had not been to his room since my arrival. I complied with his request, and found he was minutely informed of the contents of the bill I had introduced, and wished to know if it would pass; and said the news of the introduction of the bill had spread all over the city, and that it was called the War Bill or Parsons' Bill. I assured the general it would pass, and on Wednesday would be a law, and I mentioned that I regretted very much that the general entitled to command, and who all would desire should command the forces of the State, was not in a condition to take the field. To which General Jackson replied:

"'The devil in hell he is not!'

"He gritted his teeth with anguish as he uttered these words, and groaned when he ceased to speak. I told him that I hoped I was mistaken, but that I did not believe he could just then take the field. After some time I left the general. Two hours afterward I received fifty or more copies of his orders, which had been made out and printed in the meantime, and ordered the troops to rendezvous at Fayetteville, eighty miles on the way, on Thursday. At the bottom of the order was a note stating that the health of the commanding general was *restored*.

"That evening, or the next day, I saw Dr. May, General Jackson's principal physician, and inquired of him if he thought General Jackson could possibly march. Dr. May said that no other man could, and that it was uncertain whether, with his spunk and energy, *he* could; but that it was entirely uncertain what General Jackson could do in such circumstances.

"I felt much anxiety for the country and for the general; and when the general started—which was, I think, on the day before the law passed—Dr. May went with him and returned in three or four days. I called on Dr. May, upon his return, and inquired how the general had got along; whereupon the doctor stated that they had to stop the general frequently and wash him from head to foot in solutions of sugar of lead to keep down inflammation; and that he was better, and he and his troops had gone on! The Legislature then prefixed a supplemental bill to suspend all actions in which the volunteers were concerned in the courts until their return."

There, reader, you have ANDREW JACKSON—the explanation of his character, of his success, of his celebrity. If any one inquires of you what manner of man Andrew Jackson was, answer him by telling Mr. Parsons's story.

The 4th of October was the day named in the general's orders for the rendezvous at Fayetteville, a village near the northern borders of Alabama. Ten days before the day of rendezvous he dispatched his old friend and partner, Colonel Coffee, with his regiment of five hundred horse, and such mounted volunteers as could instantly join, to Huntsville, in the northern part of Alabama, to restore confidence to the frontier. Huntsville is a hundred miles or more from Nashville. On the 4th of October the energetic Coffee had reached the place, his force increased to nearly thirteen hundred men, and volunteers, as he wrote back to his commander, flocking in every hour.

The day named for the rendezvous at Fayetteville was exactly one month from that on which the commanding general received his wounds in the affray with the Bentons. He could not mount his horse without assistance when the time came for him to move toward the rendezvous. His left arm was bound and in a sling. He could not wear his coat-sleeve; nor, during any part of his military career, could he long endure on his left shoulder the weight of an epaulet. Often, in the crisis of a manœuvre, some unguarded movement would send such a thrill of agony through his attenuated frame as almost to deprive him of consciousness. It could not have been a pleasant thought that he had squandered in a paltry, puerile, private contest, the strength he needed for the defense of his country. Grievous was his fault, bitter the penalty, noble the atonement.

Traveling as fast as his healing wounds permitted, General Jackson reached Fayetteville on the 7th of October, and found that less than half of the two thousand men ordered out had assembled. But welcome tidings from Colonel Coffee awaited him. Hitherto he had chiefly feared for the safety of Mobile, and had anticipated a long and weary march into southern Alabama. He now learned from Colonel Coffee's dispatch that the Indians seemed to have abandoned their design upon Mobile, and were making their way, in two parties, toward the borders of Georgia and Tennessee. This was joyful news to the enfeebled but fiery commander. " It is surely," he wrote back to Coffee the same evening, " high gratification to learn that the Creeks are so attentive to my situation as to save me the pain of traveling. I must not be outdone in politeness, and will therefore endeavor to meet them on the middle ground."

A week was passed at Fayetteville in waiting for the troops, procuring supplies, organizing the regiments, and drilling the men; a week of intense exertion on the part of the general, to whom congenial employment brought daily restoration.

At one o'clock on Monday, the 11th of October, an express dashed into camp with another dispatch from Colonel Coffee announcing the approach of the enemy. The order to prepare for marching was given on the instant. A few minutes later the express was galloping back to Coffee's camp, carrying a few hasty lines from Jackson, to the effect that in two hours he would be in motion with all his available force. Before three he had kept his word—the army was in full career toward Huntsville. Excited more and more, as they went, by rumors of Indian murders, the men marched with such incredible swiftness as to reach Huntsville, thirty-two miles from Fayetteville, by eight o'clock the same evening! It is hard to believe that an army could march six miles an hour for five hours, but the fact is stated on what may be considered the authority of General Jackson himself. At Huntsville it was found that the news of the rapid approach of the Indians was exaggerated. The next day, therefore, the force marched leisurely to the Tennessee River, crossed it, and toward evening came up with Colonel Coffee's command, encamped on the south side of the river.

So far all had gone well. There they were, twenty-five hundred of them, in the pleasant autumn weather, upon a high bluff overlooking the beautiful Tennessee, all in high spirits, eager to be led against the enemy. There were jovial souls among them. David Crockett, then the peerless bear-hunter of the West (to be member of Congress by and by, to be national joker, and to stump the country against his present commander), was there with his rifle and hunting-shirt, the merriest of the merry, keeping the camp alive with his quaint conceits and marvelous narratives. He had a hereditary right to be there, for both his grandparents had been murdered by Creeks, and other relatives carried into long captivity by them. Merriment, meanwhile, was far from the heart of the general. Grappling now with the chronic difficulty of the campaign, he was torn with impatience and anxiety.

Twenty-five hundred men and thirteen hundred horses were on a bluff of the Tennessee, on the borders of civilization, about to plunge into pathless woods, and march, no one knew how far, into the fastnesses and secret retreats of a savage enemy! Such a body will consume ten wagon-loads of provisions every day. For a week's subsistence they require a thousand bushels of grain, twenty tons of flesh, a thousand gallons of whisky, and many hundredweight of miscellaneous stores. Assemble, suddenly, such a force in the most populous county of Oregon, as Oregon now is, and it would not be a quite easy matter, in the space of seventeen days, to organize a system of supply so that the army could march thirty miles a day into the forest and be sure of finding a day's ration waiting for them at the end of every day's march. Colonel Coffee, moreover, had been encamped for eight days upon the bluff, had swept the surrounding country of its forage, and gathered in nearly all the provisions it could furnish. All this General Jackson had expected, and hither, accordingly, he had directed the supplies from East Tennessee to be sent.

The contractor had abundant provisions, and instantly set about dispatching them. " I believe," wrote General Cocke (commander of the forces of East Tennessee) to Jackson, on the 2d of October, "a thousand barrels of flour can be had immediately. I will send it on to Ditto's Landing (Jackson's camp) without delay." To the river's side they were sent promptly enough. But the Tennessee, like most of the Western rivers, is not navigable in its upper waters in dry seasons, and the flour which General Jackson expected to find awaiting him at Coffee's bluff was still hundreds of miles up the river, " waiting for a rise." His whole stock at present amounted to only a few days' supply. To proceed seemed impossible. Nor was the cause of the delay apparent to him, since the Tennessee, where he saw it, flowed by in a sufficient stream. Chafing under the enforced delay, like a war-horse restrained from the charge after the trumpet has sounded, he denounced the contractor and the contract system, and even General Cocke, who, zealous for the service, had gone far beyond the line of his duty in his efforts to forward the supplies.

But General Jackson did better things than these. Perceiving now, only too clearly, that this matter of provisions was to be the great difficulty of the campaign, he sent back to Nashville his friend and quartermaster, Major William B. Lewis, in order that he might have some one there upon whose zeal and discretion he could entirely rely, and who would do all that man could do for his relief. Colonel Coffee, with a body of seven hundred mounted men, he sent away from his hungry camp to scour the banks of the Black Warrior, a branch of the Tombigbee. He gave the infantry who remained as hard a week's drilling as ever volunteers submitted to. Order arose from confusion; discipline began to exert its potent spell, and the mob of pioneer militia assumed something of the aspect of an army. While he was thus engaged, a friendly chief (Shelocta) came into camp with the news that hostile Creeks in a considerable body were threatening a fort occupied by friendly Indians near the Ten Islands of the Coosa. The route thither lying in part up the Tennessee, Jackson resolved, with such provisions as he had, to go and meet the expected flotilla, and, having obtained supplies, to strike at once into the heart of the Indian country and relieve the friendly fort. He lived, during these anxious days, with an eye ever on the river, heart-sick with hope deferred.

On the 19th of October the camp on the bluff broke

up. Three days of marching, climbing, and road-cutting, over mountains before supposed to be impassable, brought the little army to Thompson's Creek, a branch of the Tennessee, twenty-two miles above the previous encampment. To his inexpressible disappointment, he found there neither provisions nor tidings of provisions. In circumstances so disheartening and unexpected most men would have thought it better generalship to retreat to the settlements and wait in safety while adequate arrangements were made for the support of the army. No such thought appears to have occurred to the general. Retreat at that moment would have probably tempted the enemy to the frontiers of Tennessee, and covered them with fire and desolation. Jackson halted his force at Thompson's Creek, and while his men were employed in throwing up a fort to be used as a depot for the still expected provisions, he sat in his tent for three days writing letters the most pathetic and imploring. He wrote to General Cocke and Judge Hugh L. White, of East Tennessee; to the Governors of Tennessee and Georgia; to the Indian agents among the Cherokees and Choctaws; to friendly Indian chiefs; to General Flourney, of New Orleans; to various private friends of known public spirit—appealing to every motive of interest and patriotism that could influence men, entreating them to use all personal exertions and public authority in forwarding supplies to his destitute army. "Give me provisions," was the burden of these eloquent letters, "and I will end this war in a month." "There *is* an enemy," he wrote, "whom I dread much more than I do the hostile Creeks, and whose power, I am fearful, I shall be first made to feel—I mean the meager monster Famine. I shall leave this encampment in the morning direct for the Ten Islands, and thence, with as little delay as possible, to the junction of the Coosa and Tallapoosa;

and yet I have not on hand two days' supply of bread-stuffs."

Colonel Coffee soon after joined the general. In twelve days he had marched two hundred miles, burned two Indian towns, collected three or four hundred bushels of corn, and returned to the Tennessee without having seen a hostile Indian. Runners still arriving from the Ten Islands with entreaties from the friendly Indians for relief, Jackson, with two days' supply of bread and six of meat, resolved to march, and depend for subsistance upon chance and victory. Leaving Fort Deposit on the 25th of October, the general marched southward into the enemy's country as fast as the state of his commissariat permitted; halting when his corn quite gave out; marching again when he procured a day's supply; sending out detachments to burn villages and find hidden stores; writing letter after letter imploring succor from the settlements; always resolute, always in suspense. On one of these days, Colonel Dyer, who had been sent out with a detachment of two hundred men, returned to camp with twenty-nine prisoners and a considerable supply of corn, the spoils of a burned village. Other slight successes on the march served to keep the men in good spirits, but were not sufficient to lift for more than a moment the load of care that rested upon the heart of the general. A week brought the whole force, intact, to the banks of the Coosa, within a few miles of the Ten Islands, near which, at a town called Talluschatches, it was now known, a large body of the Indians had assembled.

Talluschatches was thirteen miles from General Jackson's camp. On the 2d of November came the welcome order to General Coffee (he had just been promoted) to march with a thousand mounted men to destroy this town. Late in the same day the detachment were on the trail, accompanied by a body of friendly Creeks wearing white feathers and white deers' tails, to distinguish them from their hostile brethren. The next morning's sun shone upon Coffee and his men preparing to assault the town.

On the evening of the same day, General Coffee, having destroyed the town, killed two hundred of the enemy, and buried five of his own men, led his victorious troops back to Jackson's camp, where he received from his general and the rest of the army the welcome that brave men give to brave men returning from triumph. Along with the returning horsemen, joyful with their victory, came into camp a sorrowful procession of prisoners, all women or children, all widows or fatherless, all helpless and destitute. They were humanely cared for by the troops, and soon after sent to the settlements for maintenance during the war.

On the bloody field of Talluschatches was found a slain mother still embracing her living infant. The child was brought into camp with the other prisoners, and Jackson, anxious to save it, endeavored to induce some of the Indian women to give it nourishment. "No," said they, "all his relations are dead; kill him too." This reply appealed to the heart of the general. He caused the child to be taken to his own tent, where, among the few remaining stores, was found a little brown sugar. This, mingled with water, served to keep the child alive until it could be sent to Huntsville, where it was nursed at Jackson's expense until the end of the campaign, and then taken to the Hermitage. Mrs. Jackson received it cordially; and the boy grew up in the family, treated by the general and his kind wife as a son and favorite.

It was General Jackson's turn next. Thirty miles from his encampment on the Coosa stood a small fort, into which, as before intimated, a party of one hundred and fifty-four friendly Creeks had fled for safety. The site of this fort is now covered by part of the town of Talladega, the capital of Talladega County, Alabama, a thriving place of several thousand inhabitants, situated on a branch of the Coosa, in the midst of beautiful mountain scenery. This region was, at the time of which we are now writing, literally a *howling* wilderness; for, while General Coffee was returning in triumph from Talluschatches, more than a thousand hostile Creeks suddenly surrounded the friendly fort and invested it so completely that not a man could escape. With only a small supply of corn, and scarcely any water, outnumbered seven to one, and unable to send intelligence of their situation, the inmates of the fort seemed doomed to massacre. The assailants appear to have comported themselves on this occasion in the manner of a cat sure of her mouse. They whooped and sported around their prey, waiting for terror or starvation to save them the trouble of conquest.

Some days passed. The sufferings of the beleaguered Indians from thirst began to be intolerable. A noted chief of the party resolved upon making one desperate effort to escape and carry the news to Jackson's camp. Enveloping himself in the skin of a large hog, with the head and feet attached, he left the fort, and went about rooting and grunting, gradually working his way through the hostile host until he was beyond the reach of their arrows; then, throwing off his disguise, he fled with the swiftness of the wind. Not knowing precisely where General Jackson was, he did not reach the camp till late in the evening of the next day, when he came in, breathless and exhausted, and told his story.

This was on the 7th of November, four days after

the affair of Talluschatches, during which the general and the troops had been busy in erecting a fortification, or depot, which was named Fort Strother. The army was still, as it had been from the beginning of the campaign, only a few days removed from starvation. Contractors had been dismissed, new ones appointed, more imploring letters written, and every conceivable effort made, and yet no system had been devised to overcome the inherent difficulties of the work. To the general's other embarrassments was now added the care of the considerable number of wounded and sick, many of whom could not be moved. There was one encouraging circumstance, however. The troops from East Tennessee, under Major-General Cocke and Brigadier-General White, had at length reached the vicinity, and a force under General White was expected to join the next day, and so bring with them some supplies. So General White himself had written. Jackson, at the moment when the messenger from the beleaguered fort arrived, was in his tent closing his reply to the coming general, to whom he imparted the new intelligence and announced his intentions with regard to it, adding that he depended upon him (General White) to protect his camp during his own absence from it.

Relying with the utmost possible confidence upon General White's arrival, Jackson, with his usual promptitude, issued orders for his whole division, except a few men to guard the post and attend the sick, to prepare for marching that very evening. He had taken the resolution to rush to the relief of the friendly Creeks, justly supposing that the massacre of such a body, within so short a distance of an American army, would intimidate all the friendly Indians, and tend to unite the Southern tribes as one man against the United States.

At one o'clock in the morning of November 8th,

eight hundred horsemen and twelve hundred foot, under command of General Jackson, stood on the bank of the Coosa, one mile above Fort Strother, ready to cross. The river was wide, but fordable for horsemen. Each of the mounted men, taking behind him one of the infantry, rode across the river and then returned for another. This operation consumed so long a time that it was nearly four o'clock in the morning before the whole force was drawn up on the opposite bank prepared to move. A long and weary march through a country wild and uninhabited brought them about sunset within six miles of Talladega. There the general thought it best to halt and give repose to the troops, taking precautions to conceal his presence from the enemy.

There was no repose for the general that night. Till late in the evening he remained awake, receiving reports from the spies sent out to reconnoitre the enemy's position, and making arrangements for the morrow's work. At midnight an Indian came into the camp with a dispatch from General White, announcing, to Jackson's inexpressible astonishment and dismay, that, in consequence of positive orders from General Cocke, he would not be able to protect Fort Strother, but must return and rejoin his general immediately. No other explanation was given. Jackson was in sore perplexity. To go forward, was to leave the sick and wounded at Fort Strother to the mercy of any strolling party of savages. To retreat, would bring certain destruction upon the friendly Creeks, and probably the whole besieging force upon his own rear. In this painful dilemma he resolved upon the boldest measures and the wisest—to strike the foe in his front at the dawn of day, and, having delivered the inmates of the fort, hasten from the battlefield to the protection of Fort Strother.

Before four in the morning the army was in full

march toward the enemy. A sudden and vigorous attack soon put to flight the besieging host, and set free the loyal Creeks, whose delight at their escape is described to have been affecting in the extreme. Besides being nearly dead from thirst, they were anticipating an assault that very day, and had no knowledge of Jackson's approach until they heard the noise of the battle. Fifteen minutes after the action became general the savages were flying headlong in every direction and falling fast under the swords of the pursuing troops. The delivered Creeks ran out of the fort, and, having appeased their raging thirst, thronged around their deliverer, testifying their delight and gratitude. The little corn that they could spare the general bought and distributed among his hungry men and horses. He had left Fort Strother with only provisions for little more than one day, and the supply obtained from the Creeks amounted to less than a meal for his victorious army.

The dead honorably buried, and the wounded placed in litters, the troops marched back to Fort Strother the day after the battle. They arrived tired and hungry, yet fondly hoping that in their absence some supplies had been collected. Not a peck of meal, not a pound of flesh had reached the fort, and they found their sick and wounded comrades as hungry as themselves. It was a bitter moment. The general was in an agony of disappointment and apprehension. The men, though returning from victory, murmured ominously. Until this day the general and his staff had subsisted upon private stores procured and transported at his own expense. Before leaving for Talladega he had directed the surgeons to draw upon these if necessary for the maintenance of the sick, and upon his return he found that all had been consumed except a few pounds of biscuit. These were immediately distributed among the hungry applicants, not one being reserved for the general. Concealing his feelings and assuming a cheerful aspect, he went among the men and endeavored to give the affair a jocular turn. He went with his staff to the slaughtering-place of the camp and brought away from the refuse there the means of satisfying his appetite, declaring with a smiling face that tripe was a savory and nutritious article of food, and that for his part he desired nothing better. For several days succeeding, while a few lean cattle were the only support of the army, General Jackson and his military family subsisted upon tripe, without bread or seasoning.

Jackson soon saw the effect of his brilliant success at Talladega. The Hillabee warriors, who had been defeated in that battle, at once sent a messenger to Fort Strother to sue for peace. Jackson's reply was prompt and characteristic. His Government, he said, had taken up arms to avenge the most gross depredations, and to bring back to a sense of duty a people to whom it had shown the utmost kindness. When those objects were attained the war would cease, but not till then. " Upon those," he continued, "who are disposed to become friendly, I neither wish nor intend to make war, but they must afford evidences of the sincerity of their professions; the prisoners and property they have taken from us and the friendly Creeks must be restored; the instigators of the war, and the murderers of our citizens, must be surrendered; the latter must and will be made to feel the force of our resentment. Long shall they remember Fort Mims in bitterness and tears."

The Hillabee messenger, who was an old Scotchman, long domesticated among the Indians, departed with Jackson's reply. It was never delivered. Before the message reached the Hillabees an event occurred which banished from their minds all thought of peace, changing them from suppliants for pardon into enemies the most resolute and deadly of all the Indians in the Southern country. General White, of East Tennessee, totally unaware of the state of feeling among the Hillabees, nay, supposing them to be inveterately hostile, marched rapidly into their country, burning and destroying. On his way he burned one village of thirty houses, and another of ninety-three. The principal Hillabee town, whence had proceeded the messenger to Jackson asking peace, and whither that messenger was to return that day, General White surprised at daybreak, killed sixty warriors, and captured two hundred and fifty women and children. Having burned the town, he returned to General Cocke, supposing that he had done the State some service.

The feelings of the Hillabee tribe may be imagined. *This*, then, is General Jackson's answer to our humble suit! *Thus* does he respond to friendly overtures! They never knew General Jackson's innocence of this deed. From that time to the end of the war it was observed that the Indians fought with greater fury and persistence than before, for they fought with the blended energy of hatred and despair. There was no suing for peace, no asking for quarter. To fight as long as they could stand, and as much longer as they could sit or kneel, and then as long as they had strength to shoot an arrow or pull a trigger, were all that they supposed remained to them after the destruction of the Hillabees.

"An army, like a serpent, goes upon its belly," Frederick of Prussia used to say. "Few men know," Marshal MacMahon is reported to have remarked after one of the Italian battles, "how important it is in war for soldiers not to be kept waiting for their rations, and what vast events depend upon an army's not going into action before it has had its coffee."

We left General Jackson at Fort Strother, giving out his last biscuit to his hungry troops and appeasing his own appetite with unseasoned tripe. Then followed ten long weeks of agonizing perplexity, during which, though the enemy was unmolested by the Tennessee troops, their general appeared in a light more truly heroic than at any other part of his military life. His fortitude, his will, alone saved the campaign. His burning letters kept the cause alive in the State; his example, resolution, activity, and courage preserved the conquests already achieved, and prepared the way for others that threw them into the shade. The spectacle of a brave man contending with difficulties is one in which the gods were said to take delight. Such a spectacle was exhibited by Andrew Jackson during these weeks of enforced inaction.

Hunger, that great tamer of beasts and men, is precisely the enemy against which amateur soldiers are least able to contend. Lounging and dozing about the camp, unable to make the slightest attempt against the foe, their first love of adventure satisfied, desirous to recount their exploits to friends at home, pining for the abundance they had left, anxious for their farms and families, and angered at the supposed neglect of the State authorities and contractors, the troops became discontented, and began to clamor for the order to return into the settlements. Jackson's force consisted of two kinds of troops, militia and volunteers. It seemed at first a proof of the safety of the purely voluntary principle that it was among the militia that the discontents took quickest root; the pride of the volunteers keeping them firm in their duty after the militia were resolved to abandon theirs. It is said, however, that some of the volunteers who, from their having accompanied the general on his fruitless march to Natchez, were looked upon as the veterans of the army, were not the last to join the malcontents, nor the most moderate in expressing their feelings. These men spoke with a kind of oracular authority, which had influence with the younger soldiers. Some of the officers, too, overcome by that bane and blight of republican virtue, the lust of popularity, secretly sided with the men and fomented their mutinous disposition. In secluded places about the camp, by the watch fires at night, wherever a group of hungry soldiers were together, they talked of their wrongs, of the uselessness of remaining where they were, and how much better it would be for the army to return home for a while, and finish the war under better auspices at a more convenient season.

In circumstances like these revolt ripens apace. Ten days of gnawing hunger and inaction at Fort Strother brought all the militia regiments to the resolution of marching back in a body to the settlements, with or without the consent of the commanding general, and a day was fixed upon for their departure. Jackson heard of it in time. On the designated morning the militia began the homeward movement; but they found a lion in the path. The general was up before them, and had drawn up on the road leading to the settlements the whole body of volunteers, with orders to prevent the departure of the militia, peaceably if they could, forcibly if they must. The militia, in this unexpected posture of affairs, renounced their intention, and, obeying the orders of the general, returned to their position and their duty.

It soon, appeared, however, that the volunteers were as much chagrined and disappointed at the success of this movement as the militia, and, ere night closed in, resolved themselves to depart on the following day. The general, apprised of their intention, was again early in the field. Imagine the surprise of the volunteers when, on taking the projected line of march, they found drawn up in hostile array to prevent them the very militia whose departure they had frustrated the day before! The militia stood firm, and the volunteers, not without some grim laughter at this practical revolt, returned to their stations. The cavalry, however, having petitioned the general for permission to retire to Huntsville long enough to recruit their famished horses, promising to return when that object was accomplished, were allowed to leave. Jackson remained in the wilderness with his thousand infantry, now sullen and enraged, and rapidly approaching the point of downright mutiny.

As was his wont in every crisis, the general tried the effect of a patriotic address. Inviting the officers of all grades to his quarters, he first laid before them the letters last received from Tennessee, which gave assurance that a plentiful supply of provisions was already on the way, and that measures were in operation which would insure a sufficiency in future. He then delivered a warm and energetic speech, extolling their past achievements, lamenting their privations, and urging them still to persevere. The conquests they had already made, he said, were of the greatest importance, and the most dreadful consequences would result from abandoning them. "To be sure," said he in conclusion, "we do not live sumptuously, but no one has died of hunger, or is likely to die; and then, how animating are our prospects! Large supplies are at Deposit, and already are officers dispatched to hasten them on. Wagons are on the way; a large number of beeves are in the neighborhood, and detachments are out to bring them in. All these resources can not fail. I have no wish to starve you— none to deceive you. Stay contentedly; and if supplies do not arrive in two days, we will all march back together, and throw the blame of our failure where it should properly lie. Until then we certainly have the means of subsisting; and if we are compelled to bear privations, let us remember that they are borne for our country, and are not greater than many, perhaps most, armies have been compelled to endure. I have called you together to tell you my feelings and my wishes. This evening think on them seriously, and let me know yours in the morning."

The officers returned to their quarters and consulted with the troops. On this occasion, whether from a spirit of rivalry or the sense of duty, the militia proved more tractable than the volunteers; for, on the return of the officers to Jackson's tent, the officers of the volunteer regiments reported that nothing short of an immediate return to the settlements could prevent the forcible departure of their men; but the militia officers declared the willingness of their troops to remain long enough to ascertain whether supplies could be obtained. "If they can," said they, "let us proceed with the campaign; if not, let us be marched back to where they can be procured."

The general thought it best to take both bodies at their word. He sent one regiment of volunteers to meet the coming provisions, ordering them to return with them as an escort. The other volunteer regiment, shamed by the superior fortitude of the militia, agreed to stay two days longer; and thus the general gained a brief respite from his torturing solicitude. These departing volunteers were the very men whom Jackson had refused to abandon at Natchez, even at the command of the Government, and for whose safe return he had pledged and risked his fortune. That they should have been the first, in his sore perplexity, to abandon him, was an event which gave him the most acute mortification.

The two days passed. No provisions arrived. The militia demanded the prompt fulfillment of the general's promise. He was now in the dilemma that Columbus would have been in if land had not been descried in three days. Overwhelmed with despondency, he lifted up his hands and exclaimed, after long brooding over his situation, " If only two men will remain with me, I will *never* abandon the post ! " One Captain Gordon replied, in a jocular manner, " You have one, general ; let us see if we can not find another." He set about seeking volunteers, and, aided by the general's staff, soon obtained the names of one hundred and nine men who agreed to remain and defend the fort. Rejoicing at this result, the general left Fort Strother in their charge, and marched himself, with the rest of the troops, toward Fort Deposit, upon the explicit understanding that, having met the expected provisions, and having satisfied their hunger, they were to return with the provision train to Fort Strother and proceed against the enemy. It was to insure the performance of this engagement that he commanded them in person.

Away they marched, haggard and hungry, but in high spirits, and praying Heaven that they might *not* meet the coming supplies—so desperate was their desire to return home. To Jackson's inexpressible joy, and to the dismay of his troops, they had not marched more than twelve miles before they saw approaching them a drove of one hundred and fifty cattle. Halt, kill, and eat, was the word. The slaughtering, the cooking, and the devouring were quickly accomplished ; and the army, filled with beef and valor, felt itself able to cope even with General Jackson. To return to Fort Strother was the furthest from their thoughts. When the order to return was given, the general himself was not in the immediate presence of the troops, and the order was not obeyed. One company moved off on the homeward road, had gone some distance, and were about to be followed by others, when word was brought to Jackson of the mutiny. Followed by his staff and a few faithful friends, he galloped in pursuit, and came by a detour to a part of the road a little in advance of the deserters, where he found General Coffee and a small force. Forming these across the road, he ordered them to fire upon the deserters if they should persist in their attempt to leave. On coming up, the homesick gentlemen gave one glance at the fiery general and the opposing force, and fled precipitately to their stations.

The manner, appearance, and language of General Jackson on occasions like this were literally terrific. Few common men could stand before the ferocity of his aspect and the violence of his words. On the present occasion, I presume that the mutineers were put to flight as much by the terrible aspect of the general as by the armed men who were with him. We can fancy the scene—Jackson in advance of Coffee's men, his grizzled hair bristling up from his forehead, his face as red as fire, his eyes sparkling and flashing; roaring out with the voice of a Stentor and the energy of Andrew Jackson, " By the immaculate God ! I'll blow the damned villains to eternity if they advance another step ! "

Trusting that the men would now do their duty, the general went among them, leaving General Coffee and his own staff to proceed with the preparations for departure. He found almost the whole brigade infected and on the point of moving toward home. Upon the instant, he resolved to prevent this or perish in the path before them. He seized a musket and rode a few paces in advance of the troops. His left arm was still in a sling. Leaning his musket on his horse's neck, he swore he would shoot the first man that attempted to proceed.

Meanwhile, General Coffee and Major Reid, suspecting that something extraordinary was occurring, ran up, and found their general in this attitude, with the column of mutineers standing in sullen silence before him, not a man daring to stir a foot forward. Placing themselves by his side, they awaited the result with intense anxiety. Gradually a few of the troops, who were still faithful, were collected behind the general, armed, and resolved to use their arms in his support. For some minutes the column of mutineers stood firm to their purpose, and it only needed one man bold enough to advance to bring on a bloody scene. They wavered, however, at length abandoned their purpose, and agreed to return to their duty. It afterward appeared that the musket which figured so effectually in this scene was too much out of order to be discharged !

The troops were not in the highest spirits nor in the most amiable humor as they marched back to Fort Strother that afternoon. Yet they marched back, and the frontiers were still safe. Jackson did not return with them, but proceeded to Fort Deposit, to inspect that post and personally hasten forward supplies. Prodigious exertions were now put forth. Major Lewis surpassed himself. Two hundred pack-horses and forty wagons were taken into service by him. From this time the operations of the army were not seriously impeded by the want of supplies. News now came that the measures so hastily adopted by the State of Tennessee had been approved by the Government at Washington, and that the whole force employed had been received into the service of the United States. Jackson rejoined his division in high spirits, and was rejoiced to find that the works at Fort Strother had been vigorously carried on in his absence. Nothing seemed now to oppose the successful prosecution of the war. A few swift marches, a few well-fought engagements, and the troops might return home, the general thought, to receive the applause of the State and the nation. Ordering General Cocke to join him at Fort Strother, with the troops from East Tennessee, he expected nothing but to renew the contest upon their arrival.

But the general was reckoning without his army. The volunteers, penetrated with the spirit of discontent, soon provided themselves with a new argument for abandoning the service. The first days of December were now passing. It was on the 10th of December, 1812, that these volunteers had entered into service, engaging, as they said, to serve one year. They accordingly made no secret of their intention to leave the camp on the 10th of December, 1813. But they were now reckoning without their general, who recalled to their recollection that they had engaged to serve one year in two! They had been subject to the call of the Government for a year, but for more than half of that period they had been at home, pursuing their own affairs. Nothing short, maintained the general, of three hundred and sixty-five days of actual service in the field could release them from their obligation before the 10th of December, 1814.

Such was the new issue between the general and the volunteers. It was warmly argued, with the inevitable effect of confirming each in the opinion that accorded with his desire. The general was clear in the belief that he was in the right; but he seems, from the beginning of this contest, to have seen that it was useless to attempt new enterprises unless seconded by the alacrity of his men. Therefore, while firmly resisting the departure of the troops, he saw the necessity of procuring new levies from the State, and to this object devoted his energies. General Roberts, Colonel Carroll, and Major

Searcy, officers high in his confidence, were dispatched to Tennessee to hasten the assembling of a new army; while Jackson wrote letter upon letter to influential friends, urging them to aid the cause by personal efforts.

But to raise a new force and march it a hundred and fifty miles into the Indian country was necessarily a work of considerable time, during which we see the general—some of his best officers away recruiting, and his right arm, General Coffee, sick at Huntsville—contending almost alone with a fractious soldiery. Defeated in their previous attempts at forcible departure, these men now tried to move their commander by argument and entreaty. A formal letter from one of the colonels, which Jackson received a few days before the dreaded 10th of December, expressed the feelings of the troops. It made known to him that the whole body of volunteers retained the unalterable opinion that they would be entitled to a legal release on the 10th. "They therefore look to their general, who holds their confidence, for an honorable discharge on that day, and that in every respect he will see that justice be done them."

An appeal like this was harder for a man of Jackson's cast of character to resist than armed mutiny. He had no choice but to resist it. It was essential to the safety of the frontiers that these men should remain in service, at least until they could be relieved by other troops. Jackson's reply to this letter was moderate and unanswerable.

"The moment," said he, "it is signified to me by any competent authority, even by the Governor of Tennessee, to whom I have written on the subject, or by General Pinckney, who is now appointed to the command, that the volunteers may be exonerated from further service, that moment I will pronounce it with the greatest satisfaction. I have only the power of pronouncing a discharge—not of giving it—in any case; a distinction which I would wish should be borne in mind. Already have I sent to raise volunteers, on my own responsibility, to complete a campaign which has been so happily begun, and thus far so fortunately prosecuted. The moment they arrive—and I am assured that, fired by our exploits, they will hasten in crowds on the first intimation that we need their services—they will be substituted in the place of those who are discontented here. The latter will then be permitted to return to their homes, with all the honor which under such circumstances they can carry along with them. But I still cherish the hope that their dissatisfaction and complaints have been greatly exaggerated. I can not, must not believe, that the 'Volunteers of Tennessee,' a name ever dear to fame, will disgrace themselves, and a country which they have honored, by abandoning her standard as mutineers and deserters; but should I be disappointed, and compelled to resign this pleasing hope, one thing I will not resign—my duty. Mutiny and sedition, so long as I possess the power of quelling them, shall be put down; and even when left destitute of this, I will still be found in the last extremity endeavoring to discharge the duty I owe my country and myself."

The afternoon of the 9th ended. The frenzy of the men to return was such that they were determined not even to wait for the morning, but to march at the very moment their last day's service had been rendered. Jackson was in his tent, not anticipating a movement that evening, when an officer suddenly entered and informed him that the whole brigade was in mutiny and preparing to march off in a body. He dashed upon paper the following order: "The commanding general being informed that an actual mutiny exists in the camp, all officers and soldiers are commanded to put it down. The officers and soldiers of the First Brigade will without delay parade on the west side of the fort, and await further orders."

He further ordered the artillery company, with their two small pieces of cannon, to take position in front and rear, and the militia to be drawn up on an eminence commanding the road upon which the volunteers intended to march. These orders were obeyed with surprising alacrity, for Jackson was now in that mood that men felt it perilous to resist. The general mounted his horse and rode up to the line of volunteers, as they stood along the western side of the fort, silent, sullen, and determined. He broke at once into an impassioned yet not angry address. He praised their former good conduct. He dwelt upon the disgrace that would fall upon themselves and their families if they should carry home with them the name of mutineers and deserters. Never should they do it but by passing over his dead body! He would do *his* duty at any cost; ay, even if he perished there before them, dying honorably at his post. "Re-enforcements," said he, "are preparing to hasten to my assistance; it can not be long before they arrive. I am, too, in daily expectation of receiving information whether you may be discharged or not. Until then you must not and shall not retire. I have done with entreaty; it has been used long enough; I will attempt it no more. You must now determine whether you will go or peaceably remain. If you still persist in your determination to move forcibly off, the point between us shall soon be decided."

He paused. No one answered; no one moved. "I demand an explicit answer," said the general. There was still no response. He ordered the artillerymen to be ready with their matches, himself remaining in front of the mutineers and within the line of fire. The men now evidently hesitated. Whispers ran along the line recommending a return to duty. Soon the officers stepped forward and assured the general that the troops were willing to remain at the fort until the arrival of re-enforcements, or of the answer to General Jackson's inquiries respecting their term of service. The men were dismissed to their quarters, and the general was once more victorious.

Jackson had triumphed only so far as to secure the presence of the men at the post. He now made an effort to restore his army to contentment. The near approach of General Cocke having strengthened his position, he resolved to permit the homesick brigade to march to Tennessee, there to be dismissed or retained as the Governor should decide.

General Cocke reached Fort Strother on the 12th of December with his division of two thousand men. Jackson learned, however, that the term of service of more than half of this body was on the very point of expiring, and that none of them had longer than a month to serve. Nor were any of them provided with clothing suitable for a winter campaign. Retaining eight hundred of these troops, who owed still a month's service, Jackson ordered General Cocke to march the rest of his division back to the settlements, there to dismiss them, and to enroll a new force, properly provided, and engaged to serve six months. He addressed the departing troops, entreating them to join the new army as soon as they had procured their clothing, and return to him and aid in completing the conquest of the enemy.

These were dark days for General Jackson. Everything went wrong. The return of so many troops, bearing with them the feelings they did, giving out that, after enduring privations, gaining victories, and holding the savages in check for two months, they had been refused an honorable dismissal and sent home almost in disgrace, threw a damper upon the efforts to raise new men and spread discontent among those already engaged. Even the horsemen of General Coffee, who had been allowed to leave Fort Strother for a while to recruit their horses at home, could not be induced to return to duty. Assembling at the call of the gallant Coffee, they heard the tale of the returning troops, caught their spirit, and became mutinous, riotous, and unmanageable. At length they broke away in a tumultuous mass toward home. General Coffee galloped in pursuit, accompanied by the eloquent Blackburn, and both addressed the fugitives with all the persuasive energy of which they were capable. But in vain. Nearly to a man the cavalry brigade rode away, rioting and wasting as they went, and were seen as an organized body no more.

Affairs were little better at Jackson's own camp. He had fourteen hundred men at Fort Strother, of whom eight hundred would be free to return home in four weeks. The remaining six hundred were militia who had been called out upon the receipt of the news of Fort Mims, by an act of the Legislature which, most unfortunately, did not specify *any* time of service. Three months, said the militia, is the term established by King Precedent. By no means, replied Jackson; the omission in the act must be supplied by the phrase *for the war*. The militia were summoned, he maintained, for the purpose of avenging Fort Mims and conquering a lasting peace. These objects accomplished, the work for which the troops were engaged would be done, and they would be entitled to an honorable discharge; but not till then.

Here were the elements of new discontents and new mutinies. The three months would expire on the 4th of

January, and already the latter half of December was gliding away. Thus, in two weeks Jackson was threatened with the loss of six hundred of his troops, and in four weeks the remaining eight hundred would certainly depart. The campaign was falling to pieces in every direction. Jackson's military career seemed about to close in disgrace, and the glory of the Tennessee volunteers to be extinguished forever. But this was not all. Disaster menaced every assailable portion of the Southwest. Letters came from General Pinckney, the chief in command in that region, ordering General Jackson to hold all his posts, since it had become a matter of the first national importance to deprive the British of their Indian allies.

How anxiously, in such circumstances, General Jackson looked for news from Tennessee may be imagined. Help from that quarter alone could save him, and that help he had implored from Governor Blount, who alone could grant it. The expected dispatch from Nashville reached Fort Strother at length, and proved to be a most disheartening response to Jackson's entreaties. The Governor feared to transcend his authority. Having called out all the troops authorized by Congress and the Legislature, what could he do more? The campaign had failed, he said, and he advised General Jackson to give up a struggle which could have no favorable issue, and return home; to wait until the General Government should provide the means requisite for carrying on the war with vigor.

Not for one instant did Jackson concur in this view of the situation. He was of that temper which gained new determination from other men's despair. The last ounce stiffened his back, but did not break it. He went to his tent and wrote to the Governor the best letter he ever wrote in his life—one of those historical epistles which do the work of a campaign in rolling back the tide of events. This eloquent epistle convinced and roused Governor Blount. He forthwith ordered a new levy of twenty-five hundred men to rendezvous at Fayetteville on the 28th of January, to serve for three months, and authorized General Cocke to obey Jackson's order for raising a new division of East Tennesseeans. The aspect of affairs in the State was immediately changed. The noise of preparation was everywhere heard. There was a furbishing of arms and a tramp of marching men in all quarters of the State. In a few days the honorable scruples of the Governor were completely set at rest by a dispatch from the Secretary of War, which more than covered all he had done, and sanctioned any further requisition of men which he might deem necessary. If Jackson could but hold his position a few weeks longer, there was every prospect of his being able once more to act with efficiency.

From the middle of December to the middle of January General Jackson was called upon to endure every description of mortification and difficulty known to border warfare. On the 4th of January his six hundred militia, in spite of warning and entreaty, and after scenes of violence similar to those already related, marched homeward. On the 14th, the eight hundred of General Cocke's division, whose term of service then expired, were earnestly besought to remain, if only for twenty days. The savages were in motion again, and threatened the frontiers of Georgia. Jackson implored these men to make *one* excursion into the enemy's country, to strike *one* blow at them, for the purpose of at least diverting or dividing their force and giving an easier victory to the Georgia troops. But no; their minds were set resolutely homeward, and away they marched, leaving him with a mere handful of men to guard the post. Moreover, the new recruits could not be induced to engage for six months. Colonel Carroll, rather than bring back no men, had enlisted a body of horse for two months only, and General Roberts returned with infantry engaged for three. These men General Jackson was obliged to accept, or be left alone in the wilderness.

On the 15th of January, then, we find the general at Fort Strother with nine hundred raw recruits, who had come out with the expectation of making a single raid into the Indian territory and then to return to narrate their exploits and draw their pay. Such troops it is dangerous to keep in inaction for a single week. The regular levies from Tennessee could not be expected for a month to come. The necessity of striking a blow at the exulting enemy was pressing. In these circumstances, Jackson, with the daring prudence that characterized his career, resolved upon instant action, and gave the order to prepare for marching against the foe.

"On the evening of the 20th I encamped at Enotachopco, a small Hillabee village about twelve miles from Emuckfau. Here I began to perceive very plainly how little knowledge my spies had of the country, of the situation of the enemy, or of the distance I was from them. The insubordination of the new troops, and the want of skill in most of their officers, also became more and more apparent. But their ardor to meet the enemy was not diminished, and I had sure reliance upon the guards, and upon the company of old volunteer officers, and upon the spies, in all about one hundred and twenty-five. My wishes and my duty remained united, and I was determined to effect, if possible, the objects for which the excursion had been principally undertaken.

"On the morning of the 21st I marched from Enota-

chopco as direct as I could for the bend of the Tallapoosa, and about two made a swift incursion into the
enemy's country, during which hard blows were dealt
them, keeping the restless men loyal to their duty, and
prepared the way for the next and decisive operations
of the war."

CHAPTER X.

THE excursion over, and the new levies from Tennessee approaching, Jackson dismissed his victorious troops, whose term of service was about to expire. He bade them farewell in an address abounding in kind and flattering expressions; and they left him feeling all that soldiers usually feel toward the general who has led them to victory.

The return of these troops, animated by such sentiments, gave a new impetus to the cause in Tennessee, and fired the troops who were on their way to the seat of war with new zeal. From all quarters came volunteers, hurrying toward the standard of the successful general, whose prospects now brightened with every day's dispatches. On the 3d of February came news that two thousand East Tennesseeans were far on their way to join him. A day or two after, a dispatch informed the general that nearly as many West Tennessee troops had reached Huntsville and waited his orders. On the 6th marched into Fort Strother the Thirty-ninth Regiment of United States infantry, six hundred strong, under Colonel Williams—a most important acquisition. Into this regiment one Sam Houston had recently enlisted as a private soldier, and made his way to the rank of ensign—the same Sam Houston who was afterward President of Texas and Senator of the United States.

In addition to this re-enforcement, there came in,

soon after, a part of General Coffee's old brigade of mounted men, and a troop of dragoons from East Tennessee. The Choctaw Indians now openly joined the peace party, and asked orders from General Jackson. There was no lack of men of any description. Long before February closed Jackson was at the head of an army of five thousand men, all within a few days' march of Fort Strother, waiting only till the general could accumulate twenty days' rations to march in and strike, as they hoped, a finishing blow at the enemy.

Six weeks of intense labor on the part of the general and his army were required to complete the preparations for the decisive movement. The middle of March had arrived. The various divisions of the army were assembled at Fort Strother, and the requisite quantity of provisions had been accumulated. A system of expresses had been established for the conveyance of information to General Pinckney and Governor Blount. With much difficulty, one man had been found competent to beat the ordinary calls on the drum, and this one drum was the sole music of the army. Deducting the strong guards to be left at the posts already established, the force about to march against the enemy amounted to about three thousand men.

The attention of the reader is now to be directed to a remarkable "bend" of the river Tallapoosa, about fifty-five miles from Fort Strother, the scene, for so many weeks, of General Jackson's strenuous endeavors.

The Tallapoosa and the Coosa are the rivers which unite in the southern part of Alabama and form the Alabama River. The bend of which we speak is about midway between the source and the mouth of the Tallapoosa. It occurs where the stream is not fordable during the spring rains, but is not wide enough to present a serious obstacle to an Indian swimmer. From the shape of this peninsula the Indians called it Tohopeka, which means *horseshoe*. It contains a hundred acres of land, since a cotton field. The neck, or isthmus, is about three hundred and fifty yards across. The ground rises somewhat from the edge of the water. It was a wild, rough piece of ground, abounding in places which would afford covert to an Indian warrior. At the time of which we write the surrounding country for a hundred miles or more was a nearly unbroken wilderness of forest, swamp, and cane, marked only by the trail of wild beasts and the "trace" of wild men. As well from its situation as its form this place was entitled to be styled the heart of the Indian country.

Here it was that the evil genius of the Creeks prompted them to assemble the warriors of all the tribes residing in that vicinity, to make a stand against the great army with which, their runners told them, General Jackson was preparing to overrun the Indian country. The long delays at Fort Strother had given them time to prepare for his reception, and they had improved that time. Across the neck of the peninsula they had built (of logs) a breastwork of immense strength, pierced with two rows of port-holes. The line of defense was so drawn that an approaching enemy would we exposed both to a direct and a raking fire. Behind the breastwork was a mass of logs and brushwood, such as Indians delight to fight from. At the bottom of the peninsula, near the river, was a village of huts. The banks of the river were fringed with the canoes of the savage garrison, so that they possessed the means of retreat as well as of defense. The greater part of the peninsula was still covered with the primeval forest. Within this extensive fortification were assembled about nine hundred warriors of various Creek tribes, and about three hundred women and children.

The Indian force was small to defend so extensive a line of fortification. But a variety of circumstances conspired to give the savage garrison confidence: such as the impregnable strength of the breastwork, its peculiar construction, the facilities afforded in the interior of the bend for the Indian mode of fighting, the partial successes gained by the Indians at Emuckfau and Enotachopco—of which they continually boasted, averring that they had made "Captain Jackson" run—and, above all, the positive and reiterated predictions of their prophets. Three of the most famous of the prophets were there, performing their incantations day and night, and keeping alive that religious fury which had played so great a part in previous battles. And besides, in case the breastwork was carried and the bend overrun, how easy to rush to the canoes and paddle across the river, laughing at their baffled assailants as they vanished into the woods on the opposite shore! So thought the Creeks.

Jackson was eleven days in marching his army the fifty-five miles of untrodden wilderness that lay between Fort Strother and the Horseshoe Bend of the Tallapoosa. Roads had to be cut, the Coosa explored, boats waited for and rescued from the shoals, high ridges crossed, Fort Williams built and garrisoned to keep open the line of communication, and numerous other difficulties overcome, before he could penetrate to the vicinity of the bend. It was early in the morning of March 27th that, with an army diminished by garrisoning the posts to two thousand men, he reached the scene and prepared to commence operations.

Perceiving at one glance that the Indians had simply penned themselves up for slaughter, his first measure was to send General Coffee with all the mounted men and friendly Indians to cross the river two miles below, where it was fordable, to take a position on the bank opposite the line of canoes, and so cut off the retreat. This was promptly executed by General Coffee, who soon announced by a preconcerted signal that he had reached the station assigned him. Jackson then planted his two pieces of cannon—one a three, the other a six-pounder—upon an eminence eighty yards from the nearest point of the breastwork, whence, at half-past ten in the morning, he opened fire upon it. His sharpshooters also were drawn up near enough to get an occasional shot at an Indian within the bend. A steady fire of cannon and rifles was kept up in front for two hours without producing any hopeful beginning of a breach in the breastwork. The little cannon balls buried themselves in the logs or in the earth between them without doing decisive harm. The Indians whooped in derision as they struck and disappeared.

Meanwhile General Coffee, not content to remain inactive, hit upon a line of conduct that proved eminently effective. He sent some of the best swimmers among his force of friendly Indians across the river to cut loose and bring away the canoes of the beleaguered Creeks. That done, he used the canoes for sending over a party of men under Colonel Morgan, with orders first to set fire to the cluster of huts at the bottom of the bend, and then to rush forward and attack the Indians behind the breastwork.

This was gallantly done. The force under Jackson soon perceived from the smoke of the burning huts and from the rattling fire behind the breastwork that General Coffee was up and doing. Soon, however, that fire was observed to slacken, and it became apparent that Morgan's force was too small to do more than distract and divide the attention of the assailed. This, however, alone was an immense advantage. Jackson's men saw it and clamored for the order to assault. The General hesitated many minutes before giving an order that would inevitably send so many of his brave fellows to their account, and the issue of which was doubtful. The order came at length, and was received with a general shout.

The Thirty-ninth Regiment, under Colonel Williams, and the brigade of East Tennesseeans, under Colonel Bunch, marched rapidly up to the breastwork and delivered a volley through the port-holes. The Indians returned the fire with effect, and, muzzle to muzzle, the combatants for a short time contended. Major L. P. Montgomery, of the Thirty-ninth, was the first man to spring upon the breastwork, where, calling upon his men to follow, he received a ball in his head and fell dead to the ground. At that critical moment young Ensign Houston mounted the breastwork. A barbed arrow pierced his thigh; but, nothing dismayed, this gallant youth, calling his comrades to follow, leaped down among the Indians and soon cleared a space around him with his vigorous right arm. Joined in a moment by parties of his own regiment, and by large numbers of the East Tennesseeans, the breastwork was soon cleared, the Indians retiring before them into the underbrush.

The wounded ensign sat down within the fortification and called a lieutenant of his company to draw the arrow from his thigh. Two vigorous pulls at the barbed weapon failed to extract it. In a fury of pain and impatience Houston cried, " Try again, and if you fail this time I will smite you to the earth!" Exerting all his strength the lieutenant drew forth the arrow, tearing the flesh fearfully, and causing an effusion of blood that compelled the wounded man to hurry over the breastwork to get the wound bandaged. While he was lying on the ground under the surgeon's hands the general rode up, and, recognizing his young acquaintance, ordered him not to cross the breastwork again. Houston begged him to recall the order, but the general repeated it peremptorily and rode on. In a few minutes the ensign had disobeyed the command and was once more with his company in the thick of that long hand-to-hand engagement which consumed the hours of the afternoon.

Not an Indian asked for quarter, nor would accept it when offered. From behind trees and logs, from clefts in the river's banks, from among the burning huts, from chance log-piles, from temporary fortifications, the desperate red men fired upon the troops. A large number plunged into the river and attempted to escape by swimming, but from Coffee's men on one bank and Jackson's on the other a hailstorm of bullets flew over the stream, and the painted heads dipped beneath its blood-stained ripples. The battle became at length a slow, laborious massacre. From all parts of the peninsula resounded the yells of the savages, the shouts of the assailants, and the reports of the firearms, while the gleam of the uplifted tomahawk was seen among the branches.

Toward the close of the afternoon it was observed that a considerable number of the Indians had found a refuge under the bluffs of the river, where a part of the breastwork, the formation of the ground, and the felled trees gave them complete protection. Desirous to end this horrible carnage, Jackson sent a friendly Indian to announce to them that their lives should be spared if they would surrender. They were silent for a moment, as if in consultation, and then answered the summons by a volley which sent the interpreter bleeding from the scene. The cannon were now brought up and played upon the spot without effect. Jackson then called for volunteers to charge, but the Indians were so well posted that for a minute no one responded to the call. Ensign Houston again emerged into view on this occasion. Ordering his platoon to follow, but not waiting to see if they would follow, he rushed to the overhanging bank which sheltered the foe and through openings of which they were firing. Over this mine of desperate savages he paused and looked back for his men. At that moment he received two balls in his right shoulder; his arm fell powerless to his side, he staggered out of the fire and lay down totally disabled. His share in that day's work was done.

Several valuable lives were afterward lost in vain endeavors to dislodge the enemy from their well-chosen covert. As the sun was going down, fire was set to the logs and underbrush, which overspread and surrounded this last refuge of the Creeks. The place soon grew too hot to hold them. Singly, and by twos and threes, they ran from the ravine, and fell as they ran before the fire of a hundred riflemen on the watch for the starting of the game.

The carnage lasted as long as there was light enough to see a skulking or a flying enemy. It was impossible to spare. The Indians fought after they were wounded, and gave wounds to men who sought to save their lives, for they thought that if spared they would be reserved only for a more painful death. Night fell at last, and recalled the troops from their bloody work to gather wounded comrades and minister to their necessities. It was a night of horror. Along the banks of the river, all around the bend, Indians—the wounded and the unhurt—were crouching in the clefts, under the brushwood, and in some instances under the heaps of slain, watching for an opportunity to escape. Many did escape, and some lay until the morning, fearing to attempt it. One noted chief, covered with wounds, took to the

water in the evening and lay beneath the surface, drawing his breath through a hollow cane until it was dark
enough to swim across. He escaped, and lived to tell
his story and show his scars many years after to the historian of Alabama, from whom we have derived the incident. In the morning, parties of the troops again
scoured the peninsula and ferreted from their hiding-
places sixteen more warriors, who, refusing still to surrender, were added to the number of the slain.

Upon counting the dead, five hundred and fifty-seven
was found to be the number of the fallen enemy within
the peninsula. Two hundred more, it was computed,
had found a grave at the bottom of the river. Many
more died in the woods attempting to escape. Jackson's
loss was fifty-five killed and one hundred and forty-six
wounded, of whom more than half were friendly Indians.
The three prophets of the Creeks, fantastically dressed
and decorated, were found among the dead. One of
them, while engaged in his incantations, had received a
grapeshot in his mouth, which killed him instantly.

One would have expected General Jackson to pause
in his operations after such an affair as that of the
Horseshoe. Nothing was further from his thoughts.
"In war," his maxim was, "till everything is done
nothing is done." On the morning after the battle he
began at once to prepare for a retrograde movement as
far as Fort Williams, the fort which he had built on his
march from Fort Strother. He had brought with him
into the heart of the wilderness but seven days' provisions. Before pushing his conquests further, it was
necessary both to procure supplies and place his long
train of wounded in a place of safety and comfort. He
was up betimes, therefore, and passed a busy morning.
His dead were sunk in the river, to prevent their being
scalped by the returning savages. Litters were prepared

for the wounded. A brief, imperfect account of the battle was dispatched to General Pinckney. Before the sun was many hours on his course all things were in readiness, and the army set out on its return.

Five days' march brought them to Fort Williams. There the wounded were cared for, the friendly Indians dismissed, and the troops publicly thanked, praised, and congratulated. The praise of the general was the theme of every tongue.

Provisions were not too abundant there in the wilderness, and supplies were brought in with incredible difficulty and toil. Jackson's next object was to form a junction with the southern army at the confluence of the Coosa and Tallapoosa, the holy ground of the Creeks, which their prophets told them no white man could tread and live. He had been assured by General Pinckney that as soon as the junction of the two armies was effected all difficulty with regard to provisions would be at an end, as superabundant supplies had been provided by the General Government. Moreover, it was on this holy ground that the only body of Creeks that still maintained a hostile attitude were assembled. For five days the troops rested from their labors at Fort Williams ; then they set out on their march through the pathless wilderness, leaving behind wagons and baggage, each man carrying eight days' provisions upon his back. Floods of rain, converting swamps into lakes, rivulets into rivers, creeks into torrents, retarded their progress, and gave the Indians time to disperse. The latter days of April, however, found the troops on the holy ground, where a junction with part of the southern army was effected.

But the war was over. The power of the Creeks was broken; half their warriors were dead, the rest were scattered and subdued in spirit. Fort Mims was indeed avenged. Jackson's amazing celerity of movement, and particularly his last daring plunge into the wilderness, and his triumph over obstacles that would have deterred even an Indian force, quite baffled and confounded the unhappy Creeks. Against such a man they felt it vain to contend. The general had no sooner reached the holy ground and procured for his tired and hungry men the supplies they needed, than the chiefs began to come into his camp and supplicate for peace. His reply to them was brief and stern. They must give proof, he said, of their submission, by returning to the north of his advanced post—Fort Williams. There they would be treated with, and the demands of the Government made known to them.

In a few days fourteen of the leading chiefs had given in their submission and taken up their sorrowful march toward the designated place. Those of the fallen tribe who despaired of making terms, and those whose spirit was not yet completely crushed, fled into Florida, and there sowed the seed of future wars.

With the establishment of Fort Jackson in the holy ground, at the confluence of the two rivers, General Jackson's task was nearly done. For a few days he was busy enough in receiving deputations of repentant and crestfallen chiefs, and in sending out strong detachments of troops to scour the country in search of hostile parties, if any such still kept the field. No hostile parties were found. The friendly Creeks, however, gave some trouble by their excess of zeal. Attributing the calamities brought upon their tribe to the massacre at Fort Mims, they were bent upon putting to death every man that had taken part in that scene of horrors. Bodies and single individuals of the hostile portion of the tribe were waylaid and killed by roving companies of their own countrymen. A war of extermination would have ensued, had not General Jackson, in his decisive manner, announced that any of the friendly party who should molest a Red Stick after he had surrendered and while he was obeying the orders of the general, should be treated as enemies of the United States. This stayed the work of blood, and the Indians continued to repair to the northern part of Alabama, which had been assigned for their temporary residence. Fort Jackson completed the line of posts which separated them from the hostile Indians, the hostile British, and the sympathizing Spaniards of Florida.

In the beginning of May, 1814, a few days after the news of the battle of the Horseshoe reached Washington, a brigadier-generalship fell vacant, which the President was induced to offer to General Jackson. Before it was known whether the offer would be accepted, the unhappy misunderstanding between the Secretary of War and General William Henry Harrison resulted in the resignation of that brave officer and honest gentleman. Whether it was the haste of the Secretary to shelve an officer disagreeable to him, or the growing *éclat* of Jackson's victories, or both of these causes together, that induced the Government to accept the resignation and offer the vacancy to Jackson, is a matter of no importance now. Jackson received the offer of the brigadiership ; and while he was considering the question of acceptance or rejection, the mail of the day following brought him the second offer, which he accepted promptly and gladly. It was a reward which he desired and felt to be due to his standing and services. The National Intelligencer of May 31, 1814, contained the announcement in the usual form :

" Andrew Jackson, of Tennessee, is appointed major-general in the army of the United States, *vice* William Henry Harrison, resigned."

The emoluments of his new rank were of importance to General Jackson, for he was by no means a rich man in 1814. The pay of a major-general in the army of the United States was twenty-four hundred dollars a year, with allowances for rations, forage, servants, and transportation, that swelled the income to an average of about six thousand five hundred dollars. It was never less than six thousand dollars. The Legislature of Mississippi Territory, about the same time, voted General Jackson a sword, which was the first of the many similar gifts bestowed upon him during his military career.

It is worthy of remark, in view of succeeding events, that no less than six generals had stood between Jackson and the likelihood of his being intrusted with the defense of the Southwest. First, General Wilkinson was transferred from New Orleans to the Northwest, where his failure was signal. Next, Brigadier-General Hampton resigned. Third, Major-General William Henry Harrison resigned. Fourth, General Flourney, who succeeded Wilkinson at New Orleans, resigned. Fifth, General Howard, of Kentucky, who was dispatched to succeed Flourney, died before reaching his post. Sixth, General Gaines, sent from Washington in haste when the first alarm for New Orleans was felt by the Administration, did not arrive till all was over. And all these singular and unexpected changes occurred within the space of a very few months.

The effects of Jackson's eight months' service upon his health were permanently injurious. In reading of his exploits we figure to ourselves a man in the enjoyment of the full tide of health. How different was the fact! From the moment of his being wounded in the affray with the Bentons to the close of the war he was so much an invalid that a man of less strength of will would probably have yielded to the disease and spent his days in nursing it. Chronic diarrhœa was the form which his complaint assumed. The slightest imprudence in eating or drinking brought on an attack, during which he suffered intensely. While the paroxysm lasted he could obtain relief only by sitting on a chair with his chest against the back of it and his arms dangling forward. In this position he was sometimes compelled to remain for hours. It often happened that he was seized with the familiar pain while on the march through the woods at the head of the troops. In the absence of other means of relief he would have a sapling half severed and bent over, upon which he would hang with his arms downward till the agony subsided. The only medicine that he took, and his only beverage then, was weak gin and water. The reader is therefore to banish from his imagination the popular figure of a vigorous warrior galloping in the pride of his strength upon a fiery charger, and put in the place of it a slight, attenuated form, a yellowish, wrinkled face, the dark-blue eyes of which were the only feature that told anything of the power and quality of the man. In great emergencies, it is true, his will was master, compelling his impaired body to execute all its resolves. But the reaction was terrible sometimes, days of agony and prostration following an hour of anxiety or exertion. He gradually learned in some degree to manage and control his disease. But all through the Creek war and the New Orleans campaign he was an acute sufferer, more fit for a sick-chamber than for the forest bivouac or the field of battle. There were times, and critical times, too, when it seemed impossible that he could go on. But at the decisive moment he always rallied, and would do what the decisive moment demanded.

General Jackson rested from his labors three weeks. As soon as his acceptance of the major-generalship reached Washington he was ordered to take command of the Southern Division of the army, if division it could be called, which consisted of three half-filled regiments. He was ordered to halt, on his way to the Southern coast, long enough to form a definite treaty with the Creeks, or rather to announce to them the terms upon which the United States would consent to a permanent peace. Colonel Hawkins, who had been the agent for the Creeks since the days of General Washington, was associated with the general in this business. On the 10th of July, General Jackson, with a small retinue, reached the holy ground once more, the place appointed for meeting the chiefs, where he assumed the command of the troops and prepared to begin the negotiation.

The instructions from the Secretary of War set forth that terms were to be dictated to the Creeks as to a conquered people. The commissioners were to demand, first, an indemnification for the expenses incurred by the United States in the prosecution of the war, by such a cession of land as might be deemed an equivalent; secondly, a stipulation on the part of the Creeks that they would cease all intercourse with any Spanish garrison or town, and not admit among them any agent or trader who did not derive his authority or license from the United States; thirdly, an acknowledgment of the right of the United States to open roads through the Creek territory, and to establish such military posts and trading-houses as might be necessary and proper; and, lastly, the surrender of the prophets and instigators of the war.

An outline of a treaty in accordance with these principles was promptly submitted by the commissioners to the council of chiefs; an engagement being added that, in consideration of the destitute condition of the tribe, supplies would be furnished by the United States until the maturity of the next crop. After a delay of a whole month in negotiation the treaty was signed by the chiefs and the commissioners, and General Jackson, accompanied by his staff and a few troops, directed his steps toward Mobile. Rumors of the great British expedition against New Orleans already alarmed the Southern country. British troops, indeed, were already in Florida.

CHAPTER XI.

IT may have surprised the reader that a commander so remarkable for celerity of movement as General Jackson should have lingered a whole month at the junction of the Coosa and Tallapoosa, concluding a treaty with the Creeks. But that was by no means his principal employment there, as shall now be shown.

All that summer he had had a watchful and frequently a wrathful eye on Florida. That the flying Creeks should have been afforded a refuge in that province first moved him to anger, for it was the nature of Andrew Jackson to finish whatever he undertook. He went, as Colonel Benton often remarked, for "a clean victory or a clean defeat." As long as there was anywhere on earth one Creek maintaining an attitude of hostility against the United States, he felt his work incomplete, and regarded any man or Governor as an enemy who gave that solitary warrior aid and comfort. Being a man with less of the spirit of the circumlocution office in him than any other individual then extant—a man, in fact, with not a shred of red tape in his composition—the impulse of his mind was to march straight into the heart of Florida and extinguish the hostile remnant of the Creeks without more ado. That, however, was a measure of which he was not yet ready to assume the whole responsibility.

While on his way from the Hermitage to Fort Jackson, a rumor reached his ears that a British vessel was at Appalachicola landing arms for distribution among the Indians. His first act, therefore, on arriving at the treaty ground, was to select, by the aid of Colonel Hawkins, some trustworthy Indians to send to Appalachicola to ascertain what was going on there. Before they returned, a piece of very tangible evidence of the truth of the rumor reached him in the form of a new musket of English manufacture, which had been given to a Creek of the peace party by a friend of his at Appalachicola only a week before. We can imagine the feelings and the manner of Jackson as he handled, examined, and descanted upon this shining weapon. The owner of the musket, upon being questioned, stated that a party of British troops was at Appalachicola, giving out arms and ammunition to all the hostile Indians that applied for them.

In fifteen days the friendly Indians returned to Fort Jackson, confirming the testimony of the new musket and its proprietor. Soon came rumors that a large force of British were expected at Pensacola, and at length positive information of the landing of Colonel Nichols, of the welcome he had received from the Spanish governor, and of his extraordinary proceedings.

"Florida must be ours," was thenceforth the burden of General Jackson's secret thoughts, communicated only to two or three of his most confidential officers. "Florida must be ours," was the burden of his letters to the Secretary of War. "If the hostile Creeks," he wrote to the Secretary, "have taken refuge in Florida, and are there fed, clothed, and protected; if the British have landed a large force, munitions of war, and are fortifying and stirring up the savages, will you only say to me, 'Raise a few hundred militia, which can be quickly done, and, with such regular force as can be conveniently collected, make a descent upon Pensacola and reduce it?' If so, I promise you the war in the South shall have a speedy termination, and English influence be forever destroyed with the savages in this quarter."

The answer of Secretary Armstrong to this letter—whether from accident or design will never be known—was six months on its way from Washington to the hands of General Jackson. It reached him at New Orleans when the campaign and the war were over. It gave him all the authority he desired.

"If this letter," he would say in after-years, "or any hint that such a course would have been even winked at by the Government, had been received, it would have been in my power to have captured the British shipping in the bay. I would have marched at once against Barrancas and carried it, and thus prevented any escape. But, acting on my own responsibility against a neutral power, it became essential for me to proceed with more caution than my judgment or wishes approved, and consequently important advantages were lost which might have been secured."

Colonel Nichols, taking no precautions whatever to conceal his designs, but rather courting publicity, General Jackson was kept well informed of what was transpiring in Florida. Early in September it was noised about in Pensacola, and soon reported to General Jackson, that Colonel Nichols had hostile designs upon Mobile. The general's mind from that moment was made up. He would dally no longer with a Secretary of War two months distant; he would take the responsibility; he would fight the Southern campaign himself as best he could, orders or no orders. Already he had written to the Governors of Tennessee, Louisiana, and Mississippi, urging them to complete the organization of their militia, "for," said he, "there is no telling when or where the spoiler may come." "Dark and heavy clouds," he said in another letter, "hover around us. The energy and patriotism of the citizens of your States must dispel them. Our rights, our liberties, and free Constitution are threatened. This noble patrimony of our fathers must be defended with the best blood of our country ; to do this, you must hasten to carry into effect the requisition of the Secretary of War, and call forth your troops without delay."

On the 9th of September, Colonel Butler, Jackson's adjutant-general, who had been sent to Tennessee to hasten the organization of the new levies in that State, received the welcome order from Jackson to call out the troops and march them with all dispatch southward toward Mobile. The call was obeyed with even greater alacrity than that of the last year, when the massacre of Fort Mims was to be avenged. General Coffee was promptly in the field once more. Such was the eagerness of the Tennesseeans to share a campaign with General Jackson, that considerable sums, ranging from thirty to eighty dollars, were paid for the privilege of being substitutes for those who could not go. On the appointed day two thousand men appeared at the rendezvous, well armed and equipped, ready to march with General Coffee, four hundred miles, to the scene of expected combat. At the same time a small body of recruits for the regular army set out from Nashville toward Mobile. Colonel Butler, as soon as he had completed his business in Tennessee, hurried forward to conduct to the same place the forces stationed at the posts which had been established during the late Creek war.

Mobile was an insignificant village of a hundred and fifty houses when Jackson arrived there to defend it, in the latter part of August, 1814. Like Pensacola, it derived whatever importance it had from the bay at the head of which it was situated, and the great river system of which that bay is the outlet.

When General Jackson reached Mobile he found it little better prepared for defense against any but an Indian foe than if war were unknown to the civilized part of mankind. There were some blockhouses and stockades in the town, but no structure that could resist artillery. Nor, indeed, was there need of any, for the place was to be defended or lost at Mobile Point, thirty miles down the bay. If Colonel Nichols and Captain Percy had touched at the Point on their way to Pensacola and landed two hundred men there, they would have given General Jackson much more trouble than they did. There was nothing to hinder their doing so at the time.

To Mobile Point Jackson repaired soon after his arrival at Mobile. There he found the remains of the fortification, then called Fort Bowyer, though the name has since been changed to Fort Morgan. Incomplete, and yet falling into ruin, without a bomb-proof, and mounting but two twenty-four pounders, six twelves, and twelve smaller pieces, it was plain that Fort Bowyer was Mobile's chance of safety. It had been untenanted for a year or more, and contained nothing of the means of defense except cannons and cannon-balls. For the information of unprofessional readers, it is enough to say that the fort was a semicircular structure, with such additional outworks as were necessary to enable it to command the all-important channel, the peninsula, and the open sea. It was surrounded by a ditch twenty feet wide. Its weak point was similar to that by which Fort Ticonderoga was once taken—it was overlooked by some tall hillocks of sand within cannon range.

Into this fort General Jackson, with all haste, threw a garrison of one hundred and sixty men, commanded by Major Lawrence, of the Second Regiment of United States Infantry, as gallant a spirit as ever stood to his country's defense. A large proportion of the little garrison were totally ignorant of gunnery, and had to learn the art by practicing it in fighting the enemy. The first twelve days in September were employed by them in repairing the essential parts of the fortification, while General Jackson was busy on shore dispatching provisions and ammunition, and counting over and over again the days that must elapse before he could reasonably expect the arrival of re-enforcements.

No signs of an enemy appeared until the morning of the 12th of September, when an out-sentinel came running in with the report that a body of British marines and Indians had landed on the peninsula, within a few miles of the fort. Colonel Nichols, it afterward appeared, was the commander of this detachment, which consisted, according to American writers, of one hundred and thirty marines and six hundred Indians; according to James, the English historian, of sixty marines and one hundred and twenty Indians. Captain Woodbine commanded the Indian part of this force. Toward evening of the same day four British vessels of war hove in sight and came to anchor near the coast, six miles from the Point. These proved to be the Hermes, Captain Percy, twenty-two guns; the Sophia, in command of Captain Lockyer, eighteen guns; the Carron, twenty guns; and the Childers, eighteen guns—the whole under the command of Captain Percy.

Night fell upon the fleet, the land force, and the anxious garrison, without any movement having been attempted on either side. The garrison slept upon their arms, every man at his post.

The next day a reconnoitering party approached within three quarters of a mile and then retired. A little after noon Colonel Nichols drew a howitzer, the only one he had with him, behind a mound seven hundred yards from the fort. He fired three shells and a cannon-ball, which splintered a piece of timber that crowned part of the rampart, but did no other damage. The garrison, without being able to see the enemy, fired a few shots in the direction of the mound. Under cover of other sand-hills Nichols then withdrew his party to a point a mile and a half distant, where he appeared to be throwing up a breastwork. Three well-aimed shots from the fort again dispersed the party and drove them beyond range, within which they did not return that day. Later in the afternoon several small boats put off from the ships, and attempted to sound the channel near Mobile Point. A few discharges of ball and grape drove them off also, and they returned to the ships. Night again closed in upon the scene, and the garrison again went to sleep upon their arms, encouraged and confident.

On the following morning, as soon as it was light enough to discern distant objects, the enemy was seen at the same place, still engaged, as it seemed, in throwing up works, the ships remaining at their former anchorage. As the morning wore away without any further movement, Major Lawrence, concluding that the enemy designed to take the fort by regular approaches, thought it most prudent to send an express to General Jackson, informing him of the enemy's arrival and asking a re-enforcement. It so chanced that Jackson had set out on that very morning to visit the fort, and had sailed to within a few miles of it when he met the boat bearing Major Lawrence's message. Back to Mobile he hurried, his bargemen straining every nerve. He reached the town late at night, where he instantly mustered a body of eighty men, under the command of Captain Laval, hurried them on board a small brig, and saw them off toward Mobile Point before he left the shore. At the fort the whole day passed in inaction. Night came on apace, and once more the beleaguered garrison lay upon their arms, wondering what the morrow would bring forth.

Day dawned upon the 15th of September. Straining eyes from the summit of the fort sought to penetrate the morning mist. Gradually the low, dark line of the enemy's bivouac, and then the dim outline of the more distant ships, became visible. There they were, unchanged from the day before. Are we to have another day, then, of puzzle and inactivity? As the morning cleared it was observed that there was an unwonted stir and movement among the enemy. There was a marching hither and thither upon the peninsula; boats were passing and repassing between the shore and the ships; and all those nameless indications were noticed which announce that something absorbing and decisive is on foot. There is a magnetism in the very air on such occasions which conveys an intimation of coming events to the high-strained nerves of belligerent men. Still, hour after hour passed on, and the ships lay at anchor, and the busy troops upon the shore made no advance.

An hour before noon the wind, which had been fresh, fell to a light breeze, favorable for a movement of the squadron. The ships now weighed anchor and stood out to sea; the little garrison looking out over the ramparts and through the portholes. For nearly three hours the ships beat up against the light wind, away from the fort, till they were hull down in the blue gulf. Have they given it up, then, without a trial? At two o'clock in the afternoon they were observed to tack, get before the wind, and bear down toward the fort in line of battle, the Hermes leading. The suspense was over. They were going to attack !

Then Major Lawrence, in the true spirit of a classical hero, called his officers together to concert the requisite measures. "Don't give up the Fort!" was adopted as the signal for the day, and it did but express the unanimous feeling of the garrison. The officers, while agreeing to defend the fort as long as it was tenable, defined also the terms upon which alone the survivors should surrender. These were the words of their resolution, deliberately concluded upon while the fleet was approaching, and the force on the peninsula was preparing for simultaneous attack :

"That in case of being, by imperious necessity, compelled to surrender (which could only happen in the last extremity, on the ramparts being entirely battered down and the garrison almost wholly destroyed, so that any further resistance would be evidently useless), no capitulation should be agreed on unless it had for its fundamental article that the officers and privates should retain their arms and their private property, and that on no pretext should the Indians be suffered to commit any outrage on their persons or property; and unless full assurance were given them that they would be treated as prisoners of war, according to the custom established among civilized nations."

The officers ratified this resolution by an oath, each man solemnly swearing to abide by it in any and every extremity. Now, every man to his post, and don't give up the fort !

At four o'clock the Hermes came within reach of the fort's great guns. A few shots were exchanged with little effect. One by one the other vessels came up and gave the garrison some practice at long range, but no great harm was done them. At half past four, Captain Percy, like the gallant sailor that he was, ran the Hermes right into the narrow channel that leads into the bay, dropped anchor within musket shot of the fort, and turned his broadside to its guns. The other vessels followed his brave example, and anchored in the channel one behind the other, all within reach of the long guns of the fort, though considerably more distant from them than the Hermes.

Then arose a thundering cannonade. Broadside after broadside from the ships; the fort replying by a steady, quick fire, that was better and better directed as the fight went on. Meanwhile Captain Woodbine, from behind a bluff in the shore, opened fire from his howitzer; but a few shots from the fort's south battery silenced him, and compelled him for a time to keep his distance.

For an hour the firing continued on both sides without a moment's pause, the fleet and the fort enveloped in huge volumes of smoke, lighted up by the incessant flash of the guns. At half past five the halyards of the Hermes's flag were severed by a shot, and the flag fell into the fire and smoke below. Major Lawrence, thinking it possible the ship might have surrendered, ceased his fire. A silence of five minutes succeeded, at the expiration of which a new flag fluttered up to the masthead of the commodore's ship, and the Sophia, that lay next her, renewed the strife by firing a whole broadside at once. In the interval every gun in the fort had been loaded, and the broadside was returned with a salvo that shook the earth. A most furious firing succeeded, and continued for some time longer without any important mishap occurring on either side.

At length a shot from the fort—a lucky shot indeed for the little garrison—cut the cable of the Hermes.

The current of the channel in which she lay caught her heavy stern and turned her bow-foremost to the fort, where she lay for twenty minutes, raked from bow to stern by a terrible fire. At this time it was that the flag-staff of the fort was shot away. The ships, it is to be presumed, either because they did not perceive the absence of the flag, or because they knew the cause of its absence, redoubled their firing at the moment; while Captain Woodbine and his whooping savages, supposing the fort had surrendered, ran up to seize their prey. A few discharges of grape drove the Indians howling back behind the hillocks out of sight, and another flag, fastened hastily to a sponging-rod, was raised above the ramparts.

The Hermes, totally unmanageable, her decks swept of every man and everything, drifted slowly along with the current for half a mile and then ran aground. Still exposed to the fire, and damaged in every part by the hail of shot she had received, it was impossible either to save or fight her. Captain Percy therefore got out his wounded men, transferred them to the Sophia, set his ship on fire, and abandoned her to her fate. Then the Sophia, which was also severely crippled, contrived with difficulty to get out of range. The two other vessels, which were not seriously harmed, hoisted sail and departed to their old anchorage off the coast. The fort guns continued to play upon the Hermes till dark, when the fire burst through her hatches and lighted up the scene with more than the brilliancy of day. At eleven o'clock she blew up, with an explosion that was heard by General Jackson at Mobile, thirty miles distant.

When the next day dawned, Nichols, Woodbine, marines and Indians, had vanished from the peninsula. The three vessels were still in sight, but early in the afternoon they weighed anchor, stood to sea, and were seen no more.

Then the heroic little garrison came forth exulting from their battered walls, surveyed the scene of the late encounter, and reckoned up their victory. Four of their number lay dead within the fort; four others were wounded in the battle; six men had been injured by the bursting of some cartridges. Both of the great twenty-four pounders were cracked beyond using. Two guns had been knocked off their carriages; one had burst; one had been broken short off by a thirty-two-pound ball. The walls of the fort showed the holes and marks of three hundred balls, and the ground about the fort was plowed into ridges. Though but twelve pieces had been brought to bear upon the fleet, the stock of cannon-balls had been diminished by seven hundred. The wreck of the gallant Hermes lay near by, her guns visible in the clear water of the channel.

The garrison was ignorant, as yet, of the name, the force, and the loss of the enemy. They knew not whence they had come, whither they were gone, nor how soon they might return in greater numbers to renew the attack. In the course of the day, two marines, deserters from the party under Colonel Nichols, came in and gave the garrison all the information they desired. They reported the British loss at one hundred and sixty-two killed and seventy wounded. This was an exaggeration. The real loss of the English, as officially given by themselves, was thirty-two killed and forty wounded. Among the wounded was Colonel Nichols himself, who lost an eye in one of his reconnoiterings. The deserters stated that the ships had returned to Pensacola, leaving the marines and Indians to march back to the same place as best they could.

After the defense of Fort Bowyer, General Jackson

had to endure six weeks of most intolerable waiting. Nothing could be done before the arrival of the troops from Tennessee. To the tedium of delay was added a torturing uncertainty with regard to the nature, the extent, and the proximity of the impending danger. If a powerful expedition should arrive, which rumor with a thousand tongues foretold, to which so many probabilities pointed, New Orleans was open to its approach, and Fort Bowyer, with its battered ramparts and cracked guns, could make but a poor and brief resistance. It is not surprising that during these weeks the chronic malady under which the general suffered should have given him many a pang, and frequently laid him prostrate for many successive hours. His attenuated form and yellow, haggard face struck every one with surprise who saw him then for the first time.

On the 25th of November came at length an express from General Coffee, announcing his arrival on the Mobile River with an army of twenty-eight hundred men. The next day Jackson joined him and took the command. Including the troops led by General Coffee, the garrison of Mobile, a body of mounted Mississippians, and a small number of Creek Indians, General Jackson found himself, by the 1st of November, in command of an army of four thousand men, of whom perhaps one thousand were troops of the regular service. A large proportion of the volunteers, not less than fifteen hundred, were mounted. It is mentioned, as a signal proof of their zeal in the service, that they willingly left their horses to pasture on the Mobile River, and served as infantry during the subsequent operations, forage being scarce on the way they were next to go.

General Jackson had resolved, without waiting for any further development of the enemy's plans, to " rout the English out of Pensacola," as he was wont to express it. The press and the people of the Southern States had been clamoring for this with increasing vehemence and unanimity ever since they had heard of the landing of Colonel Nichols. Jackson was nothing loath. In the whole range of military enterprise no expedition could have been suggested which he would have undertaken with so keen a zest as a march upon Pensacola. The treasure-chest being empty, Jackson was compelled to purchase supplies partly with money of his own and partly on the credit of the Government. On the 3d of November, rations for eight days having been distributed, he marched, with three thousand men, unencumbered with baggage, toward Pensacola, and halted, on the evening of the 6th, within a mile and a half of the place.

Not less prudent than impetuous on great occasions, Jackson immediately sent forward Major Piere, of the Forty-fourth Infantry, with a flag, to confer with Governor Maurequez. He was ordered to give a friendly and candid explanation of the object of General Jackson; which was, not to make war upon a neutral power, nor to injure the town, nor needlessly to alarm the subjects of the Spanish king, but merely to deprive the enemies of the United States of a refuge and basis of offensive operations. Major Piere was also to demand the immediate surrender of the forts, which General Jackson pledged himself to hold only in trust, and to restore uninjured as soon as the present peril of the Gulf ports was passed.

As the major approached Fort St. Michael, bearing the flag of truce, he was fired upon; upon which he retired and reported the fact to the general. Jackson then rode forward, and discovered, upon inspecting the fort, that it was garrisoned both by British and Spanish troops, though only the Spanish ensign now floated from the flagstaff. Ordering the troops to bivouac for the night, he resolved on the following day to storm the town. Upon reflecting, however, that the firing upon the flag was probably the work of the English part of the garrison, he made another attempt in the course of the evening to reach the Governor and bring him to terms. A Spanish corporal had been taken on the march, to whom Jackson now intrusted a message to the Governor, asking an explanation of the insult to the flag. Late in the evening the corporal returned with a verbal communication from the Governor, to the effect that he was powerless in the hands of the British, who alone had been concerned in firing upon the flag of truce, and that he would gladly receive any overtures the American general might be pleased to make. Jackson, rejoicing in the prospect of a bloodless and speedy success, at once dispatched Major Piere again to the town, who was soon in the Governor's presence performing his mission. Jackson had hastily written a letter to Maurequez, summing up his demands and purposes in his brief, decisive way. "I come," said he, "not as the enemy of Spain; not to make war, but to ask for peace; to demand security for my country, and that respect to which she is entitled and must receive. My force is sufficient, and my determination taken, to prevent a future repetition of the injuries she has received. I demand, therefore, the possession of the Barrancas, and other fortifications, with all your munitions of war. If delivered peaceably, the whole will be receipted for and become the subject of future arrangement by our respective governments; while the property, laws, and religion of your citizens shall be respected. But if taken by an appeal to arms, let the blood of your subjects be upon your own head! I will not hold myself responsible for the conduct of my enraged soldiers. One hour is given you for deliberation, when your determination must be had."

The Governor left Major Piere alone and consulted with his officers. He returned after a short absence, and said, apparently with reluctance—for the man was in a sore strait between two—and cared only for the preservation of his town—that the terms proposed by General Jackson could not be acceded to. In the small hours of the morning Major Piere returned to the general and reported the Governor's answer.

"Turn out the troops!" was Jackson's sole commentary upon the events of the night.

An hour before daylight the men were under arms and ready to advance. They had slept upon the main road leading into the town, a road commanded by Fort St. Michael, and exposed to the full force of a cannonade of seven British men-of-war that lay at anchor in the harbor. But let the general himself state the events of the morning:

"On the morning of the 7th," he wrote to Governor Blount a few days after, "I marched with the effective regulars of the Third, Thirty-ninth, and Fourth Infantry, part of General Coffee's brigade, the Mississippi dragoons, and part of the West Tennessee regiment, commanded by Lieutenant-Colonel Hammonds (Colonel Lowry having deserted and gone home), and part of the Choctaws, led by Major Blue, of the Thirty-ninth, and Major Kennedy, of Mississippi Territory. Being encamped on the west of the town, I calculated they would expect the assault from that quarter, and be prepared to rake me from the fort, and the British armed vessels, seven in number, that lay in the bay. To cherish this idea, I sent out part of the mounted men to show themselves on the west, while I passed in rear of the fort, undiscovered, to the east of the town. When I appeared within a mile, I was in full view. My pride was never more heightened than in viewing the uniform firmness of my troops, and with what undaunted courage they advanced, with a strong fort ready to assail them on the right, seven armed vessels on the left, strong blockhouses and batteries of cannon in their front; but they still advanced with unshaken firmness, and entered the town, when a battery of two cannon was opened upon the center column, composed of regulars, with ball and grape, and a shower of musketry from the houses and gardens. The battery was immediately stormed by Captain Laval and his company, and carried, and the musketry was soon silenced by the steady and well-directed fire of the regulars."

In storming the battery, Captain Laval fell severely wounded, but the troops pressed forward into the town and took a second battery before the party posted in it could more than three times reload. There was still some firing from behind houses and garden walls, when the Governor, in utter consternation, ran out into the streets bearing a white flag to find the general. He came up first with Colonel Williamson and Colonel Smith, commanding the dismounted troops, to whom he addressed himself with faltering speech, entreating them to spare the town, and promising to consent to whatever terms the general in command might propose. Jackson, who had halted for a moment at the spot where Captain Laval had fallen, soon rode up, and, hearing what had occurred, proceeded to the Governor's house, where he received in person the assurance that all the forts should be instantly surrendered.

Hostilities ceased. Owing to what General Jackson styled "Spanish treachery," but probably to the confusion and bewilderment that prevailed, and the consequent misunderstanding of orders, or perhaps to the irresolution of the Governor and his desire to stand excused in the eyes of his English friends, the forts were not instantly surrendered. More than once in the course of the day, Jackson, exasperated at the delay, was about to open fire upon them; but one by one the forts were given up, and late in the evening the town was fully his own—the town, but not the port which was far more important. Fort Barrancas, six miles distant, which commanded the mouth of the harbor, was in the hands of the English, and gave complete protection to their fleet. Maurequez had given a written order for its surrender, addressed to the nominal commandant, and Jackson was prepared to march, with the dawn of the next day, to receive it if the order were obeyed; to carry it by storm if it were not.

He was still in hopes that by the prompt seizure of Fort Barrancas he could catch the British fleet as in a trap, and either force it to surrender, or do it terrible damage if it should attempt to escape. But before the dawn of day a tremendous explosion was heard in the direction of the mouth of the harbor; then another explosion, not so loud; and, a few seconds later, a third. There was little doubt what had occurred. Early in the morning a party that was sent out to reconnoiter returned with the intelligence that Fort Barrancas was a heap of ruins, and that the British vessels had disappeared from the bay. Colonel Nichols, Captain Woodbine, the garrison, and some hundreds of friendly Indians had gone off with the ships, leaving their friend Maurequez to settle with the American general as best he could.

The sudden departure of the British fleet was not less alarming than disappointing to the general. Whither had they gone? The most probable supposition was that they were hastening away to attack Fort Bowyer and capture Mobile in the absence of the troops. To retain Pensacola, in the circumstances, was equally needless and impossible. Sending off a dispatch to warn the garrison of Fort Bowyer of their danger, the general at once prepared to evacuate the town and fly to the defense of Mobile. The next morning he was in full march. Not a man had been lost. Less than twenty of the troops had been wounded, of whom Captain Laval alone was obliged to be left behind to the care of Governor Maurequez. The gallant captain received every attention which his situation required. He recovered from his wound, and was living, in 1859, an honored citizen of Charleston, to tell the story of his own and his general's exploits.

Jackson waited in the vicinity of Mobile for ten days in expectation of the arrival of Colonel Nichols. That officer did not appear, and from the top of Fort Bowyer no approaching fleet was descried. At length came intelligence that Nichols, Woodbine, and their Indians had been landed at Appalachicola, where they were fortifying a position in all haste. Against them Jackson dispatched a body of troops and friendly Creeks, under Major Blue, who, after many remarkable adventures and some severe fighting, drove the savages into the interior and Colonel Nichols from the peninsula.

General Jackson, now freed from apprehension for the safety of Mobile, could direct all his thoughts to the defense of New Orleans. He left Mobile in command of General Winchester, of the regular army. Fort Bowyer was still intrusted to the brave Major Lawrence. General Coffee was ordered to move by easy marches toward New Orleans, choosing the roads and the course that promised the best forage. On the 22d of November, the general, without any escort but his staff, mounted horse and rode off in the same direction. He had a journey before him of a hundred and seventy miles, over the roads of the early years of the century. Riding a little more than seventeen miles a day, he arrived within one short stage of New Orleans on the 1st of December, 1814.

CHAPTER XII.

NEW ORLEANS was all unprepared for defense against
a powerful foe. When the first rumor of the approaching invasion reached the city, Edward Livingston, the
leading lawyer of the State, caused a meeting of the
citizens of New Orleans to be convened at Tremoulet's
coffee-house, to concert measures for defense. The
meeting occurred on the 15th of September, 1814. Upon
taking the chair, Livingston presented a series of spirited
resolutions, breathing union and defiance, and supported
them by a speech of stirring eloquence. They were
passed by acclamation. A Committee of Public Defense,
nine in number, with Edward Livingston at its head, was
appointed, and directed to prepare an address to the
people of the State. The publication of the address,
and the gift of a saber to the commandant of Fort Bowyer, were the only acts of the Committee of Public Defense that I find recorded. It may have induced the
formation of new uniformed companies of volunteers;
it may have stimulated the militia to a more vigorous
drill; it may have induced the Governor to convene the
Legislature; but its main effect was upon the feelings
and the fears of the people.

On the 5th of October the Legislature, in obedience
to the summons of Governor Claiborne, assembled at
New Orleans. Factious, and incredulous of danger, it

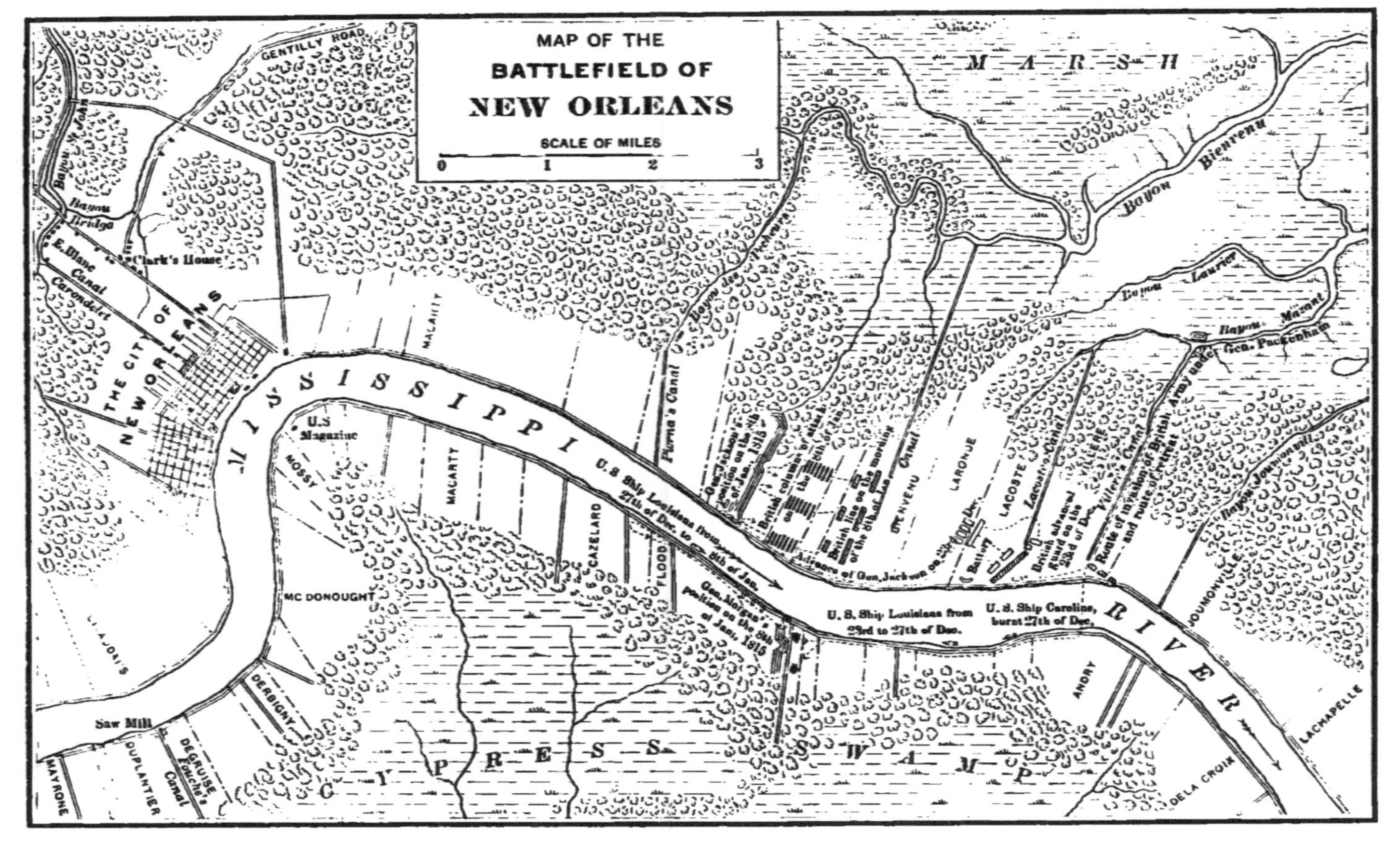

MAP OF THE
BATTLEFIELD OF
NEW ORLEANS
SCALE OF MILES
0   1   2   3
M A R S H
C Y P R E S S   S W A M P
MISSISSIPPI
RIVER
GENTILLY ROAD
THE CITY OF NEW ORLEANS
Bayou St. John
Bayou Bridge
E. Blanc Canal
Carondelet Canal
Clark's House
U.S. Magazine
MOSSY
MACARTY
MC DONOUGHT
LT. AJOIS'S
DERBIGNY
Saw Mill
MAYRONE
DUPLANTIER
DEGRUISE Fouche's Canal
CAZELARD
FLOOD
U.S. Ship Louisiana from
27th of Dec. to Jan. 8th of Jan.
Gen. Morgan's
position on the 8th
of Jan. 1815
U.S. Ship Louisiana from
23rd to 27th of Dec.
U.S. Ship Caroline,
burnt 27th of Dec.
Puma's Canal
Gen. Jackson's
position on the
8th of Jan. 1815
British columns of attack
British line on the morning
of the 8th of Jan.
Advance of Gen. Jackson on the 8th of Jan.
BIENVENU
LARONDE
LACOSTE
Lacoste's Canal
VILLERE
British advance
Road on the
22d of Dec.
Route of invasion of British Army and route of retreat
Bayou Jumonville
JOUMONVILLE
ANDRY
DELA CROIX
LACHAPELLE
Bayou Bienvenu
Bayou Laurier
Bayou Mazant under Gen. Packenham
Battery

did nothing, it attempted nothing, for the defense of the city. Disputes of the most trivial character engrossed the minds of the members. All had some fear of an insurrection of the slaves. Every man had his scheme or his system of measures, which he knew would save the city if it were adopted; but none could bring any plan to bear, or get all the opportunity he wanted for making it known. In a word, there was no central power or man in New Orleans in whom the people sufficiently confided, or who possessed the requisite lawful authority to call out the resources of the State and direct them to the single object of defeating the expected invader. There was talent enough, patriotism enough, zeal enough. The uniting man alone was wanting—a man of renown sufficient to inspire confidence—a man unknown to the local animosities, around whom all parties could rally without conceding anything to one another.

Jackson has come! There was magic in the news. Every witness testifies to the electric effect of the general's quiet and sudden arrival. There was a truce at once to indecision, to indolence, to incredulity, to factious debate, to paltry contentions, to wild alarm. He had come so worn down with disease and the fatigue of his ten days' ride on horseback that he was more fit for the hospital than the field; but there was that in his manner and aspect which revealed the master. That will of his triumphed over the languor and anguish of disease, and every one who approached him felt that the man for the hour was there.

He began his work without the loss of one minute. The unavoidable formalities of his reception were no sooner over than he mounted his horse again and rode out to review the uniformed companies of the city. These companies consisted of several hundred men, the *élite* of the city—merchants, lawyers, the sons of planters, clerks, and others, who were well equipped, and not a little proud of their appearance and discipline. The general complimented them warmly, addressed the principal officers, inquired respecting the numbers, history, and organization of the companies, and left them captivated with his frank and straightforward mode of procedure.

Returning to his quarters, the general summoned the engineers resident in the city, among others Major Latour, afterward the historian of the campaign. The vulnerable points and practicable approaches were explained and discussed, and the readiest mode of defending each was considered and determined upon. Every bayou connecting the city with the adjacent bays, and through them with the Gulf of Mexico, was ordered to be obstructed by earth and sunken logs, and a guard to be posted at its mouth to give warning of an enemy's approach. It was determined that the neighboring planters should be invited to aid in the various works by gangs of slaves. Young gentlemen pressed to headquarters offering to serve as aides to the general. Edward Livingston, whose services in that capacity had been previously offered and accepted, was with the general from the first, doing duty as aide-de-camp, secretary, translator, confidential adviser, and connecting link generally between the commander-in-chief and the heterogeneous multitude he had come to defend. Never before, in the space of a few hours, did such a change come over the spirit of a threatened and imperiled city. The work to be done was ascertained and distributed during that afternoon and evening; and it could be said that, before the city slept, every man in it able and willing to assist in preparing for the reception of the enemy, whether by mind or muscle, had his task assigned him, and was eager to enter upon its performance.

The demeanor of General Jackson on this occasion was such as to inspire peculiar confidence. It was that of a man entirely resolved, and entirely certain of being able, to do what he had come to do. He never admitted a doubt of defeating the enemy. For his own part he had but one simple plan to propose, nor would hear of any other: to make all the preparations possible in the time and circumstances; to strike the enemy wherever, whenever, and in what force soever, he might appear; and to drive him back headlong into the sea, or bring him prisoner to New Orleans. A spirit of this kind is very contagious, particularly among such a susceptible and imaginative people as the French creoles—a people not wise in council, not gifted with the instinct of legislation, but mighty and terrible when strongly commanded. The new impulse from the general's quarters spread throughout the city. Hope and resolution sat on every countenance.

Jackson was up betimes on the following morning, and set out in a barge, accompanied by aides and engineers, to see with his own eyes the lower part of the river. The principal mouth of the Mississippi was naturally but erroneously the first object of his solicitude, and he had dispatched Colonel A. P. Hayne from Mobile to the Balize, to ascertain whether the old fort there commanded the mouth of the river, and whether it could be made available for preventing the entrance of a hostile fleet. Colonel Hayne reported it useless. Some miles higher up the river, however, at a point where the navigation was peculiarly difficult, was Fort Philip, which it was supposed, and the event proved, could be rendered an impassable barrier to the enemy's ships. Thither Jackson repaired. He perceived the immense importance of the position, and, with the assistance of Major Latour, drew such plans and suggested such alterations of the works as made the fort entirely equal to the defense of the river. The stream, as every one knows, is narrow and swift, and presents so many obstacles to the ascent of large vessels, that an enemy unprovided with steamboats would scarcely have attempted to reach New Orleans by the river even if no fort was to be passed. Jackson returned to the city after six days' absence, with little apprehension of danger from that quarter.

Desirous of seeing everything for himself, he proceeded immediately upon a rapid tour of inspection along the borders of Lake Pontchartrain and Lake Borgne, those broad, shallow bays which afford to the commerce of New Orleans so convenient a back gate. He visited every bayou and fortification, suggesting additional works and stimulating the zeal of the people. He had then completed the first survey of his position, and, upon the whole, the result was assuring. He thought well of his situation. At least, he had little fear of a surprise.

Let us take one glance at the lake approaches to the Crescent City before we proceed. Lake Pontchartrain is land-locked, except where a narrow strait connects it with Lake Borgne. That strait was defended by a fortification which, it was hoped, was capable of beating off the enemy. But not by that alone. Lake Borgne, too shallow for the admission of large seagoing vessels, would be crossed by the enemy, if crossed at all, in small coasting craft or ships' boats. Accordingly, on that lake Commodore Patterson had stationed a fleet of gunboats, six in number, carrying in all twenty-three guns and one hundred and eighty-two men, the whole under the command of Lieutenant Thomas Ap Catesby Jones. Lieutenant Jones was ordered to give prompt notice of the enemy's coming, and if threatened with attack to retire before the enemy and lead him on to the entrance of the strait that led into Lake Pontchartrain, and there anchor and fight to the last extremity. With the peculiar advantages of position which the place afforded, it was confidently expected that he would be able to defeat any force of small craft that the enemy were likely to have at command.

It is evident that Lake Pontchartrain was universally regarded at the time as the most natural and obvious means of reaching the city, and the gunboats were chiefly relied upon for its defense. Upon them, too, the general mainly relied for the first information of the enemy's arrival. If the gunboats failed, the fort upon the strait was open to attack. If the gunboats failed, the vigilance of the pickets at the mouths of the bayous was the sole safeguard against a surprise. If the gunboats failed, Lake Borgne offered no obstacle to the approach of an enemy except its shallowness and its marshy shores. If the gunboats failed, nothing could hinder the enemy from gaining a foothold within a very few miles of the city, unless the sentinels should descry their approach in time to send ample notice to the general. While the gunboats continued to cruise in the lake the city had a certain ground of security, and could sleep without fear of waking to find British regiments under its windows.

But where was the army with which General Jackson was to execute his design of hurling into the Gulf of Mexico the invading host? Let us see what forces he had and what forces he expected.

The troops then in or near New Orleans, and its sole defenders as late as the middle of December, were these: Two half-filled, newly raised regiments of regular troops, numbering about eight hundred men; Major Planché's high-spirited battalion of uniformed volunteers, about five hundred in number; two regiments of State militia, badly equipped, some of them armed with fowling-pieces, others with muskets, others with rifles, some without arms, all imperfectly disciplined; a battalion of free men of color. The whole amounted to about two thousand men. Two vessels of war lay at anchor in the river, the little schooner Carolina and the ship Louisiana, neither of them manned, and no one dreaming of what importance they were to prove. Commodore Patterson and a few other naval officers were in the city, ready when the hour should come, and, indeed, already rendering yeoman's service in many capacities. General Coffee, with the army of Pensacola, was approaching the city by slow marches, contending manfully with an inclement season, swollen streams, roads almost impassable, and scant forage. He had three hundred men, nearly a tenth of his force, sick with fever, dysentery, and exhaustion. But he was coming. General Carroll, burning with zeal to join his old friend and commander, had raised a volunteer force in Tennessee early in the autumn, composed of men of substance and respectability, and, after incredible exertions and many vexatious delays, had got them afloat upon the Cumberland. The State had been so stripped of arms that Carroll's regiment had not a weapon to every ten men. So many men had gone to the wars from Tennessee, that Peter Cartwright, that valiant son of the Methodist Church militant, found his congregations thin and his ingatherings of new members far below the average. "So many of our members," he says, "went into the war, and deemed it their duty to defend our common country under General Jackson." An extraordinary rise of the Cumberland, such as seldom occurs in November, enabled General Carroll to make swift progress into the Ohio, and thence into the Mississippi, where another piece of good fortune befell him, so important that it may almost be said to have saved New Orleans. He overtook a boat-load of muskets, which enabled him to arm his men and drill them daily in their use on the roofs of his fleet of arks.

Two thousand Kentuckians, under General Thomas and General Adair, were also on their way down the Mississippi—the worst provided body of men, perhaps, that ever went fifteen hundred miles from home to help defend a sister State. A few rifles they had among them, but no clothing suitable for the season, no blankets, no tents, no equipage. Besides food, they were furnished with just one article of necessity, namely, a cooking-kettle to every eighty men! In a flotilla of boats hastily patched together on the banks of the Ohio, they started on their voyage, carrying provisions enough for exactly half the distance. They were agreeably disappointed, however, in their expectation of living a month on half rations, by overtaking a boat loaded with flour, and, thus supplied, they went on their way ragged but rejoicing.

Such was General Jackson's situation, such the posture of affairs in New Orleans, such the means and prospects of defense, on the 14th of December: two or three thousand troops in the city; four thousand more within ten or fifteen days' march; six gunboats on Lake Borgne; two armed vessels on the river; a small garrison of regulars at Fort St. Philip; another at the fort between the two lakes; the obstruction of the bayous still in progress; the citizens hopeful and resolute, most of them at work, every man where he could do most for the cause; the general returning to his quarters from his tour of inspection.

At the western extremity of the island of Jamaica there are two headlands, eight miles apart, which inclose

Negril Bay, and render it a safe and convenient anchorage. It was the rendezvous of the British fleet designed for the capture of New Orleans. November 24, 1814, was the day appointed for its final inspection and review previous to its departure for Lake Borgne. A fleet of fifty armed vessels, many of them of the first magnitude, covered the waters of the bay, and the decks of the ships were crowded with red-coated soldiers. The four regiments, numbering, with their sappers and artillerymen, three thousand one hundred men, who had fought the battle of Bladensburg, burned the public buildings of Washington, and lost their general near Baltimore the summer before, were on board the fleet. Four regiments, under General Keane, had come from England direct to re-enforce this army. Two regiments, composed in part of negro troops, supposed to be peculiarly adapted to the climate of New Orleans, had been drawn from the West Indies to join the expedition. The fleet could furnish, if required, a body of fifteen hundred marines. General Keane found himself, on his arrival from Plymouth, in command of an army of seven thousand four hundred and fifty men, which the marines of the fleet could swell to eight thousand nine hundred and fifty. The number of sailors could scarcely have been less than ten thousand, of whom a large portion could, and did, assist in the operations contemplated.

Here was a force of nearly twenty thousand men, a fleet of fifty ships carrying a thousand guns, and perfectly appointed in every particular, commanded by officers some of whom had grown gray in victory. And this great armament was about to be directed against swamp-environed New Orleans, with its ragged, half-armed defenders floating down the Mississippi, or marching wearily along through the mire and flood of the Gulf shores, commanded by a general who had seen fourteen months' service and caught one glimpse of a civilized foe. The greater part of General Keane's army were fresh from the fields of the Peninsula, and had been led by victorious Wellington into France, to behold and share in that final triumph of British arms. To these Peninsular heroes were added the Ninety-third Highlanders, recently from the Cape of Good Hope, one of the " praying regiments " of the British army, as stalwart, as brave, as completely appointed a body of men as had stood in arms since Cromwell's Ironsides gave liberty and greatness to England. Indeed, there was not a regiment of those which had come from England to form this army which had not won brilliant distinction in strongly contested fields. The *élite* of England's army and navy were afloat in Negril Bay on that bright day of November when the last review took place.

The day after the review, the Tonnant, the Ramilies, and two of the brigs weighed anchor and put to sea. The next morning the rest of the fleet followed.

Three weeks of pleasant sailing in those tropical seas brought the fleet to the entrance of Lake Borgne, the shallowness of which forbade its near approach. The American gunboats were descried, and it was seen at once by the British admiral that offensive operations were impossible as long as that little fleet commanded the lake. A force of fifty large open boats, containing a thousand men, under Captain Lockyer, were dispatched from the British fleet against the gunboat flotilla. A dead calm prevented its retreat, and there was no resource but to fight, in the open lake, this great armament. A most gallant and resolute defense was made by Lieutenant Jones and the men under his command; but nothing could avail against a force so overwhelmingly superior, and the little fleet was compelled to surrender.

This obstacle removed, the British commander prepared to transport his army across the broad expanse of the lake to the vicinity of New Orleans, a distance of eighty miles. An advance party of sixteen hundred men found their way unobserved to the mouth of the Bayou Bienvenu, a sluggish creek about twenty miles below the city. This spot had early attracted the attention of General Jackson. It was, and is, a lonely, desolate place, resorted to only by fishermen and tourists. A little colony of Spanish fishermen had built a few rude huts there for their accommodation during the fishing season. A picket, consisting of a sergeant, eight white men, and three mulattoes, had been stationed in the village by General Villeré, a planter of the neighborhood, to whom Jackson had assigned the duty of guarding the spot. No one anticipating danger in that quarter, the picket gradually relaxed their vigilance. Two British officers, Captain Spencer of the Carron and Lieutenant Peddie of the army, disguised in blue shirts and old tarpaulins, landed without exciting suspicion, bought over the Spanish fishermen and their boats, rowed up the bayou, reached the firm land along the banks of the great river, and drank of its waters. Having carefully noted all the features of the scene, questioning the negroes and others whom they met, they returned to Pine Island, whence they guided the advance of the British army to the fatal plain.

It is denied by all American writers that the picket at the fisherman's village was surprised in the manner stated by English historians. Mr. Alexander Walker, who collected his information from the men themselves, gives this account of what transpired on the night of the landing:

" Nothing occurred to attract the notice of this picket until about midnight on the 22d, when the sentinel on duty in the village called his comrade and informed him that some boats were coming up the bayou. It was no false alarm. These boats composed the advanced party of the British, which had been sent forward from the main body of the flotilla, under Captain Spencer, to reconnoiter and secure the village.

"The Americans, perceiving the hopelessness of defending themselves against so superior a force, retired for concealment behind the cabin, where they remained until the barges had passed them. They then ran out and endeavored to reach a boat by which they might escape; but they were observed by the British, who advanced toward them, seized the boat before it could be dragged into the water, and captured four of the picket. Four others were afterward taken on land. Of the four remaining, three ran into the canebrake, thence into the prairie, where they wandered about all day, until, worn down with fatigue and suffering, they returned to the village, happy to surrender themselves prisoners. One only escaped, and after three days of terrible hardships and constant perils, wandering over trembling prairies, through almost impervious canebrakes, swimming bayous and lagoons, and living on reptiles and roots, got safely into the American camp."

Having effected a landing, the British army, led by General Keane himself, began a slow and toilsome march toward the city. An English officer describes the advance in a highly interesting manner. "It was not," he says, "without many checks that we were able to proceed. Ditches frequently stopped us by running in a cross-direction too wide to be leaped, and too deep to be forded; consequently, on all such occasions, the troops were obliged to halt till bridges were hastily constructed of such materials as could be procured and thrown across. Having advanced in this manner for several hours, we at length found ourselves approaching a more cultivated region. The marsh became gradually less and less continuous, being intersected by wider spots of firm ground; the reeds gave place by degrees to wood, and the wood to inclosed fields. Upon these, however, nothing grew, harvest having long ago ended. They accordingly presented but a melancholy appearance, being covered with the stubble of sugar cane, which resembled the reeds which we had just quitted in everything except altitude. Nor as yet was any house or cottage to be seen. Though we knew, therefore, that human habitations could not be far off, it was impossible to guess where they lay or how numerous they might prove; and as we could not tell whether our guides might not be deceiving us, and whether ambuscades might not be laid for our destruction as soon as we should arrive where troops could conveniently act, our march was insensibly conducted with increased caution and regularity.

"But in a little while some groves of orange trees presented themselves, on passing which two or three farmhouses appeared. Toward these our advanced companies immediately hastened, with the hope of surprising the inhabitants and preventing any alarm from being raised. Hurrying on at double-quick time, they surrounded the buildings, succeeded in securing the inmates, and captured several horses; but, becoming rather careless in watching their prisoners, one man contrived to effect his escape. Now, then, all hope of eluding observation might be laid aside. The rumor of our landing would, we knew, spread faster than we could march, and it only remained to make that rumor as terrible as possible.

"With this view, the column was commanded to widen its files and to present as formidable an appearance as could be assumed. Changing our order in obedience to these directions, we marched not in sections of eight or ten abreast, but in pairs, and thus contrived to cover with our small division as large a tract of ground as if we had mustered thrice our present numbers. Our steps were likewise quickened, that we might gain, if possible, some advantageous position where we might be able to cope with any force that might attack us; and, thus hastening on, we soon arrived at the main road which leads directly to New Orleans. Turning to the right, we then advanced in the direction of that town for about a mile, when, having reached a spot where it was considered that we might encamp in comparative safety, our little column halted, the men piled their arms, and a regular bivouac was formed.

"The country where we had now established ourselves was a narrow plain of about a mile in width, bounded on one side by the Mississippi and on the other by the marsh from which we had just emerged. Toward the open ground this marsh was covered with dwarf-wood, having the semblance of a forest rather than a swamp; but on trying the bottom it was found that both characters were united, and that it was impossible for a man to make his way among the trees, so boggy was the soil upon which they grew. In no other quarter, however, was there a single hedgerow or plantation of any kind, excepting a few apple and other fruit trees in the gardens of such houses as were scattered over the plain, the whole being laid out in large fields for the growth of sugar cane, a plant which seems as abundant in this part of the world as in Jamaica.

" Looking up toward the town, which we at this time faced, the marsh is upon your right and the river upon your left. Close to the latter runs the main road, following the course of the stream all the way to New Orleans. Between the road and the water is thrown up a

lofty and strong embankment, resembling the dikes in
Holland, and meant to serve a similar purpose, by means
of which the Mississippi is prevented from overflowing
its banks, and the entire flat is preserved from inun-
dation. But the attention of a stranger is irresistibly
drawn away from every other object to contemplate the
magnificence of this noble river. Pouring along at the
prodigious rate of four miles an hour, an immense body
of water is spread out before you, measuring a full mile
across and nearly a hundred fathoms in depth. What
this mighty stream must be near its mouth I can hardly
imagine, for we were here upward of a hundred miles
from the ocean."

The spot upon which, at noon on the 23d of December, the British advance halted and stacked their arms
was eight miles below the city, and, at the moment of
the halt, General Jackson had received no intimation
even of the landing of an enemy. If General Keane
had pushed on, he could have taken New Orleans without firing a shot; for, although General Coffee and General Carroll had reached the town, the troops under
their command were so widely scattered in and above
the city that an adequate force could not have been assembled in time to resist the onset of the foe.

But mark: "One man contrived to effect his escape,"
records the British officer whose narrative we have
quoted above. How many a gallant life hung upon the
chances of that one man's capture! The individual invested with such sudden and extreme importance was
young Major Gabriel Villeré, the son of General Villeré,
a creole planter, upon whose plantation the British were
then halting. Major Villeré it was who had stationed
the picket at the mouth of the bayou by which the
English troops had gained the banks of the Mississippi,
and stood now upon the high-road leading to the prize

they were in search of, and within a few miles of it. He made all haste to New Orleans, joined on his way by two friends, and proceeded to headquarters. Judge Walker thus relates their interview with the general: "During all the exciting events of this campaign Jackson had barely the strength to stand erect without support; his body was sustained alone by the spirit within. Ordinary men would have shrunk into feeble imbeciles or useless invalids under such a pressure. The disease contracted in the swamps of Alabama still clung to him. Reduced to a mere skeleton, unable to digest his food, and unrefreshed by sleep, his life seemed to be preserved by some miraculous agency. There, in the parlor of his headquarters in Royal Street, surrounded by his faithful and efficient aides, he worked day and night, organizing his forces, dispatching orders, receiving reports, and making all the necessary arrangements for the defense of the city.

"Jackson was thus engaged at half past one o'clock P. M. on the 23d of December, 1814, when his attention was drawn from certain documents he was carefully reading by the sound of horses galloping down the streets with more rapidity than comported with the order of a city under martial law. The sounds ceased at the door of his headquarters, and the sentinel on duty announced the arrival of three gentlemen who desired to see the general immediately, having important intelligence to communicate.

"'Show them in,' ordered the general.

"The visitors proved to be Mr. Dussau de la Croix, Major Gabriel Villeré, and Colonel de la Ronde. They were stained with mud, and nearly breathless with the rapidity of their ride.

"'What news do you bring, gentlemen?' eagerly asked the general.

"'Important! highly important!' responded Mr. de la Croix. 'The British have arrived at Villeré's plantation, nine miles below the city, and are there encamped. Here is Major Villeré, who was captured by them, has escaped, and will now relate his story.'

"The major accordingly detailed in a clear and perspicuous manner the occurrences we have related, employing his mother tongue, the French language, which De la Croix translated to the general. At the close of Major Villeré's narrative the general exclaimed:

"'By the Eternal, they shall not sleep on our soil!'

"Then courteously inviting his visitors to refresh themselves, and sipping a glass of wine in compliment to them, he turned to his secretary and aides, and remarked:

"'Gentlemen, the British are below; we must fight them to-night!'"

Jackson proceeded to act as though everything had occurred exactly as he had anticipated. General Coffee's brigade was still encamped near the spot where they had first halted, four or five miles above the city. Major Planché's battalion was at the Bayou St. John, two miles from headquarters. The State militia, under Governor Claiborne, were on the Gentilly road, three miles away; the regulars were in the city, but variously disposed. General Carroll and his Tennesseeans appear to have been still in the boats that brought them down the river. Commodore Patterson, too, was some distance off. General Jackson dispatched a messenger to each of the corps under his command, ordering them with all haste to break up their camp and march to positions assigned them—General Carroll to the head of the upper branch of the Bienvenu, Governor Claiborne to a point farther up the Gentilly road, which road leads from the Chef-Menteur to New Orleans; the rest of the troops to a plantation just below the city. Commodore Patterson was also sent for and requested to prepare the Carolina for weighing anchor and dropping down the river.

These orders issued, the general sat down to dinner and ate a little rice, which alone his system could then endure. He then lay down upon a sofa in his office and dozed for a short time. Before three o'clock he mounted his horse and rode to the lower part of the city, where then stood Fort St. Charles, on ground now occupied by the Branch Mint Building. Before the gates of the fort he took his station, waiting to see the troops pass on their way to the vicinity of the enemy's position and to give his final orders to the various commanders. Drawn up near him was one of the two regiments of regulars, the Forty-fourth Infantry, Colonel Ross, mustering three hundred and thirty-one muskets. Around the general were gathered his six aides —Captain Butler, Captain Reid, Captain Chotard, Edward Livingston, Mr. Davezac, and Mr. Duplessis. The other regiment of regulars, the Seventh Infantry, Major Piere, four hundred and sixty-five muskets, had already marched down the road to guard it against the enemy's advance. With them were sixty-six marines, twenty-two artillerymen, and two six-pounders, under Colonel McRea and Lieutenant Spotts, of the regular artillery. Captain Beal's famous company of New Orleans riflemen, composed of merchants and lawyers of the city, were also below, defending the high-road. A cloud of dust on the levee and the thunder of horses' feet soon announced to the expectant general the approach of cavalry. Colonel Hinds, of the Mississippi Dragoons, emerged from the dust-cloud, galloping at the head of his troop, which he led swiftly by to its designated post. Coffee with his Tennesseeans was not far behind. Halting at the general's side, he conversed with him for a few minutes, and then, rejoining his men, gave the

word, "Forward at a gallop!" and the long line of backwoodsmen swept rapidly past. Next came into view a
party-colored host on foot, at a run, which proved to be
Major Planché's fine battalion of uniformed companies.
"Ah!" cried Jackson to his aide Davezac, "here come
the brave creoles." They had run all the way from the
Fort St. John, and came breathless into the general's
presence. In a moment they too had received their
orders, and were again in motion. A battalion of colored freemen, under Major Dacquin, and a small body
of Choctaw Indians, under Captain Jugeant, arrived,
halted, passed on, and the general had seen his available
force go by. The number of troops that went that afternoon to meet the enemy was twenty-one hundred and
thirty-one, of whom considerably more than half had
never been in action.

The commanders of the different corps had all received the same simple orders : to advance as far as the
Rodriguez Canal, six miles below the city and two
miles above the Villeré plantation, there to halt, take
positions, and wait for orders to close with the enemy.
The Rodriguez Canal was no more than a wide, shallow
ditch, which extended across the firm ground from the
river to the swamp.

The last corps of the army had disappeared in the
distance, and still the general lingered before the gates
of Fort St. Charles, looking, with a slight expression of
impatience on his countenance, toward that part of the
river where the sloop of war Carolina was anchored.
He saw her at length weigh her anchor and move slowly
down the stream. She had been manned within the
last few days, and well manned, as it proved, though
some of her crew only learned their duty by doing it.
Captain Henly commanded the little vessel. Commodore Patterson, however, was in no mood to stay in New

Orleans on such a night, and so went in her to the scene of action.

The general had no sooner seen the Carolina under way, than he put spurs to his horse, and galloped down the road by which the troops had gone, followed by all his staff except Captain Butler. Much against his will, Captain Butler was appointed to command in the city that night. It was four o'clock in the afternoon when the Carolina left her anchorage, and General Jackson rode away from before the gates of Fort St. Charles. The day was Friday.

CHAPTER XIII.

NIGHT BATTLE OF DECEMBER 23D.

Four o'clock in the afternoon.—Most of the American troops have reached the Rodriguez Canal; others are coming up every moment. They are all on or near the high-road which runs along the river's bank. The Second Division of the British army, consisting of the Twenty-first, the Forty-fourth, and the Ninety-third Highlanders, is nearing the fishermen's village at the mouth of the Bayou Bienvenu. The party in advance is quiescent and unsuspecting on and about the Villeré plantation. General Keane and Colonel Thornton are pacing the piazza of the Villeré mansion, Keane satisfied with his position, Thornton distrusting it.

Half past four.—The first American scouting party, consisting of five mounted riflemen, advance toward the British camp to reconnoiter. They advance too far, and retire with the loss of one horse killed and two men wounded. The first blood of the land campaign is shed; Thomas Scott, the name of the first wounded man. Major Planché's battalion of creole volunteers are now beginning to arrive.

Five o'clock.—The general is with his little army, serene, confident. He believes he is about to capture or destroy those red-coats in his front, and he communicates some portion of his own assurance to those around him. First, Colonel Hayne, inspector-general of the army, shall go forward with Colonel Hinds's hundred horsemen, to see what he can of the enemy's position and numbers. The hundred horsemen advance; dash into the British pickets; halt while Colonel Hayne takes a survey of the scene before him; wheel, and gallop back. Colonel Hayne reports the enemy's strength at two thousand. But what are these printed bills stuck upon the plantation fences?

"LOUISIANIANS! REMAIN QUIET IN YOUR HOUSES. YOUR SLAVES SHALL BE PRESERVED TO YOU, AND YOUR PROPERTY RESPECTED. WE MAKE WAR ONLY AGAINST AMERICANS!"

Signed by General Keane and Admiral Cochrane. A negro was overtaken by the returning cavalrymen, with printed copies of this proclamation upon his person, in Spanish and French. Twilight deepens into darkness. It is the shortest day of the year but two. The moon rises hazy and dim, yet bright enough for that night's work, if it will only last. The American host is very silent—silent, because such is the order; silent, because they are in no mood to chatter. The more provident and lucky of the men eat and drink what they have, but most of them neither eat nor hunger. As the night drew on the British watch fires, numerous and brilliant, became visible, disclosing completely their position, and lighting the Americans the way they were to go.

Six o'clock.—The general-in-chief has completed his scheme, and part of it is in course of execution. It was the simple old backwoods plan of cornering the enemy; the best possible for the time and place. Coffee, with his own riflemen, with Beale's New Orleans sharp-shooters, with Hinds's dragoons, was to leave the river's side, march across the plain to the cypress swamp, turn down toward the enemy, wheel again, attack them in the flank and crowd them to the river. With General Coffee, as

guide and aide, went Colonel de la Ronde, the proprietor
of one of the plantations embraced in the circle of operations. A circuitous march of five miles, over moist,
rough, obstructed ground, lay before General Coffee,
and he was already in motion. Jackson, with the main
fighting strength of the army, was to keep closer to the
river and open an attack directly upon the enemy's
position; the artillery and marines upon the high-road;
the two regiments of regulars to the left of the road;
Planché's battalion, Dacquin's colored freemen, Jugeant's
Choctaws still farther to the left, so as to complete the
line of attack across the plain. The Carolina was to
anchor opposite the enemy's camp, close in shore, and
pour broadsides of grape and round shot into their
midst. From the Carolina was to come the signal of
attack. Not a shot to be fired, not a sound uttered,
till the schooner's guns were heard. Then, Coffee,
Planché, regulars, marines, Indians, negroes, artillery,
Jackson, all advance at once, and girdle the foe with
fire!

Half past six.—The Carolina arrives opposite General Jackson's position. Edward Livingston goes on
board of her, explains the plan of attack, communicates
the general's orders to Commodore Patterson, and re-
turns to his place at the general's side. "It continuing
calm," says the commodore in his official dispatch, "got
out sweeps, and a few minutes after, having been frequently hailed by the enemy's sentinels, anchored, veered
out a long scope of cable, and sheered close in shore
abreast of their camp." The commodore's "few minutes" was three-quarters of an hour at least, according
to the other accounts. He had more than two miles
to go before reaching the spot where he "veered out the
long reach of cable"—itself an operation not done in
a moment.

Seven o'clock.—The night has grown darker than was hoped. Coffee has made his way across the plain. Behind a ditch separating two plantations he is dismounting his men. Cavalry could not be employed upon such ground in the dark. Leaving the horses in charge of a hundred of his riflemen, he is about to march with the rest to find and charge the enemy. He has still a long way to go, and wants a full hour, at least, to come up with them. General Coffee, a man of few words, and intent on the business of the hour delivers an oration in something like these words:

"Men, you have often said you could fight; now is the time to prove it. Don't waste powder. Be sure of your mark before firing."

Half past seven.—The first gun from the Carolina booms over the plain, followed in quick succession by seven others—the schooner's first broadside. It lays low upon the moist delta a hundred British soldiers, as some compute or guess. Jackson hears it, and yet withholds the expected word of command. Coffee hears it too soon, but he makes haste to respond. The English division then landing at the fishermen's village hear it and hurry tumultuously toward the scene of action, and the boats go back to Pine Island with the news. New Orleans hears it. A great crowd of women, children, old men, and slaves, assembled in the square before the State House, see the flash and listen to the roar of the guns.

Other broadsides follow, as fast as men can load. And yet, strange to say, the people on board the terrible schooner knew nothing all that night of the effect their fire produced; knew not whether they had contributed anything or nothing to the final issue of the strife. Commodore Patterson simply says: "Commenced a heavy (and, as I have since learned, most destructive) fire from our starboard battery and small-arms, which was returned most spiritedly by the enemy with congreve rockets and musketry from their whole force, when, after about forty minutes of most incessant fire, the enemy was silenced. The fire from our battery was continued till nine o'clock upon the enemy's flank while engaged in the field with our army, at which hour ceased firing, supposing, from the distance of the enemy's fire (for it was too dark to see anything on shore), that they had retreated beyond the range of our guns. Weighed and swept across the river, in hopes of a breeze the next morning, to enable me to renew the attack upon the enemy should they be returned to their encampment."

So much for the Carolina. What she did, we know. But I defy any living being to say with positiveness and in detail what occurred on shore. The contradictions between the British and American accounts, and between the various American narratives, are so irreconcilable, that the narrator who cares only for the truth pauses bewildered and knows not what to believe. But exactness of detail is not important in describing this unique battle. A more successful night attack, or one that more completely gained not the object proposed but the objects most necessary to be gained, was never made. That fact alone might suffice. Yet, let us peer into the thickening darkness, and see what we can discern of the credible, the probable, and the certain, borrowing other people's eyes when our own fail.

Jackson opened his attack with curious deliberation. He waited patiently for the Carolina's guns. And when the thunder of her broadside broke the silence of the night, he still waited. For ten minutes, which seemed thirty, he let the little schooner wage the combat alone, hoping to fix the attention of the enemy exclusively upon her.

Then—" FORWARD ! "

Down the high-road, close to the river, with the Seventh Regiment, the artillery, and the marines, Jackson advanced. A light breeze from the river blew over the plain the smoke of the Carolina's incessant fire, to which was added a fog then beginning to rise from the river. Lighted only by the flash of the guns and the answering musketry and rockets, the general pushed on, and had approached within less than a mile of the British head-quarters, when the company in advance, under Lieutenant McClelland, received a brisk fire from a British outpost lying in a ditch behind a fence near the road. Colonel Platt, quartermaster-general, who was with this company, ran to the front, and, seeing the red-coats by the flash of their own guns, cried out :

" Come out and fight like men, on open ground ! "

Without giving them time to comply with this invitation, he poured a volley into their midst, and kept up an active fire for four or five minutes. The British picket gave way, and over the fence leaped Platt's company, and occupied the post they had abandoned. This was the first success of the battle, but it was very short. In a few minutes a large party of British, two hundred it is said, came up to regain their lost position, and opened a fire upon the victorious company. Its gallant commander, Lieutenant McClelland, fell dead; Colonel Platt was wounded; a sergeant was killed; several of the men were wounded, and it was going hardly with the little band. In the nick of time, however, the two pieces of cannon were placed in position on the road and began a most vigorous fire, relieving the advanced company, and compelling the enemy to keep his distance. A second time the Americans were successful, for a moment. Soon a formidable force of British came up the road, and opened fire upon the artillerymen and marines, evidently designing to take the guns. The marines recoiled before the leaden tempest. The horses attached to the cannon, wounded by the fire, reared, plunged, became unmanageable, and one of the pieces was overturned into the ditch by the side of the road. It was a moment of frightful and nearly fatal confusion. Jackson dashed into the fire, accompanied by two of his aides, and roared out with that startling voice of his:

"Save the guns, my boys, at every sacrifice!"

The presence of the general restored and rallied the marines as another company of the Seventh came up, and the guns were "protected," says Major Eaton—which probably means drawn out of danger. All this was the work of a very few minutes. The other companies of the Seventh and the whole of the Forty-fourth, were meanwhile engaged in a miscellaneous, desultory, indescribable manner.

General Coffee, though the signal came a little too early for him, was in the thick of the fight sooner than he had expected. Having reached the Villeré plantation, he wheeled toward the river and marched in a widely extended line, each man to fight, in the Indian fashion, on his own account. He expected to come up with the enemy near the river's bank, and would have done so if the Carolina had begun her fire half an hour later. The enemy, however, had then had time to recover from their confusion, to abandon the river, and to form in various positions across the plain. General Coffee had not advanced a hundred yards from the swamp before he was astonished to find himself in the presence of the British Eighty-fifth. "A war of duels and detachments" ensued, with varying fortune; but the deadly and unerring fire of Coffee's cool riflemen, accustomed from of old to night warfare with Indians, acquainted with all the arts of covert and approach, was too much for the British infantry. From orange grove, from behind negro huts, the Eighty-fifth slowly retired toward the river, until at length they took post behind an old levee near the high-road. Bayonets alone could dislodge them thence, and the Tennesseeans had no bayonets. Coffee, too, retired to cover, and sent to the general for orders.

Captain J. N. Cooke, a British officer, who wrote a narrative of this unexampled campaign, gives a lively picture of the battle at the time when Coffee was fighting his way across the plain: "Lumps and crowds of American militia, who were armed with rifles and long hunting-knives for close quarters, now crossed the country, and by degrees getting nearer to the head-quarters of the British, they were met by some companies of the rifle corps and the Eighty-fifth Light Infantry; and here again such confusion took place as seldom occurs in war—the bayonet of the British and the knife of the American were in active opposition at close quarters during this eventful night, and, as pronounced by the Americans, it was 'rough and tumble.'

"The darkness was partially dispelled for a few moments now and then by the flashes of firearms, and whenever the outlines of men were distinguishable the Americans called out, 'Don't fire—we are your friends!' Prisoners were taken and retaken. The Americans were litigating and wrangling, and protesting that they were not taken fairly, and were hugging their firearms, and bewailing their separation from a favorite rifle that they wished to retain as their lawful property.

"The British soldiers, likewise, hearing their mother tongue spoken, were captured by this deception; when such mistakes being detected, the nearest American received a knock-down blow, and in this manner prisoners on both sides, having escaped, again joined in the fray, calling out lustily for their respective friends. Here were fighting and straggling flashes of fire darting through the gloom like the tails of so many comets.

"At this most remarkable night encounter the British were fighting on two sides of a ragged triangle, their left face pounded by the fire from the sloop and their right face engaged with the American land forces. Hallen was still fighting in front at the apex.

"At one time the Americans pushed round Hallen's right and got possession of the high-road behind him, where they took Major Mitchell and thirty riflemen going to his assistance. But Hallen was inexorable, and at no time had more than one hundred men at his disposal; the riflemen coming up from the rear by twos and threes to his assistance when he had lost nearly half his picket in killed and wounded. And behind him was such confusion, that an English artillery officer declared that the flying illumination encircling him was so unaccountably strange, that had he not pointed his brass cannon to the front at the beginning of the fight he could not have told which was the proper front of battle (as the English soldiers were often firing one upon the other, as well as the Americans), except by looking toward the muzzle of his three-pounder, which he dared not fire from the fear of bringing down friends and foes by the same discharge, seeing, as he did, the darkness suddenly illuminated across the country by the flashing of muskets at every point of the compass."

Such were the scenes enacted on the plains of the delta in the evening of December 23, 1814, for about the space of an hour and a half.

Nine o'clock.—The Carolina, as we have seen, ceases her fire. The Second Division of English troops has arrived and mingled in the battle, more than repairing the casualties of the night in the English army. The fog, rising from the river, has spread densely over the field, first enveloping Jackson's division, which was nearest the river, then rolling over the entire plain. The general has heard nothing of General Coffee since he parted with him at six o'clock. He concludes now to suspend all operations till the dawn of day. Coffee's messenger finds the general at length, and departs with an order for General Coffee to withdraw his men from the field and rejoin the right wing with all dispatch.

Ten o'clock.—The American troops have retired, and are spread over the plain a mile or more from the scene of conflict. The wounded, all of them that can be found, are brought in and conveyed toward the city. The inhabitants of New Orleans have learned enough of the issue of the fight to allay their apprehensions of immediate danger; but women still sit at home or flit about the streets in an agony of suspense to learn something of the fate of fathers, husbands, and brothers. The arrival of British prisoners is noised about, cheering all but those who have staked more than life in the contest. General Jackson has as yet no thought but to renew the battle the moment it is light enough to find the foe, and to that end sends a dispatch to General Carroll, who is guarding the city from attack from above, ordering him, if no sign of an enemy has appeared in that quarter, to join the main body instantly with all his force.

The battle over, we can reckon up its cost, while the troops, reassembled, are eagerly narrating their several adventures or performing sad duties to wounded comrades and the dead. The British have lost to-night, according to General Keane's official report, forty-six killed, one hundred and sixty-seven wounded, and sixty-four prisoners and deserters. Lieutenant De Lacy Evans, afterward member of Parliament, and more recently one of the heroes of the Crimea, was among the wounded. The American loss was—killed, twenty-four; wounded, one hundred and fifteen; missing, seventy-four.

One o'clock in the morning.—Silence reigns in both camps. There have been occasional alarms during the night and some firing, enough to keep both armies on the alert. Noise of an approaching host from the city is heard soon after one, which proves to be General Carroll and his men, who have marched down with Tennesseean swiftness. But Jackson has changed his mind. British deserters have brought information of the arrival of re-enforcements to General Keane's army, and of still further forces to arrive on the morrow. Is it prudent to risk the campaign and the city upon an open fight between twenty-five hundred raw troops without bayonets and six or seven thousand disciplined British soldiers who have bayonets and know how to use them? That question, argued around the general's bivouac at midnight, admitted of but one answer. It was resolved, then, in the midnight council on the fog-covered field, to retire at daybreak to the old position behind the Rodriguez Canal, there to throw up whatever line of defense might be possible and await the enemy's attack. The two men-of-war shall anchor off the levee and cover the high-road with their guns. If necessary, the levee shall be pierced and the plain between the two armies flooded. Hinds's dragoons, who could not join in the night battle, shall hold the position between the two armies and conceal the contemplated movements.

Slowly, very slowly, the hours of darkness wore away. "The night," says Nolte, "was very cold. Wearied by our long march and standing in the open field, we all wanted to make a fire, and at length, at the special request of our major, permission to kindle one was obtained. Within twenty minutes we saw innumerable watch fires blazing up in a line extending like a crescent from the shores of the Mississippi to the woods, and stretching far away behind the plantations of Villeré, Lacoste, and others occupied by the English, on whose minds, as well as on our own, the impression must have been produced that Jackson had many more troops under his command and near the spot than any one had supposed."

The fires were not lighted too soon, for in the fight many of Coffee's men had thrown away their long coats and stood shivering through the night in their shirt-sleeves. Indeed, both brigades of Tennesseeans were in sorry plight with regard to clothes when they arrived, and few came out of the battle with a whole garment. There will be busy sewing-circles to-morrow in New Orleans, seasoned with tales of the brave deeds done by the ragged heroes of the night battle. And all over the field shall wander, after dawn, Tennesseeans hunting up lost coats, lost tomahawks and knives, lost horses, and, alas! lost comrades, cold forever, for whom there will be proud mourning in the log-houses of Tennessee. "These poor fellows," wrote a British officer, who with General Keane walked over part of the field, "presented a strange appearance. Their hair, eyebrows, and lashes were thickly covered with hoarfrost or rime, their blood-less cheeks vying with its whiteness. Few were dressed in military uniforms, and most of them bore the appearance of farmers or husbandmen. Peace to their ashes! They had nobly died in defending their country."

CHAPTER XIV.

THE Rodriguez Canal was an old mill race partly filled up and grown over with grass. In the early days of the colony the planters built their mills on the levee, and obtained water power by cutting canals from the river to the swamp, through which poured an abundant flood during the periodical swellings of the river. The Rodriguez Canal crossed the plain where the plain was narrowest; and this circumstance it was that rendered the position chosen by General Jackson for his line of intrenchments the best which the vicinity afforded.

Daylight dawned. The fog slowly lifted. Never was the light of day welcomer to the longing sons of men. The earliest light found the main body of Jackson's army in their former position behind the canal. Everything that New Orleans could furnish in the shape of spade, shovel, pickaxe, crowbar, wheelbarrow, cart, had been sent for hours before, and the first supplies began to arrive almost as soon as the men were ready to use them. Now let there be such digging, shoveling and heaping up of earth as the Delta of the Mississippi, or any other delta, has never seen since Adam delved!

The canal was deepened and the earth thrown up on the side nearest the city. The fences were torn away, and the rails driven in to keep the light soil from falling back again into the canal. Soft palms, which had never before handled anything harsher than a pen, a fishing-rod, or a lady's waist, blistered and bled, and felt it not. Each company had its own line of embankment to throw up, which it called its castle, and strained every muscle in friendly rivalry to make it overtop the castles of the rest.

The nature of the soil rendered the task one of peculiar difficulty. Dig down three feet anywhere in that singular plain and you come to water. Earth soon became the scarcest of commodities near the lines, and had to be brought from far, after the first hours. An idea occurs to an ingenious French intellect. Cotton bales! The town is full of cotton; and lo! here, close to the lines, is a vessel laden with cotton, waiting for a chance to get to sea. The idea, plausible as it was, did not stand the test of service. The first cannonade knocked the cotton bales about in a manner that made the general more eager to get rid of them than he had been to use them. Some of the bales, too, caught fire and made a most intolerable and persistent smoke, so that, days before the final conflict, every pound of cotton was removed from the lines. A similar error was made by the enemy, who, supposing that sugar would offer resistance to cannon balls equal to sand, employed hogsheads of sugar in the formation of their batteries. The first ball that knocked a hogshead to pieces and kept on its destructive way unchecked, convinced them that sugar and sand, though often found together, have little in common.

During the 24th the entire line of defense, a mile long, was begun, and raised in some places to a height of four or five feet. The work was not interrupted by the enemy for a moment, nor was there any alarm or sign of their approach. Before night two small pieces of cannon were placed in position on the high-road.

In the course of the morning Major Latour was

ordered to cut the levee at a point one hundred yards below the lines. The water rushed through the opening and flooded the road to the depth of three feet. A day or two after, an engineer was sent below the British camp to let in the water behind them, so as to render their position an island. If the river had been as high as it occasionally is in December, and always is in the spring, the campaign would have had a ludicrous and bloodless termination, for nearly the whole plain could have been laid under water, and the enemy would have found no sufficient resting-place for the soles of so many feet. It chanced, however, that the rise of the river at this time was only temporary. The water soon fell to the level of the road; and the piercing of the levee really aided the English, by filling up and rendering more navigable the creeks in their rear, by which their supplies were brought up. For a day or two only the flooding of the road was serviceable in giving an appearance of security to the lines near the river.

Early in the morning the Carolina, from her anchorage opposite the British camp, and the Louisiana, from an advantageous position a mile above, played upon the enemy whenever a red-coat showed itself within range. General Keane found himself, to his astonishment, besieged! Not a column could be formed upon the plain, which was torn up in every direction by the Carolina's accurate and incessant fire. Never was an army more strangely, more unexpectedly, more completely paralyzed. They could do absolutely nothing but cower under embankments, skulk behind huts, lie low in dry ditches, or else retire beyond the reach of that terrible fire which they had no means of silencing or answering.

And on this busy Saturday—the day before the best day of the Christian year—while such events as these were transpiring on the Delta of the Mississippi, what a different scene was enacting at Ghent, three thousand miles away! In Senator Seward's Life of John Quincy Adams we read: " Mr. Todd, one of the secretaries of the American commissioners, and son-in-law of President Madison, had invited several gentlemen, Americans and others, to take refreshments with him on the 24th of December. At noon, after having spent some time in pleasant conversation, the refreshments entered, and Mr. Todd said: ' It is twelve o'clock. Well, gentlemen, I announce to you that peace has been made and signed between America and England.' In a few moments, Messrs. Gallatin, Clay, Carroll, and Hughes entered, and confirmed the annunciation. This intelligence was received with a burst of joy by all present. The news soon spread through the town, and gave general satisfaction to the citizens. At Paris the intelligence was hailed with acclamations. In the evening the theatres resounded with cries of ' God save the Americans!' "

Had there then been an Atlantic telegraphic cable!

The light of Christmas morning found the English army disheartened almost to the degree of despair. " I shall eat my Christmas dinner in New Orleans," said Admiral Cochrane on the day of the landing. The remark was reported by a prisoner to General Jackson, who said, " Perhaps so; but I shall have the honor of presiding at that dinner." As usual when affairs go wrong, the general in command was the scapegoat. By every camp fire, in every hut, at every outpost, the conduct of General Keane was severely criticised.

Though discouragement was the habitual feeling of the British troops from the night of the 23d until the end, yet an event on this Christmas morning occurred which for the time dispelled the prevailing gloom. This was the arrival in camp, to take command of the troops, of Major-General Sir Edward Pakenham, and with him, as second in command, Major-General Samuel Gibbs, besides several staff officers of experience and distinction. In a moment hope revived and animation reappeared. General Pakenham, the brother-in-law of the Duke of Wellington, a favorite of the duke and of the army, was of north of Ireland extraction, like the antagonist with whom he had come to contend. Few soldiers of the Peninsular War had won such high and rapid distinction as he. At Salamanca, at Badajos— wherever, in fact, the fighting had been fiercest—there had this brave soldier done a man's part for his country, often foremost among the foremost. He was now but thirty-eight years of age, and the record of his bright career was written all over his body in scars. Conspicuous equally for his humanity and for his courage, he had ever lifted his voice and his arm against those monstrous scenes of pillage and outrage which disgraced the British name at the capture of the strongholds of Spain ; hanging a man upon one occasion upon the spot, without trial or law, and thus, according to Napier, " nipping the wickedness in the bud."

General Pakenham inherited General Keane's erroneous information respecting Jackson's strength. Keeping this fact in view, his first measure seems judicious enough. To blow the Carolina out of the water was General Pakenham's first resolve. Till that is done he thinks no movement of the troops is possible. With incredible toil, nine fieldpieces, two howitzers, one mortar, a furnace for heating balls, and a supply of the requisite implements and ammunition, were brought from the fleet and dragged to the British camp. By the evening of the 26th they have all arrived, and are ready to be placed in position on the levee as soon as darkness covers the scene of operations and silences the Carolina's exasperating fire. The little schooner lay near the opposite shore of the river, just where she had dropped her anchor after swinging away from the scene of the night action of the 23d. There she had remained immovable ever since, firing at the enemy as often as he showed himself. A succession of northerly winds and dead calms rendered it impossible for Captain Henly to execute his purpose of getting nearer the British position, nor could he move the vessel higher up against the strong current of the swollen Mississippi. In a word, the Carolina was a fixture, a floating battery. What is very remarkable, considering the great annoyance caused by the fire of this schooner, she had but one gun, a long twelve, as Captain Henly reports, which could throw a ball across the river.

The headquarters of General Jackson were now at a mansion-house about two hundred yards behind the American lines. From an upper window of this house, above the trees in which it was embosomed, the general surveyed the scene below: the long line of men at work upon the intrenchments; Hinds's dragoons manœuvring and galloping to and fro between the two armies; the Carolina and Louisiana in the stream vomiting their iron thunder upon the foe. With the aid of an old telescope lent him by an aged Frenchman, which appears to have been the only instrument of the kind procurable in the place, he scanned the British position anxiously and often. He was surprised, puzzled, and perhaps a little alarmed at the enemy's prolonged inactivity. What could they be doing down there behind the plantation houses? Why should they, unless they had some deep scientific scheme on foot, quite beyond the penetration of backwoodsmen, allow him to go on strengthening his position day after day, without the slightest attempt at molestation?

It was not in the nature of Andrew Jackson to wait

13

long for an enemy to attack. Too prudent to trust his raw troops in an open fight with an army twice his number, it occurred to him on the afternoon of the 26th that there might be another and a safer way to dislodge them from their covert ; at least, to disturb them in the development of whatever scheme they might be so quietly concocting. He sent for Commodore Patterson. Upon the arrival of the commodore at headquarters, a short conference took place between the naval and the military hero. Then the gallant commodore hurries off to New Orleans. His object is to ascertain whether a few of the merchant vessels lying idle at the levee can not be instantly manned, and armed each with two thirty-two-pounders from the navy yard; and if they can, to set them floating down toward the British position, where, dropping anchor, they shall join in the cannonade, and sweep the plain from side to side with huge, resistless balls. No plantation houses, no negro huts, no shallow ditches, no attainable distance will then avail the invading army.

Commodore Patterson could not succeed in his errand in time ; but he bore in mind the general's hint, and in due time acted upon it in another way with effect.

At dawn of day on the 27th the American troops were startled by the report of a larger piece of ordnance than they had yet heard from the enemy's camp. The second shot from the great guns placed by the British on the levee during the night, white hot, struck the Carolina, pierced her side and lodged in the main hold under a mass of cables, where it could neither be reached nor quenched. And this was but the prelude to a furious cannonade, which sent the bombs and hot balls hissing and roaring about her, penetrating her cabin, knocking away her bulwarks, and bringing down rigging and spars about the ears of the astonished crew. Captain Henly replied as best he could with his single long twelve, while both armies lined and thronged the levee, watching the unequal combat with breathless interest.

No, not breathless. As often as the schooner was hit, cheers from the British troops rent the morning air; and whenever a well-aimed shot from the Carolina drove the British gunners for a moment under the shelter of the levee, shouts from the Americans applauded the devoted crew. General Jackson was at his high window spying the combat. Perceiving from the first how it must end, he sent an emphatic order to Lieutenant Thompson, of the Louisiana, to get that vessel out of range if it was in the power of man to do it. General Pakenham stood on the levee near his guns cheering on the artillerymen.

Half an hour of this work was enough for the Carolina. "Finding," says Captain Henly, in his report to Commodore Patterson, with the blunt pathos of a sailor mourning for the loss of his vessel, "that hot shot were passing through her cabin and filling-room, which contained a considerable quantity of powder, her bulwarks all knocked down by the enemy's shot, the vessel in a sinking condition, and the fire increasing, and expecting every moment that she would blow up, at a little after sunrise I reluctantly gave orders for the crew to abandon her, which was effected with the loss of one man killed and six wounded. A short time after I had succeeded in getting the crew on shore I had the extreme mortification of seeing her blow up."

The explosion was terrific. It shook the earth for miles around; it threw a shower of burning fragments over the Louisiana, a mile distant; it sent a shock of terror to thousands of listening women in New Orleans; it gave a momentary discouragement to the American troops. The English army, whom the schooner's fire had tormented for four days, raised a shout of exultation, as though the silencing of that single gun had removed the only obstacle to their victorious advance.

But the Louisiana was still above water, and apparently as immovable as the Carolina had been. Upon her the British guns were immediately turned. To avail himself of a light breeze, or intimation of a breeze, from the east, Lieutenant Thompson spread all his sails. But against that steady, strong, deep current it availed not even to slacken the ship's cable. Red-hot balls fell hissing into the water about her, and a shell burst upon her deck, wounding six of the crew. "Man the boats!" cried the commander. A hundred men were soon tugging at the oars, struggling as for more than life to tow the ship up the stream. She moved; the cable slackened and was let go; still she moved slowly, steadily, and ere long was safe out of the deadly tempest, at anchor under the western shore opposite the American lines.

Then cheer upon cheer saluted the rescued ship. The English soldiers heard the cheers as they were "falling in" three miles below. Every trace of discouragement was gone from both armies. The British now formed upon the open plain without let or hindrance. The Americans could coolly estimate the success of the cannonade at its proper value. They had lost just one available gun and saved a ship which, at one broadside, could throw eight twelve-pound balls a mile and a half. That was the result of a cannonade for which the British army had toiled and waited a day and two nights.

If the English had directed their fire first upon the Louisiana, they could have destroyed both vessels. How astonishing that any man standing where General Pakenham stood that morning could have failed to perceive a fact so obvious! The Louisiana had only to go a mile up the river to be out of danger. Half a mile made her comparatively safe. The Carolina was fully two miles below the point of safety. The half hour expended upon the schooner would have blown up the ship, and then at their leisure they could have played upon the smaller vessel. And even if Captain Henly had slipped his cable and dropped down the stream past the British camp, the vessel would have been as effectually removed as she was when her burning fragments floated by.

The 27th was a busy day in the American lines. They were still far from complete, and every man now felt that their strength would soon be put to the test. In the course of the day a twelve-pound howitzer was placed in position so as to command the high-road. In the evening a twenty-four was established farther to the left, and early next morning another twenty-four. The crew of the Carolina hurried round to the lines to assist in serving these guns, and on the morrow the Baratarians were coming down from Fort St. Johns to lend a powerful hand. The two regiments of Louisiana militia were added to the force behind the lines. All day long the shovel and the spade are vigorously plied; the embankment rises; the canal deepens. The lines nearest the river are strongest and best protected, and, besides, are concealed from the view of an approaching foe by the buildings of the Chalmette plantation, a quarter of a mile below them. These buildings, which have served hitherto as the quarters of Hinds's dragoons, will protect the enemy more than they protect us, thinks the general, and orders them to be fired when the enemy advances. It proved to be a mistake, and the order, luckily, was only executed in part. Far to the left, near the cypress swamp, the lines are weakest, though there

Coffee's Tennesseans had worked as Coffee's Tennesseans could work to make them strong.

The morning of the 28th of December was one of those perfect mornings of the Southern winter to enjoy. which it is almost worth while to live twenty degrees too near the tropic of Cancer—balmy, yet bracing; brilliant, but soft; inviting to action, though rendering mere existence happiness enough. The golden mist that heralded the sun soon wreathed itself away and vanished into space, except that part of it which hung in glittering diamonds upon the herbage and the evergreens that encircled the stubble-covered plain. The monarch of the day shone out with that brightness that neither dazzles nor consumes, but is beautiful and cheering merely. Gone and forgotten now were the lowering clouds, the penetrating fogs, the disheartening rains that for so many days and dreary, fearful nights had hung over the dark delta. The river was flowing gold. " The trees," we are told, " were melodious with the noisy strains of the ricebird, and the bold falsetto of that pride of Southern ornithology, the mocking-bird, who here alone continues the whole year round his unceasing notes of exultant mockery and vocal defiance."

Music more noisy and more defiant salutes the rising sun—the rolling drum and ringing bugle, namely, that call twelve thousand hostile men to arms. This glorious morning General Pakenham is resolved to have at least one good look at the wary and active foe that for five days has given pause to the invading army, and has not yet been so much as seen by them. With his whole force he will march boldly up to the lines, and, if fortune favors and the prospect pleases, he will leap over them into New Orleans and the House of Lords. A grand reconnoissance is the order of the day.

The American general has not used his telescope in

vain; he is perfectly aware that an early advance is intended. Five pieces of cannon he has in position. The crew of the Carolina, under Lieutenant Crawley and Lieutenant Norris, Captain Humphrey and his artillerymen, are ready to serve them. Before the sun was an hour on his way, Jackson's anxious glances toward the city had been changed into expressions of satisfaction and confidence by the spectacle of several straggling bands of red-shirted, bewhiskered, rough and desperate-looking men, all begrimed with smoke and mud, hurrying down the road toward the lines. These proved to be the Baratarians under Dominique You and Bluche, who had run all the way from the Fort St. John, where they had been stationed since their release from prison. They immediately took charge of one of the twenty-four-pounders. And, what is of far more importance, the Louisiana, saved yesterday by the resolution and skill of Lieutenant Thompson, is ready at a moment's warning to let out cable and swing round so as to throw her balls obliquely across the plain. And all this is hidden from the foemen, who will know nothing of what awaits them till they have passed the plantation houses of Chalmette and Bienvenu, only five hundred yards from the lines!

General Jackson was not kept long in suspense. The spectacle of the British advance was splendid in the extreme. "Forward they came," says the author of ' Jackson and New Orleans,' "in solid columns, as compact and orderly as if on parade, under cover of a shower of rockets and a continual fire from their artillery in front and their batteries on the levee. It was certainly a bold and imposing demonstration, for such, as we are told by British officers, it was intended to be. To new soldiers like the Americans, fresh from civic and peaceful pursuits, who had never witnessed any scenes of real warfare, it was certainly a formidable display of military power and discipline. Those veterans moved as steadily and closely together as if marching in review instead of 'in the cannon's mouth.' Their muskets, catching the rays of the morning sun, nearly blinded the beholder with their brightness, while their gay and various uniforms, red, gray, green, and tartan, afforded a pleasing relief to the winter-clad field and the sombre objects around."

Thus appeared the British host to the gazing multitude behind the American lines; for the author of the passage quoted learned his story from the lips of men who saw the sight. The British "Subaltern" tells us how the American lines looked to the advancing army, and what reception greeted it: "Moving on in merry mood, we advanced about four or five miles without the smallest check or hindrance, when at length we found ourselves in view of the enemy's army, posted in a very advantageous manner. About forty yards in their front was a canal, which extended from the morass to within a short distance of the high-road. Along their line were thrown up breastworks, not indeed completed, but even now formidable. Upon the road, and at several other points, were erected powerful batteries; while the ship, with a large flotilla of gunboats [no, sir—no gunboats], flanked the whole position from the river.

"When I say that we came in sight of the enemy, I do not mean that he was gradually exposed to us in such a manner as to leave time for cool examination and reflection. On the right, indeed, he was seen for some time; but on the left, a few houses built at a turning in the road entirely concealed him; nor was it till they had gained that turning, and beheld the muzzles of his guns pointed toward them, that those who moved in this direction were aware of their proximity to danger. But that danger was indeed near, they were quickly taught ; for scarcely had the head of the column passed the houses, when a deadly fire was opened from both the battery and the shipping. That the Americans are excellent marksmen, as well with artillery as with rifles, we have had frequent cause to acknowledge; but perhaps on no occasion did they assert their claim to the title of good artillerymen more effectually than on the present. Scarce a ball passed over or fell short of its mark, but all striking full into the midst of our ranks occasioned· terrible havoc. The shrieks of the wounded, therefore, the crash of firelocks, and the fall of such as were killed, caused at first some little confusion ; and what added to the panic was, that from the houses beside which we stood bright flames suddenly burst out. The Americans, expecting this attack, had filled them with combustibles for the purpose, and directing against them one or two guns loaded with red-hot shot, in an instant set them on fire. The scene was altogether very sublime. A tremendous cannonade mowed down our ranks and deafened us with its roar, while two large chateaux and their out-buildings almost scorched us with the flames, and blinded us with the smoke which they emitted.

" The infantry, however, were not long suffered to remain thus exposed, but, being ordered to quit the path and to form line in the fields, the artillery was brought up and opposed to that of the enemy. But the contest was in every respect unequal, since their artillery far exceeded ours both in numerical strength and weight of metal. The consequence was that in half an hour two of our field-pieces and one field mortar were dismounted ; many of the gunners were killed ; and the rest, after an ineffectual attempt to silence the fire of the shipping, were obliged to retire.

"In the meantime the infantry, having formed line, advanced under a heavy discharge of round and grape shot, till they were checked by the appearance of the canal. Of its depth they were of course ignorant, and to attempt its passage without having ascertained whether it could be forded might have been productive of fatal consequences. A halt was accordingly ordered, and the men were commanded to shelter themselves as well as they could from the enemy's fire. For this purpose they were hurried into a wet ditch, of sufficient depth to cover the knees, where, leaning forward, they concealed themselves behind some high rushes which grew upon its brink, and thus escaped many bullets which fell around them in all directions.

"Thus fared it with the left of the army, while the right, though less exposed to the cannonade, was not more successful in its object. The same impediment which checked one column forced the other likewise to pause, and, after having driven in an advanced body of the enemy and endeavored without effect to penetrate through the marsh, it also was commanded to halt. In a word, all thought of attacking was for this day abandoned, and it now only remained to withdraw the troops from their present perilous situation with as little loss as possible.

"The first thing to be done was to remove the dismounted guns. Upon this enterprise a party of seamen was employed, who, running forward to the spot where they lay, lifted them, in spite of the whole of the enemy's fire, and bore them off in triumph. As soon as this was effected, regiment after regiment stole away—not in a body, but one by one—under the same discharge which saluted their approach. But a retreat thus conducted necessarily occupied much time. Noon had therefore long passed before the last corps was brought off, and when we again began to muster twilight was approaching."

What a day for the heroes of the Peninsula and the stately Ninety-third Highlanders!—lying low in wet ditches, some of them for seven hours, under that relentless cannonade, and then slinking away behind fences, huts, and burning houses, or even crawling along on the bottom of ditches, happy to get beyond the reach of those rebounding balls, that "knocked down the soldiers," says Captain Cooke, "and tossed them into the air like old bags." And what a day for General Jackson and his four thousand, who saw the magnificent advance of the morning, not without misgivings, and then beheld the most splendid and imposing army they had ever seen sink, as it were, into the earth and vanish from their sight! This reconnoissance cost General Pakenham a loss of fifty killed and wounded. The casualties on the American side were nine killed and eight wounded.

CHAPTER XV.

SECOND ADVANCE OF THE ENGLISH.

General Pakenham had seen the American lines. The inference he drew from the sight was that the way to carry the American position was to make regular approaches to it, as to a walled and fortified city.

During the last three days of the year 1814 the British army remained inactive on the plain, two miles below the American lines and in full view of them, while the sailors were employed in bringing from the fleet thirty pieces of cannon of large caliber, with which to execute the scheme that had been resolved upon. By the evening of the 31st of December the thirty pieces of cannon from the fleet (twenty long eighteens and ten twenty-fours) had reached the British camp. All that day the Americans had been amused with a cannonade from a battery erected near the swamp, under cover of which parties of English troops attempted, but with small success, to reconnoiter the American position. As soon as it was quite dark operations of far greater importance commenced. "One half the army," says a British officer, "was ordered out and marched to the front, passing the pickets, and halting about three hundred yards from the enemy's line. Here it was resolved to throw up a chain of works; and here the greater part of this detachment, laying down their fire-locks, applied themselves vigorously to their tasks, while the rest stood armed and prepared for their defense. The night was dark, and our people maintained a profound silence; by which means not an idea of what was going on existed in the American camp. As we labored, too, with all diligence, six batteries were completed long before dawn, in which were mounted thirty pieces of heavy cannon; when, falling back a little way, we united ourselves to the remainder of the infantry, and lay down behind the rushes in readiness to act as soon as we should be wanted."

The second Sunday of this strange mutual siege had come round. The light of another New-Year's day dawned upon the world.

The English soldiers had not worked so silently during the night upon their new batteries but that an occasional sound of hammering, dulled by distance, had been heard in the American lines. The outposts, too, had sent in news of the advance of British troops, who were busy at something, though the outposts could not say what. The veterans of the American army—that is, those who had smelt gunpowder before this campaign—gave it as their opinion that there would be warm work again at daybreak.

Long before the dawn the dull hammering ceased. When the day broke, a fog, so dense that a man could discern nothing at a distance of twenty yards, covered all the plain. Not a sound was heard in the direction of the enemy's camp, nor did the American sentinels nearest their position hear or see anything to excite alarm. At eight o'clock the fog was still impenetrable, and the silence unbroken. As late even as nine the American troops, who were on slightly higher ground than the British, saw little prospect of the fog breaking away, still less of any hostile movement on the part of the foe. The veterans begin to retract their opinion. We are to have another day of waiting, think the younger soldiers, the gay creoles not forgetting that the day was the first of a new year.

The general, conceding something to the pleasure-loving part of his army, permitted a brief respite from the arduous toil of the week, and ordered a grand review of the whole army, on the open ground between the lines and his own headquarters. To-day, too, for the first time in several days, the Louisiana remained at her safe anchorage above the lines, and a large number of her crew went ashore on the western bank and took post in Commodore Patterson's new battery there. But this was not for holiday reasons. A deserter came in the night before and informed the commodore that the enemy had established two enormous howitzers in a battery on the levee, where balls were kept red hot for the purpose of firing the obnoxious vessel the moment she should come within range again. So the commodore kept his vessel safe, landed two more of her great guns, and ordered ashore men enough to work them.

Toward ten o'clock the fog rose from the American position and disclosed to the impatient enemy the scene behind the lines. A gay and brilliant scene it was, framed and curtained in fog. "The fog dispersed," remarks Captain Hill, "with a rapidity perfectly surprising; the change of scene at a theatre could scarcely be more sudden, and the bright sun shone forth, diffusing warmth and gladness." "Being at this time," says the Subaltern, "only three hundred yards distant, we could perceive all that was going forward with great exactness. The different regiments were upon parade, and, being dressed in holiday suits, presented really a fine appearance. Mounted officers were riding backward and forward through the ranks, bands were playing, and colors floating in the air—in a word, all seemed jollity and gala." The general in chief had not yet appeared upon the ground. He had been up and doing before the dawn, and was now lying on a couch at headquarters, before riding out to review the troops.

In a moment how changed the scene! At a signal from the central battery of the enemy, the whole of their thirty pieces of cannon opened fire full upon the American lines, and the air was filled with the red glare and hideous scream of hundreds of Congreve rockets! As completely taken by surprise as the enemy had been on the night of the 23d, the troops were thrown into instantaneous confusion. "The ranks were broken," continues the Subaltern, " the different corps, dispersing, fled in all directions, while the utmost terror and disorder appeared to prevail. Instead of nicely dressed lines, nothing but confused crowds could now be observed; nor was it without much difficulty that order was finally restored. Oh, that we had charged at that instant ! "

The enemy, having learned which house was the headquarters of the general, directed a prodigious fire upon it, and the first news of the cannonade came to Jackson in the sound of crashing porticoes and out· buildings. During the first ten minutes of the fire one hundred balls struck the mansion, but, though some of the general's suite were covered with rubbish, and Colonel Butler was knocked down, they all escaped and made their way to the lines without a scratch.

The Subaltern is mistaken in saying that the troops fled in all directions. There was but one direction in which to fly either to safety or to duty; for, on that occasion, the post of duty and the post of safety were the same, namely, close behind the line of defense. For ten minutes, however, the American batteries, always before so prompt with their responsive thunder, were silent, while the troops were running in haste to their several posts.

Ten guns were in position in the American lines, besides those in the battery on the other side of the river.
Upon Jackson's coming to the front, he found his artillerymen at their posts, waiting with lighted matches to
open fire upon the foe as soon as the dense masses of
mingled smoke and mist that enveloped their batteries
should roll away. "Jackson's first glance," as Mr.
Walker informs us, "when he reached the line, was in
the direction of Humphrey's battery. There stood this
right arm of the artillery, dressed in his usual plain
attire, smoking that eternal cigar, coolly leveling his
guns and directing his men.

"'Ah!' exclaimed the general, 'all is right. Humphrey is at his post, and will return their compliments
presently.'

"Then, accompanied by his aides, he walked down
to the left, stopping at each battery to inspect its condition, and waving his cap to the men as they gave him
three cheers, and observing to the soldiers:

"'Don't mind those rockets; they are mere toys to
amuse children.'"

Captain Humphrey soon caught a glimpse of the
British batteries—structures of narrow front and slight
elevation, lying low and dim upon the field; no such
broad target as the mile-long lines of the American
position. Adjusting a twelve-pounder with the utmost
exactness, he quietly gave the word, and the firing
from the American lines began. The other batteries
instantly joined in the strife. The British howitzers on
the levee and the battery of Commodore Patterson on
the opposite bank exchanged a vigorous fire. For the
space of an hour and a half a cannonade so loud and rapid
shook the delta as had never before been heard in the
Western world. Imagine fifty pieces of cannon, of large
caliber for that day, each discharged from once to thrice

a minute; often a simultaneous discharge of half a dozen pieces; an average of two discharges every second; while plain and river were so densely covered with smoke that the gunners aimed their guns from recollection chiefly, and knew scarcely anything of the effect of their fire.

Well aimed, however, were the British guns, as the American lines soon began to exhibit. Most of their balls buried themselves harmlessly in the soft, elastic earth of the thick embankment. Many flew over its summit and did bloody execution on those who were bringing up ammunition, as well as on some who were retiring from their posts. Several balls struck and nearly sunk a boat laden with stores that was moored to the levee two hundred yards behind the lines. The cotton bales of the batteries nearest the river were knocked about in all directions, and set on fire, adding fresh volumes to the already impenetrable smoke. One of Major Planché's men was wounded in trying to extinguish this most annoying fire. A thirty-two-pounder in Lieutenant Crawley's battery was hit and damaged. The carriage of a twenty-four was broken. One of the twelves was silenced. Two powder-carriages, one containing a hundred pounds of the explosive material, blew up with a report so terrific as to silence for a moment the enemy's fire and draw from them a faint cheer. And still the lines continued to vomit forth a fire that knew neither cessation nor pause, until the guns grew so hot that it was difficult and dangerous to load them. And after an hour and a half of such work as this no man in Jackson's army could say with certainty whether the English batteries had been seriously damaged.

It was nearly noon when it began to be perceived that the British fire was slackening. The American batteries were then ordered to cease firing, for the guns to cool and the smoke to roll away. What a scene greeted the anxious gaze of the troops when at length the British position was disclosed! Those formidable batteries, which had excited such consternation an hour and a half before, were totally destroyed, and presented but formless masses of soil and broken guns, while the sailors who had manned them were seen running from them to the rear ; and the army that had been drawn up behind the batteries, ready to storm the lines as soon as a breach had been made in them, had again ignominiously " taken to the ditch."

Those hogsheads of sugar were the fatal mistake of the English engineers. They afforded absolutely no protection against the fire of the American batteries, the balls going straight through them and killing men in the very center of the works. Hence it was that in little more than an hour the batteries were heaps of ruins, and the guns dismantled, broken, and immovable. The howitzers, too, on the levee, after waging an active duel with Commodore Patterson on the other side of the river, were silenced and overthrown by a few discharges from Captain Humphrey's twelve-pounders. Nothing remained for the discomfited army but to make the best of their way to their old position, and so incessant was the American fire during the afternoon that it was only when night came that all the army succeeded in withdrawing.

The British loss on the 1st of January was about thirty killed and forty wounded; the Americans, eleven killed and twenty-three wounded. Most of the American slain were not engaged in the battle, but were struck down a considerable distance behind the lines while they were looking on as mere spectators.

The cotton error was quickly repaired. Every bale of that delusive material was removed from the works and its place supplied with the black and spongy soil of the delta, which the Sunday cannonade had shown to be a perfect defense, the balls sinking into it out of sight without shaking the embankment. The lines were strengthened in every part and new cannon mounted upon them. Work was continued upon the second line, a mile and a half in the rear. Even a third line of defense was marked out and begun, still nearer the city. On the opposite bank of the river the old works were repaired and strengthened, and new ones commenced.

What the enemy would attempt next, was a mystery which General Jackson anxiously revolved in his mind and strove in all ways to penetrate. Monday, Tuesday, Wednesday, Thursday passed away, and still the hostile army made no movement which gave the American general a clew to their design, if design they had. Strong men and weak men, good men and men less good, are all alike liable to the error of judging others by themselves. During these days, therefore, Jackson inclined to the opinion that his lines would not again be attacked, and so wrote to the Secretary of War. While apparently bending all his energies to the sole object of strengthening his position, his mind was racked with fear of being surprised in another quarter. How natural such an idea! If thirty pieces of cannon could not penetrate the lines, what could? If, on the 1st of January, the American position was found impregnable, could it be deemed less so after three thousand men had worked upon it for nearly a week? Two attempts having signally and ignominiously failed, would any general risk his army and his reputation upon a third?

On Wednesday morning, January 4th, the long-looked for Kentuckians, twenty-two hundred and fifty in number, reached New Orleans. Seldom has a re-

enforcement been so anxiously expected; never did
the arrival of one create keener disappointment. They
were so ragged that the men, as they marched shivering
through the streets, were observed to hold together their
garments with their hands to cover their nakedness;
and, what was far worse, because beyond remedy, not
one man in ten was well armed, and only one man in
three had any arms at all. It was a bitter moment for
General Jackson when he heard this, and it was a bitter
thing for those brave and devoted men, who had fondly
hoped to find in the abundance of New Orleans an end of
their exposure and destitution, to learn that the general
had not a musket, a blanket, a tent, a garment, a rag, to
give them. A body of Louisiana militia, too, who had
arrived a day or two before from Baton Rouge, were in
a condition only a little less deplorable. Here was a
force of nearly three thousand men, every man of whom
was pressingly wanted, paralyzed and useless from want
of those arms that had been sent on their way down the
river sixty days before. It would have fared ill, I fear,
with the captain of that loitering boat if he had chanced
to arrive just then, for the general was wroth exceedingly. Up the river go new expresses to bring him down
in irons. They bring him at last, the astonished man,
but days and days too late. The old soldiers of this
campaign mention that the general's observations upon
the character of the hapless captain, his parentage, and
upon various portions of his mortal and immortal frame,
were much too forcible for repetition in print.

The Legislature of Louisiana and the people of New
Orleans behaved on this occasion with prompt and noble
generosity. Major Latour records what was done by
them and by the people for the relief of the destitute
soldiers: "Within one week twelve hundred blanket
cloaks, two hundred and seventy-five waistcoats, eleven

hundred and twenty-seven pairs of pantaloons, eight hundred shirts, four hundred and ten pairs of shoes, and a great number of mattresses were made up, or purchased ready made, and distributed among our brethren in arms who stood in the greatest need of them."

The enemy, meanwhile, had recovered their spirits and increased their numbers. Two regiments, the Seventh and Forty-third Infantry, numbering together seventeen hundred, under General John Lambert, had arrived from England, infusing new life into the disheartened army, and raising its force to seven thousand three hundred men. General Pakenham had formed a bold and soldierlike design, for the execution of which the whole army was preparing, and the camp was alive with expectation. The "chained dog" would at length get at his enemy and growl no more. "The new scheme," says the Subaltern, "was worthy, for its boldness, of the school in which Sir Edward had studied his profession. It was determined to divide the army : to send part across the river, who should seize the enemy's guns and turn them on themselves, while the remainder should at the same time make a general assault along the whole intrenchment. But before this plan could be put into execution it would be necessary to cut a canal across the entire neck of land from the Bayou de Catiline to the river, of sufficient width and depth to admit of boats being brought up from the lake. Upon this arduous undertaking were the troops immediately employed. Being divided into four companies, they labored by turns, day and night ; one party relieving another after a stated number of hours, in such order as that the work should never be entirely deserted. The fatigue undergone during the prosecution of this attempt no words can sufficiently describe ; yet it was pursued without repining, and at length, by unremitting exertions,

they succeeded in effecting their purpose by the 6th of
January.

The lines, then, were to be stormed! The vital
clause of the scheme was that which contemplated the
carrying of the works on the western bank first, and the
turning of Commodore Patterson's great guns upon the
back of Jackson's lines. Let that be done, and the lines
are untenable and will require little storming. If that
is not done, or not done in time, the storming of the
lines will be a piece of work such as British soldiers
have seldom attempted. The naked bodies of the
troops will have to encounter that before which sugar
hogsheads and earthworks crumbled to pieces in an
hour!

It was not till Friday evening, the 6th of the new
year, that General Jackson began to so much as suspect
the enemy's design. On that day Sailing-Master John-
son, who was posted at the Chef-Menteur, seeing a small
English brig on her way from the fleet to the Bienvenu,
laden, as he supposed, with supplies for the British army,
darted out upon her with three boats and captured her
and ten prisoners. From these prisoners the American
general learned one important fact—that the enemy was
deepening and prolonging a canal across the plain.
Then their plan began to dawn upon Jackson's mind.
Early the next morning Commodore Patterson walked
behind the levee of the western bank to a point directly
opposite the British position, and spent several hours
there in watching their movements. Upon his return
the general no longer doubted that in a very few days
or hours he would have to resist a simultaneous attack
on both sides of the river. The bustle in the enemy's
camp, and the forward state of their preparations, indicated that ere the sun of another Sunday had appeared
above the horizon they might be upon him.

On Saturday afternoon Jackson was much at his high window at headquarters observing the enemy's movements. He had done what he could do to prepare for them, and little then remained but to await the result. He had been showing the lines to his old friend General Adair, of Kentucky, and asking his opinion of them.

"Well," said Jackson to Adair, after they had gone the rounds, "what do you think of our situation? Can we defend these works, or not?"

"There is one way," replied the Kentuckian, "and but one way, in which we can hope to defend them. We must have a strong corps of reserve to meet the enemy's main attack, wherever it may be. No single part of the lines," continued Adair, "is strong enough to resist the united force of the enemy. But with a strong column held in our rear, ready to advance upon any threatened point, we can beat them off."

This was an important suggestion. Jackson adopted General Adair's idea. "He agreed," says Adair, "that I should act with the Kentuckians as a reserve corps, and directed me to select my own ground for encampment, to govern my men as I thought most proper, and that I would receive no orders but from himself."

And off to town gallops Adair on the general's own white horse, to prevail on the veteran guard to lend him some of their muskets for three days only; so that he was able to employ several hundreds of his troops in that important service.

Such was the position of affairs on Jackson's side of the river. On the western bank the prospect was less promising. Commodore Patterson was there, and he had spent the week in arduous labor; but all his exertions had been directed toward the annoyance of the enemy on the other side of the river, not to the defense of his own position. As late as Wednesday morning nothing had been done to prepare for an attack on the western bank. "During the 2d and 3d," wrote Commodore Patterson to the Secretary of the Navy, "I landed from the ship and mounted, as the former ones, on the banks of the river, four more twelve-pounders, and erected a furnace for heating shot, to destroy a number of buildings which intervened between General Jackson's lines and the camp of the enemy, and occupied by him. On the evening of the 4th I succeeded in firing a number of them and some rice-stacks by my hot shot, which the enemy attempted to extinguish notwithstanding the heavy fire I kept up, but which at length compelled them to desist. On the 6th and 7th I erected another furnace, and mounted on the banks of the river two more twenty-four pounders, which had been brought up from the English Turn by the exertions of Colonel Caldwell, of the drafted militia of this State, and brought within and mounted on the intrenchments on this side the river one twelve-pounder. In addition to which, General Morgan, commanding the militia on this side, planted two brass six-pound field-pieces in his lines, which were incomplete, having been commenced only on the 4th. These three pieces were the only cannon on the lines. All the others, being mounted on the bank of the river, with a view to aid the right of General Jackson's lines on the opposite shore, and to flank the enemy should they attempt to march up the road leading along the levee, or erect batteries on the same, of course could render no aid in defense of General Morgan's lines. My battery was manned in part from the crew of the ship and in part by militia detailed for that service by General Morgan, as I had not seamen enough to fully man them."

On Saturday afternoon, upon Commodore Patterson's reporting to General Jackson what he had observed at the enemy's camp, it was determined to send over the river, to re-enforce General Morgan, a body of Kentuckians. Colonel Davis and four hundred of those troops were detailed for that purpose. At seven o'clock in the evening, after a day of hard duty, during which they had only once broken their fast, Colonel Davis and his men marched from the lines toward New Orleans, where they were to receive their arms and cross the river by the ferry. At the city it was found that only two hundred muskets, and those old and defective, could be procured. Only two hundred men, therefore, crossed the river. It was two o'clock before they reached the western shore. Fatigued, hungry, and chilled to the bone with long waiting, they formed upon the levee, and set out for General Morgan's position. Over a road miry from the recent rains, walking sometimes knee-deep in mud and water, the Kentuckians made their way, and reached Morgan's soon after four o'clock in the morning, as unfit for any duty involving danger and exertion as can be imagined.

Even with this re-enforcement General Morgan's command amounted to no more than eight hundred and twelve men, all militia, all badly armed, posted behind works upon which four hundred men had labored for three days. Jackson should have spared a few companies of regulars for this side of the river, which had suddenly become so important; although, for his own lines, he had but three thousand two hundred men, against an army which he supposed to consist of twelve thousand disciplined troops. With another day of preparation and clear insight into the enemy's desigh he would have done something effectual for the western bank. It was too late then. The days of preparation were numbered—were passed. Fare with him as it might to-morrow, he could do no more.

Nolte tells us that Commodore Patterson, on his way from headquarters to his post on the other side of the river, said to him as he passed, " I expect you will see some fun between this and to-morrow." Nolte adds that only himself and a few others knew what was expected. But when, soon after dark, the noise of preparation in the British camp grew louder and came nearer, there could not have been much doubt in the lines that another most unquiet Sunday was in reserve for them. There was much silent preparation in Jackson's camp; a cleaning of arms, a counting out of cartridges and adjustment of flints, and a careful loading of muskets and rifles. Beside the thirty-two-pounder was heaped up a bushel or two of musket balls and fragments of iron, enough to fill the piece up to the muzzle, and which will fill it up to the muzzle if the enemy come to close quarters. Jackson walks slowly along the lines just before dark. He wears the look of a man whose mind is wholly made up, and who clearly knows what he will do in any and every case. He stops occasionally to see that the stacked muskets are all loaded, and says to Planché's men, as he goes along their part of the lines, " Don't fire till you can see the whites of their eyes ; and if you want to sleep, sleep upon your arms."

Mishap befell the party of British under Colonel Thornton, who were detailed for the attack on the western bank. The water, owing to the fall of the river, was so low in the canal that it was not until eight hours after the appointed time of embarking that enough boats were launched into the Mississippi to convey across one third of the designated force. Instead of fourteen hundred men, only four hundred and ninety-eight went over. Instead of embarking immediately after dark, it was nearly daybreak before they reached the opposite bank. Instead of landing directly opposite the British position, the swift, deceptive current swept them down a mile and a half below it. But this little band, thus balked and delayed, was led by a soldier, Colonel W. Thornton, the most daring and efficient man in the British army.

CHAPTER XVI.

AT one o'clock on the morning of this memorable day, on a couch in a room of the McCarty mansion-house, General Jackson lay asleep in his worn uniform. Several of his aides slept upon the floor in the same apartment, all equipped for the field. A sentinel paced the adjacent passage. Sentinels moved noiselessly about the building, which loomed up large, dim, and silent in the foggy night, among the darkening trees. Most of those who slept at all that night were still asleep, and there was as yet little stir in either camp to disturb their slumbers.

Commodore Patterson was not among the sleepers. Soon after dark, accompanied by his faithful aide, Shepherd, he again took his position on the western bank of the river, directly opposite to where Colonel Thornton was struggling to launch his boats into the stream, and there he watched and listened till nearly midnight. He could hear almost everything that passed, and could see by the light of the camp fires a line of red-coats drawn up along the levee. He heard the cries of the tugging sailors as they drew the boats along the shallow, caving canal, and their shouts of satisfaction as each boat was launched with a loud splash into the Mississippi. From the great commotion, and the sound of so many voices, he began to surmise that the main body of the enemy were about to cross, and that the day was to be lost or

won on his side of the river. There was terror in the
thought, and wisdom too; and, if General Pakenham
had known all that we now know, the commodore's surmise would have been correct. Patterson's first thought
was to drop the ship Louisiana down upon them. But
no; the Louisiana had been stripped of half her guns
and all her men, and had on board, above water, hundreds of pounds of powder, for she was then serving as
powder-magazine to the western bank. To man the
ship, moreover, would involve the withdrawal of all the
men from the river batteries, which, if the main attack
were on Jackson's side of the river, would be of such
vital importance to him.

Revolving such thoughts in his anxious mind, Commodore Patterson hastened back to his post, again observing and lamenting the weakness of General Morgan's
line of defense. All that he could do in the circumstances was to dispatch Mr. Shepherd across the river
to inform General Jackson of what they had seen and
what they feared, and to beg an immediate re-enforcement. Informing the captain of the guard that he had
important intelligence to communicate, Shepherd was
conducted to the room in which the general was sleeping.

"Who's there?" asked Jackson, raising his head as
the door opened.

Mr. Shepherd gave his name and stated his errand,
adding that General Morgan agreed with Commodore
Patterson in the opinion that more troops would be required to defend the lines on the western bank.

"Hurry back," replied the general, as he rose, "and
tell General Morgan that he is mistaken. The main attack will be on this side, and I have no men to spare.
He must maintain his position at all hazards."

Shepherd recrossed the river with the general's answer, which could not have been very reassuring to

Morgan and his inexperienced men, not a dozen of whom had ever been in action.

Jackson looked at his watch.

" Gentlemen," said he to his dozing aides, " we have slept enough. Rise. I must go and see Coffee."

The order was obeyed very promptly. Sword-belts were buckled, pistols resumed, and in a few minutes the party were ready to begin the business of the day. There was little for the American troops to do but to repair to their posts. By four o'clock in the morning, along the whole line of works, every man was in his place and everything was ready. A little later General Adair marched down the reserve of a thousand Kentuckians to the rear of General Carroll's position, and, halting them fifty yards from the works, went forward himself to join the line of men peering over the top of the embankment into the fog and darkness of the morning. The position of the reserve was fortunately chosen. It was almost directly behind that part of the lines which a deserter from Jackson's army had yesterday told General Paken- ham was their weakest point! And the deserter was half right. He had deserted on Friday, before there had been any thought of the reserve, and he omitted to mention that Coffee and Carroll's men, over two thou- sand in number, were the best and coolest shots in the world.

Not long after the hour when the American general had been roused from his couch, General Pakenham, who had slept an hour or two at the Villeré mansion, also rose, and rode immediately to the bank of the river, where Thornton had just embarked his diminished force. He learned all that the reader knows of the delay and difficulty that had there occurred, and lingered long upon the spot listening for some sound that should indi- cate the whereabouts of Thornton. But no sound was heard, as the swift Mississippi had carried the boats far down out of hearing. Surely Pakenham must have known that the vital part of his plan was for that morning frustrated. Surely he will hold back his troops from the assault until Thornton announces himself. The story goes that he had been irritated by a taunt of Admiral Cochrane, who had said that if the army could not take those mud-banks, defended by ragged militia, *he* would do it with two thousand sailors armed only with cutlasses and pistols. And, besides, Pakenham believed that nothing could resist the calm and determined onset of the troops he led. He had no thought of waiting for Thornton, unless perhaps till daylight.

Before four o'clock the British troops were up and in the several positions assigned them.

What was the humor of the troops? As they stood there performing that most painful of all military duties, *waiting*, there was much of the forced merriment with which young soldiers conceal from themselves the real nature of their feelings. But the older soldiers augured ill of the coming attack. Colonel Mullens, of the Forty-fourth, openly expressed his dissatisfaction. "My regiment," said he, "has been ordered to execution. Their dead bodies are to be used as a bridge for the rest of the army to march over."

And, what was worse, in the dense darkness of the morning he had gone by the redoubt where were deposited the fascines and ladders, and marched his men to the head of the column without one of them. Whether this neglect was owing to accident or design concerns us not. For that and other military sins Mullens was afterward cashiered. Colonel Dale, too, of the Ninety-third Highlanders, a man of far different quality from Colonel Mullens, was grave and depressed.

"What do you think of it?" asked the physician of

the regiment, when word was brought of Thornton's detention.

Colonel Dale made no reply in words. Giving the doctor his watch and a letter, he simply said, "Give these to my wife; I shall die at the head of my regiment." Soon after four, General Pakenham rode away from the bank of the river, saying to one of his aides, " I will wait my own plan no longer."

He rode to the quarters of General Gibbs, who met him with another piece of ominous intelligence. "The Forty-fourth," Gibbs said, "had not taken the fascines and ladders to the head of the column ; but he had sent an officer to cause the error to be rectified, and he was then expecting every moment a report from that regiment." General Pakenham instantly dispatched Major Sir John Tylden to ascertain whether the regiment could be got into position in time. Tylden found the Forty-fourth just moving off from the redoubt, "in a most irregular and unsoldierlike manner, with the fascines and ladders. I then returned," adds Tylden in his evidence, "after some time, to Sir Edward Pakenham, and reported the circumstance to him ; stating that by the time which had elapsed since I left them they must have arrived at their situation in column."

This was not half an hour before dawn. Without waiting to obtain absolute certainty upon a point so important as the condition of the head of his main column of attack, the impetuous Pakenham commanded, to use the language of one of his own officers, " that the fatal, ever-fatal rocket should be discharged as a signal to begin the assault on the left." A few minutes later a second rocket whizzed aloft, the signal of attack on the right.

Daylight struggled through the mist. Soon after six o'clock both columns were advancing at the steady, solid, British pace to the attack; the Forty-fourth nowhere, straggling in the rear with the fascines and ladders. The column soon came up with the American outposts, who at first retreated slowly before it, but soon quickened their pace and ran in, bearing their great news, and putting every man in the works intensely on the alert, each commander anxious for the honor of first getting a glimpse of the foe and opening fire upon him.

Lieutenant Spotts, of battery number six, was the first man in the American lines who descried through the fog the dim red line of General Gibbs's advancing column, far away down the plain close to the forest. The thunder of his great gun broke the stillness. Then there was silence again, for the shifting fog, or the altered position of the enemy, concealed him from view once more. The fog lifted again, and soon revealed both divisions, which with their detached companies seemed to cover two thirds of the plain, and gave the Americans a repetition of the military spectacle which they had witnessed on the 28th of December. Three cheers from Carroll's men. Three cheers from the Kentuckians behind them. Cheers continuous from the advancing column, not heard yet in the American lines.

Steadily and fast the column of General Gibbs marched toward batteries numbered six, seven, and eight, which played upon it at first with but occasional effect, often missing, sometimes throwing a ball right into its midst and causing it to reel and pause for a moment. Promptly were the gaps filled up; bravely the column came on. As they neared the lines the well-aimed shot made more dreadful havoc, "cutting great lanes in the column from front to rear," and tossing men and parts of men aloft, or hurling them far on one side. At length, still steady and unbroken, they came within range of the small arms, the rifles of Carroll's Tennesseeans, the muskets of Adair's Kentuckians, four lines of sharpshooters, one behind the other. General Carroll, coolly waiting for the right moment, held his fire until the enemy were within two hundred yards, and then gave the word—"Fire!"

At first with a certain deliberation, afterward in haste, always with effect, the riflemen plied their terrible weapon. The summit of the embankment was a line of fire, except where the great guns showed their liquid, belching flash. The noise was peculiar and altogether indescribable—a rolling, bursting, echoing noise, never to be forgotten by a man that heard it. Along the whole line it blazed and rolled; the British batteries showering rockets over the scene; Patterson's batteries on the other side of the river joining in the concert.

The column of General Gibbs, mowed by the fire of the riflemen, still advanced, Gibbs at its head. As they caught sight of the ditch some of the officers cried out:

"Where are the Forty-fourth? If we get to the ditch, we have no means of crossing and scaling the lines!"

"Here comes the Forty-fourth! Here comes the Forty-fourth!" shouted the general; adding in an undertone, for his own private solace, that if he lived till to-morrow he would hang Mullens on the highest tree in the cypress wood.

Reassured, these heroic men again pressed on in the face of that murderous fire. But this could not last. With half its number fallen, and all its commanding officers disabled except the general, its pathway strewed with dead and wounded, and the men falling faster and faster, the column wavered and reeled (so the American riflemen thought) like a red ship on a tempestuous sea. At about a hundred yards from the lines the front ranks halted, and so threw the column into disorder, Gibbs shouting in the madness of vexation for them to re-form and advance. There was no re-forming under such a fire. Once checked, the column could not but break and retreat in confusion.

Just as the troops began to falter, General Pakenham rode up from his post in the rear toward the head of the column. Meeting parties of the Forty-fourth running about distracted, some carrying fascines, others firing, others in headlong flight, their leader nowhere to be seen, Pakenham strove to restore them to order, and to urge them on the way they were to go.

" For shame ! " he cried bitterly ; " recollect that you are British soldiers. *This* is the road you ought to take ! " pointing to the flashing and roaring —— in front.

Riding on, he was soon met by General Gibbs, who said :

" I am sorry to have to report to you that the troops will not obey me. They will not follow me."

Taking off his hat, General Pakenham spurred his horse to the very front of the wavering column, amid a torrent of rifle-balls, cheering on the troops by voice, by gesture, by example. At that moment a ball shattered his right arm, and it fell powerless to his side. The next, his horse fell dead upon the field. His aide, Captain McDougal, dismounted from his black creole pony, and Pakenham, apparently unconscious of his dangling arm, mounted again, and followed the retreating column, still calling upon them to halt and re-form. A few gallant spirits ran in toward the lines, threw themselves into the ditch, plunged across it, and fell scrambling up the sides of the soft and slippery breastwork.

Once out of the reach of those terrible rifles, the column halted and regained its self-possession. Laying aside their heavy knapsacks, the men prepared for a second and more resolute advance. They were encouraged, too, by seeing the Highlanders marching up in solid phalanx to their support with a front of a hundred men, their bayonets glittering in the sun, which had then begun to pierce the morning mist. At a quicker step, with General Gibbs on its right, General Pakenham on the left, the Highlanders in clear and imposing view, the column again advanced into the fire. A fearful slaughter ensued! There was one moment, when that thirty-two-pounder, loaded to the muzzle with musket balls, poured its charge at point-blank range right into the head of the column, literally leveling it with the plain—laying low, it was afterward computed, two hundred men. The American line, as one of the British officers remarked, looked like a row of fiery furnaces!

The heroic Pakenham had not far to go to meet his doom. He was three hundred yards from the line when the real nature of his enterprise seemed to flash upon him, and he turned to Sir John Tylden and said:

"Order up the reserve."

Then, seeing the Highlanders advancing to the support of General Gibbs, he, still waving his hat, but waving it now with his left hand, cried out:

"Hurrah! brave Highlanders!"

At that moment a mass of grapeshot, with a terrible crash, struck the group of which he was the central figure. One of the shots tore open the general's thigh, killed his horse, and brought horse and rider to the ground. Captain McDougal caught the general in his arms, removed him from the fallen horse, and was supporting him upon the field, when a second shot struck the wounded man in the groin, depriving him instantly of consciousness. He was borne to the rear and placed in the shade of an old live-oak ; and there, after gasping a few minutes, yielded up his life without a word, happily ignorant of the sad issue of all his plans and toils.

A more painful fate was that of General Gibbs. A few moments after Pakenham fell Gibbs received his death-wound, and was carried off the field writhing in agony and uttering fierce imprecations. He lingered all that day and the succeeding night, dying in torment on the morrow. Nearly at the same moment General Keane was painfully wounded in the neck and thigh, and was also borne to the rear. Colonel Dale, of the High-landers, fulfilled his prophecy, and fell at the head of his regiment. The Highlanders, under Major Creagh, wavered not, and advanced steadily, but too slowly, into the very tempest of General Carroll's fire, until they were within one hundred yards of the lines. There, for cause unknown, they halted and stood, a huge and glittering target, until five hundred and forty-four of their number had fallen, then broke and fled in horror and amazement to the rear. The column of General Gibbs did not advance after the fall of their leader. Leaving heaps of slain behind them, they, too, forsook the bloody field, rushed in utter confusion out of the fire, and took refuge at the bottom of wet ditches and behind trees and bushes on the borders of the swamp.

But not all of them ! Major Wilkinson, followed by Lieutenant Lavack and twenty men, pressed on to the ditch, floundered across it, climbed the breastwork, and raised his head and shoulders above its summit, upon which he fell, riddled with balls. The Tennesseeans and Kentuckians defending that part of the lines, struck with admiration at such heroic conduct, lifted his still breathing body and conveyed it tenderly behind the works.

"Bear up, my dear fellow," said Major Smiley, of the Kentucky reserve; "you are too brave a man to die."

"I thank you from my heart," whispered the dying man. "It's all over with me. You can render me a favor; it is to communicate to my commander that I fell on your parapet, and died like a soldier and a true Englishman."

Lavack reached the summit of the parapet unharmed, though with two shot-holes in his cap. He had heard Wilkinson, as they were crossing the ditch, cry out:

"Now, why don't the troops come on? The day is our own."

With these last words in his ears, and not looking behind him, he had no sooner gained the breastwork than he demanded the swords of two American officers, the first he caught sight of in the lines.

"Oh, no," replied one of them; "you are alone, and therefore ought to consider yourself *our* prisoner."

Then Lavack looked around, and saw what is best described in his own language:

"Now," he would say, as he told the story afterward to his comrades, "conceive my indignation, on looking round, to find that the two leading regiments had vanished as if the earth had opened and swallowed them up."

The earth *had* swallowed them up, or was waiting to do so, and the brave Lavack was a prisoner. Lieutenant Lavack further declared that when he first looked down behind the American lines he saw the riflemen "flying in a disorderly mob," which all other witnesses deny. Doubtless there was some confusion there, as every man was fighting his own battle, and there was much struggling to get to the rampart to fire, and from the rampart to load. Moreover, if the lines had been surmounted by the foe, a backward movement on the part of the defenders would have been in order and necessary.

Thus, then, it fared with the attack on the weakest part of the American position. Let us see what success rewarded the enemy's efforts against the strongest.

Colonel Rennie, when he saw the signal rocket ascend, pressed on to the attack with such rapidity that the American outposts along the river had to run for it, Rennie's vanguard close upon their heels. Indeed, so mingled seemed pursuers and pursued that Captain Humphrey had to withhold his fire for a few minutes, for fear of sweeping down friend and foe. As the last of the Americans leaped down into the isolated redoubt British soldiers began to mount its sides. A brief hand-to-hand conflict ensued within the redoubt between the party defending it and the British advance. In a surprisingly short time the Americans, overpowered by numbers and astounded at the suddenness of the attack, fled across the plank and climbed over into safety behind the lines. Then was poured into the redoubt a deadly and incessant fire, which cleared it of the foe in less time than it had taken them to capture it; while Humphrey, with his great guns, mowed down the still advancing column, and Patterson, from the other side of the river, added the fire of his powerful batteries.

Brief was the unequal contest. Colonel Rennie, Captain Henry, Major King, three only of this column, reached the summit of the rampart near the river's edge.

"Hurrah, boys!" cried Rennie, already wounded, as the three officers gained the breastwork, "hurrah, boys! the day is ours."

At that moment Beale's New Orleans sharpshooters, withdrawing a few paces for better aim, fired a volley, and the three noble soldiers fell headlong into the ditch.

That was the end of it. Flight, tumultuous flight—some running on the top of the levee, some under it, others down the road, while Patterson's guns played upon them still with terrible effect. The three slain officers were brought out of the canal behind the lines, when, we are told, a warm discussion arose among the Rifles for the honor of having "brought down the colonel." Mr. Withers, a merchant of New Orleans, and the crack shot of the company, settled the controversy by remarking:

"If he isn't hit above the eyebrows, it wasn't my shot."

Upon examining the lifeless form of Rennie it was found that the fatal wound was indeed in the forehead. To Withers, therefore, was assigned the duty of sending the watch and other valuables found upon the person of the fallen hero to his widow, who was in the fleet off Lake Borgne. Such acts as these made a lasting impression upon the officers of the British army. When Washington Irving was in Paris, in 1822, Colorel Thornton, who led the attack on the western bank, referred to the sending back of personal property of this kind in terms of warm commendation.

A story connected with the advance of Colonel Rennie's column is related by Judge Walker: "As the detachments along the road advanced, their bugler, a boy of fourteen or fifteen, climbing a small tree within two hundred yards of the American lines, straddled a limb and continued to blow the charge with all his power. There he remained during the whole action, while the cannon balls and bullets plowed the ground around him, killed scores of men, and tore even the branches of the tree in which he sat. Above the thunder of the artillery, the rattling of the musketry fire, and all the din and uproar of the strife, the shrill blast of the little bugler could be heard; and even when his companions had fallen back and retreated from the field he continued true to his duty and blew the charge with undiminished vigor. At last, when the British had entirely abandoned the ground, an American soldier passing from the lines captured the little bugler and brought him into camp, where he was greatly astonished when some of the enthusiastic creoles, who had observed his gallantry, actually embraced him, and officers and men vied with each other in acts of kindness to so gallant a little soldier."

The reserve, under General Lambert, was never ordered up. Major Tylden obeyed the last order of his general, and General Lambert had directed the bugler to sound the advance. A chance shot struck the bugler's uplifted arm and the instrument fell to the ground. The charge was never sounded. General Lambert brought forward his division far enough to cover the retreat of the broken columns and to deter General Jackson from attempting a sortie. The chief command had fallen upon Lambert, and he was overwhelmed by the unexpected and fearful issue of the battle.

How long a time elapsed between the fire of the first American gun and the total rout of the attacking columns? Twenty-five minutes! Not that the American fire ceased or even slackened at the expiration of that period. The riflemen on the left and the troops on the right continued to discharge their weapons into the smoke that hung over the plain for two hours. But in the space of twenty-five minutes the discomfiture of the enemy in the open field was complete. The battery alone still made resistance. It required two hours of a tremendous cannonade to silence its great guns and drive its defenders to the rear.

The scene behind the American works during the fire can be easily imagined. One half of the army never fired a shot. The battle was fought at the two extremities of the lines. The battalions of Planché, Dacquin, and Lacoste, the whole of the Fourty-fourth regiment, and one half of Coffee's Tennesseeans, had nothing to do but to stand still at their posts and chafe with vain impatience for a chance to join in the fight. The batteries alone at the center of the works contributed anything to the fortunes of the day. Yet that is not quite correct. " The moment the British came into view, and their signal rocket pierced the sky with its fiery train, the band of the Battalion d'Orleans struck up 'Yankee Doodle,' and thenceforth throughout the action it did not cease to discourse all the national and military airs in which it had been instructed."

When the action began, Jackson walked along the left of the lines, speaking a few words of good cheer to the men as he passed the several corps.

"Stand to your guns. Don't waste your ammunition. See that every shot tells. Let us finish the business to-day."

Such words as these escaped him now and then, the men not engaged cheering him as he went by. As the battle became general, he took a position on ground slightly elevated, near the center, which commanded a view of the scene. There, with mind intensely excited, he watched the progress of the strife. When it became evident that the enemy's columns were finally broken, Major Hinds, whose dragoons were drawn up in the rear, entreated the general for permission to dash out upon them in pursuit. It was a tempting offer to such a man as Jackson. But prudence prevailed, and the request was refused.

At eight o'clock, there being no signs of a renewed attack, and no enemy in sight, an order was sent along the lines to cease firing with the small arms. The general, surrounded by his staff, then walked from end to end of the works, stopping at each battery and post and addressing a few words of congratulation and praise to their defenders. It was a proud, glad moment for these men when, panting from their labor, blackened with smoke and sweat, they listened to the general's burning words and saw the light of victory in his countenance. With particular warmth he thanked and commended Beale's little band of riflemen, the companies of the Seventh, and Humphrey's artillerymen, who had so gallantly beaten back the column of Colonel Rennie. Heartily, too, he extolled the wonderful firing of the divisions of General Carroll and General Adair, not forgetting Coffee, who had dashed out upon the black skirmishers in the swamp and driven them out of sight in ten minutes.

This joyful ceremony over, the artillery, which had continued to play upon the British batteries, ceased their fire for the guns to cool and the dense smoke to roll off. The whole army crowded to the parapet and looked over into the field. What a scene was gradually disclosed to them! That gorgeous and imposing military array, the two columns of attack, the Highland phalanx, the distant reserve—all had vanished like an apparition. Far away down the plain the glass revealed a faint red line still receding. Nearer to the lines "we could see," says Nolte, "the British troops concealing themselves behind the shrubbery, or throwing themselves into the ditches and gullies. In some of the latter, indeed, they lay so thickly that they were only distinguishable in the distance by the white shoulder-belts, which formed a line along the top of their hiding-place."

Still nearer, the plain was covered and heaped with dead and wounded, as well as with those who had fallen paralyzed by fear alone. "I never had," Jackson would say, "so grand and awful an idea of the resurrection as on that day. After the smoke of the battle had cleared off somewhat I saw in the distance more than five hundred Britons emerging from the heaps of their dead comrades all over the plain, rising up, and still more distinctly visible as the field became clearer, coming forward and surrendering as prisoners of war to our soldiers. They had fallen at our first fire upon them without having received so much as a scratch, and lay prostrate as if dead until the close of the action."

The American army were appalled and silenced at the scene before them. The writhings of the wounded, their shrieks and groans, their convulsive and sudden tossing of limbs, were horrible to see and hear. Seven hundred killed, fourteen hundred wounded, five hundred prisoners, were the result of that twenty-five minutes' work. Jackson's loss was eight killed and thirteen wounded. Two men were killed at the left of the lines, two in the isolated redoubt, and four in the swamp pursuing the skirmishers.

General Jackson had no sooner finished his round of congratulations, and beheld the completeness of his victory on the eastern bank, than he began to cast anxious glances across the river, wondering at the silence of Morgan's lines and Patterson's guns. They flashed and spoke at length. Jackson and Adair, mounting the breastwork, saw Thornton's column advancing to the attack, and saw Morgan's men open fire upon them vigorously. All is well, thought Jackson.

"Take off your hats and give them three cheers!" shouted the general, though Morgan's division was a mile and a half distant.

The order was obeyed, and the whole army watched the action with intense interest, not doubting that the gallant Kentuckians and Louisianians on that side of the river would soon drive back the British column, as they themselves had just driven back those of Gibbs and Rennie. These men had become used to seeing British columns recoil and vanish before their fire. Not a thought of disaster on the western bank crossed their elated minds.

Yet Thornton carried the day on the western bank. Even while the men were in the act of cheering, General Jackson saw with mortification, never forgotten by him while he drew breath, the division under General Morgan abandon their position and run in headlong flight toward the city. Clouds of smoke soon obscured the scene, but the flashes of the musketry advanced *up* the river, disclosing to General Adair and his men the humiliating fact that their comrades had not rallied, but were still in swift retreat before the foe. In a moment the elation of General Jackson's troops was changed to anger and apprehension.

Fearing the worst consequences, and fearing them with reason, the general leaped down from the breast-work and made instant preparations for sending over a powerful re-enforcement. At all hazards the western bank must be regained. All is lost if it be not. Let but the enemy have free course up the western bank, with a mortar and a twelve-pounder, and New Orleans will be at their mercy in two hours! Nay, let Commodore Patterson but leave one of his guns unspiked, and Jackson's lines, raked by it from river to swamp, are untenable! All this, which was immediately apparent to the mind of General Jackson, was understood also by all of his army who had reflected upon their position. Indeed, by ten o'clock in the morning the British were masters of the western bank, although, owing to the want of available artillery, their triumph for the moment was a fruitless one. On one of the guns captured in General Morgan's lines the victors read this inscription: "Taken at the surrender of Yorktown, 1781." In a tent behind the lines they found the ensign of one of the Louisiana regiments, which still hangs in Whitehall, London, bearing these words: "Taken at the battle of New Orleans, Jan. 8th, 1815."

General Lambert, stunned by the events of the morning, was morally incapable of improving this important success. And it was well for him and for his army that he was so. Soldiers there have been who would have seen in Thornton's triumph the means of turning the tide of disaster and snatching victory from the jaws of defeat. But General Lambert found himself suddenly invested with the command of an army which, besides having lost a third of its effective force, was almost destitute of field officers. The mortality among the higher grade of officers had been frightful. Three major-generals, eight colonels and lieutenant-colonels, six majors, eighteen captains, and fifty-four subalterns, were among the killed and wounded. In such circumstances, Lambert, instead of hurrying over artillery and re-enforcements, and marching on New Orleans, did a less spirited but a wiser thing: he sent over an officer to survey General Morgan's lines, and ascertain how many men would be required to hold them. In other words, he sent over an officer to bring him back a plausible excuse for abandoning Colonel Thornton's conquest. And during the absence of the officer on this errand the British general resolved upon a measure still more pacific.

General Jackson, meanwhile, was intent upon dispatching his re-enforcement. It never for one moment occurred to his warlike mind that the British general would relinquish so vital an advantage without a desperate struggle, and accordingly he prepared for a desperate struggle. Organizing promptly a strong body of troops, he placed it under the command of General

Humbert, a refugee officer of distinction who had led the French revolutionary expedition into Ireland in 1798, and was then serving in the lines as a volunteer. Humbert, besides being the only general officer that Jackson could spare from his own position, was a soldier of high repute and known courage, a martinet in discipline, and a man versed in the arts of European warfare. About eleven o'clock the re-enforcement left the camp, with orders to hasten across the river by the ferry at New Orleans and march down toward the enemy, and, after effecting a junction with General Morgan's troops, to attack him and drive him from the lines. Before noon Humbert was well on his way.

Soon after midday, some American troops who were walking about the blood stained field in front of Jackson's position perceived a British party of novel aspect approaching. It consisted of an officer in full uniform, a trumpeter, and a soldier bearing a white flag. Halting at the distance of three hundred yards from the breastwork, the trumpeter blew a blast upon his bugle, which brought the whole army to the edge of the parapet, gazing with eager curiosity upon this unexpected but not unwelcome spectacle. Colonel Butler and two other officers were immediately dispatched by General Jackson to receive the message thus announced. After an exchange of courteous salutations, the British officer handed Colonel Butler a letter directed to the American commander-in-chief, which proved to be a proposal for an armistice of twenty-four hours, that the dead might be buried and the wounded removed from the field. The letter was signed "Lambert," a device, as was conjectured, to conceal from Jackson the death of the British general in command.

The sprinkling of Scottish blood that flowed in Jackson's veins asserted itself on this occasion. Time was now an all-important object with him, since Humbert and his command could not yet have crossed the river, and Jackson's whole soul was bent on the regaining of the western bank.

"Lambert?" thought the general. "Who is Lambert?"

Major Butler was ordered to return to the flag of truce, and to say that Major-General Jackson would be happy to receive any communication from the commander-in-chief of the British army; but as to the letter signed "Lambert," Major-General Jackson, not knowing the rank and powers of that gentleman, must beg to decline corresponding with him.

The flag departed, but returned in half an hour with the same proposal, signed "John Lambert, commander-in-chief of the British forces." Jackson's answer was prompt and ingenious. Humbert, by this time, he thought, if he had not crossed the river, must be near crossing, and might, in a diplomatic sense, be considered crossed. Jackson therefore consented to an armistice on the eastern bank, expressly stipulating that hostilities were not to be suspended on the western side of the river, and that neither party should send over re-enforcements until the expiration of the armistice!

When this reply reached General Lambert he had not yet received the report from the western bank, and was still in some degree undecided as to the course he should pursue there. With the next return of the flag, therefore, came a request from Lambert for time to consider General Jackson's reply. To-morrow morning, at ten o'clock, he would send a definite answer. The cannonade from the lines continued through the afternoon, and the troops stood at their posts, not certain that they would not again be attacked.

Early in the afternoon the officer returned from his

inspection of the works on the western bank, and gave it as his opinion that they could not be held with less than two thousand men. General Lambert at once sent an order to Colonel Gubbins to abandon the works, and to recross the river with his whole command. The order was not obeyed without difficulty, for by this time the Louisianians, urged by a desire to retrieve the fortunes of the day and their own honor, began to approach the lost redoubts in considerable bodies.

With what alacrity Commodore Patterson and General Morgan then rushed to their redoubts and batteries; with what assiduity the sailors bored out the spikes of the guns, toiling at the work all the next night; with what zeal the troops labored to strengthen the lines; with what joy Jackson heard the tidings, may be left to the reader to imagine.

The dead in front of Jackson's lines, scattered and heaped upon the field, lay all night a spectacle of horror to the American outposts stationed in their midst. Many of the wounded succeeded in crawling or tottering back to their camp. Many more were brought in behind the lines and conveyed to New Orleans, where they received every humane attention. But probably some hundreds of poor fellows, hidden in the wood or lying motionless in ditches, lingered in unrelieved agony all that day and night, until late in the following morning. As soon as it was dark, many uninjured soldiers, who had lain in the ditches and shrubbery, rejoined their comrades in the rear.

The news of the great victory electrified the nation, and raised it from the lowest pitch of despondency. All the large cities were illuminated in the evening after the glad tidings reached them. Before the rejoicings were over came news still more joyful—that the commissioners at Ghent had signed a treaty of peace. The war was at an end. A courier was promptly dispatched from Washington to New Orleans to convey to General Jackson the news of peace. Furnished by the postmaster-general with a special order to his deputies on the route to facilitate the progress of the messenger by all the means in their power, he traveled with every advantage, and made great speed. He left Washington on the 15th of February, thirty-eight days after the battle. He has a fair month's journey before him, which he will perform in nineteen days.

CHAPTER XVII.

How pleasant it would be to dismiss now the conqueror home to his Hermitage, to enjoy the congratulations of his neighbors and the plaudits of a nation whose pride he had so keenly gratified! His work was not done. The next three months of his life at New Orleans were crowded with events, many of which were delightful, many of which were painful in the extreme.

The trials of the American army, so far as its patience was concerned, began, not ended, with the victory of the 8th of January. The rains descended and the floods came upon the soft delta of the Mississippi, converting both camps into quagmires. Relieved of care, relieved from toil, yet compelled to keep the field by night and day, the greater part of the American army had nothing to do but endure the inevitable miseries of the situation. Disease began its fell work among them—malignant influenza, fevers, and, worst of all, dysentery. Major Latour computes that during the few weeks that elapsed between the 8th of January and the end of the campaign, five hundred of Jackson's army died from these complaints—a far greater number than had fallen in action. While the enemy remained there was no repining. The sick men, yellow and gaunt, staggered into the hospitals when they could no longer stand to their posts, and lay down to die without a murmur.

For ten days after the battle the English army remained in their encampment, deluged with rain and flood, and played upon at intervals by the American batteries on both sides of the river. They seemed to be totally inactive. They were not so. General Lambert, from the day of the great defeat, was resolved to retire to the shipping. But that had now become an affair of extreme difficulty, as an English officer explains :

"In spite of our losses," he says, "there were not throughout the armament a sufficient number of boats to transport above one half of the army at a time. If, however, we should separate, the chances were that both parties would be destroyed; for those embarked might be intercepted, and those left behind would be obliged to cope with the entire American force. Besides, even granting that the Americans might be repulsed, it would be impossible to take to our boats in their presence, and thus at least one division, if not both, must be sacrificed.

"To obviate this difficulty, prudence required that the road which we had formed on landing should be continued to the very margin of the lake, while appearances seemed to indicate the total impracticability of the scheme. From firm ground to the water's edge was here a distance of many miles, through the very center of a morass where human foot had never before trodden. Yet it was desirable at least to make the attempt; for if it failed we should only be reduced to our former alternative of gaining a battle or surrendering at discretion.

"Having determined to adopt this course, General Lambert immediately dispatched strong working parties, under the guidance of engineer officers, to lengthen the road, keeping as near as possible to the margin of the creek. But the task assigned to them was burdened with difficulties. For the extent of several leagues no firm footing could be discovered on which to rest the foundation of a path, nor any trees to assist in forming hurdles. All that could be done, therefore, was to bind together large quantities of reeds and lay them across the quagmire, by which means at least the semblance of a road was produced, however wanting in firmness and solidity; but where broad ditches came in the way, many of which intersected the morass, the workmen were necessarily obliged to apply more durable materials. For these, bridges composed in part of large branches, brought with immense labor from the woods, were constructed, but they were, on the whole, little superior in point of strength to the rest of the path, for, though the edges were supported by timber, the middle was filled up only by reeds."

It required nine days of incessant and arduous labor to complete the road. The wounded were then sent on board, except eighty who could not be removed. The abandoned guns were spiked and broken. In the evening of the 18th the main body of the army commenced its retreat. "Trimming the fires," continues the British officer, "and arranging all things in the same order as if no change were to take place, regiment after regiment stole away, as soon as darkness concealed their motions; leaving the pickets to follow as a rear guard, but with strict injunctions not to retire till daylight began to appear. As may be supposed, the most profound silence was maintained; not a man opening his mouth except to issue necessary orders, and even then speaking in a whisper. Not a cough or any other noise was to be heard from the head to the rear of the column; and even the steps of the soldiers were planted with care, to prevent the slightest stamping or echo."

With an ignominious wallow in the mire ("the whole army," as another narrator remarks, "covered with mud from the top of the head to the sole of the foot") the Wellington heroes ended their month's exertions in the delta of the Mississippi. They were in mortal terror of the alligators, it appears, whose domain they had intruded upon. "Just before dark, on the night of the retreat," says Captain Cooke, "I saw an alligator emerge from the water and penetrate the wilderness of reeds which encircled us on this muddy quagmire as far as the eye could reach. The very idea of the monster prowling about in the stagnant swamp took possession of my mind in a most forcible manner; to look out for the enemy was a secondary consideration. The word was, 'Look out for alligators!' Nearly the whole night I stood a few paces from the entrance of the hut, not daring to enter, under the apprehension that an alligator might push a broad snout through the reeds and gobble me up. The soldiers slept in a lump. At length, being quite worn out from want of sleep, I summoned up courage to enter the hut, but often started wildly out of my feverish slumbers, involuntarily laying hold of my naked sword, and conjuring up every rustling noise among the reeds to be one of those disgusting brutes, with a mouth large enough to swallow an elephant's leg."

The retreat was so well managed (General Lambert was knighted for it soon after) that the sun was high in the heavens on the following morning before the American army had any suspicion of the departure of the enemy. And when it began to be suspected, some further time elapsed before the fact was ascertained. Their camp presented the same appearance as it had for many days previous. Sentinels seemed to be posted as before, and flags were flying. The American general and his aides, from the high window at headquarters, surveyed the position through the glass, and were inclined to think that the enemy were only lying low, with a view to draw the troops out of the lines into the open plain. The veteran General Humbert, a Frenchman, surpassed the acuteness of the backwoodsmen on this occasion. Being called upon for his opinion, he took the glass and spied the deserted camp.

"They are gone," said he, with the air of a man who is certain.

"How do you know?" inquired the general.

The old soldier replied by directing attention to a crow that was flying close to what had been supposed to be one of the enemy's sentinels. The proximity of the crow showed that the sentinel was a "dummy," and so ill-made, too, that it was not even a good scarecrow. The game was now apparent, yet the general ordered out a party to reconnoiter. While it was forming, a British medical officer approached the lines, bearing a letter from General Lambert, which announced his departure, and recommended to the humanity of the American commander the eighty wounded men who were necessarily left behind. There could now be little doubt of the retreat, but Jackson was still wary, and restrained the exultant impetuosity of the men, who were disposed at once to visit the abandoned camp. Sending Major Hinds's dragoons to harass the retreat of the army, if it had not already gone beyond reach, and dispatching his surgeon-general to the wounded soldiers left to his care, the general himself, with his staff, rode to the enemy's camp. He saw that they had indeed departed, and that his own triumph was complete and irreversible. Fourteen pieces of cannon were found deserted and spoiled, and much other property, public and private. For one item, three thousand cannon balls were picked up on the field and piled behind the American ramparts by the Kentuckian troops.

The general visited the hospital and assured the wounded officers and soldiers of his protection and care— a promise which was promptly and amply fulfilled. "The circumstances of these wounded men," says Mr. Walker, "being made known in the city, a number of ladies rode down in their carriages with such articles as were deemed essential to the comfort of the unfortunates. One of these ladies was a belle of the city, famed for her charms of person and mind. Seeing her noble philanthropy and devotion to his countrymen, one of the British surgeons conceived a warm regard and admiration, which subsequent acquaintance ripened into love. This surgeon settled in New Orleans after the war, espoused the creole lady whose acquaintance he had made under such interesting circumstances, and became an esteemed citizen and the father of a large family." Dr. J. C. Kerr was the hero of this romantic story. He lived until within these few years. A son of his was that Victor Kerr who was executed at Havana with General Lopez and Colonel Crittenden in 1851—his last words, "I die like a Louisianian and a freeman!"

Two days later the main body of the American troops returned to New Orleans. "The arrival of the army," says Major Latour, who saw the spectacle, "was a triumph. The noncombatant part of the population of New Orleans—that is, the aged, the infirm, the matrons, daughters, and children—all went out to meet their deliverers, to receive with felicitations the saviors of their country. Every countenance was expressive of gratitude; joy sparkled in every feature on beholding fathers, brothers, husbands, sons, who had so recently saved the lives, fortunes, and honor of their families by repelling an enemy come to conquer and subjugate the country.

Nor were the sensations of the brave soldiers less lively on seeing themselves about to be compensated for all their sufferings by the enjoyment of domestic felicity. They once more embraced the objects of their tenderest affections, were hailed by them as their saviors and deliverers, and felt conscious that they had deserved the honorable title. How light, how trifling, how inconsiderable did their past toils and dangers appear to them at this glorious moment! All was forgotten, all painful recollections gave way to the most exquisite sensations of inexpressible joy."

A few days after the return of the army the general went in state to the cathedral. "A temporary arch," continues Major Latour, "was erected in the middle of the grand square, opposite the principal entrance of the cathedral. The different uniformed companies of Planché's battalion lined both sides of the way, from the entrance of the square toward the river to the church. The balconies of the windows of the city hall, the parsonage house, and all the adjacent buildings, were filled with spectators. The whole square and the streets leading to it were thronged with people. The triumphal arch was supported by six columns. Among those on the right was a young lady representing Justice, and on the left another representing Liberty. Under the arch were two young children, each on a pedestal, holding a crown of laurel. From the arch in the middle of the square to the church, at proper intervals, were ranged young ladies representing the different States and Territories composing the American Union, all dressed in white, covered with transparent veils, and wearing a silver star on their foreheads. Each of these young ladies held in her right hand a flag inscribed with the name of the State she represented, and in her left a basket trimmed with blue ribbons and full of flowers.

Behind each was a shield suspended on a lance stuck in the ground, inscribed with the name of a State or Territory. The intervals had been so calculated that the shields, linked together with verdant festoons, occupied the distance from the triumphal arch to the church.

"General Jackson, accompanied by the officers of his staff, arrived at the entrance of the square, where he was requested to proceed to the church by the walk prepared for him. As he passed under the arch he received the crowns of laurel from the two children, and was congratulated in an address spoken by Miss Kerr, who represented the State of Louisiana. The general then proceeded to the church, amid the salutations of the young ladies representing the different States, who strewed his passage with flowers. At the entrance of the church he was received by the Abbé Dubourg, who addressed him in a speech suitable to the occasion, and conducted him to a seat prepared for him near the altar. A *Te Deum* was chanted with impressive solemnity, and soon after a guard of honor attended the general to his quarters, and in the evening the town, with its suburbs, was splendidly illuminated."

The day and night were given up to pleasure, both by the soldiers and the people. The next day discipline resumed its sway. The Tennessee troops were encamped on their old ground above the city. New troops kept coming by squads and companies, and the boat load of arms arrived for them. The general addressed himself to the task of rendering the country secure against a second surprise, in case the enemy should attempt a landing elsewhere. New works were ordered in exposed localities. New Orleans was saved, but the Southwest was still the country menaced, and it was not to be supposed that the British fleet and army, re-enforced by a thousand new troops, would retire from the coast without an attempt to retrieve the campaign. Not a thought, not the faintest presentiment of immediate peace, occurred to any one. The question was not whether the enemy would make a new attempt, but whether New Orleans or Mobile would be its object.

For the first three weeks after the triumphal return of the army to New Orleans little occurred to disturb the public harmony. Martial law was rigorously maintained, and all the troops were kept in service. The duty at the lines and below the lines was hard and disagreeable, but, whatever murmurs were uttered by the troops, the duty was punctually performed. The mortality at the hospitals continued to be very great. The business of the city was interrupted in some degree by the prevalence of martial law, and still more by the retention in service of business men. But so long as there was no whisper of peace in the city, the restraint was felt to be necessary, and was submitted to without audible complaining. During this interval some pleasant things occurred, which exhibit the general in a favorable light.

On February 4th, Edward Livingston, Mr. Shepherd, and Captain Maunsel White were sent to the British fleet to arrange for a further exchange of prisoners, and for the recovery of a large number of slaves, who, after aiding the English army on shore, had gone off with them to their ships. They were charged also with a less difficult errand. General Keane, when he received his wounds on the 8th of January, lost on the field a valuable sword, the gift of a friend. He stated the circumstance to General Jackson, and requested him to restore the sword. It was an unusual request, thought the general, but he complied with it, adding polite wishes for General Keane's recovery. General Keane acknowledged the restoration of the sword in courteous terms.

Mr. Livingston returned to New Orleans with the news of peace on the 19th of February. The city was thrown into joyful excitement, and the troops expected an immediate release from their arduous toils. But they were doomed to disappointment. The package which Admiral Malcolm had received contained only a newspaper announcement of peace. There was little doubt of its truth, but the statements of a newspaper are as nothing to the commanders of fleets and armies. To check the rising tide of feeling, Jackson, on the very day of Livingston's return, issued a proclamation, stating the exact nature of the intelligence, and exhorting the troops to bear with patience the toils of the campaign a little longer. "We must not," said he, "be thrown into false security by hopes that may be delusive. It is by holding out such that an artful and insidious enemy too often seeks to accomplish what the utmost exertions of his strength will not enable him to effect. To place you off your guard and attack you by surprise is the natural expedient of one who, having experienced the superiority of your arms, still hopes to overcome you by stratagem. Though young in the 'trade' of war, it is not by such artifices that he will deceive us."

This proclamation seems rather to have inflamed than allayed the general discontent. Two days after the return of Livingston a paragraph appeared in the Louisiana Gazette to the effect that "a flag had just arrived from Admiral Cochrane to General Jackson, officially announcing the conclusion of peace at Ghent between the United States and Great Britain, and virtually requesting a suspension of arms." For this statement there was not the least foundation in truth, and its effect at such a crisis was to inflame the prevailing excitement. Upon reading the paragraph Jackson caused to be prepared an official contradiction, which he sent by an aide-de-camp to the offending editor, with a written order requiring its insertion in the next issue of the paper.

This was regarded by the rebellious spirits as a new provocation.

In this posture of affairs some of the French troops hit upon an expedient to escape the domination of the general. They claimed the protection of the French consul, M. Toussard. The consul, nothing loath, hoisted the French flag over the consulate, and dispensed certificates of French citizenship to all applicants. Naturalized Frenchmen availed themselves of the same artifice, and for a few days Toussard had his hands full of pleasant and profitable occupation. Jackson met this new difficulty by ordering the consul and all Frenchmen who were not citizens of the United States to leave New Orleans within three days, and not to return to within one hundred and twenty miles of the city until the news of the ratification of the treaty of peace was officially published! The register of votes of the last election was resorted to for the purpose of ascertaining who were citizens and who were not. Every man who had voted was claimed by the general as his "fellow-citizen and soldier," and compelled to do duty as such.

This bold stroke of authority aroused much indignation among the anti-martial law party, which on the 3d of March found voice in the public press. A long article appeared .anonymously in one of the newspapers, boldly but temperately and respectfully calling in question General Jackson's recent conduct, and especially the banishment of the French from the city. Here was open defiance. Jackson accepted the issue with a promptness all his own. He sent an order to the editor of the Louisiana Courier, in which the article appeared, commanding his immediate presence at headquarters. The name of the author of the communication was demanded and given. It was Mr. Louaillier, a member of the Legislature, a gentleman who had distinguished himself by his zeal in the public cause, and who had been particularly prominent in promoting subscriptions for the relief of the ill-clad soldiers. Upon his surrendering the name the editor was dismissed.

At noon on Sunday, the 5th of March, two days after the publication of the article, Mr. Louaillier was walking along the levee, opposite one of the most frequented coffee-houses in the city, when a Captain Amelung, commanding a file of soldiers, tapped him on the shoulder and informed him that he was a prisoner. Louaillier, astonished and indignant, called the bystanders to witness that he was conveyed away against his will by armed men. A lawyer, P. L. Morel by name, who witnessed the arrest from the steps of the coffee-house, ran to the spot, and was forthwith engaged by Louaillier to act as his legal adviser in this extremity. Louaillier was placed in confinement. Morel hastened to the residence of Judge Dominick A. Hall, of the District Court of the United States, to whom he presented, in his client's name, a petition for a writ of *habeas corpus*. The judge granted the petition, and the writ was immediately served upon the general. Jackson instantly sent a file of troops to arrest the judge, and, before night, Judge Hall and Mr. Louaillier were prisoners in the same apartment of the barracks.

So far from obeying the writ of *habeas corpus*, General Jackson seized the writ from the officer who served it and retained it in his own possession, giving to the officer a certified copy of the same. Louaillier was at once placed on his trial before a court-martial upon the following charges, all based upon the article in the

Louisiana Courier: Exciting to mutiny; general misconduct; being a spy; illegal and improper conduct; disobedience to orders; writing a willful and corrupt libel against the general; unsoldierly conduct; violation of a general order.

Nor were these the only arrests. A Mr. Hollander, partner in business of our friend Nolte, expressed himself somewhat freely in conversation respecting Jackson's proceedings, and suddenly found himself a prisoner in consequence.

On Monday, March 6th, the day after the arrest of Louaillier and Judge Hall, the courier arrived at New Orleans who had been dispatched from Washington nineteen days before to bear to General Jackson the news of peace. He had traveled fast by night and day, and most eagerly had his coming been looked for. His packet was opened at headquarters and found to contain no dispatches announcing the conclusion of peace, but an old letter, of no importance then, which had been written by the Secretary of War to General Jackson some months before. It appeared that in the hurry of his departure from Washington the courier had taken the wrong packet. The blank astonishment of the general, of his aides, and of the courier, can be imagined. The only proof the unlucky messenger could furnish of the genuineness of his mission and the truth of his intelligence was an order from the Postmaster-General requiring his deputies on the route to afford the courier bearing the news of peace all the facilities in their power for the rapid performance of his journey. In ordinary circumstances this would have sufficed. But the events of yesterday had rendered the circumstances extraordinary. The general resolved still to hold the reins of military power firmly in his hands. New Orleans was still a camp, and Judge Hall a soldier.

Jackson wrote, however, to General Lambert on the same day, stating precisely what had occurred, and inclosing a copy of the Postmaster-General's order, "that you may determine," said the general, "whether these occurrences will not justify you in agreeing, by a cessation of all hostilities, to anticipate a happy return of peace between our two nations, which the first direct intelligence must bring to us in an official form."

The week had nearly passed away. Judge Hall remained in confinement at the barracks. General Jackson resolved on Saturday, the 11th of March, to send the judge out of the city and set him at liberty, which was done.

Brief was the exile of the banished judge. The very next day—Monday, March 13th—arrived from Washington a courier with a dispatch from the Government announcing the ratification of the treaty of peace, and inclosing a copy of the treaty and of the ratification. Before that day closed the joyful news was forwarded to the British general, hostilities were publicly declared to be at an end, martial law was abrogated, and commerce released. "And in order," concluded the general's proclamation, "that the general joy attending this event may extend to all manner of persons, the commanding general proclaims and orders a pardon for all military offenses heretofore committed in this district, and orders that all persons in confinement under such charges be immediately discharged."

Louaillier was a prisoner no longer. Judge Hall returned to his home. On the day following, the impatient militia and volunteers of Tennessee, Kentucky, Mississippi, and Louisiana were dismissed with a glorious burst of grateful praise.

I shall not dwell upon the subsequent proceedings of Judge Hall. March 22d, in the United States District Court, on motion of Attorney John Dick, it was ruled and ordered by the court that "the said Major-General Andrew Jackson show cause on Friday next, the 24th of March, instant, at ten o'clock A. M., why an attachment should not be awarded against him for contempt of this court, in having disrespectfully wrested from the clerk aforesaid an original order of the honorable the judge of this court for the issuing of a writ of *habeas corpus* in the case of a certain Louis Louaillier, then imprisoned by the said Major-General Andrew Jackson, and for detaining the same. Also, for disregarding the said writ of *habeas corpus* when issued and served, in having imprisoned the honorable the judge of this court, and for other contempts, as stated by the witnesses."

General Jackson appeared in court attended by a concourse of excited people. He wore the dress of a private citizen. "Undiscovered amid the crowd," Major Eaton relates, "he had nearly reached the bar, when, being perceived, the room instantly rang with the shouts of a thousand voices. Raising himself on a bench and moving his hand to procure silence, a pause ensued. He then addressed himself to the crowd, told them of the duty due to the public authorities, for that any impropriety of theirs would be imputed to him, and urged, if they had any regard for him, that they would on the present occasion forbear those feelings and expressions of opinion. Silence being restored, the judge rose from his seat, and remarking that it was impossible and unsafe to transact business at such a moment and under such threatening circumstances, directed the marshal to adjourn the court. The general immediately interfered, and requested that it might not be done. 'There is no danger here; there shall be none. The same arm that protected from outrage this city against the invaders of the country, will shield and protect this court or perish in the effort.'

"Tranquillity was restored, and the court proceeded to business. The district attorney had prepared and now presented a file of nineteen questions to be answered by the prisoner. 'Did you not arrest Louaillier?' 'Did you not arrest the judge of this court?' 'Did you not seize the writ of *habeas corpus?*' 'Did you not say a variety of disrespectful things of the judge?' These interrogatories the general utterly refused to answer, to listen to, or to receive. He told the court that in a paper previously presented by his counsel he had explained fully the reasons that had influenced his conduct. That paper had been rejected without a hearing. He could add nothing to that paper. 'Under these circumstances,' said he, 'I appear before you to receive the sentence of the court, having nothing further in my defense to offer.'"

Whereupon Judge Hall pronounced the judgment of the court. It is recorded in the words following: "On this day appeared in person Major-General Andrew Jackson, and, being duly informed by the court that an attachment had issued against him for the purpose of bringing him into court, and the district attorney having filed interrogatories, the court informed General Jackson that they would be tendered to him for the purpose of answering thereto. The said General Jackson refused to receive them, or to make any answer to the said interrogatories. Whereupon the court proceeded to pronounce judgment; which was, 'That Major-General Andrew Jackson do pay a fine of one thousand dollars to the United States.'"

The general was borne from the courtroom in triumph; or as Major Eaton has it, "he was seized and forcibly hurried from the hall to the streets, amid the reiterated cries of 'Huzza for Jackson!' from the immense concourse that surrounded him. They presently met a

carriage in which a lady was riding, when, politely taking her from it, the general was made, spite of entreaty,
to occupy her place. The horses being removed, the carriage was drawn on and halted at the coffee-house, into
which he was carried, and thither the crowd followed,
huzzaing for Jackson and menacing violently the judge.
Having prevailed on them to hear him, he addressed
them with great feeling and earnestness; implored them
to run into no excesses; that if they had the least gratitude for his services, or regard for him personally, they
could evince it in no way so satisfactorily as by assenting, as he most freely did, to the decision which had just
been pronounced against him."

Upon reaching his quarters he sent back an aide-de-
camp to the courtroom with a check on one of the city
banks for a thousand dollars. And thus the offended
majesty of the law was supposed to be avenged.

It is not to be inferred, from the conduct of the
people in the courtroom, that the course of General
Jackson in maintaining martial law so long after the
conclusion of peace was morally certain, was generally
approved by the people of New Orleans. It was not.
It was approved by many, forgiven by most, resented by
a few. An effort was made to raise the amount of the
general's fine by a public subscription, to which no one
was allowed to contribute more than one dollar. But
Nolte tells us (how truly I know not) that, after raising
with difficulty one hundred and sixty dollars, the scheme
was quietly given up. He adds that the courtroom on
the day of the general's appearance was occupied chiefly
by the special partisans of the general.

On the 6th of April General Jackson and his family
left New Orleans on their return to Tennessee. On approaching Nashville the general was met by a procession
of troops, students, and citizens, who deputed one of

their number to welcome him in an address. At Nashville a vast concourse was assembled, among whom were many of the troops who had served under him at New Orleans. The greatest enthusiasm prevailed. Within the courthouse Mr. Felix Grundy received the general with an eloquent speech, recounting in glowing periods the leading events of the last campaigns. The students of Cumberland College also addressed the general. The replies of General Jackson to these various addresses were short, simple, and sufficient.

And so we dismiss the hero home to his beloved Hermitage, there to recruit his impaired energies by a brief period of repose. He had been absent for the space of twenty-one months, with the exception of three weeks between the end of the Creek War and the beginning of the campaign of New Orleans.

CHAPTER XVIII.

FOUR months' rest at the Hermitage. In the cool days of October we find the general on horseback once more, riding slowly through Tennessee, across Virginia, toward the city of Washington—the whole journey a triumphal progress. At Lynchburg, in Virginia, the people turned out *en masse* to greet the conqueror. A number of gentlemen rode out of town to meet him, one of whom saluted the general with an address, to which he briefly replied. Escorted into the town on the 7th of November, he was received by a prodigious assemblage of citizens and all the militia companies of the vicinity, who welcomed him with an enthusiasm that can be imagined. In the afternoon a grand banquet, attended by three hundred persons, was served in honor of the general. Among the distinguished guests was Thomas Jefferson, then seventy-two years of age, the most revered of American citizens then living. His residence was only a long day's ride from Lynchburg, and he had come to join in the festivities of this occasion. The toast offered by the ex-President at the banquet at Lynchburg has been variously reported, but in the newspapers of the day it is uniformly given in these words: " Honor and gratitude to those who have filled the measure of their country's honor." General Jackson volunteered a toast which was at once graceful and significant: " James Monroe, late Secretary of War "—graceful, because Mr.

Monroe was a Virginian, a friend of Mr. Jefferson, and had nobly co-operated with himself in the defense of New Orleans; significant, because Mr. Monroe was a very prominent candidate for the presidency, and the election was drawing near.

To horse again the next morning. Nine days' riding brought the general to Washington, which he reached in the evening of November 17th. He called the next morning upon the President and the members of the Cabinet, by whom he was welcomed to the capital with every mark of cordiality and respect. His stay at Washington, I need not say, was an almost ceaseless round of festivity. A great public dinner was given him, which was attended by all that Washington could boast of the eminent and the eloquent. He was lionized severely at private entertainments, where the stateliness of his bearing and the suavity of his manners pleased the gentlemen and won the ladies. And this was to be one of the conditions of his lot thenceforward to the end of his life. He was the darling of the nation. Nothing had yet occurred to dim the luster of his fame. His giant popularity was in the flush of its youth. He could go nowhere without incurring an ovation, and every movement of his was affectionately chronicled in the newspapers.

General Jackson was to remain in the army! Upon the conclusion of peace with Great Britain the army was reduced to ten thousand men, commanded by two major-generals, one of whom was to reside at the North and command the troops stationed there, and the other to bear military sway at the South. The generals selected for these commands were General Jacob Brown for the Northern division, and General Andrew Jackson for the Southern, both of whom had entered the service at the beginning of the late war as generals of militia. General Jackson's visit to Washington on this occasion was in obedience to an order, couched in the language of an invitation, received from the Secretary of War soon after his return from New Orleans; the object of his visit being to arrange the posts and stations of the army. The feeling was general at the time that the disasters of the War of 1812 were chiefly due to the defenseless and unprepared condition of the country, and that it was the first duty of the Government, on the return of peace, to see to it that the assailable points were fortified. " Let us never be caught napping again "; " In time of peace prepare for war," were popular sayings then. On these and all other subjects connected with the defense of the country the advice of General Jackson was asked and given. His own duty, it was evident, was first of all to pacify, and if possible satisfy, the restless and sorrowful Indians in the Southwest. The vanquished tribe, it was agreed, should be dealt with forbearingly and liberally. The general undertook to go in person into the Indian country and remove from their minds all discontent. He did so.

It is not possible to overstate his popularity in his own State. He was its pride, boast, and glory. Tennesseeans felt a personal interest in his honor and success. His old enemies either sought reconciliation with him or kept their enmity to themselves. His rank in the army, too, gave him unequaled social eminence; and, to add to the other felicities of his lot, his fortune now rapidly in-. creased, as the entire income of his estate could be added to his capital, the pay of a major-general being sufficient for the support of his family. He was forty-nine years old in 1816. He had riches, rank, power, renown, and all in full measure.

But in 1817 there was trouble again among the Indians—the Indians of Florida, the allies of Great Britain during the War of 1812, commonly known by the name of Seminoles. Composed in part of fugitive Creeks, who scouted the treaty of Fort Jackson, they had indulged the expectation that on the conclusion of peace they would be restored by their powerful ally to the lands wrested from the Creeks by Jackson's conquering army in 1814. This poor remnant of tribes once so numerous and powerful had not a thought, at first, of attempting to regain the lost lands by force of arms. The best testimony now procurable confirms their own solemnly reiterated assertions that they long desired and endeavored to live in peace with the white settlers of Georgia. All their "talks," petitions, remonstrances, letters, of which a large number are still accessible, breathe only the wish for peace and fair dealing. The Seminoles were drawn at last into a collision with the United States by a chain of circumstances with which they had little to do, and the responsibility of which belongs not to them.

Fourteen miles east of Fort Scott, in Georgia, but near the Florida line, on lands claimed by the United States under the treaty of Fort Jackson, was a Seminole village called by the settlers Fowltown. The chief of this village of forty-five warriors was supposed to be, and was, peculiarly embittered against the whites. The red war-pole had been erected by his warriors, around which they danced the war-dance. The Fowltown chief was resolved to hold his lands, and resist by force any further encroachments, and had said as much to Colonel Twiggs, the commandant of Fort Scott. "I warn you," he said to Colonel Twiggs, early in November, "not to cross, nor cut a stick of wood, on the east side of the Flint. That land is mine. I am directed by the powers above and the powers below to protect and defend it. I shall do so." A few days after, General Gaines arrived at Fort Scott with a re-enforcement of regular troops, when the talk of the Fowltown chief was reported to him. General Gaines, "to ascertain," as he said, "whether his hostile temper had abated," had previously sent a runner to the chief to request him to come to him at Fort Scott. The chief replied: "I have already said to the officer commanding at the fort all I have to say. I will not go."

General Gaines immediately detached a force of two hundred and fifty men, under command of Colonel Twiggs, with orders "to bring to me the chief and his warriors, and, in the event of resistance, to treat them as enemies."

On the morning of November 21st, before the dawn of day, the detachment reached Fowltown. The warriors fired upon the troops without waiting to learn their errand. It could not be expected to occur to the benighted Seminole mind that a large body of troops, arriving near their town in the darkness of a November morning, could have any but a hostile errand. The fire of the Indians, which was wholly without effect, was "briskly returned" by the troops, when the Indians took to flight, with the loss of two men and one woman killed, besides several wounded. Colonel Twiggs entered and searched the abandoned town. Among other articles found in the house of the chief were a scarlet coat of the British uniform, a pair of golden epaulets, and a certificate in the handwriting of Colonel Nichols, declaring that the Fowltown chief had ever been a true and faithful friend of the British. Colonel Twiggs took post near the town, erected a temporary stockade, and waited for further orders. Shortly afterward the town was burned by General Gaines himself.

The die was cast. The revenge of the Seminoles for this seizure of Fowltown and the slaughter of its warriors and the woman was swift, bloody, and atrocious.

Nine days after, a large open boat, containing forty United States troops, seven soldiers' wives, and four little children, under command of Lieutenant Scott, of the Seventh Infantry, was warping slowly up the Appalachicola River. They were within one mile of reaching the junction of the Chattahoochee and Flint, and not many miles from Fort Scott. To avoid the swift current, the soldiers kept the boat close to the shore. They were passing a swamp densely covered with trees and cane. Suddenly, at a moment when not a soul on board suspected danger, for not an Indian nor trace of an Indian had been seen, a heavy volley of musketry from the thickets within a few yards of the boat was fired full into the closely compacted party. Lieutenant Scott and nearly every man in the boat were killed or badly wounded at the first fire. Other volleys succeeded. The Indians soon rose from their ambush and rushed upon the boat with a fearful yell. Men, women, and children were involved in one horrible massacre, or spared for more horrible torture. The children were taken by the heels and their brains dashed out against the sides of the boat. The men and women were scalped, all but one woman, who was not wounded by the previous fire. Four men escaped by leaping overboard and swimming to the opposite shore, of whom two only reached Fort Scott uninjured. Laden with plunder, the savages re-entered the wilderness, taking with them the woman whom they had spared. In twenty minutes after the first volley was fired into the boat, every creature in it but five was killed and scalped, or bound and carried off.

The Seminoles had tasted blood, and thirsted like tigers for more. Still haunting the banks of the river, they attacked, a few days later, a convoy of ascending boats, under Major Muhlenberg, killing two soldiers and wounding thirteen. For four or five days and nights the boats lay in the middle of the stream, immovable, for not a man could show himself for an instant above the bulwarks without being fired upon. With difficulty, and after great suffering on the part of the sick and wounded, the fleet was rescued from its horrible situation by a party from Fort Scott.

Before the year closed Fort Scott itself was threatened. A desultory and ineffectual fire was kept up upon it for several days. The garrison, being short of provisions, and forming a most exaggerated estimate of the numbers of the enemy, feared to be obliged to abandon the post. This was war indeed. The Government at Washington was promptly informed of these terrible events by General Gaines, who advised the most vigorous measures of retaliation. It chanced that, just before these dispatches reached Washington, the Secretary of War, Mr. John C. Calhoun, not anticipating serious trouble from the Indians, had sent orders to General Gaines to proceed to Amelia Island. General Gaines was accordingly compelled to leave the frontiers at a time when his presence there was most needed. The Government, fearing the effect at such a moment of the absence of a general officer from the scene of hostilities, resolved upon ordering General Jackson to take command in person of the troops upon the frontiers of Georgia.

On the 22d of January, General Jackson and his "guard" left Nashville amid the cheers of the entire population. The distance from Nashville to Fort Scott is about four hundred and fifty miles. In the evening of March 9th, forty-six days after leaving Nashville, he reached Fort Scott with eleven hundred hungry men. No tidings yet of the Tennessee troops under Colonel Hayne! There was no time to spend, however, in waiting or surmising. The general found himself at Fort Scott in command of two thousand men, and his whole stock of provisions one quart of corn and three rations of meat per man. There was no supply in his rear, for he had swept the country on his line of march of every bushel of corn and every animal fit for food. He had his choice of two courses only: to remain at Fort Scott and starve, or to go forward and find provisions. It is not necessary to say which of these alternatives Andrew Jackson selected. "Accordingly," he wrote, "having been advised by Colonel Gibson, quartermaster-general, that he would sail from New Orleans on the 12th of February with supplies, and being also advised that two sloops with provisions were in the bay, and an officer had been dispatched from Fort Scott in a large keel-boat to bring up a part of their loading, and deeming that the preservation of these supplies would be to preserve the army, and enable me to prosecute the campaign, I assumed the command on the morning of the 10th, ordered the live stock to be slaughtered and issued to the troops, with one quart of corn to each man, and the line of march to be taken up at twelve meridian."

It was necessary to cross the swollen river, an operation which consumed all the afternoon, all the dark night succeeding, and a part of the next morning. Five days' march along the banks of the Appalachicola—past the scene of the massacre of Lieutenant Scott—brought the army to the site of the old Negro Fort on Prospect Bluff. On the way, however, the army, to its great joy, met the ascending boat-load of flour, when the men had their first full meal since leaving Fort Early, three weeks before. Upon the site of the Negro Fort, General Jackson ordered his aide, Lieutenant Gadsden, of the engineers, to construct a fortification, which was promptly done, and named by the general Fort Gadsden, in honor, as he said, of the "talents and indefatigable zeal" of the builder. No news yet of the great flotilla of provisions from New Orleans. "Consequently," wrote the general,

"I put the troops on half rations, and pushed the completion of the fort for the protection of the provisions in the event of their arrival, intending to march forthwith to the heart of the enemy and endeavor to subsist upon him. In the meantime I dispatched Major Fanning of the corps, of artillery, to take another look into the bay, whose return on the morning of the 23d brought the information that Colonel Gibson, with one gunboat and three transports and others in sight, were in the bay. On the same night I received other information that no more had arrived. I am therefore apprehensive that some of the smaller vessels have been lost, as one gunboat went to pieces, and another, when last spoken, had one foot of water in her."

The Tennessee volunteers did not arrive, but had been heard from. "The idea of starvation," wrote General Jackson, "has stalked abroad. A panic appears to have spread itself everywhere." Colonel Hayne had heard that the garrison of Fort Scott were starving, and had passed into Georgia for supplies, despite the willingness of the men "to risk the worst of consequences on what they had to join me." General Gaines, however, joined the army at Fort Gadsden, though in sorry plight. "In his passage down the Flint," explains Jackson, "he was shipwrecked, by which he lost his assistant adjutant-general, Major C. Wright, and two soldiers drowned. The general reached me six days after, nearly exhausted by hunger and cold, having lost his baggage and clothing, and being compelled to wander in the woods four days and a half without anything to subsist on, or any clothing except a pair of pantaloons. I am happy to have it in my power to say that he is now with me, at the head of his brigade, in good health."

Nine days passed, and still the general was at Fort Gadsden waiting for the great flotilla. It occurred to

him that possibly the Governor of Pensacola might have
opposed its ascent of the river or molested it in the bay.
He wrote a very polite but very plain letter to the Governor on the 25th of March.   "I wish it to be distinctly
understood," he observed, "that any attempt to inter-
rupt the passage of transports can not be viewed in any
other light than as a hostile act on your part. I will not
permit myself for a moment to believe that you would
commit an act so contrary to the interests of the King
your master.   His Catholic Majesty, as well as the Government of the United States, is alike interested in
chastising a savage foe who have too long warred with
impunity against his subjects as well as the citizens of
this republic, and I feel persuaded that every aid which
you can give to promote this object will be cheerfully
tendered."

The Governor in due time replied that he would permit the transports to pass this time, on condition of their
paying the usual duties, but never again.   "If extraordinary circumstances," he concluded, " should require any
further temporary concessions, not explained in the
treaty, I request your Excellency to have the goodness
to apply in future, for the obtaining of them, to the
proper authority, as I, for my part, possess no power
whatever in relation thereto."

Before the day closed on which the general wrote his
plain letter to the Governor of Pensacola he had the
pleasure of hearing that the provision flotilla had arrived,
and of welcoming to Fort Gadsden its commanding officers, Colonel Gibson of the army and Captain McKeever
of the navy.   He was writing a dispatch at the time to
the Secretary of War, which he hastened to close with this
most gratifying intelligence: " I shall move to-morrow,"
he said, " having made the necessary arrangements with
Captain McKeever for his co-operation in transporting

my supplies around to the Bay of St. Marks, from which place I shall do myself the honor of communicating with you. Should our enemy attempt to escape with his supplies and booty to the small islands, and thence to carry on a predatory warfare, the assistance of the navy will prevent his escape."

General Jackson on the following day was in full march toward St. Marks. He left Fort Gadsden on the 26th of March, was joined by one regiment of Tennesseans on the 1st of April, and on the same day had a brush with the enemy. A "number" of Indians, we are told in the official report, were discovered engaged in the peaceful employment of "herding cattle." An attack upon these dusky herdsmen was instantly ordered. One American killed and four wounded, fourteen Indians killed and four women prisoners, were the results of this affair. The army advanced upon the town to which the herdsmen belonged, and found it deserted. "On reaching the square, we discovered a red pole planted at the council house, on which was suspended about fifty fresh scalps, taken from the heads of extreme age down to the tender infant, of both sexes; and in an adjacent house those of nearly three hundred men, which bore the appearance of being the barbarous trophies of settled hostility for three or four years past." *

General Gaines continued the pursuit on the following day, and gathered a prodigious booty. "The red pole," says the adjutant's report, "was again found planted in the square of Fowltown, barbarously decorated with human scalps of both sexes, taken within the last six months from the heads of our unfortunate citizens. General McIntosh, who was with General Gaines

---

* These scalps were doubtless the accumulation of many years and of previous wars. The Seminoles had not taken ten scalps since the War of 1812, exclusive of those of Lieutenant Scott's party.

routed a small party of savages near Fowltown, killed one negro and took three prisoners, on one of whom was found the coat of James Champion, of Captain Cumming's company, Fourth Regiment of Infantry, who was killed by the Indians on board of one of our boats descending the river to the relief of Major Muhlenburg. The pocket-book of Mr. Leigh, who was murdered at Cedar Creek on the 21st of January last, was found, in Kinghajah's town, containing several letters addressed to the deceased, and one to General Glascock. About one thousand head of cattle fell into our hands, many of which were recognized by the Georgia militia as having brands and marks of their citizens. Nearly three thousand bushels of corn were found, with other articles useful to the army. Upward of three hundred houses were consumed, leaving a tract of fertile country in ruin, where these wretches might have lived in plenty but for the vile machinations of foreign traders, if not agents."

On the 6th of April the army reached St. Marks, and halted in the vicinity of the fort. The general sent in to the Governor his aide-de-camp, Lieutenant Gadsden, bearing a letter explanatory of his objects and purposes. He had come, he said, "to chastise a savage foe, who, combined with a lawless band of negro brigands, had been for some time past carrying on a cruel and unprovoked war against the citizens of the United States." He had already met and put to flight parties of the hostile Indians. He had received information that those Indians had fled to St. Marks and found protection within its walls; that both Indians and negroes had procured supplies of ammunition there; and that the Spanish garrison, from the smallness of its numbers, was unable to resist the demands of the savages. "To prevent the recurrence of so gross a violation of neutrality, and to exclude our savage enemies from so strong a hold as

St. Marks, I deem it expedient to garrison that fortress with American troops until the close of the present war. This measure is justifiable on the immutable principle of self-defense, and can not but be satisfactory, under existing circumstances, to his Catholic Majesty the King of Spain."

The Governor replied that he had been made to understand General Jackson's letter only with the greatest difficulty, as there was no one within the fort who could properly translate it. He denied that the Indians and negroes had ever obtained supplies, succor, or encouragement from Fort St. Marks. On the contrary, they had menaced the fort with assault because supplies had been refused them. With regard to delivering up the fort intrusted to his care, he had no authority to do so, and must write on the subject to his Government. Meanwhile he prayed General Jackson to suspend his operations. "The sick your Excellency sent in," concluded the polite Governor, "are lodged in the Royal Hospital, and I have afforded them every aid which circumstances admit. I hope your Excellency will give me other opportunities of evincing the desire I have to satisfy you. I trust your Excellency will pardon my not answering you as soon as requested, for reasons which have been given you by your aide-de-camp. I do not accompany this with an English translation, as your Excellency desires, because there is no one in the fort capable thereof, but the before-named William Hambly proposes to translate it to your Excellency in the best manner he can."

This was delivered to General Jackson on the morning of the 7th of April. He instantly replied to it by taking possession of the fort! The Spanish flag was lowered, the Stars and Stripes floated from the flagstaff, and American troops took up their quarters within the fortress. The Governor made no resistance, and indeed could make none. When all was over, he sent to General Jackson a formal protest against his proceedings, to which the general briefly replied: "The occupancy of Fort St. Marks by my troops previous to your assenting to the measure became necessary from the difficulties thrown in the way of an amicable adjustment, notwithstanding my assurances that every arrangement should be made to your satisfaction, and expressing a wish that my movements against our common enemy should not be retarded by a tedious negotiation. I again repeat what has been reiterated to you through my aide-de-camp, Lieutenant Gadsden, that your personal rights and private property shall be respected, that your situation shall be made as comfortable as practicable while compelled to remain in Fort St. Marks, and that transports shall be furnished, as soon as they can be obtained to convey yourself, family, and command to Pensacola."

Alexander Arbuthnot, a Scotch trader among the Indians, was found within the fort, an inmate of the Governor's own quarters. It appears that on the arrival of General Jackson he was preparing to leave St. Marks. His horse, saddled and bridled, was standing at the gate. General Jackson had no sooner taken possession of St. Marks than Arbuthnot became a prisoner. " In Fort St. Marks," wrote General Jackson, " an inmate in the family of the Spanish commandant, an Englishman by the name of Arbuthnot was found. Unable satisfactorily to explain the object of his visiting this country, and there being a combination of circumstances to justify a suspicion that his views were not honest, he was ordered into close confinement."

For two days only the army remained at Fort St. Marks. Suwanee, the far-famed and dread Suwanee, the town of the great chief Boleck, or Bowlegs, the refuge of negroes, was General Jackson's next object.

It was one hundred and seven miles from St. Marks, and the route lay through a flat and swampy wilderness, little known and destitute of forage. On the 9th of April, leaving a strong garrison at the fort, and supplying the troops with rations for eight days, the general again plunged into the forest—the white troops in advance, the Indians, under General McIntosh, a few miles in the rear.

The army made slow progress, wading through extensive sheets of water ; the horses starving for want of forage, and giving out daily in large numbers. Late in the afternoon of the third day the troops reached a " remarkable pond," which the Indian guides said was only six miles from Suwanee town. " Here," says the general, " I should have halted for the night had not six mounted Indians (supposed to be spies), who were discovered, effected their escape. This determined me to attempt by a forced movement to prevent the removal of their effects, and, if possible, themselves from crossing the river, for, my rations being out, it was all-important to secure their supplies for the subsistence of my troops." At sunset, accordingly, the lines were formed, and the whole army rushed forward.

But the prey had been forewarned. A letter from Arbuthnot to his son had reached the place and had been explained to Bowlegs, who had been ever since employed in sending the women and children across the broad Suwanee into those inaccessible retreats which render Florida the best place in the world for such warfare as Indians wage. The troops reached the vicinity of the town, and in a few minutes drove out the enemy and captured the place. The pursuit was continued on the following morning by General Gaines ; but the foe had vanished by a hundred paths, and were no more seen.

In the evening of April 17th the whole army encamped on the level banks of the Suwanee. In the dead of night an incident occurred which can here be related in the language of the same young Tennessee officer who has already narrated for us the capture of the chiefs and their execution. Fortunately for us, he kept a journal of the campaign. This journal, written at the time partly with a decoction of roots and partly with the blood of the journalist*—for ink was not attainable—lay for forty years among his papers, and was copied at length by the obliging hand of his daughter for the readers of these pages. "About midnight of April 18th," wrote our journalist, "the repose of the army, then bivouacked on the plains of the old town of Suwanee, was suddenly disturbed by the deep-toned report of a musket, instantly followed by the sharp crack of the American rifle. The signal to arms was given, and where but a moment before could only be heard the measured tread of the sentinels and the low moaning of the long-leafed pines, now stood five thousand men, armed, watchful, and ready for action. The cause of the alarm was soon made known. Four men, two whites and two negroes, had been captured while attempting to enter the camp. They were taken in charge by the guard, and the army again sank to such repose as war allows her votaries. When morning came it was ascertained that the prisoners were Robert C. Ambrister, a white attendant named Peter B. Cook, and two negro servants—Ambrister being a nephew of the English governor, Cameron, of the Island of New Providence, an ex-lieutenant of British marines, and suspected of being engaged in the business of counseling and furnishing munitions of war to the Indians in furtherance of their

---

* Mr. J. B. Rodgers, of South Rock Island, Tennessee.

contest with the United States. Ignorant of the situation of the American camp, he had blundered into it while endeavoring to reach Suwanee town to meet the Indians, being also unaware that the latter had been driven thence on the previous day by Jackson."

Ambrister was conducted to St. Marks and placed in confinement, together with his companions. The fact that through Arbuthnot the Suwanee people had escaped, thus rendering the last swift march comparatively fruitless, was calculated, it must be owned, to exasperate the mind of General Jackson.

The Seminole War, so called, was over, for the time. On the 20th of April the Georgia troops marched homeward to be disbanded. On the 24th, General McIntosh and his brigade of Indians were dismissed. On the 25th, General Jackson, with his Tennesseeans and regulars, was again at Fort St. Marks. It was forty-six days since he had entered Florida, and thirteen weeks since he left Nashville.

General Jackson, on his homeward march, halted at the fortress of St. Marks, to decide the fate of the prisoners Ambrister and Arbuthnot. He had determined to accord them the indulgence of a trial, and now selected for that purpose a " special court " of fourteen officers, who were ordered to " record all the documents and testimony in the several cases, and their opinion as to the guilt or innocence of the prisoners, and what punishment, if any, should be inflicted."

At noon on the 28th of April the court convened. The members were sworn, and Arbuthnot was arraigned. The charges brought against him were three in number. First charge: Exciting the Creek Indians to war against the United States. Second charge: Acting as a spy, aiding and comforting the enemy, and supplying them with the means of war. Third charge: Exciting the

Indians to murder and destroy William Hambly and Edmund Doyle, and causing their arrest with a view to their condemnation to death and the seizure of their property, on account of their active and zealous exertions to maintain peace between Spain, the United States, and the Indians, they being citizens of the Spanish Government.

The evidence adduced was of two kinds, documentary and personal. The letters and papers that were found on board the prisoner's schooner were all submitted to the court. They proved that the prisoner had sympathized with the Seminoles; that he had considered them an injured people; that he had written many letters entreating the interference in their behalf of English, Spanish, and American authorities; that he had given them notice of the approach of General Jackson's army, and advised them to fly; that he had on all occasions exerted whatever influence he possessed to induce the Indians to live in peace with one another and with their neighbors.

Arbuthnot in his defense called the captain of his vessel, who testified that no arms had been brought to the province by the prisoner, and but small quantities of powder and lead; and that Ambrister had seized the prisoner's schooner and used it for purposes of his own. Arbuthnot's address to the court at the conclusion of the trial was respectful, calm, and able. He commented chiefly upon the hearsay character of the evidence. The "trial" over, the prisoner was removed, and the court deliberated. Two thirds of the court concurred in the following opinion and sentence: "The court, after mature deliberation on the evidence adduced, find the prisoner, A. Arbuthnot, guilty of the first charge, and guilty of the second charge, leaving out the words 'acting as a spy'; and, after mature reflection, sentence him, A. Arbuthnot, to be suspended by the neck until he is dead."

Ambrister was next arraigned. He was accused of aiding and comforting the enemy, and of "levying war against the United States," by assuming command of the Indians and ordering a party of them "to give battle to an army of the United States." It was proved against Ambrister that he had come to Florida to "see the negroes righted"; that he had captured Arbuthnot's schooner, plundered his store, and distributed its contents among his negro and Indian followers; that he had written to New Providence asking that arms and ammunition might be sent to the Indians; and that he had sent a party to "oppose" the American invasion. The last-named fact was proved by a sentence in one of his own letters to the Governor of New Providence. "I expect," wrote Ambrister, March 20, 1818, "that the Americans and Indians will attack us daily. I have sent a party of men to oppose them."

The prisoner made no formal defense, but merely remarked that, "inasmuch as the testimony which was introduced in this case was very explicit, and went to every point the prisoner could wish, he has nothing further to offer in his defense, but puts himself upon the mercy of the honorable court."

The honorable court pronounced him guilty of the principal charge, and sentenced him to be shot. But we are told that, "one of the members of the court requesting a reconsideration of his vote on the sentence, the sense of the court was taken thereon and decided in the affirmative, when the vote was again taken, and the court sentenced the prisoner to receive fifty stripes on his bare back, and to be confined with a ball and chain to hard labor for twelve calendar months."

The trials, which began at noon on the 26th, terminated late in the evening of the 28th, when the proceedings of the court were submitted to the commanding general. On the following morning, before the dawn of day, General Jackson and the main body of his army were in full march for Fort Gadsden. He left at St. Marks a garrison of American troops. The following order with regard to the court and the prisoners it had tried, issued just before his departure, was dated

"CAMP, FOUR MILES NORTH OF ST. MARKS, *April* 29, 1818.

"The commanding general approves the finding and sentence of the court in the case of A. Arbuthnot, and approves the finding and first sentence of the court in the case of Robert C. Ambrister, and disapproves the reconsideration of the sentence of the honorable court in this case.

"It appears, from the evidence and pleading of the prisoner, that he did lead and command within the territory of Spain (being a subject of Great Britain) the Indians in war against the United States, those nations being at peace. It is an established principle of the laws of nations that any individual of a nation making war against the citizens of any other nation, they being at peace, forfeits his allegiance and becomes an outlaw and pirate. This is the case of Robert C. Ambrister, clearly shown by the evidence adduced.

"The commanding general orders that brevet Major A. C. W. Fanning, of the corps of artillery, will have, between the hours of 8 and 9 o'clock, A. M., A. Arbuthnot suspended by the neck with a rope until he is dead, and Robert C. Ambrister to be shot to death, agreeably to the sentence of the court."

The sentences of the general were immediately executed. It is difficult to characterize aright this deplorable tragedy. Arbuthnot was put to death for acts every one of which was innocent, and some of which were eminently praiseworthy. Even Ambrister's fault was one which General Jackson himself would have been certain to commit in the same circumstances. He sent a party to "oppose" the invasion of the province ; and even his seizure of Arbuthnot's schooner seems to have been done to provide his followers with the means of defense. Arbuthnot was convicted upon the evidence of men who had the strongest interest in his conviction. And who presided over the court ? Was it not General Gaines, whose treatment of the Fowltown warriors, first arrogant and then precipitate, was the direct cause of the war and all its horrors ?

Of all the men concerned in this tragedy, General Jackson was perhaps the least blameworthy. We can survey the transaction in its completeness, but he could not. He carried out of the War of 1812 the bitterest recollections of Nichols and Woodbine, who had given protection, succor, and honor to the fugitive Creeks. A train of circumstances led him to the conclusion that Arbuthnot and Ambrister were still doing the work in Florida that Nichols and Woodbine had begun in 1814. He expressly says, in one of his dispatches, that at the beginning of his operations he was " strongly impressed with the belief that this Indian war had been excited by some unprincipled foreign agents," and that the Seminoles were too weak in numbers to have undertaken the war unless they had received assurances of foreign support. Woodbine had actually been in Florida the summer before, brought thither by Arbuthnot. To the " machinations " of these men General Jackson attributed the massacre of Lieutenant Scott, and considered them equally guilty. They were at length in his power, and he then selected fourteen of his officers to examine the evidence against them. After three days' investigation those officers brought in a verdict that accorded exactly with his own previous convictions, as well as with the representations of men who surrounded his person and had an interest in confirming his impressions.

This is not a justification, for it is not permitted to any man to make mistakes of the kind that costs human lives. The execution of Ambrister had some slight shadow of justice, but that of poor Arbuthnot had none, and the violent death of that worthy old man must remain a blot upon the memory of Andrew Jackson. The executions created in England such general and extreme indignation that nothing but the prudence of the ministry prevented a war between the two countries. At home these sad events were little understood, and after a debate of a whole month upon them in Congress the conduct of the general was approved.

In 1821, when Florida, after some years of negotiation, was ceded to the United States, General Jackson was appointed Governor of that Territory by President Monroe. He accepted the appointment, resigned his commission in the army, and set out on his journey. Delays vexatious but unavoidable occurred in the delivery of the province, and even after he had taken possession the Governor was in the worst possible humor. Mrs. Jackson, who accompanied her fiery lord on this occasion, wrote home in August: "There never was a man more disappointed than the general has been. In the first place, he has not the power to appoint one of his friends; which, I thought, was in part the reason of his coming. But far has it exceeded every calculation; it has almost taken his life. Captain Call says it is equal to the Seminole campaign. Well, I knew it would be a ruining concern. I shall not pretend to describe the toils, fatigue, and trouble. Those Spaniards had as lieve die as give up their country. He has had terrible scenes.

The Governor has been put in the calaboose, which is a terrible thing, really." Yes, the Spanish Governor, Colonel Callava, who of all the governors of Pensacola was by far the most agreeable and the most respectable character, had indeed been put into the calaboose. He was a Castilian, of a race akin to the Saxon, of light complexion, a handsome, well-grown man, of dignified presence and refined manners. If an angel from heaven had appeared to General Jackson in the guise of a Spanish governor he would not have liked him, so rooted was his prejudice against Spanish governors. And that Spanish governor from heaven would have found it difficult to so far forget or overlook what General Jackson had formerly done in Florida as to regard the general with an entirely friendly eye. The presence, therefore, of Colonel Callava in Pensacola—particularly after what had occurred previous to the surrender—furnished the material for a grand explosion, provided the Governor and the ex-Governor should by any accident come into collision.

We need not dwell upon the details of this affair, which was more ludicrous than tragic. In a few months General Jackson resigned his office and resumed the life of a planter on the fertile shores of the Cumberland River. He reached the Hermitage November 3, 1821, unspeakably disgusted with his brief exercise of civil authority. He was then fifty-four years of age. Already he had lived, as it were, two lives. He had first assisted to subdue the Western wilderness, and then taken the lead in defending it. He had first broken the power of the Southern Indians, and then, by a series of treaties, regulated the terms upon which they were to live in neighborhood with the conquering race. He had first won by his diligence and skill a fair private estate, and then acquired, by his valor and conduct in war, national

renown and intense popularity. He might well think
that he had done his part, had borne his share of private
and public burdens, and might now, with impaired health
and strength, sit down under his own vine and fig-tree
and rest. That such was his sincere desire and real intention there are sufficient reasons to believe. Civil
service he appears always to have accepted unwillingly,
and resigned gladly. Nothing but a summons to the
field ever completely overcame his reluctance to leave
his happy home; and now that the aspect of the world
was such as to promise a lasting peace to his country,
he had, doubtless, no thought but to pass his remaining
days in the pleasant labors of his farm and the tranquil
enjoyment of his home.

CHAPTER XIX.

A CANDIDATE FOR THE PRESIDENCY.

THE presidential campaign of 1824 was the least instructive one that ever occurred, because it was the most exclusively personal. But it was far from being the least exciting. The long lull in the political firmament had given every one a desire for a renewal of the old excitements, and there was everywhere an eager buzz of preparation. During the last three years of Mr. Monroe's second term the great topic of conversation throughout the country was, Who shall be our next President? Five candidates were frequently mentioned, each of whom had devoted partisans: William H. Crawford, of Georgia, Secretary of the Treasury; John Quincy Adams, Secretary of State; John C. Calhoun, Secretary of War; Henry Clay, Speaker of the House of Representatives; De Witt Clinton, Governor of New York—all strong, able, and popular men. But the name of Jackson had no sooner been presented to the nation by the Legislature of Tennessee, than it was discovered that his popularity was about to render him a most formidable competitor. To promote his presidential prospects his friends caused him to be elected to the Senate of the United States. Pennsylvania soon seconded his nomination, and most of the Southern States showed a strong inclination to support him. Mr. Calhoun withdrew his own name in favor of the victor of New Orleans, and consented to stand for the vice-presidency. The pros-

pects of General Jackson were further improved by Mr.
Crawford being stricken with paralysis, which totally
prostrated him, and, in effect, narrowed the contest to
Adams and Jackson.

John C. Calhoun was elected Vice-President by a
great majority. He received 182 electoral votes out of
261. All New England voted for him except Connecticut and one electoral district of New Hampshire. General Jackson received thirteen electoral votes for the
vice-presidency, and was the choice of two entire states
for that office—Connecticut and Missouri.

Now for the presidency. Mr. Adams was the choice
of seven States, General Jackson of eleven States, Mr.
Clay of three States, Mr. Crawford of three States. Still
no majority. The population of the United States in
1820 was about nine and a half millions. The population of the three States which gave a majority for Mr.
Clay was 1,212,337. The population of the three States
which preferred Mr. Crawford was 1,497,029. The population of the seven States which gave a majority for Mr.
Adams was 3,032,766. The population of the eleven
States which voted for General Jackson was 3,757,756.
It thus appears that General Jackson received more
electoral votes, the vote of more States, and the votes
of more people, than any other candidate. Add to these
facts that General Jackson was the second choice of
Kentucky, Missouri, and Georgia, and it must be admitted that he came nearer being elected by the people
than any other candidate. He was, moreover, a gaining
candidate; every month added to his strength.

The result was not known in all its details when the
time came for Senator Jackson to begin his journey to
Washington in the fall of 1824. That he was confident,
however, of being the successful candidate, was indicated
by Mrs. Jackson's accompanying him to the seat of gov-

ernment. They traveled in their own coach-and-four, I believe, on this occasion. The opposition papers, at least, said so, and descanted upon the fact as an evidence of aristocratic pretensions; considering it antidemocratic to employ four horses to draw a load that four horses sometimes could not tug a mile an hour, and were a month in getting to Washington.

The people having failed to elect a President, it devolved upon the House of Representatives, voting by States, each State having one vote to elect one from the three candidates who had received the highest number of electoral votes. A majority of States being necessary to an election, some one candidate had to secure the vote of thirteen States. The great question was to be decided on the 9th of February, 1825.

The result, when announced by the tellers, surprised almost every one—surprised many of the best-informed politicians who heard it. Upon the first ballot, Mr. Adams received the vote of thirteen States, which was a majority. Maryland and Illinois, which had given popular majorities for Jackson, voted for Adams. Kentucky, Ohio, and Missouri, which had given popular majorities for Clay, voted for Adams. Crawford received the vote of four States—Delaware, North Carolina, Georgia, and Virginia. General Jackson, for whom eleven States had given an electoral majority, received the vote of but seven States in the House.

Was General Jackson, indeed, so heartily acquiescent in his defeat as he seemed to be? He was disappointed and indignant, believing that he had been defrauded of the presidency by a corrupt bargain between Mr. Adams and Mr. Clay. In this belief General Jackson lived and died. His partisans took up the cry, and made it the chief ground of opposition to Mr. Adams's administration.

General Jackson was renominated for the presidency by the Legislature of Tennessee before Mr. Adams had served one year. The general resigned his seat in the Senate, and entered heartily into the schemes of his friends. His popularity, great as it was before, seemed vastly increased by his late defeat, and by the belief, industriously promulgated, that he had been cheated of the office to which the people desired to elevate him.

The campaign of 1828 opened with a stunning flourish of trumpets. Louisiana, like New York, was a doubtful and troublesome State. In 1827 the Legislature of Louisiana, which had refused to recognize General Jackson's services in 1815, invited him to revisit New Orleans, and unite with it in the celebration of the 8th of January, 1828, on the scene of his great victory.

The reception of General Jackson at New Orleans on this occasion was, I presume, the most stupendous thing of the kind that had ever occurred in the United States. Delegations from States as distant as New York were sent to New Orleans to swell the *éclat* of the demonstration. "The morning of the auspicious day," wrote an eyewitness, "dawned upon New Orleans. A thick mist covered the water and the land, and at ten o'clock began to rise into clouds; and when the sun at last appeared, it served only to show the darkness of the horizon threatening a storm in the north. It was at that moment the city became visible, with its steeples, and the forest of masts rising from the waters. At that instant, too, a fleet of steamboats was seen advancing toward the Pocahontas, which had now got under way, with twenty-four flags waving over her lofty decks. Two stupendous boats, lashed together, led the van. The whole fleet kept up a constant fire of artillery, which was answered from several ships in the harbor and from the shore. General Jackson stood on the back gallery of the Pocahontas, his head uncovered, conspicuous to the whole multitude, which literally covered the steamboats, the shipping, and the surrounding shores. The van which bore the Revolutionary soldiers and the remnant of the old Orleans Battalion passed the Pocahontas, and, rounding to, fell down the stream, while acclamations of thousands of spectators rang from the river to the woods and back to the river.

" In this order the fleet, consisting of eighteen steamboats of the first class, passed close to the city, directing their course toward the field of battle. When it was first descried, some horsemen only, the marshals of the day, had reached the ground; but in a few minutes it seemed alive with a vast multitude, brought thither on horseback and in carriages, and poured forth from the steamboats. A line was formed by Generals Planché and Labaltat, and the committee repaired on board the Pocahontas, in order to invite the general to land and meet his brother-soldiers and fellow-citizens. I have no words to describe the scene which ensued."

The festivities continued four days, at the expiration of which the general and his friends re-embarked on board the Pocahontas and returned homeward.

The campaign now set in with its usual severity. General Jackson was accused of every crime, offense, and impropriety that man was ever known to be guilty of. His whole life was subject to the severest scrutiny. Every one of his duels, fights, and quarrels was narrated at length. His connection with Aaron Burr was, of course, a favorite theme. The military executions which he had ordered were all recounted.* John Binns, of Phila-

---

* On February 21, 1815, in an open place near the (then) village of Mobile, the execution occurred of six militiamen, officers and privates,

delphia, issued a series of handbills, each bearing the outline of a coffin-lid, upon which was printed an inscription recording the death of one of these victims. Campaign papers were first started this year. One, entitled We the People, and another, called The Anti-Jackson Expositor, were particularly prominent. The conduct of General Jackson in Florida during his governorship of that Territory was detailed.

The number of electoral votes in 1828 was two hundred and sixty-one. One hundred and thirty-one was a majority. General Jackson received one hundred and seventy-eight; Mr. Adams, eighty-three.

In all Tennessee, Adams and Rush obtained less than three thousand votes. In many towns every vote was cast for Jackson and Calhoun. A distinguished member of the North Carolina Legislature told me that he happened to enter a Tennessee village in the evening of the last day of the presidential election of 1828. He found the whole male population out hunting, the object of the chase being two of their fellow-citizens. He inquired by what crime these men had rendered themselves so obnoxious to their neighbors, and was informed that they had voted against General Jackson! The village, it appeared, had set its heart upon sending up a unanimous vote for the general, and these two voters had frustrated its desire. As the day wore on, the whisky flowed more and more freely, and the result was a universal chase after the two voters, with a view

---

convicted by a court-martial of "mutiny." A body of troops numbering fifteen hundred were drawn up to witness the scene; the men were blindfolded, and each man knelt upon his coffin. Thirty-six soldiers were detailed for the purpose, six to fire at each. The sentence was duly carried out, and for several years the country was excited over the event, and much adverse criticism of General Jackson found expression in the newspapers.—EDITOR.

to tarring and feathering them. They fled to the woods, however, and were not taken.

The news of General Jackson's election to the presidency, I was informed by Major Lewis, created no great sensation at the Hermitage, so certain beforehand were its inmates of a result in accordance with their desires. Mrs. Jackson quietly said:

"Well, for Mr. Jackson's sake, I am glad; for my own part, I never wished it."

The people of Nashville, greatly elated by the success of their general, resolved to celebrate it in the way in which they had long been accustomed to celebrate every important event in his career. A banquet unparalleled should be given in honor of his last triumph. The day appointed for this affair was the 23d of December, the anniversary of the night battle below New Orleans. General Jackson accepted the invitation to be present. Certain ladies of Nashville, meanwhile, were secretly preparing for Mrs. Jackson a magnificent wardrobe, suitable, as they thought, for the adornment of her person when, as mistress of the White House, she would be deemed the first lady in the nation. She was destined never to wear those splendid garments.

For four or five years the health of Mrs. Jackson had been precarious. She had complained occasionally of an uneasy feeling about the region of the heart; and, during the late excitements, she had been subject to sharper pains and palpitation. She died December 22d, late in the evening. Her husband was shocked and grieved beyond expression. It was long, as I was assured by her favorite servant Hannah, before he would believe that she had really breathed her last.

The sad news reached Nashville early on the morning of the 23d, when already the committee of arrangements were busied with the preparations for the general's reception. "The table was well-nigh spread," said one of the papers, "at which all was expected to be hilarity and joy, and our citizens had sallied forth on the morning with spirits light and buoyant, and countenances glowing with animation and hope, when suddenly the scene is changed: congratulations are turned into expressions of condolence, tears are substituted for smiles, and sincere and general mourning pervades the community."

General Jackson never recovered from the shock of his wife's death. He was never quite the same man afterward. It subdued his spirit and corrected his speech. Except on occasions of extreme excitement, few and far between, he never again used what is commonly called "profane language," not even the familiar phrase, "By the Eternal." There were times, of course, when his fiery passions asserted themselves; when he uttered wrathful words; when he wished even to throw off the robes of office, as he once said, that he might call his enemies to a dear account. But these were rare occurrences. He mourned deeply and ceaselessly the loss of his truest friend, and was often guided in his domestic affairs by what he supposed would have been her will if she had been there to make it known.

CHAPTER XX.

Haggard with grief and watching, "twenty years older in a night," as one of his friends remarked, the President-elect was compelled to enter without delay upon the labor of preparing for his journey to Washington. His inaugural address was written at the house of Major Lewis, near Nashville. But one slight alteration was made in this document after the general reached the seat of government. Before leaving home, the general drew up a series of rules for the guidance of his administration, one of which was that no member of his Cabinet should be his successor. The party left Nashville on a Sunday afternoon about the middle of January. The journey to Washington—every one knows what it must have been. The complete, the instantaneous acquiescence of the people of the United States in the decision of a constitutional majority was well illustrated on this occasion. The steamboat that conveyed the general and his party down the Cumberland to the Ohio and up the Ohio to Pittsburg—a voyage of several days —was saluted or cheered as often as it passed a human habitation. At Cincinnati it seemed as if all Ohio, and at Pittsburg as if all Pennsylvania, had rushed forth to shout a welcome to the President-elect. Indeed, the whole country appeared to more than acquiesce in the result of the election.

The day of the inauguration was one of the brightest

and balmiest of the spring. Mr. Webster, in his comic manner, remarks: "I never saw such a crowd here before. Persons have come five hundred miles to see General Jackson, and they really seem to think that the country is rescued from some dreadful danger!" The ceremony over, the President drove from the Capitol to the White House, followed soon by a great part of the crowd who had witnessed the inauguration. Judge Story, a strenuous Adams man, did not enjoy the scene which the apartments of the "palace," as he styles it, presented on this occasion. "After the ceremony was over," he wrote, "the President went to the palace to receive company, and there he was visited by immense crowds of all sorts of people, from the highest and most polished down to the most vulgar and gross in the nation. I never saw such a mixture. The reign of King Mob seemed triumphant. I was glad to escape from the scene as soon as possible."

Soon after General Jackson arrived at the seat of government he informed Edward Livingston, of Louisiana, that Mr. Van Buren was the foreordained Secretary of State of the incoming Administration, and offered him the choice of the seats remaining. Mr. Livingston, just then elected to the Senate, preferred his senatorship to any office in the Government except the one already appropriated. In distributing the six great offices, General Jackson assigned two to the North, two to the West, and two to the South.

Mr. Van Buren accepted the first place without hesitation, resigned the governorship of New York after holding it seventy days, and entered upon his duties at Washington three weeks after the inauguration. Samuel D. Ingham, of Pennsylvania, was appointed to the second place in the Cabinet—that of Secretary of the Treasury. John H. Eaton, Senator from Tennessee, was appointed

Secretary of War. General Jackson was, from the first, determined to have in his Cabinet one of his own Tennessee circle of friends, and Mr. Eaton was the one selected. The Navy Department was assigned to John Branch, for many years a Senator from North Carolina. John Macpherson Berrien, of Georgia, was appointed Attorney-General. William T. Barry, of Kentucky, was appointed Postmaster-General. Such was the first Cabinet of the new President. With the exception of Mr. Van Buren, its members had no great influence over the measures of their chief, and play no important part in the general history of the times.

No sooner had General Jackson announced the names of the gentlemen who were to compose his Cabinet, than an opposition to one of them manifested itself of a peculiar and most virulent character. Mr. Eaton, the President's friend and neighbor, was the object of this opposition, the grounds of which must be particularly stated, for it led to important results. A certain William O'Neal kept at Washington for many years a large, old-fashioned tavern, where members of Congress in considerable numbers boarded during the sessions of the national Legislature. William O'Neal had a daughter, sprightly and beautiful, who aided him and his wife in entertaining his boarders. Peg O'Neal, as she was called, was so lively in her deportment, so free in her conversation, that, had she been born twenty years later, she would have been called one of the " fast " girls of Washington.

When Major Eaton first came to Washington as a Senator of the United States, in the year 1818, he took board at Mr. O'Neal's tavern, and continued to reside there every winter for ten years. He became acquainted, of course, with the family, including the vivacious and attractive Peg. When General Jackson came to the city as Senator in 1823, he also went to live with the O'Neals, whom he had known in Washington before it had become the seat of government. For Mrs. O'Neal, who was a remarkably efficient woman, he had a particular respect. Even during his presidency, when he was supposed to visit no one, it was one of his favorite relaxations, when worn out with business, to stroll with Major Lewis across the "old fields" near Washington to the cottage where Mrs. O'Neal lived in retirement, and enjoy an hour's chat with the old lady. Mrs. Jackson, also, during her residence in Washington in 1825, became attached to Mrs. O'Neal and to her daughter.

In the course of time Miss O'Neal became the wife of Purser Timberlake, of the United States Navy, and the mother of two children. In 1828 came the news that Mr. Timberlake, then on duty in the Mediterranean, had cut his throat in a fit of melancholy, induced, it was said, by previous intoxication. On hearing this intelligence, Major Eaton, then a widower, felt an inclination to marry Mrs. Timberlake, for whom he had entertained an attachment quite as tender as a man could lawfully indulge for the wife of a friend and brother-mason. He took the precaution to consult General Jackson on the subject. "Why, yes, major," said the general, "if you love the woman, and she will have you, marry her, by all means." Major Eaton mentioned, what the general well knew, that Mrs. Timberlake's reputation in Washington had not escaped reproach, and that Major Eaton himself was supposed to have been too intimate with her. "Well," said the general, "your marrying her will disprove these charges, and restore Peg's good name." And so, perhaps, it might, if Major Eaton had not been taken into the Cabinet.

Eaton and Mrs. Timberlake were married in January, 1829, a few weeks before General Jackson arrived at the seat of government. As soon as it was whispered about Washington that Major Eaton was to be a member of the new Cabinet, it occurred with great force to the minds of certain ladies, who supposed themselves to be at the head of society at the capital, that in that case Peg O'Neal would be the wife of a Cabinet minister, and, as such, entitled to admission into their own sacred circle.

From the moment the scandal reached his ears the new President made Mr. Eaton's cause his own. He sent a confidential agent to New York to investigate one of the stories. He wrote so many letters and statements in relation to this business that Major Lewis, who lived in the White House, was worn out with the nightly toil of copying. The entire mass of the secret and confidential writings relating to Mrs. Eaton, all dated in the summer and autumn of 1829, and most of them originally in General Jackson's hand, would fill about one hundred and sixty of these pages. And besides these, there was a large number of papers and documents not deemed important enough for preservation. General Jackson, indeed, brought to the defense of Mrs. Eaton all the fire and resolution with which, forty years before, he had silenced every whisper against Mrs. Jackson. He considered the cases of the two ladies parallel. His zeal in behalf of Mrs. Eaton was a manifestation or consequence of his wrath against the calumniators of his wife. At length the President of the United States brought this matter before his Cabinet. The members of the Cabinet having assembled one day in the usual place, the accusers were brought before them, when the President endeavored to demonstrate that Mrs. Eaton was ·'as chaste as snow." Whether the efforts of the President had or had not the effect of convincing the ladies of Washington that Mrs. Eaton was worthy of admission into their circle, shall in due time be related. Upon a point of that nature ladies are not convinced easily. Meanwhile, the suitors for presidential favor are advised to make themselves visible at the lady's receptions. A card in Mrs. Eaton's card-basket is not unlikely to be a winning card.

CHAPTER XXI.

IT is delightful to observe with what a scrupulous conscientiousness the early Presidents of this republic disposed of the places in their gift. Washington demanded to be satisfied on three points with regard to an applicant for office : Is he honest ? Is he capable ? Has he the confidence of his fellow-citizens ? Not till these questions were satisfactorily answered did he deign to inquire respecting the political opinions of a candidate. Private friendship between the President and an applicant was absolutely an obstacle to his appointment, so fearful was the President of being swayed by private motives. " My friend," he says, in one of his letters, " I receive with cordial welcome. He is welcome to my house and welcome to my heart; but, with all his good qualities, he is not a man of business. His opponent, with all his politics so hostile to me, *is* a man of business. My private feelings have nothing to do in the case. I am not George Washington, but President of the United States. As George Washington, I would do this man any kindness in my power ; as President of the United States, I can do nothing." The example of General Washington was followed by his successors.

Up to the hour of the delivery of General Jackson's inaugural address it was supposed that the new President would act upon the principles of his predecessors. In his former letters he had taken strong ground against partisan appointments, and when he resigned his seat in the Senate he had advocated two amendments to the Constitution, designed to limit and purify the exercise of the appointing power. One of these proposed amendments forbade the re-election of a President, and the other the appointment of members of Congress to any office not judicial.

The sun had not gone down upon the day of his inauguration before it was known in all official circles in Washington that the "reform" alluded to in the inaugural address meant a removal from office of all who had conspicuously opposed, and an appointment to office of those who had conspicuously aided, the election of the new President. The work was promptly begun. Colonel Benton will not be suspected of overstating the facts respecting the removals, but he admits that their number, during this year (1829) was six hundred and ninety. His estimate of six hundred and ninety does not include the little army of clerks and others who were at the disposal of some of the six hundred and ninety. The estimate of two thousand includes all who lost their places in consequence of General Jackson's accession to power; and, though the exact number can not be ascertained, I presume it was not less than two thousand. Colonel Benton says that of the eight thousand postmasters, only four hundred and ninety-one were removed; but he does not add, as he might have added, that the four hundred and ninety-one vacated places comprised nearly all in the department that were worth having. Nor does he mention that the removal of the postmasters of half a dozen great cities was equivalent to the removal of many hundreds of clerks, bookkeepers, and carriers.

In the eagerness of his desire to "stand by his friends," the President was brought into collision with the

Bank of the United States, a truly imposing and powerful institution in 1829. Its capital was thirty-five millions. The public money deposited in its vaults averaged six or seven millions; its private deposits, six millions more; its circulation, twelve millions; its discounts, more than forty millions a year; its annual profits, more than three millions. Besides the parent bank at Philadelphia with its marble palace and hundred clerks, there were twenty-five branches in the towns and cities of the Union, each of which had its president, cashier, and board of directors. The employees of the bank were more than five hundred in number, all men of standing and influence, all liberally salaried. In every county of the Union, in every nation on the globe, were stockholders of the Bank of the United States. One fifth of its stock was owned by foreigners. One fourth of its stock was held by women, orphans, and the trustees of charity funds—so high, so unquestioned was its credit. Its bank notes were as good as gold in every part of the country. From Maine to Georgia, from Georgia to Astoria, a man could travel and pass these notes at every point without discount. Nay, in London, Paris, Rome, Cairo, Calcutta, or St. Petersburg, the notes of the Bank of the United States were worth a fraction more or a fraction less than their value at home, according to the current rate of exchange. They could usually be sold at a premium at the remotest commercial centers. It was not uncommon for the stock of the bank to be sold at a premium of forty per cent. The directors of this bank were twenty-five in number, of whom five were appointed by the President of the United States. The bank and its branches received and disbursed the entire revenue of the nation. At the head of this great establishment was the once renowned Nicholas Biddle.

General Jackson had no thought of the bank until

he had been President two months. He came to Washington anticipating but a single term, during which the question of rechartering the bank was not expected to come up. The bank was chartered in 1816 for twenty years, which would not expire until 1836, three years after General Jackson hoped to be at the Hermitage once more, never to leave it. The first intercourse, too, between the bank and the new Administration was in the highest degree courteous and agreeable. A large payment was to be made of the public debt early in the summer, and the manner in which the bank managed that affair, at some loss and much inconvenience to itself, but greatly to the advantage of the public and to the credit of the Government, won from the Secretary of the Treasury a warm eulogium.

But while this affair was going on so pleasantly, trouble was brewing in another quarter. Isaac Hill, from New Hampshire, then Second Comptroller of the treasury, was a great man at the White House. He had a grievance. Jeremiah Mason, one of the three great lawyers of New England, a Federalist, a friend of Daniel Webster and of Mr. Adams, had been appointed to the presidency of the branch of the United States Bank at Portsmouth, New Hampshire—much to the disgust of Isaac Hill and other Jackson men of that State. Isaac Hill desired the removal of Mr. Mason, and the appointment in his place of a gentleman who was a friend of the new Administration.

Mr. Hill caused petitions to be addressed to the directors of the bank, in which Mr. Mason was accused of partiality, haughtiness, mismanagement, and his removal demanded. Mr. Biddle went himself to Portsmouth, where he spent six days in investigating the charges, and satisfied himself that they were groundless. He informed the Secretary of the Treasury, who had addressed him on the subject, that the directors would not remove a faithful servant for political reasons. So the Bank of the United States triumphed over Isaac Hill and the Administration. It was a dear victory.

Near the close of the new President's first message was the famous passage which sounded the first note of war against the United States Bank: "The charter of the Bank of the United States expires in 1836, and its stockholders will most probably apply for a renewal of their privileges. In order to avoid the evils resulting from precipitancy in a measure involving such important principles and such deep pecuniary interests, I feel that I can not, in justice to the parties interested, too soon present it to the deliberate consideration of the Legislature and the people. Both the constitutionality and the expediency of the law creating this bank are well questioned by a large portion of our fellow-citizens; and it must be admitted by all that it has failed in the great end of establishing a uniform and sound currency."

The Senate retorted by rejecting the nomination of Isaac Hill to the second comptrollership of the Treasury, which the President amended by causing Mr. Hill to be elected Senator from New Hampshire. Many other nominations were rejected, and the great bank in many ways frustrated and defied the President. After years of loud and vehement strife, the rechartering of the United States Bank was prevented by him, and it ceased to exist as a national institution.

Congress met on the 7th of December, 1829. Such was the strength of the Administration in the House of Representatives, that Andrew Stephenson was re-elected to the speakership by one hundred and fifty-two votes out of one hundred and ninety-one. This Congress, however, came in with the Administration, and had been elected when General Jackson was elected. This was the session signalized by the great debate between Mr. Hayne and Mr. Webster, the first of many debates upon nullification.

It had been a custom in Washington, for twenty years, to celebrate the birthday (April 13th) of Thomas Jefferson, the apostle of democracy. As General Jackson was regarded by his party as the great restorer and exemplifier of Jeffersonian principles, it was natural that they should desire to celebrate the festival, this year, with more than usual *éclat*. It was so resolved. A banquet was the mode selected; to which the President, the Vice-President, the Cabinet, many leading members of Congress, and other distinguished persons, were invited. When the regular toasts were over, the President was called upon for a volunteer, and gave it: "Our Federal Union: It must be preserved."

Mr. Calhoun gave the next toast: "The Union: Next to our liberty the most dear: may we all remember that it can only be preserved by respecting the rights of the States, and distributing equally the benefit and burden of the Union."

It was supposed, at the time, that the toast offered by the President was an impromptu. On the contrary, the toast was prepared with singular deliberation, and was designed to produce the precise effect it did produce. Major Lewis favors the reader with the following interesting reminiscence: "This celebrated toast, 'The Federal Union: It must be preserved,' was a cool, deliberate act. The United States Telegraph, General Duff Green's paper, published a programme of the proceedings for the celebration the day before, to which the general's attention had been drawn by a friend, with the suggestion that he had better read it. This he did in the course of the evening, and came to the conclusion that the celebration was to be a nullification affair altogether. With this impression on his mind, he prepared early the next morning (the day of the celebration) three toasts, which he brought with him when he came into his office, where he found Major Donelson and myself reading the morning papers. After taking his seat he handed them to me and asked me to read them, and tell him which I preferred. I ran my eye over them and then handed him the one I liked best. He handed them to Major Donelson also, with the same request, who, on reading them, agreed with me. He said he preferred that one himself, for the reason that it was shorter and more expressive. He then put that one into his pocket, and threw the others into the fire. That is the true history of the toast the general gave on the Jefferson birthday celebration in 1830, which fell among the nullifiers like an exploded bomb!"

The year 1829 had not closed before General Jackson was resolved to do all that in him lay to secure the election of Mr. Van Buren as his successor to the presidency. Nor did that year come to an end before he began to act in furtherance of the project. "All through the summer and fall of 1829," writes Major Lewis, "General Jackson was in very feeble health, and in December of the same year his friends became seriously alarmed for his safety. It occurred to me that General Jackson's name, though he might be dead, would prove a powerful lever, if judiciously used, in raising Mr. Van Buren to the presidency. I therefore determined to get the general, if possible, to write a letter to some friend, to be used at the next succeeding presidential election (in case of his death), expressive of the confidence he reposed in Mr. Van Buren's abilities, patriotism, and qualifications for any station, even the highest within the gift of the people. He accordingly wrote a letter to his old friend Judge Overton, and handed it to me to copy, with authority to make such alterations as I might think proper. After copying it (having made only a few verbal alterations) I requested him to read it, and, if satisfied with it, to sign it. He read it, and said it would do, and then put his name to it, remarking as he returned it to me:

"'If I die, you have my permission to make such use of it as you may think most desirable.'"

The letter to Judge Overton contained these words: "Permit me here to say of Mr. Van Buren, that I have found him everything that I could desire him to be, and believe him not only deserving my confidence but the confidence of the nation. Instead of his being selfish and intriguing, as has been represented by some of his opponents, I have ever found him frank, open, candid, and manly. As a counselor, he is able and prudent; republican in his principles, and one of the most pleasant men to do business with I ever saw. He, my dear friend, is well qualified to fill the highest office in the gift of the people, who in him will find a true friend ard safe depository of their rights and liberty."

Judge Overton, I believe, never knew the purpose for which this letter was written. The copy retained was signed by General Jackson and placed among the secret papers of Major Lewis, where it reposed until copied for the readers of these pages.

A new man was summoned to the councils of the President—Lewis Cass, Governor of the Territory of Michigan, who was installed as head of the Department of War in July. The vacant attorney-generalship was conferred upon Mr. Roger B. Taney, then Attorney-General of Maryland, afterward the Chief Justice of the Supreme Court of the United States. Mr. Taney was a lawyer of the first distinction in his native State. He was one of the Federalists who had given a zealous support to General Jackson in 1828.

At the next session of Congress the Senate confirmed the nominations of Edward Livingston, Louis McLane, Levi Woodbury, Lewis Cass, and Roger B. Taney, to their respective places in the Cabinet. Not so the nomination of Mr. Van Buren to the post of British minister. Mr. Calhoun, at that time, in common with most of the opposition, attributed to the machinations of Mr. Van Buren his rupture with the President and the dissolution of the Cabinet. Mr. Clay and Mr. Webster were of the opinion that it was Mr. Van Buren who had induced the President to adopt the New York system of party re movals. The leaders of the Senate resolved upon the rejection of Mr. Van Buren.

The rejection secured Mr. Van Buren's political fortune. His elevation to the presidency, long before desired and intended by General Jackson, became from that hour one of his darling objects. The "party," also, took him up with a unanimity and enthusiasm that left the wire-pullers of the White House little to do. Letters of remonstrance and approbation, signed by influential members of the party, were sent over the sea to Mr. Van Buren, who soon found that his rejection was one of the most fortunate events of his public life.

The last important act of President Jackson's first term was his veto of the bill to recharter the United States Bank, which he accompanied by a message of singular effectiveness. Concerning the financial and legal principles laid down in this important document financiers and lawyers differ in opinion. The office of the present chronicler is to state that the bank-veto message of President Jackson came with convincing power upon a majority of the people of the United States. It settled the question. It was the singular fortune of the bank-veto message to delight equally the friends and foes of the bank. The opposition circulated it as a campaign document! Duff Green published it in his extra Telegraph, calling upon all the opponents of the Administration to give it the widest publicity, since it would damn the Administration wherever it was read. The New York American characterized it thus: "It is indeed and verily beneath contempt. It is an appeal of ignorance to ignorance, of prejudice to prejudice, of the most unblushing partisan hostility to the obsequiousness of partisan servility. No man in the Cabinet proper will be willing to share the ignominy of preparing or approving such a paper."

Nicholas Biddle himself was enchanted with it, for he thought it had saved the bank by destroying the bank's great enemy. "You ask," he wrote to Henry Clay, "what is the effect of the veto? My impression is, that it is working as well as the friends of the bank and of the country could desire."

The result of the election astonished everybody. Not the wildest Jackson man in his wildest moment had anticipated a victory quite so overwhelming. Two hundred and eighty-eight was the whole number of electoral votes in 1832. General Jackson received two hundred and nineteen—seventy-four more than a majority. Mr. Van Buren, for the vice-presidency, received one hundred and eighty-nine electoral votes—forty-four more than a majority.

CHAPTER XXII.

THE SECOND TERM.

THE triumphant re-election of General Jackson in 1832 was a sore disappointment to Mr. Calhoun, and to his friends the "nullifiers" of South Carolina.

The War of 1812 left the country burdened with a debt of one hundred and thirty millions of dollars, and blessed with a great number of small manufactories. The debt and the manufactories were both results of the war. By cutting off the supply of foreign manufactured articles, the war had produced upon the home manufacturing interests the effect of a prohibitory tariff. To pay the interest of this great debt, and occasional installments of the principal, it was necessary for the Government to raise a far larger revenue than had ever before been collected in the United States. The new manufacturing interests asked that the duties should be so regulated as to afford some part of that complete protection which the war had given it. The peace, that had been welcomed with such wild delight in 1815, had prostrated entire branches of manufacture to which the war had given a sudden development.

Among those who advocated the claims of the manufacturers in the session of 1815-'16, and strove to have the protective principle permanently incorporated into the revenue legislation of Congress, the most active, the most zealous, was John C. Calhoun, member of the House of Representatives from South Carolina. He

spoke often on the subject and he spoke unequivocally.
Mr. Clay, who was then the friend, ally, and messmate
of Mr. Calhoun, admitted that the Carolinian had surpassed himself in the earnestness with which he labored
in the cause of protection. One of his arguments was
drawn from the condition of Poland at the time. "The
country in Europe" said he, "having the most skillful
workmen, is broken up. It is to us, if wisely used, more
valuable than the repeal of the Edict of Nantes was to
England. She had the prudence to profit by it; let us
not discover less political sagacity. Afford to inge-
nuity and industry immediate and AMPLE PROTECTION,
and they will not fail to give a preference to this free
and happy country."

The protectionists, led by Messrs. Clay and Calhoun,
triumphed in 1816. In the tariff bill of 1820 the principle was carried further, and still further in those of 1824
and 1828. But about the year 1824 it began to be
thought that the advantages of the system were enjoyed
chiefly by the Northern States, and the South hastened
to the conclusion that the protective system was the
cause of its lagging behind. There was, accordingly, a
considerable Southern opposition to the tariff of 1824,
and a general Southern opposition to that of 1828. In
the latter year, however, the South elected to the presidency General Jackson, whose votes and whose writings
had committed him to the principle of protection. Southern politicians felt that the general, as a Southern man,
was more likely to further their views than Messrs.
Adams and Clay, both of whom were peculiarly devoted
to protection.

As the first years of General Jackson's administration
wore away without affording to the South the "relief"
which they had hoped from it, the discontent of the
Southern people increased. Circumstances gave them a

new and telling argument. In 1831 the public debt had been so far diminished as to render it certain that in three years the last dollar of it would be paid. The Government had been collecting about twice as much revenue as its annual expenditures required. In three years, therefore, there would be an annual surplus of twelve or thirteen millions of dollars. The South demanded with almost a united voice, that the duties should be reduced so as to make the revenue equal to the expenditure, and that, in making this reduction, the principle of protection should be, in effect, abandoned. Protection should thenceforth be "incidental" merely. The session of 1831–'32 was the one during which Southern gentlemen hoped to effect this great change in the policy of the country. The President's message, as we have seen, also announced that, in view of the speedy extinction of the public debt, it was high time that Congress should prepare for the threatened surplus.

The case was one of real difficulty. It was a case for a statesman. To reduce the revenue thirteen millions, at one indiscriminate swoop, might close half the workshops in the country. At the same time, for the United States to go on raising thirteen millions a year more than was necessary for carrying on the government would have been an intolerable absurdity.

Mr. Clay, after an absence from the halls of Congress of six years, returned to the Senate in December, 1831 —an illustrious figure, the leader of the opposition, its candidate for the presidency, his old renown enhanced by his long exile from the scene of his well-remembered triumphs. The galleries filled when he was expected to speak. He was in the vigor of his prime. He never spoke so well as then, nor as often, nor so long, nor with so much applause. But he either could not or dared not undertake the choking of the surplus. What wise, complete, far-reaching measure *can* a candidate for the presidency link his fortunes to ? He wounded, without killing it; and he was compelled, at a later day, to do what it had been glorious voluntarily to attempt in 1832. He proposed merely that "the duties upon articles imported from foreign countries, and not coming into competition with similar articles made or produced within the United States, be forthwith abolished, except the duties upon wines and silks, and that those be reduced." After a debate of months' duration, a bill in accordance with this proposition passed both Houses, and was signed by the President. It preserved the protective principle intact; it reduced the income of the Government about three millions of dollars; and it inflamed the discontent of the South to such a degree that one State, under the influence of a man of force, became capable of—nullification.

The President signed the bill, as he told his friends, because he deemed it an approach to the measure required. His influence, during the session, had been secretly exerted in favor of compromise. The President thought that the just course lay between the two extremes of abandoning the protective principle and of reducing the duties in total disregard of it.

Here was the opportunity of the nullifiers. A convention of the people of South Carolina met at Columbia, November 19, 1832, which passed an "ordinance" declaring that the tariff law of 1828, and the amendment to the same of 1832, were "null, void, and no law, nor binding upon this State, its officers or citizens," and that no duties enjoined by that law or its amendment ' shall be paid, or permitted to be paid, in the State of South Carolina, after the first day of February, 1833."

The message of the new Governor indorsed the acts of the convention in the strongest language possible.

"I recognize," said Governor Hayne, "no allegiance as paramount to that which the citizens of South Carolina owe to the State of their birth or their adoption." He said more: "If the sacred soil of Carolina should be polluted by the footsteps of an invader, or be stained with the blood of her citizens, shed in her defense, I trust in Almighty God that no son of hers, native or adopted, who has been nourished at her bosom, or been cherished by her bounty, will be found raising a parricidal arm against our common mother."

The Legislature instantly responded to the message by passing the acts requisite for carrying the ordinance into practical effect. The Governor was authorized to accept the services of volunteers, who were to hold themselves in readiness to march at a moment's warning. The State resounded with the noise of warlike preparation. Blue cockades with a palmetto button in the center appeared upon thousands of hats, bonnets, and bosoms. Medals were struck ere long, bearing this inscription: "John C. Calhoun, First President of the Southern Confederacy." The Legislature proceeded soon to fill the vacancy created in the Senate of the United States by the election of Mr. Hayne to the governorship. John C. Calhoun, Vice-President of the United States, was the individual selected, and Mr. Calhoun accepted his seat. He resigned the vice-presidency, and began his journey to Washington in December, leaving his State in the wildest ferment.

The President baffled and brought to naught the misguided men who originated and sustained this alarming complication. General Winfield Scott was quietly ordered to Charleston, for the purpose, as the President confidentially informed the collector, "of superintending the safety of the ports of the United States in that vicinity." Other changes were made in the disposition of naval and military forces, designed to enable the President to act with swift efficiency if there should be occasion to act. If ever a man was resolved to accomplish a purpose, General Jackson was resolved on this occasion to preserve intact the authority with which he had been intrusted. Nor can any language do justice to the fury of his contemptuous wrath against the author and fomenter of all this trouble.

Congress met on the 3d of December, 1832. Mr. Calhoun had not reached Washington, and his intention to resign the vice-presidency was not known there. The message reveals few traces of the loud and threatening contentions amid which it was produced. The troubles in South Carolina were dismissed in a single paragraph, which expressed a hope of a speedy adjustment of the difficulty.

While Congress was listening to this calm and suggestive message, the President was absorbed in the preparation of another document, and one of a very different description. A pamphlet containing the proceedings of the South Carolina Convention reached him on one of the last days of November. It moved him profoundly; for this fiery spirit loved his country as few men have loved it. Though he regarded those proceedings as the fruit of John C. Calhoun's ambition and resentment, he rose on this occasion above personal considerations, and conducted himself with that union of daring and prudence which had given him such signal success in war. He went to his office alone, and began to dash off page after page of the memorable proclamation which was soon to electrify the country. He wrote with that great steel pen of his, and with such rapidity, that he was obliged to scatter the written pages all over the table to let them dry. A gentleman who came in when the President had written fifteen or twenty pages, observed that three of them were glistening with wet ink at the same moment. The warmth, the glow, the passion, the eloquence of that proclamation were produced then and there by the President's own hand.

To these pages were added many more of notes and memoranda which had been accumulating in the Presidential hat for some weeks, and the whole collection was then placed in the hands of Mr. Livingston, the Secretary of State, who was requested to draw up the proclamation in proper form. Major Lewis writes to me: " Mr. Livingston took the papers to his office, and in the course of three or four days brought the proclamation to the general, and left it for his examination. After reading it, he came into my room and remarked that Mr. Livingston had not correctly understood his notes; there were portions of the draft, he added, which were not in accordance with his views, and must be altered. He then sent his messenger for Mr. Livingston, and pointed out to him the passages which did not represent his views, and requested him to take it back with him and make the alterations he had suggested. This was done, and, the second draft being satisfactory, he ordered it to be published. I will add that, before the proclamation was sent to press to be published, I took the liberty of suggesting to the general whether it would not be best to leave out that portion to which, I was sure, the State-rights party would particularly object. He refused. " ' Those are my views,' said he with great decision of manner, 'and I will not change them nor strike them out.' "

This celebrated paper was dated December 11, 1832. The word proclamation does not describe it. It reads more like the last appeal of a sorrowing but resolute father to wayward, misguided sons. Argument, warning, and entreaty were blended in its composition. It began by calmly refuting, one by one, the leading positions of the nullifiers. The *right to annul* and the *right to secede*, as claimed by them, were shown to be incompatible with the fundamental idea and main object of the Constitution, which was " to form a more perfect Union." That the tariff act complained of did operate unequally was granted, but so did every revenue law that had ever been or could ever be passed. The right of a State to secede was strongly denied. " To say that any State may at pleasure secede from the Union, is to say that the United States are not a nation." The individual States are not completely sovereign, for they voluntarily resigned part of their sovereignty. " How can that State be said to be sovereign and independent whose citizens owe obedience to laws not made by it, and whose magistrates are sworn to disregard those laws, when they come in conflict with those passed by another ? "

Finally, the people of South Carolina were distinctly given to understand that, in case any forcible resistance to the laws were attempted by them, the attempt would be resisted by the combined power and resources of the other States. For one word, however, of this kind, there were a hundred of entreaty. " Fellow-citizens of my native State," exclaimed the President, " let me not only admonish you, as the First Magistrate of our common country, not to incur the penalty of its laws, but use the influence that a father would over his children whom he saw rushing to certain ruin. In that paternal language, with that paternal feeling, let me tell you, my countrymen, that you are deluded by men who are either deceived themselves or wish to deceive you."

Such were the tone and manner of this celebrated proclamation. It was clear in statement, forcible in argument, vigorous in style, and glowing with the fire of a genuine and enlightened patriotism. The proclamation was received at the North with an enthusiasm that seemed unanimous, and was nearly so. The opposition press bestowed the warmest encomiums upon it. Three days after its appearance in the newspapers of New York, an immense meeting was held in the Park for the purpose of stamping it with metropolitan approval. Faneuil Hall, in Boston, was quick in responding to it, and there were Union meetings in every large town of the Northern States. In Tennessee, North Carolina, Virginia, Maryland, Delaware, Missouri, Louisiana, and Kentucky the proclamation was generally approved as an act, though its extreme Federal positions found many opponents.

In South Carolina, however, it did but inflame the prevailing excitement. The Legislature of that State, being still in session, immediately passed the following resolution :

" *Whereas*, The President of the United States has issued his proclamation, denouncing the proceedings of this State, calling upon the citizens thereof to renounce their primary allegiance, and threatening them with military coercion, unwarranted by the Constitution and utterly inconsistent with the existence of a free State : Be it, therefore,

" *Resolved*, That his Excellency the Governor be requested forthwith to issue his proclamation, warning the good people of this State against the attempt of the President of the United States to seduce them from their allegiance, exhorting them to disregard his vain menaces, and to be prepared to sustain the dignity and protect the liberty of the State against the arbitrary measures proposed by the President."

Governor Hayne issued his proclamation accordingly, and a most pugnacious document it was. When the

proclamation reached Washington, the President forthwith replied to it by asking Congress for an increase of
powers adequate to the impending collision. The message in which he made this request, dated January 16,
1833, gave a brief history of events in South Carolina
and of the measures hitherto adopted by the Administration; repeated the arguments of the recent proclamation and added others; stated the legal points
involved, and asked of Congress such an increase of
executive powers as would enable the Government, if
necessary, to close ports of entry, remove threatened
custom-houses, detain vessels, and protect from State
prosecution such citizens of South Carolina as should
choose or be compelled to pay the obnoxious duties.

Mr. Calhoun was in his place in the Senate-chamber
when this message was read. He had arrived two weeks
before, after a journey which one of his biographers
compares to that of Luther to the Diet of Worms. He
met averted faces and estranged friends everywhere on
his route, we are told; and only now and then some
daring man found courage to whisper in his ear, "If you
are sincere, and are sure of your cause, go on, in God's
name, and fear nothing." Washington was curious to
know, we are further assured, what the arch-nullifier
would do when the oath to support the Constitution of
the United States was proposed to him. "The floor of the
Senate-chamber and the galleries were thronged with
spectators. They saw him take the oath with a solemnity and dignity appropriate to the occasion, and then
calmly seat himself on the right of the chair, among his
old political friends, nearly all of whom were now ar-
rayed against him."

After the President's message had been read, Mr. Calhoun rose to vindicate himself and his State, which he
did with that singular blending of subtlety and force,

truth and sophistry, which characterized his later efforts. He declared himself still devoted to the Union, and said that, if the Government were restored to the principles of 1798, he would be the last man in the country to question its authority.

A bill conceding to the President the additional powers requested in his message of January 16th was promptly reported and finally passed. It was nicknamed, at the time, the " Force Bill," and was debated with the heat and acrimony which might have been expected. As other measures of Congress rendered this bill unnecessary, and it had no practical effect whatever, we need not dwell upon its provisions nor review the debates upon it. It passed, by majorities unusually large, late in February.

The 1st of February, the dreaded day which was to be the first of a fratricidal war, had gone by, and yet no hostile and no nullifying act had been done in South Carolina. How was this? Did those warlike words mean nothing? Was South Carolina repentant? It is asserted by the old Jacksonians that one citizen of South Carolina was exceedingly frightened as the 1st of February drew near, namely—John C. Calhoun. The President was resolved, and avowed his resolve, that the hour which brought the news of one act of violence on the part of the nullifiers, should find Mr. Calhoun a prisoner of state upon a charge of high treason. And not Calhoun only, but every member of Congress from South Carolina who had taken part in the proceedings which had caused the conflict between South Carolina and the General Government. Whether this intention of the President had any effect upon the course of events, we can not know. It came to pass, however, that, a few days before the 1st of February, a meeting of the leading nullifiers was held in Charleston, who passed resolutions to this effect: That, inasmuch as measures were then pending in Congress which contemplated the reduction of duties demanded by South Carolina, the nullification of the existing revenue laws should be postponed until after the adjournment of Congress; when the convention would reassemble, and take into consideration whatever revenue measures may have been passed by Congress. The session of 1833 being the "short" session, ending necessarily on the 4th of March, the Union was respited thirty days by the Charleston meeting.

Which of these two bills was most in accordance with Mr. Calhoun's new opinions? Which of them could he most consistently have supported? Not Mr. Clay's. Yet it was Mr. Clay's bill that he did support and vote for; and Mr. Clay's bill was carried by the aid of his support and vote.

Mr. Calhoun left Washington, and journeyed homeward post-haste, after Congress adjourned. Traveling night and day by the most rapid public conveyances, he succeeded in reaching Columbia in time to meet the convention before they had taken any additional steps. Some of the more fiery and ardent members were disposed to complain of the Compromise Act, as being only a halfway, temporizing measure; but when his explanations were made, all felt satisfied, and the convention cordially approved of his course. The nullification ordinance was repealed, and the two parties in the State abandoned their organizations and agreed to forget all their past differences. So the storm blew over.

One remarkable result of the pacification was that it strengthened the position of the leading men of both parties. The course was cleared for Mr. Van Buren. The popularity of the President reached its highest point. Mr. Calhoun was rescued from peril, and a degree of his former prestige was restored to him. The collectors of political pamphlets will discover that, as late as 1843, he still had hopes of reaching the presidency by uniting the South in his support and adding to the united South Pennsylvania. With too much truth he claimed, in subsequent debates, that it was the hostile attitude of South Carolina which alone had enabled Mr. Clay to carry his compromise.

Mr. Clay, as some readers may remember, won great glory at the North by his course during the session of 1833. He was received in New York and New England, this year, with that enthusiasm which his presence in the manufacturing States ever after inspired. The warmth of his reception consoled him for his late defeat at the polls, and gave new hopes to his friends. But the Colossus of the session was Daniel Webster, well named then, the expounder of the Constitution. In supporting the Administration in all its anti-nullification measures, he displayed his peculiar powers to the greatest advantage. The subject of debate was the one of all others the most congenial to him, and he rendered services then to his country to which his country in 1860 recurred with gratitude. "Nullification kept me out of the Supreme Court all last winter," he says in one of his letters in 1833. He mentions, also, that the President sent his own carriage to convey him to the Capitol on one important occasion. After the adjournment he visited the great West, where he was welcomed with equal warmth by the friends and the opponents of the Administration.

When all was over, General Jackson wrote that letter to the Rev. A. J. Crawford, of Georgia, which later events rendered the most celebrated of all his writings. May 1, 1833, is the date of this famous production:

"I have had," wrote the President, "a laborious task here, but nullification is dead, and its actors and courtiers will only be remembered by the people to be execrated for their wicked designs to sever and destroy the only good Government on the globe, and that prosperity and happiness we enjoy over every other portion of the world. Haman's gallows ought to be the fate of all such ambitious men who would involve the country in a civil war, and all the evils in its train, that they might reign and ride on its whirlwinds and direct the storm. The free people of the United States have spoken, and consigned these wicked demagogues to their proper doom. Take care of your nullifiers you have among you. Let them meet the indignant frowns of every man who loves his country. The tariff, it is now well known, was a mere pretext. Its burdens were on your coarse woolens; by the law of July, 1832, coarse woolens was reduced to five per cent for the benefit of the South. Mr. Clay's bill takes it up, and closes it with woolens at fifty per cent, reduces it gradually down to twenty per cent, and there it is to remain, and Mr. Calhoun and all the nullifiers agree to the principle. The cash duty and home valuation will be equal to fifteen per cent more, and after the year 1842 you will pay on coarse woolens thirty-five per cent. If this is not protection, I can not understand it. Therefore, the tariff was only the pretext, and disunion and a Southern confederacy the real object. *The next pretext will be the negro or the slavery question.*"

Not content to let the Bank of the United States peacefully die upon the expiration of its charter in 1836, the President resolved in 1833 to remove from it the public money, and thus sever its connection with the Government. The sub-Treasury had not yet been thought of, or only thought of. The complete divorce which that simple expedient effected between bank and State came too late to save the country from four years of most disastrous "experiment." The plan proposed in 1833 was, instead of depositing the public money in the Bank of the United States and its twenty-five branches, to deposit it in a similar number of State banks. We can not wonder that every member of the Cabinet except two, besides some important members of the kitchen cabinet and a large majority of the President's best friends, opposed it from the beginning to the end.

The measure occurred to the President while he was conversing, one day early in the year 1833, with Mr. Blair, of the Globe, who hated the bank only less than the President himself did. "Biddle," said Mr. Blair, "is actually using the people's money to frustrate the people's will. He is using the money of the Government for the purpose of breaking down the Government. If he had not the public money he could not do it."

The President said, in his most vehement manner: "He sha'n't have the public money! I'll remove the deposits! Blair, talk with our friends about this, and let me know what they think of it."

The deposits were removed accordingly, and the public money was placed in the State banks all over the country. These State banks, as a Senator remarked, "soon began to feel their oats." The expression is homely, but not inapt. The extraordinary increase in the public revenue during the next two years added immense sums to the available capital of those banks, and gave a new and undue importance to the business of banking. Banks sprang into existence like mushrooms in a night. The pet banks seemed compelled to extend their business, or lose the advantage of their connection with the Government. The great bank felt itself obliged to expand, or be submerged in the general inflation. It expanded twelve millions during the next two years. All the other banks expanded, and all men expanded, and all things expanded. Many causes conspired to produce the unexampled, the disastrous, the demoralizing inflation of 1835 and 1836; but I do not see any escape from the conclusion that the inciting cause was the vast amounts of public treasure that, during those years, were "lying about loose" in the deposit banks. General Jackson desired a currency of gold and silver. Never were such floods of paper money emitted as during the continuance of his own fiscal system. He wished to reduce the number and the importance of banks, bankers, brokers, and speculators. The years succeeding the transfer of the deposits were the golden biennium of just those classes. In a word, his system, as far as my acquaintance with such matters enables me to judge, worked ill at every moment of its operation, and upon every interest of business and morality. To it, more than to all other causes combined, we owe the inflation of 1835 and 1836, the universal ruin of 1837, and the dreary and hopeless depression of the five years following.

In November, 1836, General Jackson beheld the consummation of his most cherished hopes in the election of Mr. Van Buren to the presidency.

Signs of coming revulsion in the world of business were so numerous and so palpable during this year that it is wonderful so few observed them. The short crops of 1836 and the paper inflation had raised the price of the necessaries of life to a point they had never reached before, and have never reached since. Flour was sold in lots, at fifteen dollars a barrel; in single barrels, at sixteen; in smaller quantities, at eighteen. The growing scarcity of money had already compelled manufacturers to dismiss many of their workmen; and thus, at a moment when financiers cherished the delusion that the country was prosperous beyond all previous example, large numbers of worthy mechanics and seamstresses were suffering from want.

To the last day of his residence in the presidential mansion General Jackson continued to receive proofs that he was still the idol of the people. The eloquence of the opposition had not availed to lessen his general popularity in the least degree. We read of one enthusiastic Jacksonian conveying to Washington, from New York, with banners and bands of music, a prodigious cheese as a present to the retiring chief. The cheese was four feet in diameter, two feet thick, and weighed fourteen hundred pounds—twice as large, said the Globe, as the great cheese given to Mr. Jefferson on a similar occasion. The President, after giving away large masses of his cheese to his friends, found that he had still more cheese than he could consume. At his last public reception he caused a piece of the cheese to be presented to all who chose to receive it—an operation that filled the White House with an odor that is pleasant only when there is not too much of it. Another ardent lover of the President gave him a light wagon composed entirely of hickory sticks with the bark upon them. Another presented an elegant phaeton made of the wood of the old frigate Constitution. The hickory wagon the general left in Washington, as a memento to his successor. The Constitutional phaeton he took with him to the Hermitage, where I saw it, faded and dilapidated, in 1858.

The farewell address of the retiring President was little more than a *résumé* of the doctrines of his eight annual messages. The priceless value of the Union; the danger to it of sectional agitation; the evils of a splendid and powerful government; the safety and advantages of plain and inexpensive institutions; the perils of a surplus revenue; the injustice of a high tariff; the unconstitutionality of that system of internal

improvements which the Maysville veto had checked;
the curse of paper money; the extreme desirableness of
a currency of gold and silver—were the leading topics
upon which the President descanted. "My own race,"
said he, "is nearly run; advanced age and failing health
warn me that before long I must pass beyond the reach
of human events, and cease to feel the vicissitudes of
human affairs. I thank God that my life has been spent
in a land of liberty, and that he has given me a heart to
love my country with the affection of a son. And, filled
with gratitude for your constant and unwavering kindness, I bid you a last and affectionate farewell."

CHAPTER XXIII.

GENERAL JACKSON was seventy years of age when he retired from the presidency. He was a very infirm old man, seldom free from pain for an hour, never for a day. Possessed of a most beautiful and productive farm and a hundred and fifty negroes, he yet felt himself to be a poor man on his return to the Hermitage. "I returned home," he writes to Mr. Trist, "with just ninety dollars in money, having expended all my salary, and most of the proceeds of my cotton crop; found everything out of repair; corn, and everything else for the use of my farm, to buy; having but one tract of land besides my homestead, which I have sold, and which has enabled me to begin the new year (1838) clear of debt, relying on our industry and economy to yield us a support, trusting to a kind Providence for good seasons and a prosperous crop."

During the next few years he lived the life of a planter, carefully directing the operations of his farm, enjoying the society of his adopted son and his amiable and estimable wife. They and their children were the solace of his old age.

The commercial disasters of 1837 and the depression that succeeded had not seriously inconvenienced General Jackson, with his magnificent farm and his hundred and fifty negroes. He repeatedly expressed the opinion that no one failed in that great revulsion who ought not to have failed. Not the faintest suspicion that any measure of his own had anything to do with it ever found lodgment in his mind. He laid all the blame upon Biddle, paper money, and speculation. In 1842, when business men began once more to hope for prosperous seasons, and the country awoke from its long lethargy, General Jackson became an anxious and embarrassed man through the misfortunes of his son. Money was not to be borrowed in the Western country even then, except at an exorbitant interest. He applied, in these circumstances, to his fast friend, Mr. Blair, of the Globe, who was then a man of fortune. Ten thousand dollars was the sum which the general deemed sufficient for his relief. Mr. Blair not only resolved on the instant to lend the money, but to lend it on the general's personal security, and to make the loan as closely resemble a gift as the general's delicacy would permit it to be. Mr. Rives desired to share the pleasure of accommodating General Jackson, and the loan was therefore made in the name of Blair and Rives. Upon reading Mr. Blair's reply to his application, the old man burst into tears. He handed the letter to his daughter, and she, too, was melted by the delicate generosity which it revealed. General Jackson, however, would accept the money only on conditions which secured his friends against the possibility of loss.

Not long after these interesting events, further relief was afforded General Jackson by the refunding of the fine which he had paid at New Orleans, in 1815, for the arrest of Judge Hall, and for refusing to obey the writ of *habeas corpus* issued by him. The fine was originally one thousand dollars, but the accumulated interest swelled the amount to twenty-seven hundred. Senator Linn, of Missouri, introduced the bill for refunding the money, and gave it an earnest and persevering support. In the House the measure was strenuously supported by

Mr. Stephen A. Douglas, of Illinois, and Mr. Charles J. Ingersoll, of Pennsylvania, to both of whom General Jackson expressed his gratitude in the warmest terms. The bill was passed in the Senate by a party vote of twenty-eight to twenty—Mr. Calhoun voting with the friends of the ex-President; in the House, by one hundred and fifty-eight to twenty-eight.

The religious tendencies of General Jackson were strengthened by the example of his wife, and much more by her affecting death at the moment when he needed her most. He gave her his solemn promise to join the church as soon as he had done with politics, and the letters which he wrote during his presidency to members of his own family abound in religious expressions. The promise which he made to his wife he remembered, but did not strictly keep. In August, 1838, he wrote to one who had addressed him on the subject: " I would long since have made this solemn public dedication to Almighty God, but knowing the wickedness of this world, and how prone men are to evil, that the scoffer of religion would have cried out, ' Hypocrisy! he has joined the church for political effect,' I thought it best to postpone this public act until my retirement to the shades of private life, when no false imputation could be made that might be injurious to religion." He passed two or three years, however, "in the shades of private life" before he performed the act referred to in this letter.

In 1842 he fulfilled the promise he had made to his wife, and joined the Presbyterian Church, Rev. Dr. Edgar, of Nashville, performing the ceremony at the little brick edifice on the Hermitage farm. Dr. Edgar informed me that the usual questions respecting doctrine and experience were satisfactorily answered by the candidate. Then there was a pause in the conversation. The clergyman said, at length:

"General, there is one more question which it is my duty to ask you. Can you forgive all your enemies ?"

The question was evidently unexpected, and the candidate was silent for a while.

"My political enemies," said he, "I can freely forgive; but as for those who abused me when I was serving my country in the field, and those who attacked me for serving my country—doctor, that is a different case."

The doctor assured him that it was not. Christianity, he said, forbade the indulgence of enmity absolutely and in all cases. No man could be received into a Christian church who did not cast out of his heart every feeling of that nature. It was a condition that was fundamental and indispensable. After a considerable pause the candidate said that he thought he could forgive all who had injured him, even those who had assailed him for what he had done for his country in the field.

From this time to the end of his life General Jackson spent most of his leisure hours in reading the Bible, biblical commentaries, and the hymn-book, which last he always pronounced in the old-fashioned way, *hime*-book. The work known as "Scott's Bible" was his chief delight; he read it through twice before his death. Nightly he read prayers in the presence of his family and household servants.

Great was the joy of General Jackson at the election of Mr. James K. Polk in 1844. In a field adjoining the Hermitage he entertained two hundred guests at dinner, in honor of the event. His anxiety, however, on the subject of the annexation of Texas appeared to increase rather than diminish after the election. On the first day of the last year of his life he wrote a long letter to his friend Blair, urging him to use all his influence to induce Congress to act with promptitude in the matter.

The well-known correspondence between Commodore Elliot and General Jackson, with regard to the sarcophagus of the Roman emperor, occurred in the spring of the last year of the general's life. "Last night," wrote the blunt sailor [March 18, 1845], "I made something of a speech at the National Institute (Washington, D. C.), and have offered for their acceptance the sarcophagus which I obtained in Palestine, brought home in the Constitution, and believed to contain the remains of the Roman Emperor Alexander Severus, with the suggestion that it might be tendered you for your final resting-place. I pray you, general, to live on in the fear of the Lord; dying the death of a Roman soldier; an emperor's coffin awaits you."

The general replied: "With the warmest sensations that can inspire a grateful heart, I must decline accepting the honor intended to be bestowed. . I can not consent that my mortal body shall be laid in a repository prepared for an emperor or a king. My republican feelings and principles forbid it; the simplicity of our system of government forbids it; every monument erected to perpetuate the memory of our heroes and statesmen ought to bear evidence of the economy and simplicity of our republican institutions, and the plainness of our republican citizens, who are the sovereigns of our glorious Union, and whose virtue is to perpetuate it. True virtue can not exist where pomp and parade are the governing passions; it can only dwell with the people—the great laboring and producing classes that form the bone and sinew of our confederacy. I have prepared an humble depository for my mortal body beside that wherein lies my beloved wife, where, without any pomp or parade, I have requested, when my God calls me to sleep with my fathers, to be laid."

During the first six years after his retirement from the presidency, General Jackson's health was not much worse than it had usually been in Washington. Every attack of bleeding at the lungs, however, left him a little weaker than he had ever been before, and his recovery was slower and less complete. During the last two years of his life he could never be said to have rallied from these attacks, but remained always very weak, and knew few intervals, and those very short, of relief from pain. A cough tormented him day and night. He had all the symptoms of consumption. One lung was consumed entirely, and the other was diseased. Six months before his death, certain dropsical symptoms, which had threatened him for years, were painfully developed. The patience which he displayed during those years of dissolution sometimes approached the sublime. No anguish, however severe, however protracted, ever wrung from this most irascible of men a fretful or a complaining word.

He saw the light of Sunday morning—June 8th—a still, brilliant, hot day. He had been worse the day before, and Dr. Esselman had remained all night at the Hermitage. "On Sunday morning," writes Dr. Esselman, "on entering his room, I found him sitting in his armchair, with his two faithful servants, George and Dick, by his side, who had just removed him from his bed. I immediately perceived that the hand of death was upon him. I informed his son that he could survive but a few hours, and he immediately dispatched a servant for Major William B. Lewis, the general's devoted friend. Mr. Jackson informed me that it was the general's request that, in case he grew worse, or was thought to be near his death, Major Lewis should be sent for, as

he wished him to be near him in his last moments. He
was instantly removed to his bed, but before he could be
placed there he had swooned away. His family and servants, believing him to be dead, were very much alarmed
and manifested the most intense grief; however, in a
few seconds reaction took place, and he became conscious, and raised his eyes, and said: 'My dear children,
do not grieve for me; it is true, I am going to leave
you; I am well aware of my situation; I have suffered
much bodily pain, but my sufferings are but as nothing
compared with that which our blessed Saviour endured
upon that accursed cross, that we might all be saved
who put our trust in him.' He first addressed Mrs.
Jackson (his daughter-in-law), and took leave of her, re-
minding her of her tender kindness manifested toward
him at all times, and especially during his protracted illness. He next took leave of Mrs. Adams (a widowed
sister of Mrs. Jackson, who had been a member of the
general's family for several years), in the most kind and
affectionate manner, speaking also of her tender devotion toward him during his illness. In conclusion, he
said, 'My dear children, and friends, and servants, I
hope and trust to meet you all in heaven, both white
and black.' The last sentence he repeated—'both white
and black,' looking at them with the tenderest solicitude.
With these words he ceased to speak, but fixed his eyes
on his granddaughter, Rachel Jackson (who bears the
name of his own beloved wife), for several seconds."

Major Lewis arrived about noon. "Major," said the
dying man, in a feeble voice, but quite audibly, "I am
glad to see you. You had like to have been too late."
The crowd of servants on the piazza, who were all day
looking in through the windows, sobbed, cried out, and
wrung their hands. The general spoke again: "What
is the matter with my dear children? Have I alarmed

you? Oh, do not cry. Be good children, and we will all meet in heaven."

These were his last words. He lay for half an hour with closed eyes, breathing softly and easily. Major Lewis stood close to his head. The family were about the bed, silently waiting and weeping. George and the faithful Hannah were present. Hannah could not be induced to leave the room. "I was born and raised on the place," said she, "and my place is here." At six o'clock the general's head suddenly fell forward and was caught by Major Lewis. The major applied his ear to the mouth of his friend, and found that he had ceased to breathe. He had died without a struggle or a pang. Major Lewis removed the pillows, drew down the body upon the bed, and closed the eyes. Upon looking again at the face, he observed that the expression of pain which it had worn so long had passed away. Death had restored it to naturalness and serenity. The aged warrior slept.

Two days after, he was laid in the grave by the side of his wife, of whom he had said, not long before he died, "Heaven will be no heaven to me if I do not meet my wife there." All Nashville and the country round about seemed to be present at the funeral. Three thousand persons were thought to be assembled on the lawn in front of the house, when Dr. Edgar stepped out upon the portico to begin the services. The preacher related, with impressive effect, the history of the late religious life of the deceased, and pronounced upon his character an eloquent but a discriminating eulogium. A hymn which the general had loved concluded the ceremonies. The body was then borne to the garden and placed in the tomb long ago prepared for its reception. "I never witnessed a funeral of half the solemnity," wrote a spectator at the time. The tablet which covers the remains bears this inscription:

GENERAL

ANDREW JACKSON,

Born on the 15th of March, 1767,

Died on the 8th of June, 1845.

When the news of the death of General Jackson reached Washington, the President of the United States ordered the departments to be closed for one day; and Mr. Bancroft, the Secretary of the Navy and Acting Secretary of War, directed public honors to be paid to the memory of the ex-President at all the military and naval stations. In every large town in the country there were public ceremonies in honor of the deceased, consisting usually of an oration and a procession. In the city of New York the entire body of the uniformed militia, all the civic functionaries, the trades and societies, joined in the parade. The record of the solemnities performed in the city of New York, in honor of Andrew Jackson, forms an octavo volume of three hundred and three pages. Twenty-five of the orations delivered on this occasion, in various towns and cities, were published in a volume entitled "Monument to the Memory of General Andrew Jackson."

Thus lived and died Andrew Jackson, the idol of his party, often the pride and favorite of his country. His best friends could not deny that he had deplorable faults, nor his worst enemies that he possessed rare and dazzling merits. He rendered his country signal services, and brought upon the government of that country an evil which it will be extremely difficult to remedy. No man will ever be quite able to comprehend Andrew Jackson who has not personally known a Scotch-Irishman. More than he was anything else, he was a north-of-Irelander

—a tenacious, pugnacious race; honest, yet capable of dissimulation; often angry, but most prudent when most furious; endowed by nature with the gift of extracting from every affair and every relation all the strife it can be made to yield; at home and among dependents, all tenderness and generosity; to opponents, violent, ungenerous, prone to believe the worst of them; a race that means to tell the truth, but, when excited by anger or warped by prejudice, incapable of either telling, or remembering, or knowing the truth; not taking kindly to culture, but able to achieve wonderful things without it: a strange blending of the best and the worst qualities of two races. Jackson had these traits in an exaggerated degree: as Irish as though he were not Scotch; as Scotch as though he were not Irish.

It was curious that England and America should both, and nearly at the same time, have elevated their favorite generals to the highest civil station. Wellington became Prime Minister in 1827; Jackson, President in 1829. Wellington was tried three years, and found wanting, and driven from power, execrated by the people. His carriage, his house, and his statue, were pelted by the mob. Jackson reigned eight years, and retired with his popularity undiminished. Wellington was not in accord with his generation, and was surrounded by men who were, if possible, less so; while Jackson, besides being in sympathy with the people, had the great good fortune to be influenced by men who had learned the rudiments of statesmanship in the school of Jefferson.

Autocrat as he was, Andrew Jackson loved the people, the common people, the sons and daughters of toil, as truly as they loved him, and believed in them as they believed in him. He had a perception that the toiling millions are not a class in the community, but *are* the community. He felt that government should exist only for the benefits of the governed; that the strong are strong only that they may aid the weak; that the rich are rightfully rich only that they may so combine and direct the labors of the poor as to make labor more profitable to the laborer. He did not comprehend these truths as they are demonstrated by philosophers, but he had an intuitive and instinctive perception of them. And in his most autocratic moments he really thought that he was fighting the battle of the people, and doing their will while baffling the purposes of their representatives. If he had been a man of knowledge as well as force, he would have taken the part of the people more effectually, and left to his successors an increased power of doing good, instead of better facilities for doing harm.

The domestic life of this singular man was blameless. He was a chaste man at every period of his life. His letters, of which many hundreds still exist, contain not a sentence, not a phrase, not a word, that a girl may not properly read. A husband more considerately and laboriously kind never lived. As a father he was only too indulgent; his generosity to his adopted children was inexhaustible. To his slaves he was master, father, physician, counselor, all in one; and though his overseers complained that he was too lenient, yet his steady prosperity for so many years, and the uniform abundance of his crops, seem to prove that his servants were not negligent of their master's interest. He had a virtuous abhorrence of debt, and his word was as good as his bond. In all his private transactions, from youth to hoary age, he was punctiliously honest.

Most of our history for the last hundred years will not be remembered for many centuries; but perhaps among the few things oblivion will spare may be some outline of the story of Andrew Jackson—the poor Irish immigrant's orphan son; who defended his country at

New Orleans, and, being elected President therefor, kept that country in an uproar for eight years; and, after being more hated and more loved than any man of his day, died peacefully at his home in Tennessee, and was borne to his grave followed by the benedictions of a large majority of his fellow-citizens.

INDEX.

THE END.